'After I ————————————————————————————— row
— that I would rather spit-ro———————————————— ning
else about the Jeremy Thorpe Affair. ————————— on
my word with more pleasure. As boldly conceived as it is vividly
realised, *Beneath the Streets* is a delight'
John Preston, *The Critic*

'A gripping thriller, interwoven with a really important thread about
the condition of being gay in the 1970s'
Harriett Gilbert, A Good Read, BBC Radio 4

'Adam Macqueen's gripping debut novel is based on a provocative
counterfactual question... He depicts his grim milieu engagingly – the
70s have seldom seemed so grotty and threatening – and this very
English scandal has wit and invention to spare'
The Observer

'Really well done. The detail and the authenticity is all there: London
as a really scary, edgy, ugly place. The atmosphere is brilliant... As a
portrait of a world I thought it was really fantastic, and I also read it
with my computer by my side because I was constantly looking up
the real-life figures and I was constantly shocked and amazed by how
much of this is true'
David Nicholls

'What if Jeremy Thorpe had succeeded in murdering Norman Scott?
That's the gripping premise behind this smart story of corruption,
murder and establishment cover-up'
***iPaper*, 40 best books of the year**

'Adam Macqueen's excellent debut thriller takes us back to 1976,
a time of very British scandals. Former rent boy Tom Wildeblood
is a thoroughly likeable hero, and the seedy allure of the period is
convincingly rendered, while the plot skilfully mixes fact with fiction'
Mail on Sunday

BENEATH THE STREETS

ADAM MACQUEEN

Lightning Books

Published in 2020
by Lightning Books Ltd
Imprint of EyeStorm Media
312 Uxbridge Road
Rickmansworth
Hertfordshire
WD3 8YL

www.lightning-books.com

Reprinted 2020

British Library Cataloguing in Publication Data
A catalogue record for this book is available from the British Library.

Printed by CPI Group (UK) Ltd, Croydon CR0 4YY

ISBN: 9781785631733

For Michael.
For everything.

Many of the characters in these pages, from pimps to peers of the realm, share their names and certain biographical details with real people.

That is all they share.
What follows is a work of fiction.

ONE

SOME PEOPLE DREAM of retiring to a cottage in the countryside. Me, I have to settle for a cottage underneath the pavements of Soho.

It was dark, like it always is. As fast as the council put new bulbs in, the punters take them out. The street light from above made it just far enough down the stairs that you could make out the stern notice: No Loitering – Please Adjust Your Dress Before Leaving. Someone had vainly tried to scrub out the question marker-penned on the tiles below it: *What if I'm not wearing one today?* As I descended, the familiar fug rolled out and filled my nostrils: the ammonia sting of piss with an undertone of something else, the rich, hot, masculine scent of secrecy and sex.

The urinal closest to the entrance was free, and I took up position there until I could work out what was what. Flopped it out for appearance's sake, but didn't even try to go. I hadn't had as much as a cup of tea since breakfast time, and knew I needed to save what few drops I might be able to squeeze out as evidence if the police came clattering down the steps, like they did increasingly often these days. *What, me, officer? I'm just minding my own business and having a piss, as you can clearly see. If you wouldn't mind letting me finish I'll zip up and be on my way.* Word is that the law says that as long as its pointing downwards not upwards they have to let you go, but I wouldn't put money on it. In my experience what a policeman actually sees and what gets written in his notebook bear very little resemblance to each other. And a magistrate will only believe one version, and it won't be the one you remember.

The old geezer standing next to me lost no time in checking me out, shuffling across for a better view and even reaching out an exploratory hand, but I batted it away without any trouble. I could tell by the wrinkles and liverspots on the back of it he must be seventy if he was a day. He wasn't what I was looking for.

With my eyes beginning to adjust to the gloom I could see we had a full house: every urinal taken, the cubicles fully occupied by the sound of things, and a couple of blokes hanging around the sinks, one washing his hands over and over and the other stood by the hand towel, giving it a yank down to make the drum spin and screech every so often just for appearance's sake. But the longer I lingered – getting close to half-mast; I can't help it, these places have that effect on me – I could see that the place was working like a relay race: no sooner would one of the doors behind us bang open than one (or, if he was lucky, two) of the men in the row beside me would peel away and go in to the vacated cubicle; instantly one of the blokes at the sinks would step in to take his place, all of it working like clockwork, with never a word said or a beat missed. The randy old git soon started chancing his arm again, so when a vacancy opened up three stops down the line I stepped out and nipped into it, not even bothering to do up my trousers. The compulsive hand-washer had started for the gap at the same time, but he had more distance to cover on the puddled and treacherous floor. He let out a tut of frustration and diverted into the space I had just left, but he obviously didn't fancy Methuselah much either because within a minute he'd zipped up and gone back to his Lady Macbeth act.

Meanwhile I'd had the chance to check out the view to either side. The bloke on my left was a burly labourer type, or at least that was how I filled in the gaps in my peripheral vision, with an impressive erection that he was working up all by himself, close to what looked like the point of no return. To my right was a middle-aged chap in a business suit, nervously sucking on a cigarette and playing with a cock that was as thin and unimpressive as he was. I could tell from the jiggling pinstripes that he would be home within the hour, taking off his jacket in a hallway in Surbiton or Orpington or one of those other places that only exist as names on railway departure boards, making excuses to his wife about broken rails or ASLEF go-slows while she fetched him his gin and tonic and told him what a poor hardworking dear he was. I'd been with plenty like him when I was still on the game. A suit and a decent pair of shoes usually meant they were good for the money, and not likely to turn nasty, because a scene in public could harm them more than it could you. But that wasn't why I was here tonight – I don't do that any more – so when he pointed both his prick and a pleading expression in my direction I just turned and stared straight ahead, with an occasional cautionary glance stage left to make sure my jeans were well out of the range of what was about to erupt at any second. They were new, genuine Orange Tab Levi's from Kensington Market. You're not supposed to wash them ever, so I wasn't about to have some stranger spunk all over them after I'd only had them a few days. Especially if it wasn't even me making it happen.

The City Slicker wasn't giving up, though. He abruptly went no hands to fumble in the pocket of his suit, pulling out a packet of fags and offering them in my direction. I thought about it for a second – didn't want him feeling I owed him – but ended up taking one anyway. So did the bloke on his right, and when the suit leaned over to light it for him (gold lighter, very flash) the flame flared up and illuminated his face and I knew straight away I had found what I had come here for.

Blond hair, parted in the middle and hanging down as far over the collar of his work jacket as I guessed his bosses would let him get away with. Big, full pouting lips like Richard Beckinsale. And dark eyes that for just a moment before the flame was snapped out, had caught mine. Which meant the game was on. This was the man I was having tonight.

And my luck was in. I hadn't taken more than two drags on my fag before the workman on my left finished what he was about, flicked whatever hadn't already made it that far in the general direction of the urinal and thumped off up the steps without even washing his hands. I sidestepped into the space he had left, careful as to where I was putting my feet, and to my delight the pretty boy slid swiftly round the back of the city gent before he could realise what was happening and parked himself in my place, grinning across at me with a delighted smile that could break a heart softer than mine.

'All right?' I whispered.

'Yeah, I'm all right, are you?' he hissed back.

I looked down. He was more than all right. A sudden

coughing fit overcame me, shattering the quietness of the cottage, and alarming the man on my left so much that he buttoned up and scurried off up to the street quick sharp. It didn't matter: another figure was already thumping down the stairs to replace him, having to turn his bulky form sideways on the stairs so the escapee could squeeze past. I gave him a quick glance of acknowledgement as he took up his place beside me, but my attention was all to my right. My new friend had reached out an arm to slap me on the back when I started coughing, but as I recovered he let it slide down to rest half in and half out of the waistband of my jeans while his other hand came round to grope at the front of them.

'Too strong for you?' he whispered with a grin. He might have been talking about the cigarette, or he might not.

I looked him straight in the eye and shook my head. 'I can take it.' His grin widened.

One of the cubicles had come free, its door hanging invitingly open. I jerked my head in its direction, and he nodded. We tossed our barely-touched cigarettes into the urinal to fizz out together – suit man must have been furious – and went inside.

The stench of sex was even stronger in there. These must be some of the least crapped-in toilets in the whole of London, though I doubt the cleaners prefer what they have to mop up instead. He pushed me ahead of him as we went in, my knees running up painfully against the lavatory pan, but as he slammed the door to I managed to twist round so we were facing each other, stretching out my own arm to double-check on the lock at the same time.

One elephant.

His mouth was on mine, open, his hot tongue searching for a way in. I could feel his end-of-work-day stubble scraping against the smoothness of my own chin.

13

Two elephants.

I reached down with both hands for my belt buckle, fumbled it open. With my flies already gaping, my trousers should have plummeted straight for the floor, but I was reckoning without my new bellbottoms: they were so tight on my thighs that they just rumpled up there and I had to reach down with the one hand I wasn't keeping on the door to try to force them further. I loved the way they looked on, but I had to admit they were not the most practical outfit for my current activities.

Three elephants.

He mistook what I was reaching for and started grinding his crotch into mine, which I must admit distracted my attention for the space of elephants four and five. Finally I managed to get my jeans down to my ankles, where they engulfed my plimsolls and pooled out over the damp floor. Looked like I was going to have to wash them after all.

Six elephants, and at last he detached from my mouth with an audible pop and a gasp. But no sooner had he taken in some air than he transferred his attention to my neck, kissing and sucking at it like a man possessed while presenting me with a mouthful of feathercut I had to twist my head to avoid. Christ, he was trying to give me a love-bite. Did he think we were dating or something?

Seven elephants.

His own trousers, brown flares made out of some sort of polyester you could barely get a grip on at all, thankfully didn't suffer the same design fault as mine. They slipped down easily enough, and his Y-fronts went with them.

Eight elephants.

He was still stabbing insistently and fleshily into my own crotch and it was time to give him what he was looking for. I squirmed around, pushing my own pants down as I did so and arching my back and pushing my bare arse into him until he was pressed right up against the cubicle's wall. My own forehead was braced against the cold surface of the partition opposite. It felt sticky. I tried not to think about that.

Nine elephants.

He gave a gasp as I reached behind me with my left hand and took his cock in a vice-like grip, guiding it inexorably towards where it wanted to go, at the same time reaching out my right hand to flick open the lock on the cubicle door.

Ten elephants.

The door was booted in and a blinding bright light bathed us both for a fraction of a second, leaving the darkness afterwards more black than ever before. I could feel him go rigid, but I kept a firm grip on the part of him that had been rigid already, bracing my own legs so he was pinned where he stood. Besides, there was nowhere for him to go as the flashbulb went off again, and again, and a fourth time for luck: the figure in the doorway was so vast he filled it entirely: the wall behind offered no escape bigger than the four-inch gap at the bottom or the glory-hole drilled by the bogroll dispenser. Unless he fancied flushing himself down the toilet itself, he was well and truly trapped.

'Mr Terry Hopkins? Of 32 Leominster Gardens, NW9?' The photographer spoke in a brisk, businesslike voice. From behind him came the sounds of a stampede as the cottage was vacated.

'Wh-what?' Hopkins was literally shrinking as he spoke. I let go of his rapidly deflating cock and turned sideways to yank up my trousers, taking my time with my belt buckle so I didn't have to look in his direction.

'Apologies for startling you, but I'm afraid it was necessary.' The fat man tapped his camera and stood aside to let me slip past him and out of the cubicle, heading straight for the stairs. 'Your wife's solicitor will be in touch in a few days.'

I didn't look back as I surfaced into the sharp cold of the winter evening. Women and men in hats and scarves milled along the pavement. A bus blasted past, its steamed-up windows aglow, commuters packed inside as tight as pilchards. I turned to my right and set off at a brisk trot, wanting to put as much distance between myself and Mr Terry Hopkins of Leominster Gardens as I could. In the Shakespeare's Head the drinkers were knocking back their pints obliviously; two separate worlds of men, both seeking out companionship, comfort and an escape from the daily grind, separated by just a few feet of concrete and the width of the world. The punters from the cottage had surfaced and dispersed back into anonymity, swallowed up by the city. At street-level we can all pass for ordinary men.

I hurried under the big sign I had been so thrilled to recognise when I first came to London a few years earlier: *Carnaby Street Welcomes the World*. The shops were all shut, their interiors darkened, their frontages, once so fresh and exciting, now faded and worn. The brightly coloured patterned paving was blotted with piles of black rubbish bags awaiting collection. Welcome to London, 1976: try swinging if you must, but you'd better beware of the consequences.

TWO

HARVEY MET ME in the doorway on the far side of Lord John like we'd arranged. He was out of breath, his camera bumping against his chest on its strap as he waddled along. His coat was flapping open: there was no need to hide it now.

'Well done, nice job,' he wheezed as he drew up. 'Those'll come out perfect.'

'Just watch how hard you kick the door next time,' I muttered. 'Few inches further over and you'd have taken my head off.'

He shook his head. 'I thought you were positioned perfectly. The perfect composition for a compromising position.'

I think he meant it as a compliment, but I wasn't in the mood to take one. 'Can I just get my money, please?'

Harvey doesn't like carrying cash when he's out on jobs like these – he's under the mistaken impression that even the most desperate cottager would go anywhere near his trouser pockets

– so we had to go back to his office on Denmark Street before he could pay me. I tried to keep a few steps behind him as we walked through Soho, in spite of how slowly he huffs and puffs along. I didn't want people thinking we were together. Anywhere else, we might have been mistaken for father and son. On these streets, people would assume something even worse.

The shops on Carnaby Street might have closed for the night, but a few blocks east the businesses were only just starting to get going. As I followed Harvey's broad back through the narrow streets, the competing neon turned him into a chameleon, bathing his beige mackintosh and bald pate in alternating shades of pink and yellow, blue and green. Enticement was everywhere as we passed: *Erotic Escapades; Striptease Spectacular; Non-Stop Live Revue; Love Shop & Cinema; We Never Close!* The girls in the doorways called out to Harvey as he waddled by, holding up an apologetic hand and firing the occasional 'maybe another time, darling': they took one look at me and knew better than to bother.

I'd been working for Harvey for a year or so now. I started when I was still doing rent, but quickly realised he would pay me more for *not* having sex with married men than they would for having it. All right, it's not what most people would call honest work, but there's not that many openings out there for someone who left school before they could get any qualifications and whose only experience is four years selling his arse on the Dilly. I have to settle for what I can get. Story of my bloody life.

Only trouble is it's not regular work – Harvey only needs my services once every few weeks. He's got two or three women on his books too: calls them the honeys in his honeytrap and pays them twenty-five quid a pop to my twenty, which isn't exactly fair since they don't take the same risks I have to. All they've got to do is sit around in some hotel bar and do their seducing in plain sight, with drinks bought for them and no risk of getting arrested in the middle of it. Trouble is, there's no trade union for my particular line of work, and plenty of younger, prettier boys who'd be only too eager to take the work if I called myself out on strike. Still, twenty quid is twenty quid, even with prices shooting up the way they are. It all helps pay the bills, as they say, or at least it would if I was stupid enough to settle down anywhere long enough for any bills to find me.

To be honest I don't think this is exactly what Harvey hoped he'd be doing when he went into the private detective business either – I think he had something more in the Mickey Spillane line in mind – but divorces are pretty much his bread and butter, along with tracking down the odd small businessman who's done a flit owing money to someone bigger. If some drop-dead dame actually did walk into Harvey's office saying she'd been framed I think he'd probably fall off his chair in surprise.

I know what you're thinking. Don't I feel sorry for the men? Well I don't know, do you feel sorry for their wives? It's not like I'm putting the idea in their heads for the first time – the way it works is that the wife comes to Harvey with a pretty strong suspicion of what her husband's up to, and then he spends a couple of days following them to make sure before he calls me in. Apparently Terry Hopkins was a regular in every cottage within walking distance of the shop he worked in on Regent Street. Harvey had watched him do the full circuit in his lunch-hour two days running, and even pop out for a quickie on his tea break.

Besides it's not like we're the only ones at it: the plod seem to be sending their prettiest young coppers round the cottages more and more now to flash their crown jewels about, and then pile in mob-handed the second some poor sod takes the bait. I suppose it's easier than trying to catch any real criminals. Not to mention the fact that half of the rent boys in London specialise in blackmailing their clients: no sooner have they got your trousers down than they've had your wallet out of the pocket and are reading you the address off your driving licence and promising to pay your wife a visit unless you pony up regular payments to keep them quiet.

Not me, I hasten to add. That was never my game. Pay up and you got the goods as advertised, that was the way I always played it. More fool me, probably.

Anyway, perhaps if they don't like it, they shouldn't have got married in the first place. They've had their chance at having it all – the normal life, the wife, the kids – and it's hardly down to me if they decide to throw it all away. Some of us never got to choose.

I always knew I was never going to go that way. They say some people are born gay, some get turned gay and the really lucky ones get gayness thrust upon them, but with me it was definitely the first one. I can't remember a time when I didn't feel different. Preferring Ilyia Kuriakin to Napoleon Solo but not being able to explain why. Sneaking my mum's catalogues up to the bedroom to look at the pants and vests. By the time the rest of the boys at school were picking up guitars and trying to be John Lennon, I knew I was more interested in what I'd like to do to George Harrison.

Of course then I thought I was the only one. You didn't get homosexuals in Berkshire. Still don't, I shouldn't think, at least not if you asked my family. You used to hear grown-ups saying the odd thing about men who were 'a bit funny' or 'got done for interfering' – my ears would always prick up, but I quickly learned that asking questions got you told off and made your ears burn with a special sort of shame that you couldn't explain or understand.

Thankfully I'd long since grown immune to all that. These days there wasn't much that could shock me: I scarcely even turned my head to look at the windows of the various 'Love Shops' and 24-hour-cinemas we passed on our zig-zag route through the Soho streets. With just one exception: as we passed under the Pillars of Hercules I slowed down and peered enviously into the side-windows of Foyles, planning my visit for first thing tomorrow when I had Harvey's cash in my pocket.

I love books. Always have done. 'Always got his nose buried in a book', the teachers at my primary school used to say. They couldn't see that I didn't have much choice: if you weren't the sort of boy who liked football and British Bulldog, you were pretty much ostracised and had to make your own entertainment. I must have ploughed through every single book in the Book Corner at least twice. Even the *Illustrated Children's Bible*. The dinner ladies used to joke about me having a vocation because I spent so many playtimes studying it, and not one of them noticed that it was always the page with Jesus stripped of his garments.

Nothing's changed in the years since. I've still always got a book on the go. The other lads on the Dilly would take the piss out of me because I always had a paperback in my pocket: the Bookworm, some of them used to call me, but it never really caught on.

Foyles is my favourite place in the whole of London. You can lose yourself in its crazy rabbit warren of shelves for a whole day if you keep moving and avoid the assistants, and finish a whole book in the warm and have it back on the shelf by closing time without anyone being any the wiser. It's easy to lift them too, at least the paperbacks, which will slip into a jacket pocket or down the back of your trousers if your coat is long enough: that way you can finish them at your leisure and the second-hand shops on the other side of the road will always give you a few pence for them when you're done.

Harvey was crossing Charing Cross Road now, and I hurried to catch him up as he headed into Denmark Street where he has his office. *Harvey Lewenstein, Private Investigator* says the brass plaque by the door, but you'd have to be looking for it to spot it: it's the shabby side door of a guitar shop and his actual office is right up in the attic. The middle floors are rehearsal rooms, which means there's usually some kind of racket going on whatever time of day you visit, but tonight's was the worst I'd heard yet. It sounded like the group had decided to attack their instruments rather than play them, or maybe attack the singer *with* them, given the strangulated yelps he was emitting.

'Tell me about it,' muttered Harvey once we were clear of the first landing and could hear ourselves speak. 'Bunch of filthy beggars they are, in and out at all hours, leaving the front door wide open. And I think some of them might be staying overnight. Need to have a word with the landlord.' At that point climbing the stairs became too much of an effort for him to talk as well, and we went up the last two flights accompanied only by his asthmatic wheezing and the considerably less rhythmic thumping of the drums.

He made a great palaver of unlocking his office door, which actually does have a glass panel with his name engraved on it – 'It's what the customers expect,' he told me crossly when I laughed at it on my first visit. Sadly that's where any resemblance to a black-and-white gumshoe movie ends, because the interior is covered in woodchip wallpaper that was either painted yellow or has just got stained that way over the years.

I plumped myself down on the threadbare settee in front of

Harvey's desk, retrieved the duffel bag he had let me leave there during our excursion, and watched as he flicked through all the keys once more to find the right one for the cash box he keeps in the top drawer.

I could have pointed out which one it was – I've got a good memory for things like that – but he'd only get shirty. The first job I did for him, he actually made me turn my back so I wouldn't see where he got the cash box from. For a supposed detective he really doesn't get how mysteries work. There's only two desks in the room – his and his secretary's – and I knew perfectly well which one he was standing behind.

'One, two, three, four, five and five and ten is twenty.' Harvey slapped the notes down on the table, then counted them through once again to make sure before handing them over. I stashed the one-pound notes in my jeans pocket, and tucked the bigger ones into my sock just in case I ran in to anyone unfriendly.

Harvey was laboriously writing an entry out in the ledger he keeps of all his transactions. He lives in terror of being arrested for living off immoral earnings, saying it would be the death of his old mum. I'm not sure why, because the ledger also features a regular outgoing for 'ground rent' which goes straight into the pocket of a local copper, Sergeant Mullaney, when he does his rounds of all the local business each week, on the understanding that he will 'see them right'. In any case it doesn't bother me. If the police or anyone else go looking for the name I sign under, they're not going to find anyone.

Assistance with investigations: T. Wildeblood Esq. Harvey pushed the ledger across the desktop and proffered his fountain pen, not taking his eyes off it until it was safely back in his jacket pocket. 'All right Tommy, piss off now, some of us have got homes to go to.'

23

I took my time getting up and shouldering my bag. 'It's Tom now,' I told him. I had decided that if I was too old to go on the game, I didn't need to go by a kid's name any more either.

'Is it indeed?' He gave a yellow grin. 'All right Tommy, whatever you say.'

I flicked a V-sign in his direction and set off down the noisy staircase.

THREE

FIRST THINGS FIRST: get something in my belly. I hadn't eaten all day, but with Harvey's cash burning a hole in my pocket (and sock) I could afford a proper blow-out. I strolled round the corner and up Tottenham Court Road to the Dionysus, where I ignored the great glistening wad of cat meat revolving behind the counter and ordered the best hake and chips in London with plenty of salt and vinegar. Cod was off, as usual.

I made to take my meal over to one of the shiny tabletops, but the bloke came out from behind the counter waving his hairy arms around and yelling at me to get out: 'I don't want you lot hanging around in here – give the place a reputation.' I tried telling him I wasn't on the game any more but he was having none of it. 'That's what you all say, go on, bugger off,' he told me as he shoved me out into the night. He pronounced bugger 'bukka'. I wonder how long he'd been in England before he learned that phrase.

I walked back down the road instead, holding the newspaper-wrapped package inside my jacket like a hot-water-bottle until I reached the fountains outside Centre Point, risking piles by perching on their frigid concrete rim to unwrap it. Grease spots bloomed across weeks-old headlines about OPEC and the IRA. I can't be doing with newspapers: the world around me is depressing enough without needing to know what's going on in the rest of it. But when I spotted a nice big photo of John Curry posing with his gold medal I did scan the accompanying text as I ate. I wanted to see if they had addressed the obvious, but of course it was nowhere to be seen – this was a *family* paper, just look at page 3 if you don't believe them.

Across the road a queue was growing outside the Astoria. According to the shonkily applied letters on the illuminated sign above the entrance it was showing *Emmanuelle II*: the line below was mostly giggling couples dotted with the odd dirty old man who hadn't worked out he could see proper pornos if he cared to stroll just a couple of blocks further. At the foot of Tottenham Court Road the shopfronts were little more than lean-tos, the storeys above them jagged like a mouth full of pulled teeth, a great emptiness stretching back to the block behind. What German bombs had destroyed, three decades of British indifference had failed to put back. Behind me was the vast stabbing finger of Centre Point, every one of its floors in pitch blackness. It had been sitting empty for as long as I had been in London, and for years before that I'd been told. And tonight, like every night, there would be people, some of them boys I knew by name, bedding down in the underpass beneath it. If you're looking for justice in this world, you're definitely in the wrong part of London.

Still, at least tonight I wasn't going to be one of them. I finished my dinner, licking my fingers and pressing them into the folds of the paper to make sure I got every last salty scrap, and was wondering whether I was going to have to spend another 30p on a pint in the Golden Lion or the Bricklayers just to keep warm when a Number 73 went past me with a familiar fat figure sitting on its top deck. Harvey, off to what he likes to pretend is his bachelor pad in Stoke Newington, though his mother in the basement would tell you a different story. I chucked the greasy ball of paper into the water behind me, hopped down from the wall and headed back towards Gerrard Street.

I'd been living in a squat in Camden until recently. It wasn't a bad gaff, as long as you weren't too attached to your personal belongings and could put up with the overwhelming smell of patchouli oil, but I'd got back a few evenings earlier and found my housemates had held a meeting in my absence – a committee, they called it – and my stuff was all bundled up in the hall and a long-haired couple were already doing a John and Yoko in my bed. Turned out my former pals had decided I was showing insufficient commitment to the United Secretariat of the Fourth International to remain a part of their collective. What that meant in practice was that someone had gone snooping in my room and discovered the piles of *Red Weekly* I was supposed to have been selling each week piled up under the mattress, which they'd helped to hoist up nicely out of the draught that came in under the door. My housemates worked out that I must have been paying my subs out of the cash I made from selling my body, and it doesn't get more capitalist than that. To be honest it only gave them the excuse they'd been looking for: for all their talk of breaking down society's structures, hippies are usually a bit funny around homos and there was one bloke on the top floor who made a big deal about going on Women's Lib marches, but had never even been able to meet my eye.

27

So it was O.U.T spells out and out you go. I wasn't over-bothered about leaving the squat, but I wasn't about to go back to sleeping on the streets in the middle of winter either. I know you can usually pick up someone who'll let you stay the night, but frankly I'd had enough of sleeping with men who make Arthur Mullard look like a catch and I really couldn't be bothered with the hassle if I wasn't getting paid for it. So instead I'd fallen back on a lucky lift from a few months before.

I reached the front door of Harvey's building – the band upstairs were still clattering on – and crouched down as if I was tying my shoelaces. Instead I extracted a pair of shiny Yale keys from my sock, being careful not to dislodge the wad of notes that were also in there. I slid the first key into the lock, pushed the door and slipped into the dark and noisy hallway.

I'd nicked the keys out of Harvey's secretary Alison's desk when she'd made the mistake of leaving me alone in the office a few weeks ago. I hadn't gone there intending to lift anything – I'd turned up for a job, after getting a message at the Bricklayers Arms that Harvey wanted to see me, only he was out for lunch and there was just her bashing away on her typewriter. The stuck-up cow had made it so clear she didn't really trust me to stay in the office while she went out for her own lunch hour that I felt duty-bound to go through her desk drawers while she was gone. The spare keys were the only interesting thing in there – although I did take the chance to empty her dry shampoo out of the window to teach her a lesson – so I pocketed them, got copies made at the locksmiths on St Martin's Lane, and then let myself back in to return the originals that very same evening, having a good look through Harvey's paperwork while I was at it. That's how I found out the girls were on a higher rate than me.

Anyway, the keys were coming in useful now, because for

most of the week, and so far without either Harvey or Alison having the slightest suspicion, I had been kipping down on the settee in the office. I'd nearly bricked myself today when I got the message that Harvey wanted to see me, thinking I must have left something behind that had given the game away, so I was even more than usually pleased to find out he wanted me for a job.

I climbed the stairs, awareness of my intruder status making me take each tread as softly as possible, even though there was no chance of anyone hearing me over the din coming from the first floor. The key to the office door was just as good a fit, and I was soon safely inside. I had to leave the blinds open so the daylight would wake me well before Alison arrived to open up in the morning – it would be the end of everything if she found me still snoring away – but the last couple of nights I'd risked switching Harvey's desk lamp on for my bedtime reading. I can't get to sleep without reading. Well, or a wank, but I wasn't going to risk that here.

I kicked off my plimsolls, shucked off my jeans and made myself as comfortable as I could on the lumpy cushions, draping my jacket over myself like a blanket. Rummaging in the bag that now contains all my worldly goods I extracted an orange-and-white paperback. It was an old favourite, pretty much the only thing I made sure to take with me when my dad threw me out, and the only thing I've managed to keep hold of ever since. This one I wouldn't flog off for all the tea in China. It's the book that saved my life.

The cover was pretty much hanging off it now, but I knew the text on it off by heart. *A first-hand account of what it means to be a homosexual, and to be tried in a controversial case and imprisoned.* And stamped beneath that: *Property of Berkshire Public Libraries.* That's where I had come across it all those

29

years ago. My parents didn't read anything other than the *Daily Express,* and were bewildered by how keen I was on books. 'He doesn't get it from us,' they used to tell their friends, just like later on they would be pointing out what else I hadn't got from them. Anyway, they soon worked out that a library ticket would keep me quiet and out of their hair, and before too long I was spending every Saturday morning and most of the school holidays in our local branch. And that's where I'd come across this. I was innocently browsing the non-fiction shelves, and found myself riven to the spot, petrified by the shock of seeing such a thing there in its ordinary Penguin cover just like all the others, standing in plain sight in such a respectable, official place, just a few streets away from my own family home.

I didn't dare even take it down from the shelf, just jammed it straight back in between its innocent neighbours, convinced the whole library must be staring at me. Was I even allowed? The very title seemed to suggest I wasn't: *Against The Law.* I had only just graduated from the buff pink of a junior ticket to the grown-up green, but surely even being officially an Adult Reader didn't mean you were allowed to look at this sort of thing?

I remember I left without taking out a single book that day, too flustered to do anything but dump those I had already gathered on a trolley and flee. But after a sleepless night I came back the next morning, when I knew it would be quiet, and I snatched the incredible book down and took it over to the table at the furthest end of the reference library where no one ever sat, hid it inside an innocent-looking volume of the *Children's Britannica* and read it from cover to cover for the first time that very day. I was 11.

I am no more proud of my condition than I would be of having a glass eye or a hare-lip. On the other hand, I am no more ashamed of it than I would be of being colour-blind or of writing with my left hand. It is essentially a personal problem, which only becomes a matter of public concern when the law makes it so.

It was June 1967, the start of the holidays. Out there, very much somewhere else and unbeknownst to any of us until long afterwards, something called the Summer of Love was going on. And in the stuffy airlessness of Latchmere Road Public Library and Reading Rooms, my own idea of love was changing forever.

The truth is that an adult man who has chosen a homosexual way of life has done so because he knows that no other course is open to him. It is easy to preach chastity when you are not obliged to practise it yourself, and it must be remembered that, to a homosexual, there is nothing intrinsically shameful or sinful in his condition.

There was nothing wrong with me. I couldn't help how I felt.

The number of homosexuals in England and Wales has never been satisfactorily estimated. Some statisticians have given a figure of 150,000; others, of over a million. If the Kinsey Report, based on inquiries in America, is accepted as a rough indication, the figure for England and Wales can be estimated at 650,000.

There were other people like me out there. Lots of them. I wasn't alone.

Looking back now I reckon one of them must have been working somewhere senior in that library. God knows who: the staff were all old women in twinsets the spit of Mrs Mary Whitehouse, and the doorkeeper still wore his war medals on his rather less impressive uniform. But who else could have smuggled this secret message of hope to boys like me in amongst the Willard Prices and Mills and Boons and Patience Strongs? At the time I was too caught up in my own feelings, too blown away by my new discovery, to think anything of the sort: instead I worried that the book itself was a trap, that at any second the full weight of the library authorities, the pursed-lipped shushing ladies and the ranked masses of headmasters and vicars and parents and police behind them would come crashing down on me and haul me away for public humiliation. After all, that was what happened to this extraordinary man, as I learned as I read on through the morning and into the afternoon, ears burning, heart thumping, too scared to continue but unable to stop. He had had his home raided and ransacked, his love letters broadcast to the world, his name plastered all over the newspapers, and he had been thrown in prison. And yet he had not backed down. He had stood up in front of the world and said 'I am a homosexual'; he had put it down again in black and white in this book, published only a year after I had been born, so that everyone could understand it. And the more I thought about it – the more I read his words, over and over again, in the privacy of my bedroom, having liberated them from the library stuffed inside my shirt because the idea of standing at the issue desk face-to-face with another human being and having my name indelibly attached to them was just too terrifying – the more I felt I had a duty to do the same. I kept the book stashed between my mattress and the base of the bed where no one would find it, and each night I would read a few paragraphs like a catechism before sliding it under my pillow so that it would always be in comforting reach in the night. Somehow I always found the right words in there to reassure me, to comfort me, to point me in the right direction to go.

So that's why I chose the name I go by. Tom Wildeblood. It's not the name my mother and father would know me by. But then they don't know me at all. They proved that just a few weeks later when Richard Baker shattered the peace of an evening at home by announcing that the government had voted to legalise 'homosexual acts' between consenting adults, and my father stood up and furiously slammed the TV off while my mother complained about feeling 'physically sick', and I sat there bright red and desperately trying not to cry. And I was more than happy to hammer the point home five angry, row-filled years later by packing my stuff and clearing off out of their lives forever.

The din from downstairs had ceased a while ago, and the familiar words of the book had lulled me to the point where I could almost forget quite how uncomfortable a bed the threadbare two-seater made. I yawned, and stretched, and was just reaching out for the switch on the anglepoise when I froze and was suddenly wide awake again.

Someone was coming up the stairs.

FOUR

SHIT. SHIT. SHIT. Harvey must have come back. He must have forgotten something. I should have waited longer. Should have gone to the Golden Lion and stayed till closing time to make sure. Should have, would have, could have. But instead I was trapped here, frozen to the spot, flat on my back like a beetle, listening to the footsteps coming steadily up the stairs and my heart thumping loud in my ears, each beat of them bringing disaster closer and closer. There was nowhere for me to go. Nothing I could do. Even as I stared, transfixed, at the etched pane in the door a shape appeared and grew taller, bigger, sharper, closer, until it was directly outside the glass –

And then stopped, and knocked.

Why would Harvey knock before coming in to his own office? was the mad thought that flitted through my mind for a moment before it clicked. In a single fluid movement I leapt off the sofa and grabbed my trousers – no time to put them on – and got myself behind the safety of the desk.

'Come in!' I ordered, in a voice rather higher-pitched than I had intended.

The door swung open. The man standing hesitantly on the threshold was about ten years older than Harvey, and several stone lighter. He was dressed in high-waisted trousers and a blue blazer over a paisley shirt. He had thin, wispy hair with a bluish tint, and the saddest eyes I have ever seen.

'I wasn't sure you'd be open so late,' he said apologetically. 'I've been walking around for hours, wondering what to do, but then when I came past and saw your front door was open…'

'No…no…no peace for the wicked,' I stammered, cursing the band and trying desperately to remember if Harvey's desk had an open front or not. I reached beneath the tabletop and tugged the tail of my shirt down as far as it would go. 'What can we do for you?'

'I…I… Oh dear.' He plucked a white handkerchief from the breast pocket of his blazer and pressed it to his mouth, flapping a hand in the direction of the sofa in a gesture which dispelled any doubts I might have had that he was a queen. 'I wonder – could I?'

I nodded, slightly over-eagerly. 'By all means. Just shove all that stuff out of the way.' He took his time, plucking my jacket up and folding it neatly, before he turned and sat down, perching on the very edge of the cushions, knees clamped together and twisted daintily to the left. Yanking my own arms up above the level of the desktop, I tried to compose my own top half into as authoritative a pose as possible.

'Oh! It looks as if I've come to the right place.'

For a second I thought he had spotted my bare legs, but he was nodding at the book, which was still sitting on the edge of the desk where I'd left it. 'Ah!' I exclaimed. 'Just…research.'

He nodded sadly. 'I went down to Winchester for a day to see the trial. Such a dreadful injustice. Of course, it's all different these days. For your generation.'

Oh yeah? I thought to myself, but I didn't say anything. I wouldn't turn twenty-one for another six months.

The visitor seemed to be considering the same subject. A look of doubt crossed his face. 'I rather expected you'd be older,' he ventured.

I gave him as reassuring a smile as I could manage. 'I'm the junior partner,' I bluffed. 'Tommy Lewenstein. Tom.'

'Ah.' He looked reassured. 'My name is Crichton. Malcolm Crichton.' He rose from the sofa and offered me a hand, which, unable to get up, I had to stretch across the desk to shake. It was like gripping a handful of autumn leaves.

'And what can we do for you, Mr Crichton?' I seemed to have adopted the royal pronoun in my new role as the unsuspecting Harvey's Boy Wonder. With a sinking feeling in my stomach I realised I was trapped in the part now. Whatever Crichton was after, I had to somehow ensure he went away happy and never darkened this doorstep again. I couldn't even send him away and tell him to come back tomorrow, because the first thing he would say was 'your son told me…' and from there even Harvey's detective skills were probably up to working out what had been going on.

Thankfully the old man seemed oblivious to the churning that was going on in both my belly and my mind. His eyes on the carpet, he was twisting the handkerchief around his fingers, lost in a torment of his own. When he finally spoke his voice was so soft I had to lean forward to hear him. 'I had a friend. A young friend. He died.'

'I'm sorry to hear that.'

'I was very fond of him. I'd hoped… I'd hoped I might spend the rest of my life with him.'

'Right.' I folded my arms on the desktop and tried to look sympathetic. If all this bloke wanted was a shoulder to cry on, I could provide that, as long as he promised not to look down. I might even be able to get rid of him within half an hour.

Then he went and piqued my interest. 'He was…he worked as a prostitute.'

'Really?'

Crichton looked up with a sheepish smile, mistaking my tone. 'I am not ashamed to admit that I pay for companionship on occasion, Mr Lewenstein. When one gets to my stage in life, one's options are rather limited.'

'No, no, of course, nothing wrong with that,' I assured him.

'But what Stephen and I had developed into something… rather special.' He gave a wistful smile. 'Latterly he would come and visit my home quite of his own accord. He said he enjoyed spending time with me.'

And I bet you never thought to count the spoons afterwards, I thought, but I kept it to myself. Punters like Crichton were every rent boy's dream: I'd had a couple myself. A soft touch, we used to call them. Someone so besotted you could rely on them not just for regular payments but for bonuses too: gifts, meals out, even a roof over your head. All you had to do was keep telling them what they wanted to hear and you could get yourself looked after for life. I knew lads who had been bought cars, taken on holidays to Tangiers or Amsterdam: there was even talk of one guy who had been bought his own flat in Chelsea and given up the game forever, though no one you spoke to ever seemed to have actually met him. It was all pretty harmless unless the punter got jealous; then things could get nasty. Maybe that was what had happened to this Stephen.

Crichton might well not have been the only sugar daddy he was stringing along.

I knew better than to suggest as much. The old man was obviously devastated, dabbing at his eyes with the unfurled handkerchief. 'We'd even discussed me legally adopting him,' he spluttered. 'Stephen loved the idea. He had no family of his own, you see.'

Now I felt distinctly less sympathetic. I've not got much time for the normal nuclear family set-up, given my own experience of it, but what Crichton was suggesting sounded a lot less wholesome. 'So what happened to him?' I asked, a bit more harshly than I intended.

The old man looked up at me, his eyes brimming. 'It was on Tuesday. I hadn't seen him since the weekend – we'd had the most glorious time together. We came up to the West End and went round the shops. He was helping me choose things for the house, ready for him to move in. He was going to have his own room, decorated just as he liked. And then on the Monday morning he said he had to go, he wouldn't say where, just that he had someone to see.'

Now I wondered if the mysterious Stephen had just staged his own disappearing act because Crichton was getting too clingy. I reached for the pad that Harvey keeps on his desk, realised too late that there was no pen to go with it, and had to bluff it out. 'Do you have any idea who that person might have been?' I asked. It sounded like the sort of thing detectives say.

The old man shook his head. 'He never liked to discuss his work with me. I think he was worried about making me jealous.' A soppy smile dislodged the tears and set them running down his cheeks. 'Not that I would have been. I understood, he was a young man, we all have needs.' He paused to blow his nose before continuing.

'Monday was such a dismal day, if you remember. But Tuesday was rather a fine morning, although it was cold of course, and I decided to go out for a walk. I live near the Heath, you see. And I happened to pass near the Men's pond.'

Sounds like Stephen was not the only one attending to his needs elsewhere, I thought uncharitably. There was no more notorious cruising ground than Hampstead Heath: no more guaranteed pick-up point than the area round the 'clothing optional' pond. But I quickly realised Crichton was avoiding my eye not from embarrassment, but from genuine anguish. 'I could see a commotion from a distance. I'm not as fast on my feet as I used to be, but I hurried there as quick as I could, thinking I might be able to help in some way. I was an ambulance driver in the war, you see, and I thought perhaps my first aid...' He tailed off and shook his head. 'But it was far too late. I could see that even when they were pulling him out of the water. He was blue.'

He was rocking back and forth, all composure gone. Any hope of getting rid of him quickly was gone, but I no longer cared: I had been drawn in. 'And it was Stephen?' I prompted.

He nodded, not even bothering to attend to the tears that were running freely now. 'I didn't recognise him at first. Or perhaps I didn't want to. But when they turned him over, and I saw his face...'

'I'm sorry,' I said helplessly.

'He was covered in bruises. His poor eye was all puffed up. The policemen tried to say it was just the effect of the water, but it was obvious. They kept saying he must just have gone for a swim and drowned. They were saying it as soon as they arrived, before they'd even looked at him, at his... body. It was as if they had already made up their minds.'

'But you don't believe that?'

He looked at me incredulously. 'In *February*?'

I did my best to look non-committal. Probably nine out of every ten rent boys I've ever met have been regular users of something: speed more often than not, glue for those who can't afford it, and China White for those who've got money to burn. Thankfully, I'd always been the tenth out of the ten. But I'd been around the rest of them enough to know that when you're on that stuff you'll do almost anything: going for a dip might seem like a good idea even if you had to break the ice to do so.

Crichton, however, was vehemently shaking his head. 'Besides, Stephen would never take his clothes off in public. He was terribly sensitive about his body. He hated to be naked even with me. He always insisted on having the lights off when we… made love. And he would put his pants and his vest back on as soon as we had finished. Every time.'

'Right.' A rent boy with body issues was nothing unusual. Half the boys on the Dilly were bringing up their lunches to keep themselves looking as skinny as possible.

'And his clothes were nowhere to be seen.' Crichton continued. 'The policemen weren't interested, they didn't care, but I walked all the way round the pond with one of the other gentlemen who found him and his clothes simply weren't there. It was the other chap who pointed it out: whoever attacked him must have taken them. Without his clothes there was no way to identify Stephen.'

I frowned. 'But you could identify him, of course.'

A look of shame and anguish clouded the old man's face. 'I couldn't say anything. How could I? Stephen was only seventeen.' He slumped forwards, holding his head in his hands. 'I couldn't… the police. You see, I have a record. It was nothing, really, a dalliance, back in my national service days. But for people like me…'

'I understand,' I said quietly. And I did. People like Crichton: people like me. I'd been beaten up and robbed and worse since coming down to London, but I'd never once have considered going to the police, and nor would any other gay man I know. You'd just as soon stick your head in a crocodile's mouth.

'And that's why I came to you.' Crichton sat up and honked loudly into his sodden handkerchief. 'Will you help me?'

So involved had I become in his story that I'd almost forgotten the ridiculous situation I'd got myself into. I frantically tried to backtrack. 'Well, I'm not sure that I – it's not really the sort of thing we – our area of expertise,' I gabbled.

The old man fumbled in his trouser pocket and pulled out a wallet thick with notes. 'Whatever your fees, I'm prepared to pay.'

My eyes widened. 'We'd be delighted to,' I assured him.

FIVE

IF I HAD HALF THE sense I was born with, this is where the story would end. I'd have taken Malcolm Crichton's money, promised him a receipt in the post and skipped off into the sunset never to darken Harvey Lewenstein's doorstep again, with only my conscience to trouble me.

It's what I had every intention of doing. I named the first figure that came into my head – twenty-five quid a day plus expenses, with a week to be paid in advance – and rapidly regretted not asking for more when Crichton counted out a hundred and fifty in crisp tenners on the desktop and still had plenty left in his wallet. Still, the wad I stashed in my usual hiding place as I left the office bright and early the next morning left me so loaded I was limping, and ready for a proper spending spree. I'm the same whenever I get cash: burn through it before someone can take it off you, that's my motto. No more lumpy sofa for me: I would book myself a hotel room for the next few nights. And I was going to splash out on some clothes, too: the time had come to get myself a decent leather jacket like I'd always wanted.

Thing is, Crichton gave me a photo too: a Polaroid he said he had taken of Stephen a few weeks earlier. I found myself looking at it while I tucked into the full works with extra fried bread at Mario's café. He was a beautiful boy, all right: stretched out artfully across a candlewick bedspread in a pose he had borrowed from the teen magazines, the sleeves of his T-shirt rolled up at the shoulder to show off his skinny arms. No track marks, I noted. But that didn't mean he hadn't been smoking, snorting or popping pills, either then or on the day he died. Blond, shoulder-length hair framing a cherubic face, but for all his attempts to ape David Cassidy or Donny Osmond there was something off in his expression. The smile didn't reach all the way to his eyes.

Or maybe it was just that I had spent too long staring at it, I thought to myself, slipping the picture back into my pocket along with Crichton's business card. *Professor Malcolm Crichton, Courtauld Institute of Art,* it read, with half an alphabet's worth of letters after his name. He'd urged me to call the number on it, day or night, as soon as I knew anything. Fat chance. Still, I hadn't thrown the card away.

Thing was, if there really was someone going round bumping off rent boys, I'd quite like to know about it: I still had friends on the Dilly.

But even if I was to try and follow it up, I didn't have the first clue how. I might have managed somehow to convince Crichton that I was a credible detective – there were points in our conversation the night before where I'd even almost believed it myself – but in the cold light of day the whole thing just looked impossible. I wouldn't know where to start. For a few moments as I chased the last smears of egg yolk round the plate I even considered going back to Harvey and confessing all, offering to split the money fifty-fifty, but I quickly thought through the likely consequences – losing not just one but both the well-paid jobs that were all I had going for me right now, as well as a place to sleep – and dismissed the idea. Instead I paid up, leaving a tip that sent Mario's eyebrows up somewhere near his receding hairline and had him chirping an uncharacteristic 'come again!', and headed out towards the tube station to do some serious spending.

A very enjoyable morning followed as I wound my way up and down the length of Camden High Street, splashing out on any bits and pieces that caught my eye and trying on every leather jacket available until I found one that both made me look sufficiently like James Dean and had inside pockets big enough to carry a book in without spoiling the lines. It looked good in the shop, and even better as I checked myself out in the mirror on the back of my hotel room door a few hours later. I'd booked myself in to the Regent Palace just off Piccadilly where they knew me of old, forking out for five nights in advance mostly to impress the woman on the desk who clearly didn't think I could afford to rent one of her rooms for more than the usual hour. Determined to get as much use out of the facilities as I could, I'd run myself a scalding bath and wallowed in it for a good forty minutes before putting on all my new clobber in one go and having a good old preen.

Still, there's not much point having natty new threads unless there's someone else around to admire them, so when I got bored of looking at myself and the four walls of my new abode I headed down to the street in search of familiar faces. While I was there, I told myself, there couldn't be any harm in flashing Stephen's photo around and letting people know what had

44

happened to him. Kind of a public service, really.

It was around four in the afternoon and the Dilly was just starting to come to life. The huge illuminated signs were flashing their messages uselessly into the daylight: *Enjoy Coca-Cola, Cinzano, Skol* – all in the same glass if you like. The tourists were gathering on the steps of the statue to take photos of one other: when they got home every single one of them would tell the unlucky sods they forced to look at them that it was Eros, but they would all be wrong. The lad with the wings and the arrows was actually Anteros, his brother. I'd read that in a history of London I'd pinched ages ago and it always tickled me. No better god to watch over the boys of Piccadilly than Anti-Eros. The opposite of love.

There were a few young chickens stretched out on the railings around the traffic island where the statue stood. Not many. It was early yet, and half the boys who worked the meat rack would still be so strung out they still thought it was the night before. Besides, punters don't get so horny in the cold. I used to work these railings when I first came down to London, till I worked out you got a classier kind of punter on the sunny side of the street over by Swan and Edgar (not to mention more escape routes from the police). I figured Stephen was new to the scene – I was certainly sure I'd never seen him around – so I thought I might tip off the other newcomers and warn them to be careful. Check out me, looking out for the younger generation. I took up a position in between a couple of them, leaning on the railings as if I was admiring the view of the traffic, and spoke to the nearest one, a lad with wild hair and a Crombie several sizes too big for him: 'Nice day for it.'

It felt weird. A reversal of my usual position. He looked at me suspiciously, eying me up and down, then made his decision. 'It's ten quid for a blow, five for a wank.'

'No, no, you're all right,' I reassured him. 'I'm just trying to find out about someone.' I pulled the photo of Stephen out of my new jacket and held it towards him. 'Do you know this lad?'

He squinted at the Polaroid, then at me. 'You Old Bill?' he asked doubtfully.

'No, nothing like that. It's just that – you should know he's come to a bad end.'

The boy just shook his head and took off at a fast pace towards the steps to the underground. I sighed, but didn't bother to follow. He'd probably mistaken me for one of the Jesus freaks who made occasional forays here, spreading fire and brimstone and attempting to save all our souls. Anyway, the kid wouldn't be going far: the usual routine was to alternate the meat rack with circuits of the station concourse, checking the toilets to see if any likely clients were hanging around, staying on the move to keep out the cold and reduce the chance of being done for loitering. He would be back, and maybe I could explain then. I turned and directed the photo and my friendliest smile to the boy on my other side, a skinny little queen in eyeliner and a shabby suede coat. 'I don't suppose you know this lad?'

He said nothing. Didn't even turn, just carried on staring straight ahead.

I tried again. 'I'm not looking for business, just a chat.'

This time he turned away, pointedly, and stared in the opposite direction. Bloody hell. In my day it was only the seriously ugly punters that got the blanking treatment: I knew I was getting on a bit, but did I really look *that* bad?

Fuck it. I'd tried. I put the photo away and went in search of a friendly face instead. I found one lurking near the newsstand outside the tourist shops on the corner of Shaftesbury Avenue: a dapper Jamaican, the collars of his orange shirt pulled out wide over the shoulders of a double-breasted blue coat that actually looked sufficient to keep out the February cold. We waved to each other from opposite sides of the pelican crossing and as I arrived on his side of the road he came forward to greet me with a complicated handshake, all fist-bumps and clutching of thumbs, and laughed as I got it wrong like I always did.

'How are you, Ray?'

'Good, man, good. We missing you down 'ere.' He pronounced it 'ee-yah'. I smiled and nodded at the group of black boys who were lingering behind him by the railings round the steps down to the underground station: I knew most of them by name but knew better than to address them except through Ray.

'I miss you too,' I lied. 'How's trade?'

'We get by, we get by.' Ray's gang – a family, he calls them, not totally inaccurately – come in from Brixton and work the day shift in the Dilly. He won't have them working nights: says it's too risky with the police and the dealers and drunk punters, so they all trot off home on the tube at 6pm like regular commuters. He won't let any of them touch drugs while they're working either, and he makes them go for regular check-ups at the clap clinic. It's a real professional outfit that Ray runs, and he takes a generous cut of his boys' earnings in return, but, to be fair, they all get their bed and board and live in some style. I was invited down to their place for Christmas one year. More food than I've ever seen, washed down with enough Beaujolais and brandy to sink a battleship. It was incredible. Could almost have tempted me to join the family, except I'd seen how he keeps his kids in line.

We bantered for a while, exchanging gossip about various old Dilly faces, before I brought up the subject of Stephen. 'By the way, I should warn you,' I said as I pulled the photo out again, 'one of the chickens got himself killed a couple of days back. Got pulled out of Hampstead Pond, but it looked like he'd been bashed about a fair bit before he went in the water. D'you recognise him?'

Ray looked at the Polaroid, sucking air through his teeth. 'I can't say I do, man.'

'Might be worth mentioning to the boys though.'

He mistook my meaning, turning and whistling to bring the tallest of the lads behind him scurrying over. 'Hello Paul,' I smiled, and he shot me a shy grin back.

'You seen dis boy?' Ray handed him the photograph.

Paul nodded quickly, but said nothing. His eyes flicked nervously from side to side.

Ray tutted in frustration. '*Where* you see him?'

The boy spoke so softly I had to strain to hear him. 'I think he's one of the Playland kids.'

Ray pursed his lips, his eyebrows raised. 'There's your answer.'

'Shit,' I muttered as Paul scuttled back to his post by the underground entrance. Playland was an arcade just round the corner in Coventry Street. It was notorious as a place for underage rent – well, we were all underage, but I'm talking *seriously* underage, 12, 13, even as young as 10 if the rumours were to be believed. They're pimped by a bunch of blokes who keep them in hostels all over London run by some supposedly religious outfit. The Vice Squad had raided the arcade a couple of years before and we'd all expected it to be shut down, but nothing seemed to come of it and before long all the old familiar faces were back in amongst the one-armed bandits and pinball machines, and a whole host of new and frighteningly young ones had arrived to join them. The boss of the place was meant to be seriously well-connected – someone even told me he was a Lord – and everyone assumed he'd stumped up enough money to make the whole thing go away. And in the meantime, while he and his friends walked free, the cops had cracked down on

48

the rest of us, doubling the number of undercover officers they had trolling the Dilly and arresting anyone who dared even look in their direction in a less than manly manner.

All of which hammered home the message that we were on our own. And that meant we had a duty to look after ourselves, and each other. We, I realised with a sinking feeling, in this case meaning I.

Ray sucked air back through pursed lips again, before asking the obvious question: 'What dis got to do with you, Tommy?'

'I've made a promise to someone,' I found myself saying. 'To find out what happened to him, if I can.'

Ray shook his head slowly, gazing up at the illuminated advertisements above our heads as they cycled through their endless circuit. 'A man should be careful who he go making promises to. A promise can be a dangerous thing. Get you into trouble. Other people's trouble.' His eyes returned earthwards and seemed to take in my appearance for the first time. 'Nice jacket, Tommy.'

'Thanks, Ray.' I screwed up the handshake again as I took my leave. I could tell he was watching me as I walked round the corner into Coventry Street, but he didn't say another thing.

SIX

THE LETTERS OF THE Playland sign were picked out in alternating bright yellow and orange lights, the leg of the Y extending downwards in to an arrow, the bulbs chasing one another endlessly downwards like a beckoning finger, ushering all comers into the gaping entrance below. Waves of discordant noise rolled out as I crossed the threshold: the snap and clatter of pinball machines, the rattle of reels on the one-armed bandits and the background hum of pop hits drowned out by shrill fanfares which erupted from the machines as their internal mechanics momentarily locked into the lucky sequence before clattering on.

There were boys all around the place. Boys gathered in twos and threes around the pinball machines, one mashing the buttons as his companions stood shoulder to shoulder to urge him on. Boys roaming amongst the fruit machines too, their dull red glow reflected in blank, empty eyes. One boy who looked barely into puberty was dully slotting coppers from a plastic pot into the penny falls machine, not seeming to care where they fell: his coins piled up uselessly on the top shelf as it slid back and forth, back and forth. Directly above him was one of the large red-on-white signs that festooned the ceiling of the arcade: *Strictly No Admittance To Under-18s*. The only people I could see in the place that looked over that age were the sweaty bloke in a stained singlet sitting in the glass-walled change booth and a man in a dark belted overcoat slotting coins into an old-fashioned one-armed bandit against the far wall. He was wearing black leather gloves too, as if he was scared of catching something. Probably wise.

I dug in my pocket and pulled out a handful of coins, which at least was plentiful after my spending spree that morning. The machines in Playland were ancient and barely maintained: half of them hadn't even been adapted for the new money and had hand-scrawled notices Sellotaped next to their slots: *Shilling coins only*. I had a couple among my change, and fed them into the machine nearest me, disinterestedly watching the pieces of fruit as they spun. Within a minute one of the roaming boys had made a beeline for me and was behind my shoulder.

'You want to hold that one,' he murmured after a few seconds, stretching a bony finger towards a pair of cherries on the first reel.

'Do I?' I pressed the button obediently. 'I don't really know what I'm doing. I don't understand these machines.'

'I can help you,' he said, without much enthusiasm. 'P'raps I'll bring you luck today.' It sounded like a line he had had drummed into him.

I let the reels shudder to a halt – the cherries joined by a lemon and one bar, which won me the sum total of nothing –

before reaching into my pocket. 'Actually I'd like to show you something.'

He gave an involuntary flinch as I turned towards him. 'It's all right,' I assured him, 'It's just a photo of someone. D'you know him?'

The boy shook his head a bit too quickly. Now I got a proper look at him, he looked even younger than Stephen in the picture: he had a similar mop of blond hair but a pinched, closed face, growing more closed by the second.

'You're sure? I think he used to come in here,' I prompted.

He stared down at his scuffed plimsolls and the garishly patterned carpet. 'I dunno.' It looked like there was a fight going on within him: he wanted to get away from me, but I guessed he was worried about what would happen to him if he failed to turn a trick. I looked around the arcade: the sweaty man was steadily watching us both from the change cage, and the bloke with the gloves had moved across from the bank of fruit machines at the far end of the room to take up position at one on the opposite side of the row from us.

I lowered my voice. 'What's your name, mate?'

'Martin,' he almost whispered, raising his eyes slightly, but not high enough to meet mine.

'Listen, Martin, you don't have to be here. If people are making you do things you don't want to do, you don't have to. I've been where you are, and there are other ways, safer places –'

My voice was cut off as an arm wrapped round my neck. 'That's enough,' barked a voice directly into my ear, and I was yanked back and dragged towards the back of the arcade, my feet desperately scrabbling for purchase on the sticky carpet. I couldn't breathe. I was vaguely aware of the boys around the pinball machines staring in my direction as I was pulled past them, but my eyes were swimming and all my thoughts were on trying to lessen the crushing pressure on my throat. My fingers were scrabbling at the arm that held me, but it was as strong as iron and clad in some sort of slippery material that I couldn't get a grip on. And then the flashing lights of the machines seemed to warp and combine, melting into a yawning tunnel with a strange blackness at its centre, and my legs gave way completely as I began to pass out.

Reality burst back like a firework along with a great burst of oxygen as the pressure on my neck was released and I was spun around and slammed back hard against a wall. The relief was shortlived: my assailant had transferred his grip to my shirtfront, which he yanked up in a gloved fist so that I was on shaky tiptoes. With his other hand he was holding something against my cheek which stung my skin: it was too close to my eye to see it properly, but it looked like a flick knife.

'Think you can come in here and steal my boys off me, do you?' he hissed. His face was inches from my own. His breath stank of stale cigarettes. He had pulled me around a corner in the back of the arcade where a high wall of darkened machines sporting Out of Order signs meant we couldn't be seen from the street. The only person who could see what was happening was the man in the change cage. As I looked pleadingly in his direction he locked his eyes on mine and very deliberately reached out to turn up the volume on the music. *Save – your – kisses for me, save all your kisses for me*, sang Brotherhood of Man as the blade bit into my cheek.

'I wasn't. I wasn't I promise,' I gasped, tasting blood as it ran down into the side of my mouth.

'I've seen you out there,' he spat. 'Too old to sell your own arse any more, so you think you'll start running some boys of your own. Should have stuck to your own turf, *mate*. Now I'm gonna have to teach you to show some *respect*.' He pivoted the knife slowly so that only the very point of the blade was resting on my cheekbone, aimed straight towards my eye. I heard someone cry out, a high-pitched, girlish wail, and realised it was me. Less than 24 hours earlier I'd been having difficulty summoning up enough urine to piss convincingly: right now that wasn't a problem at all.

'I really wasn't, you've got it wrong, that's not why I'm here at all,' I gabbled, desperate to explain.

'Don't lie to me, you little pansy. I heard what you were saying to Marty.' He exerted the tiniest bit of pressure on the knife and the movement went through my whole body. I screwed my eyes shut, but forced myself to carry on talking. The truth was all I had to defend myself with.

'I'm not, I'm not I promise, I just came in to warn them – to warn all of you. If you look in my pocket you'll find a photo. It's of a boy called Stephen, he used to… I think he was one of yours. Please, honestly, it's the truth. The inside pocket, the left one. Please.'

The man made no move to take the photo, but there was an almost imperceptible lightening of the pressure on the blade. 'Stephen? What do you know about Stephen?'

'Nothing!' With a gulp I realised that without intending to, I'd found myself not just a suspect, but a motive too. If this was how the guy behaved when he thought someone was trying to poach one of his charges, how was he likely to react to one of them announcing he wanted to take early retirement? Maybe I wasn't so bad at this detective business after all. Shame I'd left it so late to find out.

The salt of tears was mingling with the metallic taste of blood in my mouth, but I couldn't see any choice but to press on. 'All I know is that he's been killed. They've found his body.'

There was a silence. I risked opening my eyes. The man

appeared to be thinking. It looked as if Stephen's death had come as news to him, but I wasn't about to dismiss him as chief suspect, at least while he was still holding a weapon up against my face.

'When?' he finally barked.

'Tuesday. That was when they found him, anyway. Monday morning was the last time anyone saw him. Unless you know otherwise.'

He grunted, then muttered, to himself as much as to me: 'Nah, we haven't seen him since before the weekend.'

'The police pulled him out of the men's pond on Hampstead Heath,' I added. Other than the involvement of Malcolm Crichton, this thug now knew everything that I knew. God, I'd have been useless in the army, like my father always used to tell me. Never mind only giving your name, rank and serial number, it turns out that at the very first hint of torture I spill everything.

It seemed to have done the job, though. The man withdrew the blade and relaxed his grip on my collar, but only so he could use his gloved left hand to give me a cuff on the uncut side of my head. 'If I find out you're lying to me, it won't just be that pretty face I'm cutting. I'll have your cock off as well. You understand?'

'I understand.' I cringed back against the wall, pressing my own hand to my cheek. It came away bright red.

'I need to make some calls.' The knife closed and disappeared into his coat pocket as he stepped away and yanked open a fire door in the wall beside me. A dark-haired teenager practically fell out of it, only keeping his balance because the man grabbed him. He was gabbling apologies before he was even upright: 'Sorry Phil, sorry, Phil, sorry.'

'What the fuck are you playing at?' the man snarled, shoving him stumbling into the dead fruit machines. He shot a glance up the open stairway. 'Is he finished with you?'

'All done.' The boy hurried off into the main part of the arcade, head down, slight shoulders up, trying to shrink his emaciated frame even smaller, take up even less room in the world.

Phil paused, one foot on the bottom tread of the staircase, and pointed a leather-clad finger in my direction. 'And you. I'll be watching out for you. If I see you in here again, it's your body they're gonna be pulling out of the water. Got it?'

'Got it,' I confirmed, and got the hell out of Playland. I didn't stop running until I was all the way down at the other end of Haymarket.

SEVEN

'CHRIST, TOMMY, what happened to you?'

I swivelled the only eye that was available to me to look at the new arrival, but the movement was still too much for the woman who was bathing my wound. 'Keep still!' she snapped, grabbing a handful of my hair to ensure I complied.

'Sorry Shirley. Hi Mark.'

Mark, a slightly chippy Welshman in his late 20s, came over and squatted in front of me, his expression an equal mix of sympathy and outrage. 'Was it–?'

'I wasn't gay-bashed,' I said quickly. It was about the tenth time I'd answered that question this evening. 'It was...it was a work thing.'

Mark drew back, disappointment clouding his handsome face. 'I thought you were getting out of all that?'

'I am,' I muttered, wincing as Shirley substituted the watery cotton wool wad for one soaked in TCP. 'I'm trying to.'

'We worry about you.' Mark stood up, yanking down his drainpipe jeans where they had ridden up. 'I'm not judging you, you know, it's a valid lifestyle choice, but the risks…'

'I know,' I said firmly, not wanting to get back into a conversation I'd had what felt like a hundred times before. There's only so much group therapy-speak I can bear. I changed the subject. 'Nice T-shirt.'

'Thanks.' Mark looked down proudly at the two figures who were framed between the straps of his red braces. The image was smudged and badly-applied, but you could clearly make out two pendulous cocks hanging out from their cowboy outfits, almost touching one another. 'It's new. Got it in the Kings Road.'

'Bet you kept your coat done up on the bus though.'

He smirked. 'Not all the way. I'll save you a seat.'

He moved away to the half-occupied circle of orange plastic chairs which had been arranged in the middle of the hall. Many more were stacked along the walls: the hall could apparently hold up to a hundred people, but we seldom needed more than a dozen or so seats. Still, the community centre at least had a decent first-aid kit, which enabled Shirley, who was an ambulance driver in real life, to make a better job of dressing the cut on my cheek than I had managed in my hotel room with nothing more than some hard toilet paper and a pack of plasters from Boots.

'That's the best I can do for now,' she said briskly as she pressed the last bit of surgical tape into place and released my hair. 'I think it's going to leave a scar, though.'

'That's all right. I was far too pretty for this world anyway.'

She did her best to return my grin, but she was giving me the same irritating look of concern as Mark. 'Do be careful, won't you, Tom?'

'Scout's honour.' I gave her the salute, but she didn't find that funny at all, straightening up and waggling the red and white box. 'I'd better get this back before we start.'

'Yep.' I stood up and walked over to the circle. Mark had been as good as his word, and I sank gratefully into the chair next to his. The only other options were the seats on either side of Trevor, an earnest, middle-aged queen who is nice enough in his own way but has possibly the worst halitosis on the planet. I felt slightly guilty when Shirley returned from the kitchen and paused before sitting down next to him, trying to angle her body to avoid the worst of the fumes.

I had started coming to CHE meetings not long after I first moved into the squat. The community centre was just down the road from us and I'd been quite impressed at the way they kept doggedly replacing the posters on the board outside on a daily basis as they got torn down. Then one night the local National Front decided to push the message home by spray-painting graffiti across the whole of the front of the centre, and when I walked past some of the members of the group were there trying to scrub off the swastikas and swearwords and I offered to help, and got talking to them and that was that. Mark was there, and I remember he made me laugh but shocked me a bit too when he suggested leaving the words 'Poofs Out' across the doors because it wouldn't actually be a bad mission statement for the group. Our full title is the Campaign For Homosexual Equality (Camden branch), but everyone calls it CHE, as in Guevara, which gives it a revolutionary air that the rest of the members don't always quite live up to.

I'd been going along most Friday evenings ever since. It was nice to meet other gay men – gay people, I should say, because as well as Shirley there are two other lesbians who are regulars – who had more than one thing on their mind. It can all get a bit heavy at times – Mark and a couple of the other members can turn anything into a political issue if you give them the chance, and they're none of them happier than when they're stitching a banner – but tonight I figured I might be able to turn all that fervour to my advantage. My experience at Playland had hardened my determination to do something – I still wasn't quite sure what – about Stephen's death. I don't like bullies, never have. But its only recently that I've found the support of others that will help me stand up to them.

First, though, I would have to wait for Any Other Business. Our chairman Neil, a jobsworth whose day job is pushing bits of paper around for the council, keeps a tight control of our formal meetings, and would probably impose an agenda and minutes on the disco nights too if he could get away with it. So I had to sit through long discussions of the polite no thank you letter Neil had received from Thames TV to his suggestion that they might like to follow-up *The Naked Civil Servant* with a programme portraying 'a wider cross-section of the homosexual community who do not feel that Quentin Crisp fully represents them'; how last Saturday's picket of the Oxford Street branch of BHS in protest at the chain sacking a trainee manager for membership of his local CHE group had gone; what the theme should be for our presence at the Gay Pride march that summer ('it's never too early to start sewing!') and, most interminably, whether or not we should have anything to do with the local Gay Liberation Front, whose extra-parliamentary ideology was apparently completely at odds with our own commitments to the democratic process, but who did have a duplicating machine which would be useful when it came to producing the newsletters. They have the hall on Mondays.

Finally, by the point in the evening where everyone was starting to look enviously at the tea urn and custard creams laid out on paper plates in the corner, it was my turn.

'Um… I wanted to tell you about a guy who was killed a few days ago. A boy really, he said he was seventeen but I think he might have been even younger. At least, we think he was killed. He was found floating in the water but he had bruises all over his head and face.' It was the first time I'd spoken up at one of these meetings by myself – I'm not backwards about coming forward in the discussions, but this felt totally different – and I felt that despite all the time I'd had to prepare what I was going to say, I was getting it badly wrong. My thinking was that since looking into Stephen's life had proved to be a dangerous occupation, I should maybe start with his death instead, and that some of my fellow CHE members might be able to offer me a bit of guidance as to what questions to ask and who to ask them. Like I said, Shirley's an ambulance driver, and Neil works for the GLC, and there's another member who's something to do with the law, a barrister's clerk I think, only he wasn't there that night. But every single one of them was a lot more grown-up and together than I was.

'Who was he?' I was grateful to Mark for cutting in with a sensible question that got me back on track.

'He was a rent boy. His name was Stephen – I don't know his surname. And that's not necessarily his real name, either, a lot of us, I mean a lot of them, use made-up names when they're doing business.'

'And where was he found?' asked Neil, who looked slightly put out that Mark had stepped in to lead the discussion.

'In the men's pond on the Heath.' A murmur went round the group: most of them were regular visitors in the summer months and those that weren't knew all about the place's reputation.

'Was he from round there?' Neil asked, reaching into his briefcase to pull out the pamphlet with the details of all the other CHE groups around the city and country.

'No. Well – I don't think so. But he had been staying up there, with… I probably shouldn't tell you his name, because I'm not sure he'd like that, but a client. A regular client.'

'And you think he might have killed him?' asked Mark bluntly.

'Oh! No. No, I'm sure he had nothing to do with it. It was him who told me he was dead.' I was explaining this all so badly. 'No, but he was there when the body – when Stephen – was pulled out. He said there were all sorts of suspicious circumstances. There were the bruises, like I said, and he was naked, and apparently he had a real thing about not letting anyone see him in the nude. And also his clothes were nowhere to be found.'

'Which would make it more difficult to identify his body,' cut in Shirley. I was pleased to see she was at least taking it seriously.

'Yeah. Um…d'you know where they would have taken him? His body?'

She nodded. 'Probably the morgue at the Royal Free. You want me to ask around?'

'Could you?'

'No problem. There's a cute pathology technician down there I'm almost certain is a dyke.' She grinned.

'The thing is, apparently even though there were all these weird things about it, the police just weren't interested. They said he must just have gone for a swim and drowned.'

'That's easy enough to find out from the post-mortem,' Shirley cut in. 'If there's no water in the lungs, that'll show he was dead before he went in the water.'

I looked at her gratefully. 'Would they definitely do one though? A post-mortem?'

She nodded. 'Should do. There's usually an inquest with any sudden or unexplained deaths. I'll see what I can find out.'

'That would be great, thanks. It just…it all seems a bit suspicious, that's all.'

I tailed off, limply, but Mark took over with enough energy for both of us. 'Well, it's obviously bollocks, isn't it!' he erupted. 'He was blatantly gaybashed, wasn't he?' He turned to address the circle. 'This is exactly the sort of thing I've been talking about. They're ready to hassle us or arrest us on the slightest excuse, and when it comes to an actual serious crime committed against a gay man they couldn't care less. We don't count. It's not just that we're worth less than normal people, it's that we're worth *nothing*.'

'I don't think 'normal' is necessarily a useful –' started Neil, but there was no stopping Mark now. His Welsh accent got more pronounced when he was angry. I quite liked it. 'We need to take a stand. We need to do something. This week it's Tommy's friend. Next week it could be you, or me, or any one of us. I mean, Tommy, did you even think to go to the police about that?'

He was pointing at the cut on my cheek. Surprised, I put my fingers up to Shirley's expertly-applied dressing: 'No! No, I mean, I couldn't –'

'Right!' exclaimed Mark, rolling the R beautifully. 'Even when we're the victims of violence, it would never occur to us to go to the police, because we know they're just as much the enemy as the bastards that do stuff like this.' I thought this was pushing it a bit – having tangled with both, I'd much rather take my chances with the Vice Squad's finest than the psycho in Playland – but I wasn't about to interrupt him. 'It's time we said we've had enough. For god's sake, isn't that what we're supposed to be about – getting bloody equality?'

He sat back in his chair, crossing his arms. Several heads were nodding around the circle, but an uncomfortable silence reigned until Neil coughed and said 'Well, I suppose I could draft a letter…'

'*Fuck* letters!' barked Mark. 'When was the last time writing a letter made a difference?'

'Dreyfus,' said Trevor suddenly and smellily, but everyone ignored him. Mark turned towards me again. 'Tom, it's my day off tomorrow. Let's go into the police station and bloody well *demand* they do something. Refuse to leave if they don't. Who else is in?'

He looked round at the rest of the circle, who shuffled sheepishly. 'I'm on an early shift,' Shirley apologised. 'I can't really – not with my job,' someone else muttered.

Mark let out a theatrical sigh. 'All right then. You and me, Tommy. Is it a date?'

'It's a date,' I beamed thankfully.

It wasn't until an hour or so afterwards, once the adrenaline had worn off on the bus home, that it occurred to me that it actually might be.

EIGHT

I MET MARK at his flat in Kentish Town at eleven the next morning. It was a one-bedroom place above an Indian takeaway, and the whole place smelled of curry. 'They're nice lads, came over from Uganda,' he told me as he spooned sugar into two mugs in the tiny kitchenette that was crammed into the corner of his sitting room. 'The problem is it makes me feel hungry all the time.' He'd been apologising for the place ever since he opened the door, first of all for the size and then the state of it, then for the pair of freestanding electric rings he boiled the kettle on and the chips in the glass mugs he served the coffee in. 'It's all a bit Katherine Whitehorn here,' he joked, and I laughed along, even though I didn't know what that meant.

The flat was actually pretty tidy. He'd draped coloured scarves over the lamps, which gave it a nice atmosphere, and I was pleased to see a well-stocked bookcase crammed in next to the sofa, with spine-crazed copies of *The Rats* and *The Lord of the Rings* sitting alongside *Society and the Healthy Homosexual*, *Giovanni's Room* and all the other usual suspects. The cowboy t-shirt he'd been wearing last night was hanging on a wire hanger from the picture rail above the TV like it was a painting: Mark caught me looking at it and said something about fashion being a type of art itself, which I agreed with even though I thought it was probably just that he liked looking at willies.

I was glad that at least he wasn't wearing it today: I couldn't see it going down well at the police station. Instead he'd smartened up for the occasion: he was wearing a light blue shirt with a dark blue tie that between them perfectly set off the colour of his eyes. But he still had the badges he always wore on the lapel of his duffel coat when he put it on to set off: his silver gay rights lambda, the USDAW logo and the orange sun saying 'Nuclear Power No Thanks'. I'd done my best to look respectable myself, putting on a new short-sleeved shirt with blue and white stripes I'd picked up during yesterday's shopping spree. I still had my leather jacket on though. There was no way I was leaving that behind at the fleapit hotel to get nicked.

We caught the number 24 from the stop outside his flat and had the top deck to ourselves most of the way up to Hampstead. Weirdly we were avoiding the topic of what we were off to do: Mark's bravado from last night seemed to have faded away in the cold light of day and he looked nearly as nervous as I felt. Instead we talked about anything and everything else: how long he'd been living in the flat (three years, the first of them with a boyfriend who was now off the scene); where he was from (Swansea) and whether he ever went back there (yes, but, not often and only when his dad was away for work).

It was only when we got off the bus and walked up the hill towards the massive red-brick edifice of the police station with its honour guard of panda cars lined up outside that we couldn't avoid the subject any longer. 'Who's going to do the talking?' Mark asked.

'I don't mind,' I said, even though I did. I was hugely grateful for Mark's support (although, if I was honest, I would have preferred it if one of the better-qualified CHE members had volunteered to come along than an assistant in an army surplus store) but this was, when it came down to it, my battle to fight. Or at least, the battle Malcolm Crichton had paid me to fight on his behalf.

'All right. Come here then.' Mark pulled me behind one of the plane trees that lined the street and surprised me with a kiss full-on on the lips. 'For luck, yeah?'

I smiled gratefully, rubbed the rectangular shape of the book in my jacket pocket for a bit of extra good fortune, and walked over to the police station and up the steps with him following just behind me.

The reception was kitted out in grey lino with blue plastic chairs that were bolted to the floor. It was empty except for the uniformed officer behind the desk, who had thinning sandy hair and a moustache. He was sifting through some paperwork, and he made a point of carrying on when we arrived at the desk so that we had to wait for him to look up.

'How can I help you gents?' he finally asked, eyeing us both without enthusiasm.

'It's about someone who was murdered,' I blurted. That got his attention. He hauled a pad across the countertop towards him and pulled out a pen.

'When was this?'

'On Monday. You took his body away on Tuesday morning.'

He paused, his pen hovering above the pad. 'So this is an incident the police are already aware of?'

'Yes. He was found in the men's pond on the Heath.'

The policeman sighed and made a big show of returning the pen to his uniform pocket. 'Right. You'd need to speak to the officer in charge of the investigation.'

I was about to ask who that was when Mark cut in. 'So you are investigating it, then?'

The policeman gave him a cold look, taking in both badges and jutting chin. 'Figure of speech, son. Cases like this, there's often not a lot *to* investigate.'

All Mark's nervous energy had come rushing back. 'Cases like what? Cases involving gays, you mean? Go on, say it, you might as well! What about the bruises on his face? What are you doing to try to find the people who attacked him?'

The policeman placed hands like hams very deliberately down on the counter and leaned forward. 'As far as we know, there's no evidence that anyone attacked anyone. Unless, of course, you know different.' His gaze shifted to me. 'What happened to your face, sonny?'

'Shaving cut,' I said quickly before Mark could make things any worse.

He smirked. 'You don't look old enough to shave. So this chap in the pond, was he a friend of yours?' Somehow he managed to pack the word 'friend' with so much disdain it sounded like an insult.

'Friend of a friend,' I muttered. 'Look, we just want to know what you're doing about investigating his death. Because the whole thing seems pretty suspicious to us, and –'

'It does, does it?' the policeman interrupted, raising his voice. 'Shall I tell you what looks a bit suspicious to me? Your *friend of a friend* ends up in the water somewhere that's known for being a benders' hangout, and then two young fellas like you turn up, one of them with visible injuries, and start getting all emotional about it. I start to wonder about things like lover's tiffs, but then maybe that's just my dirty mind. Where were the two of you on Monday night?'

'Oh, that is just *typical*…' Mark began, but I laid a hand on his arm to stop him. The policeman's eyes followed my movement.

'You said we could talk to the officer in charge of the investigation,' I said in as calm a tone as I could manage. 'We'd like to do that, please.' I realised my hand was still resting on Mark's arm – I could feel it twitching with anger – and quickly returned it to my side.

'He's a very busy man,' the officer said after a long, frigid pause. 'I'm not sure he's available.'

'Would you mind trying, please?' I was trying to stay as polite as possible while Mark seethed beside me. I appreciated his anger, but I'd had a lot more first-hand experience of dealing with the filth than he had, and I knew losing your rag was never a good idea.

The policeman still looked like he might refuse, but finally he pulled out his pen again and barked 'Names?'

'Thomas Wildeblood, Wilde with an 'e' like Oscar, and yes, I've heard all the jokes. And this is Mark…' I realised I didn't know Mark's second name, but he sulkily supplied it: 'Adamson'.

The policeman raised a sardonic eyebrow, but he did at least pick up the telephone. 'Thank you, constable,' I smarmed. 'Sergeant!' he barked, but he started to dial anyway.

I steered Mark to the rank of seats nearest to the counter and got him sat down, risking a reassuring rub of his knee while the sergeant was absorbed with the phone. It was picked up after just a few rings. We could clearly hear the voice at the other end say 'Watkins.'

'It's Mac on the front desk, Sir. We've got a couple of gentlemen come in asking about the floater that was pulled out of the pond the other morning.'

A frustrated sigh crackled from the receiver. 'Is it bloody Special Branch again? You can tell them I've already given them everything we've got.'

'No sir,' the sergeant replied, glaring across the room at us. 'Definitely not Special Branch this time. Just a *couple* of members of the public.' This time there was no mistaking it: he'd chosen the word deliberately.

'Well, you can tell them it's out of our hands. Nothing to do with us any more. They want to know anything, they can try Scotland Yard. And if they can get any answers from them, they're doing better than me, because they were telling me fuck all.' The phone was slammed down, and the burr of the dialling tone echoed through the empty reception.

The desk sergeant looked nearly as disgruntled as his colleague had sounded. He dropped the receiver back into its cradle and shot us an unfriendly glance. 'I'm afraid no one's available to speak to you.'

Instinct told me Mark was ready to erupt again. It also told me that it would do us no good at all. 'Thank you for your help, sergeant,' I trilled brightly, and slipped my arm through Mark's to make a particularly pointed exit from the station.

He was bubbling with rage and frustration. He exploded before we had even got down the police station steps and kept up an inarticulate flow of fury all the way down the hill to the bus stop, alternating 'How dare they' with 'second-class citizens' and even the odd 'fascist state' in there too. I wasn't at all sure the situation was quite as straightforward as he was making out, but I knew better than to prompt an argument at this stage, and kept quiet in the hope he would get it all out of his system.

He didn't. A couple of sideways glances from passers-by at us walking arm in arm allowed him to vent some of his feelings by loudly inquiring what the fuck they thought they were looking at, but all the way back to Kentish Town on the bus– more crowded this time and enforcing silence upon us – I could feel his leg quivering hotly against mine. By the time we got back up the stairs to his flat and through the front door, it was pretty obvious what I needed to do. I clamped my hands around the side of his head, taking a moment to enjoy the feel of his freshly razor-cropped back and sides, pulled him close and stuck my tongue deep into his mouth, pushing back against all the energy that was fizzing off him with a practised passion I could easily summon up within myself.

He held back for a second in surprise, but then returned my kiss with equal vigour, his hands scrabbling at the front of my shirt and popping the buttons open as I ran my own hands down his back and onto the perfect twin rounds of his buttocks, pulling him close and crushing our hard bodies together.

Afterwards, when we were lying in sticky silence on the double bed that filled his tiny bedroom almost from wall to wall, me trailing a hand lazily down through the surprisingly thick hair on his chest and him absently tweaking one of my own bare nipples, he asked if he could see me again.

'You see me every week at CHE', I said. I genuinely didn't understand the question.

'No, but I mean…' He propped himself up on his elbow so he could look me in the face. 'We could go out. For a drink, or to the pictures or something.'

I shrugged. 'Yeah. Ok. That would be nice.' I realised it actually would.

He smiled, reached down and tugged on my flaccid dick. 'Although I suppose we'd have to be careful where we go. You're not 21 yet, are you?'

I shook my head. 'Not till August. Does it bother you?'

He snorted. 'An unjust law's no law at all.'

It sounded like he was quoting something, but I didn't know what. I overcompensated: 'Anyway, it's hardly like you've stolen my innocence for the very first time!'

'Hmm.' He wasn't meeting my eye. I tried again to lighten the mood. 'Don't worry, this is a freebie!'

It had sounded all right in my head, but when I saw his weak attempt at a smile I had to admit that it wasn't that funny. I rolled over to face him. 'I wasn't lying when I said I was giving it up, you know. I really am.'

'I'm glad.' He was still avoiding my eyes, looking down at my cock in his hand instead. 'I worry about you.'

'You don't need to,' I tried to reassure him, but I knew both of us were picturing poor Stephen in the freezing water with bruises all over his face.

Fortunately at that moment the phone rang, and Mark rolled over me and padded out, still naked, into the tiny hallway to answer it. I lay back and looked around the room. Most of his clothes were hanging on a rail at the foot of his bed which filled most of the remaining floorspace. I wondered idly how many of them would fit me.

'Shirley, hello,' I could hear him saying in the hallway. 'Oh right. I don't need to as it happens, he's actually here with me, you can tell him yourself. Hang on. *Tom*?'

I sat up, looked round for my underpants, failed to find them and wrapped the scratchy blanket around myself instead. We'd paused long enough to switch on the electric fire in the bedroom, its orange glow throwing a false sunset over our lovemaking, but the rest of the flat was freezing and I winced as I stepped from the carpet onto the cold cork tiles of the hallway. Mark was cupping his balls in one hand and holding out the receiver towards me with the other. He scuttled back into the warm bed as soon as I took it from him.

'Hello?'

'Hello Tommy,' said Shirley, and I could tell from her voice she was grinning. 'Fancy finding you there.'

'Ha ha, very funny,' I said tersely. Bang went any chance of keeping that secret – by the time of our next meeting, everyone in CHE would know me and Mark had had sex.

'I won't keep you,' she continued, still evidently beaming. 'It's just about that purple plus you asked me to find out about.'

'Purple plus?' For a second I thought she was talking about drugs and had got me muddled with someone else.

'Sorry, ambulance lingo. The dead body that was brought in the other day. Well, I asked at the Royal Free, and no joy I'm afraid.'

'They didn't take him there?'

'Oh no, they did, but he didn't stay long. He was due for a post-mortem yesterday, but it was cancelled and his body's already gone off for cremation.'

'Who cancelled it?'

'They got a call from the coroner's office saying there was no need because the investigation had already been closed, no inquest required. The guys in the mortuary were surprised, because they said by the look of him someone had given him a right going over.'

So it sounded like Crichton hadn't been exaggerating. '*They* didn't think he drowned, then?'

She sniggered. 'I asked the lad that bagged him if he could have just fallen in the water, and his exact words were "only if he hit every branch on every tree on the Heath on his way down".'

I suppose the jokey tone Shirley puts on is her way of coping with her job. But I couldn't really complain: I've laughed hard enough at the stories she tells in the pub before.

'Anyway, the undertakers turned up to collect him that same afternoon, and they had all the right paperwork, so off he went. Pauper's funeral, and the council usually do them as a job lot at the end of the week so he's probably already gone up the chimney I'm afraid.'

Shirley rang off with a cheeky 'I'll leave you two to it then!' but I was too deep in thought to even bother to come up with a retort. Post-mortems, coroners, special branch – all this sort of thing was Greek to me, but even I could tell that something wasn't right. What I wasn't sure about, yet, was what it was.

'Get in here and bring that blanket back!' called Mark. And since I couldn't think of anything better to do right at that moment, I did.

NINE

I WENT TO SEE Malcolm Crichton that weekend. It felt like the right thing to do.

I went to his home, because obviously there was no way he could come by what he thought was my office. It was in a big mansion block on Highgate Hill. Nearly every inch of the walls of the flat was crammed with paintings, some of them properly old and dark and expensive-looking, and almost every one of them of naked men.

'I'm something of an authority on the male nude,' Crichton said when I pointed this out. I thought of saying 'aren't we all', but let him continue instead. 'I published what's still considered to be one of the definitive works: *The Male Form After Michelangelo*. I'm sure I've a copy somewhere if you'd like to see.' He set down the tray he was carrying on the smoked glass coffee table in his living room and went unerringly to the correct shelf of the stuffed bookcase beside the paper-strewn desk in the corner.

'Very nice,' I said appreciatively as I leafed through its large pages, which were filled with black and white photos of old paintings of men in various states of undress, most of them, according to the captions, saints undergoing torture. And it was, though to be honest you'd get better value for money from under the counter of nearly any shop in Soho.

Crichton smiled modestly and poured the coffee. He had made it in one of those posh metal jugs you put on the stove, and he served it in proper bone china cups and saucers. There were even little tongs to dole out the sugar lumps. One thing was for sure: Stephen would have wanted for nothing if he had taken up the invitation to move in. It was nearly enough to make me start thinking enviously about Crichton's spare room myself.

I filled him in on what I supposed I had to call my investigations over the past few days, leaving out the incident with the flick knife and describing Mark as 'my associate' rather than, well, whatever he actually was now (I wasn't quite sure myself). The old man didn't seem surprised to hear about Playland, which made me suspect he had been too embarrassed at our first meeting to admit that was where he had picked Stephen up. If he had, he could have saved me a lot of trouble: although the cut on my cheek was beginning to heal, I was still taking very circuitous routes around town to make sure I went nowhere near the place. If I hadn't paid for so many nights in advance at the Regent Palace I would have cleared out of Piccadilly altogether: as it was I was creeping in and out of the back entrance of the hotel and keeping my head down as much as possible.

Crichton did perk up when it came to what we had learned

at the police station: he looked positively bewildered at the mention of Special Branch – as, for different reasons, was I.

'But surely that's the section of the police that deals with national security, terrorism, that sort of thing?'

'Mmm.' I tried to look unsurprised, though this was news to me. I'd assumed from the name they just dealt with cases that were particularly, well, special, like some sort of super-CID. 'Can you think of any reason why they would be interested in Stephen or yourself?'

Crichton spread his hands wide. 'I teach the history of art at the Courtauld Institute. What possible interest could Special Branch have in someone like me?'

'And what about Stephen?'

'I hardly think…' He paused, and the genuine grief that I had perceived in Crichton on our first meeting now seemed for the first time to take on an edge of something else – self-preservation, perhaps. 'Of course, I knew very little about the rest of his life.'

'Where was he from?'

'Somewhere in the north, I believe. He had quite a pronounced accent. Yorkshire perhaps? But you must understand, we rarely discussed his life outside of our own…relationship.'

'He never talked about where he grew up, what he had done before you met?'

Crichton shook his head. 'Stephen preferred not to. We were always looking to the future rather than the past.'

He gave a smile that he probably thought was wistful. From where I was sitting it just came over as smug. Much as it might help the old man to cast himself as Stephen's knight in shining armour, the fact of the matter was that he was still renting him out by the hour. I decided to push the point.

'You really can't remember anything? It might help me to

understand why he died.'

The smile faltered and drooped. Crichton thought for a moment before saying slightly sulkily: 'He did once mention a home.'

'Family, you mean? Where were they?'

'No – not home, *a* home. Or rather *the* home, was how he referred to it.' Crichton began to fuss over the coffee cups, avoiding my eyes. 'I suggested that we might try something. And he said that was the one thing he wouldn't do, he hadn't done that since 'he was in the home'. He became rather upset.'

'What was that?' I was sure it would be spanking: it's always spanking with posh blokes.

Crichton was blushing now, fluttering a hand in front of his mouth. 'I wanted to – it was quite innocent – romantic in a way – just to bathe him. Sponge his back. Like my own father used to when I took my bath as a child. It wasn't even a sexual thing.'

Oh yeah? I thought. I'd had a client once who said exactly the same while he was asking me to powder his bottom and put him in a nappy. I gave him his money back and told him to piss off. Just like I'd told Neil and the rest of the group a few months ago that if they agreed to meet with the Paedophile Information Exchange, who were trying to get themselves affiliated to CHE, it would be the last time I came anywhere near their meetings. There's a fine line in every transaction when you're on the street, but sometimes there's a whacking great thick one.

I kept my face stony. 'But he wouldn't let you.'

Crichton couldn't meet my eye. 'No. He became quite distressed. In fact he locked himself in the bathroom and wouldn't come out for some hours.'

'You said before that he didn't like taking his clothes off.' It came out slightly more accusatory than I had intended.

'No. I had once hoped he might agree to pose for a few

studies. In fact I purchased a camera specially.'

'You wanted him to pose naked?'

He shot me a hurt look. 'Nude. Just for my own personal use – I had an idea that we might imitate a few of the classical poses.' He waved a hand at the painted flesh that surrounded us. 'But Stephen wasn't happy with the idea, and you must understand that I would never try to persuade him into doing anything he didn't want to do.'

You wouldn't need to if your wallet was doing the talking, I thought, but I kept silent.

'He did at least let me take a few snaps of him fully clothed,' Crichton said sadly. 'Well of course you know, you have one of them. So I do at least have something to remember him by.'

I had a feeling that in the long term this version of Stephen, the romantic vision, the forever young one that Crichton could project all his fantasies and fetishes on to, would probably work out better for him than the flesh and blood one who wouldn't even reveal that flesh in full. But the more I learned about the boy, the more determined I was to find out what had happened to him. For his own sake, if not for the sad, silly old man sitting in front of me in the armchair, living off past glories and surrounded by picture-perfect boys whose torment had been transformed into something beautiful.

'You said he had his own room. Could I look in there?'

'Of course.' Crichton led me out into the cluttered hallway and opened a door. 'He tended to sleep in my bedroom when he visited, but I wanted him to have a space of his own. He hadn't used it yet. It's full of the things we bought that weekend before he… I won't come in if you don't mind.'

The room was not what I expected. Small, its only furniture was a single bed, the covers folded crisply back, and a chest of drawers with a few personal items sitting on top in a regimented row. It had the feel of an army barracks. Or a cell. I'd been expecting evidence of lavish spending: instead there were only cheap toiletries – a bottle of shampoo, a bar of soap, a hairbrush still in its plastic wrapper. I pulled open the drawers. White and blue t-shirts, cheap brands, all neatly folded and laid out with the same military precision. Just one of the paintings on the walls outside was probably worth more money than Stephen had ever seen in his lifetime. Crichton was evidently besotted, and more than happy to splash the cash. But it looked like the boy wasn't milking him at all.

I left the flat feeling I knew even less than I had when I arrived. On the bus back into town I totted up the little I knew so far about the dead boy: from up north, spent at least some of his time in a children's home, where bad things had happened to him. Then, like so many other lost boys before him, sucked in by the gravitational pull of London and pounced on by the vultures around Playland, who were always ready to feed on the young and the vulnerable, the abused and the usable. Then he meets someone who could have fulfilled all his apparently modest wants and needs and asked for relatively little in return – only for it all to be abruptly snuffed out.

Had he really been about to move in with Crichton? Did he have another bolthole, maybe a more luxurious one, set up elsewhere? Had his pimps found out he was plotting an escape and taken their revenge? Or had someone else, someone that neither the old man nor I knew about, got jealous and intervened?

Careful now, I chided myself. I was beginning to think like the sergeant in Hampstead, with his taunts about lover's tiffs. It might just be that Stephen had fallen foul of the ever-present risk taken by those in our line of work and ended up in the wrong place at the wrong time with the wrong man. Each of us takes our life in our hands every time we turn a trick: there's not a boy on the Dilly that couldn't tell you a tale of being robbed or roughed-up or raped by a client who turned nasty: a closet case working out his own frustrations, a sadist who was after kicks that money can't buy or just a common or garden psychopath. It happens all the time.

But if it was as ordinary as all that, why wasn't Stephen's body still sitting in the hospital morgue? And why should Special Branch give a stuff about his death?

So absorbed was I in my thoughts that I was barely aware of my surroundings as I hopped off the bus and cut through the backstreets towards my hotel room. Maybe I'd been lulled into a false sense of security by the receding pain in my cheek and the fact the cut had healed sufficiently that morning for me to dispense with Shirley's by now rather grotty dressing. Maybe I was just getting careless. But somehow I had made it all the way up to my corridor on the top floor before I became aware of someone approaching me fast from behind, and a voice I'd last heard in the Playland arcade said 'I've been looking for you.'

TEN

'CHRIST, YOU made me jump!'

It was the skinny kid from upstairs, the one that had fallen out of the door when psycho Phil yanked it open. He looked nearly as scared now as he had then, cringing away from me, as I spun round to face him. I realised I was holding up my room key clamped in my fist like a weapon and lowered my arm.

'I'm sorry. I'm sorry,' he gabbled again.

'It's all right, forget about it.' I tried to hush him. There were plenty of rabbit hutch rooms crammed on to this corridor, and the way this place worked, most of them would be occupied at this time of day by at least two people who wouldn't appreciate being disturbed. 'You just shouldn't creep up on people like that. Too light on your feet, that's the problem.' Now I got a proper look at him in daylight rather than the Technicolor glow of the arcade, he looked seriously underweight.

'I'm sorry,' he said again. 'I saw you going up the stairs, and I had to catch up with you. Is it true what you said about Stephen? That he's dead?'

That brought me up short. 'You were listening, were you? Yeah. I'm afraid so.'

Which is when he surprised me for the second time by bursting into immediate, snotty and noisy tears. I grabbed him with one hand – my fingers nearly met as they closed round his arm – and scrabbled the key into the lock of my room with the other, pushing him in ahead of me and shutting the door behind us. If he was a spy for his bosses at Playland, they would know precisely where to find me now, but I felt I had to take that chance.

'Look, sit down, please stop crying.' I steered him towards the bed – it wasn't far, the room was the size of a shoebox – went to sit next to him, thought better of that configuration and stood up again, rifling in my pockets for a handkerchief that I knew wasn't there. 'I'm sorry you had to find out that way.'

'Was he murdered?' the boy hiccupped through his tears.

'I don't know,' I said helplessly. 'I think so. I'm trying to find out why.' There was a thin towel hanging on the back of the door, put there so I would remember to take it with me when I went to the bathroom down the corridor. I plucked it down and handed it to the boy, and he buried his face in it. The sobbing began to subside.

'What's your name?' I asked him when I felt it was safe.

'Peter.' He pressed the towel's harsh corners into his eyes as if he was trying to force the tears back in.

'Have you been with a punter, Peter?'

He nodded. 'Just finished when I saw you. They'll be expecting me back at the arcade.'

I patted his shoulder. 'It's OK. Say he couldn't get it up so it took longer than usual.' He looked up at me quizzically and I explained, 'I used to be on the game myself.'

He nodded, and I felt it was OK to sit down next to him now. The bedsprings shifted with an audible creak.

'How long have you been working out of Playland?'

He sniffed. 'Couple of months. I ran away from home. They said they had a place for me to stay. They were nice to me. At first.'

'That's how it works.' The Playland boys were bussed in from a load of hostels around London run by some weird religious charity: the staff called themselves social workers and even wore weird Salvation Army-type uniforms when they hung around the big railway stations offering to help kids with nowhere to go. Before the new arrivals knew it they were turning tricks in the arcade, making a double profit for the men who took the lion's share of their earnings and all the supplementary benefit they could claim from the government for board and lodging.

'How long had Stephen been there?'

'Not much longer than me. We shared a room in the hostel. Us and a couple of other boys. They used to pick on me, but he sorted them out. He looked out for me.'

'When did you last see him?'

He ran the sleeve of his denim jacket across his nose, the towel forgotten in his lap. 'Friday. Not this Friday, the one before. He went off to see Malcy. That was this bloke he had a regular arrangement with, see. Used to pay him to stay for the whole weekend.'

I nodded. 'I've met him.'

Peter looked at me warily. 'D'you think he did it?'

'No. No, I don't think so. Why, what had Stephen said about him?'

'He said he'd asked him to move in with him. Malcy had,

84

I mean. He had a big place in a posh bit of London, wanted Stephen to stay with him all the time, be like his boyfriend.'

'And did Stephen want to?'

He nodded his head. 'He liked him. Said he was nice to him, mostly. Only he was worried it was going to be a bit…one-sided, that was what he said.'

Bathtime flashed through my mind. 'How do you mean?'

'Well, Malcy had all this money. And Stephen said that he didn't want to feel like he was, like, his servant or something, like he had to pay him to be there.'

'Right,' I said, slightly surprised.

'So he wanted to be able to pay his own way, have money of his own,' Peter continued, surprising me even more.

'So how was he going to do that? Carry on doing rent on the side?' I knew plenty of blokes who treated it like a part-time job, doing two or three days a week on the Dilly before heading back to the suburbs, in several cases to their oblivious wives and children. But Peter was shaking his head.

'No, he reckoned he had a way to make a lot of money really quickly. There was this bloke he said would pay him to keep quiet if he threatened to go to the papers and tell them about him.'

That made me sit up straight. 'Who was that, Peter?'

I could feel him shrinking away from me, fearful of my reaction. 'I don't know his name. A politician.'

'A politician?'

He nodded, desperate to please. 'Stephen said he'd seen him on the telly. Said he hadn't realised till then how famous and important he was, and he reckoned he'd pay him a decent wedge so as people didn't find out what he'd been up to. Said he had phoned him at parliament and told him he had to pay up or else. He was really excited about it.'

'Did he say what this man's name was?' Peter shook his head vigorously. 'Was it someone he'd been introduced to at Playland?'

Peter shook his head. 'I don't think so. But Stephen used to meet up with people on the side, too, so he could keep the money instead of handing it over to Phil and the others. Used to try to get me to do the same, do threesomes and that with him, but I was too scared. You've seen what Phil's like.'

I raised a hand involuntarily to the cut on my face. The memory seemed to bring the boy's fear flooding back and he rose from the bed. 'I've got to get back.'

'Wait! Can I at least buy you something to eat? You look starving.'

I'd never yet met the young Dilly boy that didn't jump at the offer of a trip to Pizzaland. And this kid so obviously needed looking after. But he was shaking his head. 'No, I can't. He'd kill me if he saw me with you.'

'All right. But let me at least give you the money for a decent meal.' I stood up too, to reach into the pocket of my jeans, which meant without meaning to I was blocking his way to the door. I could see how antsy it was making him. 'Will you come and see me again, Peter? If you find out anything? Or just…if you need to talk?'

'Yeah,' he muttered, looking past me to the exit. 'Maybe. I don't know.'

I reached out and put my hands on his sloping shoulders. He shied away like they were electrodes, but I kept them there, lowering my eyes so they were level with his. 'You've been really brave, Peter. I'm sorry I upset you. But before you go, is there anything else you can remember Stephen saying about this politician? Anything at all?'

'No. Only that he was on telly all the time. And that he had an important job.'

'In the government?'

'I think so. No. Maybe. Is that the Liberals?'

'No.' I knew that much, although I realised with a start of shame I wasn't sure which side were in power at the moment. There seemed to have been non-stop general elections recently, and like I say, I didn't read the papers.

'Is that what Stephen said? That this man was a Liberal?'

'I think so. Yeah.' The boy was actually shaking. 'Can I go now, *please*?'

'Of course you can.' I released his shoulders and held out a pound note towards him, but the moment I let go he squirmed past me and out of the room, the door banging shut behind him. I could hear his running footsteps all the way down the corridor to the stairs.

ELEVEN

I WAS DUE TO SEE Mark the following evening. We were going to see *Jaws*. Everyone had been telling me I had to see it ever since it came out, usually before saying they wouldn't spoil it for me and then giving a detailed run-down of all the scary bits anyway. Mark had already seen it too, but he said he'd like to see it again.

I met him from work – he was an assistant at Laurence Corner, the army surplus shop – and we were due to see the early showing at La Continentale, but we'd barely made it further than the top of Tottenham Court Road before he got so excited about what my visitor had had to tell me that we abandoned all plans and settled in at a pub on Warren Street to discuss it further.

'And he definitely said it was a Liberal?' he asked as I came back to our table with our pints and a packet of peanuts to share.

The barman had given me a big wink when he plucked them off the busty beauty hanging behind the bar, revealing about three square inches of her cardboard cleavage. Weird how straight people get their kicks.

'He thought so.' I downed a good couple of inches of beer to give me the Dutch courage for my next admission. 'They're the opposition, right? I don't really follow politics.'

'No, the Tories are the opposition. The Liberals are *in* opposition, but they've only got about a dozen MPs.'

At least that had to narrow down the list of suspects. I picked up a beermat and spun it between my fingers, watching the Double Diamond logo revolve so I didn't have to look Mark directly in the eye. 'So is it still Harold Wilson in charge?' I knew about him all right. He seemed to have been around forever, puffing away at his pipe on the news since I was a little kid. My dad had loathed him.

'You really don't follow politics, do you?' He was grinning in a way I didn't much like.

'It's just hard to keep up,' I muttered, my ears burning. 'There've been loads of elections recently, haven't there.' I actually did very well at school – was predicted good grades in my 'O' Levels, only I cleared out before I could take them, and after that I went straight into selling my body because I knew no one would be interested in my brain.

'It's OK.' Mark wiped the grin off his face, and leant forward to put his hand on mine, stopping the furiously spinning beermat. 'Don't worry: I'm probably just a bit *too* into this stuff.' He indicated the badges on his lapel. 'Yes, Wilson's still Prime Minister, more's the pity. Sooner he gets out of the way and lets Michael Foot show him what a *real* socialist looks like, the better.'

'And if the Liberals have only got a few seats, they don't really matter?'

'They wouldn't, normally.' He pulled back his hand, extracting the beermat from mine as an excuse for the contact in case anyone was looking, and laid it down on the table, pressing his index finger onto it. 'Look, Labour are in government because they've got the most MPs – just.' He pulled his own beermat from under his glass and slid it forward to sit beside the other one. 'But the Conservatives got very nearly as many seats at the last election – and you're right, that was the second one we had in a year… You must have been old enough to vote that November?'

I tried to think back to what I had been doing in the autumn of 1974. Ugly old men for money, mostly. 'I was a bit busy,' I muttered.

Mark frowned. 'You should always exercise your democratic rights, Tom. Even if it's just to spoil your ballot paper.' I think if anyone else had started lecturing me like this, I would have walked out, but Mark caught my look and quickly pushed forward his pair of beermats. 'So this is Labour, and this is the Tories. They've got a new leader since, a woman, but there's no way she's going to last so you don't need to worry about her. But the thing is, Labour have been losing seats ever since the election. Remember that MP who drowned in America?'

I nodded. That had been such a big story even I had clocked it: it was like something out of Agatha Christie, with the bloke leaving his clothes on a beach and disappearing and all sorts of theories about spy rings and mafia hitmen swirling around. No one had ever found his body, and they reckoned it had probably been eaten by sharks.

'Well, he was one of theirs. And Woolwich went Conservative in a by-election last year too, which means their majority is down to one right now. So Wilson's hanging on by the skin of his teeth.' He reached over to the empty table beside us to pick up a third beermat and carefully tore one of the corners off, laying it down between the two mats in front of him and sliding it from one to the other. 'That means the Liberals, even though they've only got a handful of MPs, can make all the difference according to which party they vote with in parliament. They nearly went into coalition with the Tories back in 1974. They still might next time.'

I frowned at the bit of cardboard as if it could really hold the answers. 'How many did you say there were – a dozen?'

He shrugged. 'About that.'

'So the bloke Stephen was blackmailing must be one of them?'

'Presumably.'

'Any ideas?'

He took a long, thoughtful pull on his pint before putting it down – on the Conservatives, this time, I noticed. 'I have heard rumours about Jeremy Thorpe.'

'Who?'

'Their leader. You must have seen him. Always wears a hat. Travels around in a hovercraft.'

I must have looked baffled, because he laughed at me again, but in a nicer way this time. 'Not *all* the time. But I'm sure you would recognise him. He used to present *This Week* on ITV.'

I started forward, nearly spilling my beer. 'Peter said this guy was always on TV.'

Mark nodded. 'Sounds like Thorpe. He's always turning up on all the political programmes. And I remember once he did a party political broadcast with Jimmy Savile.'

'So what have you heard? That he's gay?'

He wrinkled his nose. 'Supposedly. But you know what gossip's like. Say the name of anyone off the telly to a group of gay men and one of them will tell you for sure he's a closet queen. Someone the other week was trying to convince me Richard Chamberlain was gay, for god's sake.'

I snorted. 'Doctor Kildare?'

He grinned. 'I know.'

'But you think Thorpe might be?'

'I don't know. I can believe it about Ted Heath. But Thorpe's married – to some sort of minor royal, I think.'

I pointed a triumphant finger at him. 'So he'd have money! It would have been worth Stephen's while trying to blackmail him!'

'Maybe.' Mark looked less convinced, but I was champing at the bit now.

'No, no, it would be a big scandal, wouldn't it, if someone married into the royal family turned out to be gay?'

He sniggered. 'That depends if you believe the rumours about Lord Snowdon or not.'

'But anyway, the leader of a political party – you're not going to tell me that would be allowed?'

'Allowed? It should be,' he bristled, coming over all Gay Lib all of a sudden. 'What's it got to do with anything? But yeah, you're probably right. The Liberals don't exactly live up to their name. And there's a Labour MP called Maureen Colquhoun who's a lesbian: she said a couple of weeks ago that she wanted to be called "Ms" rather than "Mrs" Colquhoun in parliament, and the papers *crucified* her for it. And that shit Nigel Dempster got hold of her and her girlfriend's housewarming party invitations and wrote a really poisonous article about them in the *Mail*. They won't be happy until they've forced her to resign. So you're probably right.'

I looked at him, impressed. 'You really do know your politics, don't you?'

He shrugged. 'I keep up with it. I'm in the party. No point

just paying your subs and not getting involved.' He tipped his nearly empty pint pot in my direction. '*You* should join. There's really exciting things happening in the Young Socialists at the moment.'

This sounded dangerously close to the sort of talk I had heard enough of back in the squat. My tactic then, as now, was to change the subject. 'Are we having another pint?'

Mark looked at his watch, and around at the smoky pub. 'Why not? If we have a couple more here we can go to the 8 o'clock showing instead. Same again?'

The film was just as good as everyone said it was. I still jumped when the head came out of the bottom of the boat, even though I knew it was going to happen. Only rather than sharks, I found it made me think of Stephen instead. *When they turned him over and I saw his face...*

I went back to Mark's afterwards. I felt I owed him for all the information he'd given me (I'd paid for my own cinema ticket, mind).

Afterwards, when we were lying beside one another in the dark, he said: 'Can I ask you something?'

'Yeah.'

'What were you doing there? In the hotel where this Peter found you?'

'I've been staying there.'

His voice was hesitant. 'For work?'

Oh god, I thought. He's jealous.

'No. I told you, I don't do that any more.' I turned on my side, and cold air rushed in beneath the blankets to fill the space between our bodies. 'If you must know, it's the only place I've got to stay just at the moment.'

There was a moment of silence in the darkness, and then he suddenly shifted across the bed himself. The light came on.

'Seriously?' He was sitting up, looking down at me. 'You mean you're homeless?'

I bunched the covers up around my chin. 'No, I just told you, I'm staying at the hotel.'

'But you haven't got anywhere permanent to live?'

'Not at the minute, no. I'll sort something out soon.' I stared determinedly at the floral wallpaper on my side of the bed.

'But…' He thought for a moment, then the bed see-sawed again as he jumped out, rounded it and disappeared out of the room, still stark naked. Tutting, I re-tucked the covers around myself and lay there feeling about as far from sleep as it is possible to be.

Mark came back in and squatted down in front of me. He was holding a key on a ring which he dangled in front of my face. 'Here.'

'What's that?' I said grumpily.

'It's my spare key. Take it.' He jiggled it impatiently.

I kept my hands stubbornly clasped between my bare legs beneath the covers. 'I don't need it. I'm fine.'

'Take it anyway, just in case.' He bobbed his head down till his eyes were level with mine. 'Please? I'm not saying you have to move in permanently, or anything like that. It's early days, I know. But I worry about you enough already without thinking of you out on the streets.'

I sat up slowly in the bed, still making no move to take the key. 'What would you want me to do?'

'Do?' He looked genuinely puzzled. 'Not get your face slashed? Not get murdered?'

'No, but I mean – for you. In return?' I couldn't help thinking about Malcolm Crichton and his bathtime fetish, which was ridiculous. There was only about ten years between me and Mark.

He shook his head. 'I just told you.'

'I do all right by myself you know. I have done for a long time. I don't need you to…take me under your wing or whatever.' And, I could have added but didn't, if I wanted to be a kept man – which I don't – I think I could do a bit better than a shop assistant with a flat above a takeaway.

He sighed, palming the key and dropping back into a cross-legged position on the carpet but not taking his eyes off me. 'Tommy, I like you,' he said. 'I like you as a friend, and I like you as a lover. And I'll like it for as long as you want to be either of those, or both. We don't need to get hung up on bougie stuff like commitment or exclusivity. Us lot get to make up our own rules, remember?'

'Right.' I was familiar with this riff from CHE meetings: its loudest advocates tended to be blokes like Neil or Trevor who stood the least chance of ever putting it into practice.

Now he was looking at me in the annoying way he always does before he makes a point in the group discussions. 'Tommy, have you ever actually had a lover before?'

'Um, yeah,' I spluttered. 'Rent boy, remember?'

He shook his head. 'I don't mean that. I mean a relationship.'

'Well, yeah,' I muttered. There were one or two blokes I'd seen on a regular basis. I'd even given them the odd freebie.

'We're equals, OK? You don't owe me anything, and I don't owe you anything. If we spend time together, it should be because we both want to.'

I grunted.

'Now, will you please just take this before I freeze to death?' He held out the key once more. Slowly, I snaked a hand out from under the covers to take it from him. I had only paid for the Regent Palace up until the following morning, and I had already burned through so much of Malcolm Crichton's money that I was starting to worry about what I would do when it ran out.

'Good.' He sprang up and vaulted over me onto the empty side of the bed. 'Now we can both sleep more easily.'

'Yeah.' I dropped the key onto the bedside table and twisted over to face him again as he turned off the light.

I assumed we were going to have sex again, but we ended up just lying there with our arms around each other. It sounds weird but it was really nice.

TWELVE

I HAD A NAME. Jeremy Thorpe. And by mid-morning the next day I had a face to put to it too. The Politics section in Foyles is hidden away right at the centre of the labyrinth on one of the upper floors, but I know my way around better than most of the staff these days. I found him in the *Times Guide to the House of Commons*: the Right Honourable Jeremy Thorpe, no less, which I thought at first must be something to do with the royal connection Mark had mentioned until I noticed that half the other MPs in there seemed to be called it too.

And Mark had been right: I did recognise him, but mostly because of the hat, a weirdly old-fashioned trilby with a twisted brim that made the black-and-white photo look like someone's great-grandfather in the family album. Like Wilson, he was another one of those figures who popped up all over the place whether you were interested in politics or not: I could remember seeing him being interviewed on the telly when I was a kid, and

Michael Parkinson calling him a 'bit of a Fancy Dan' because of the clothes he wore. I'd asked my mum what it meant, and my father had cut in to say 'it means he's a slippery beggar who's too clever for his own good.' God knows what he'd say about him if he knew what I'd heard now.

Thorpe's face was long and strangely pinched: you could clearly see the skull beneath the skin of his face. His dark eyes had a cold look to them. Or maybe I was just reading too much into the inch-wide portrait: if you stare too long at anyone wondering if they're a murderer they probably start to look worse than Charles Manson.

I checked the price on the back of the book: £4.50. They must think I'm made of money. I considered quietly tearing the page with Thorpe out but I'm a bit funny about damaging books, so instead I slid the whole thing into the inside pocket of my leather jacket – it was a hardback, so it only just fitted – zipped up the front and minced out, down the stairs, past the oblivious staff on the tills and out of the building. One of the other advantages of Foyles is that you never seem to see the same member of staff twice, which means they don't get the chance to clock you for a regular and make you turn out your pockets. Besides, they have such a ridiculous system for buying stuff – you have to queue up to get a sales docket from one place and then go and hand over your money somewhere else entirely – that it's a wonder anyone pays at all.

My plan was to do a circuit of all the likely pubs and pick-up joints showing Thorpe's picture around and seeing if anyone recognised him. The person I could really do with talking to was Peter – I could see if Thorpe's name or photograph jogged any memories – but going anywhere near Playland was out of the question. I wondered if I could get a message in to the boy somehow. Give someone the money to pose as a punter and bring him out to meet me somewhere safe so we could chat. Mark passed briefly through my mind, but I dismissed the possibility. There was no way I was going to get him involved with that scene. He was good at talking the talk about the dangers gay men face in their daily lives, but he was an innocent abroad when it came to the world I had lived in for the past few years. And I wasn't about to do anything that put him at risk.

None of my many friends on the Dilly would be any good either – their faces were too well known, making them just likely to end up on the wrong end of Phil's knife, suspected of trying to steal his business like I had been.

Instead, after nipping back to the Regent Palace to pick up my worldly goods, I decided to work methodically across Soho from West to East, starting with one of my favourite old haunts on Poland Street. It wasn't long after opening time when I descended the rickety steps to the Down Below Club, invariably known to its regular patrons as the Up Your Bum.

'Oh, vada what the cat dragged in,' drawled the familiar figure who unlocked the door.

'Hello Clarrie.' I pecked one rouged cheek, then the other as she stood aside to let me in 'How've you been?'

'All the better for seeing you, ducks.' Claribel – born Charles, but he wouldn't answer to that, any more than he'd let you call him anything but 'she' or 'her' – was a local legend, proper old-time Soho. She'd been behind the bar at the Up Your Bum for as long as anyone could remember, bottle-black hair permed and a full face of slap whatever the time of day. She had really kept an eye out for me when I first arrived in London. Now she stood back to give me an appraising glance up and down.

'Well, isn't she butch nowadays,' was her judgement. 'Someone's come by a bit of handbag.'

'What, this?' I fingered the lapels of my leather jacket. 'All right, isn't it?'

'Bona darling. You're a real dish. Now take the weight off your lallies, buy poor old Claribel a bevvie and tell her *all* about what you've been up to. You don't write, you don't call…'

I settled down on the barstool she was indicating and slid a pound note across the bar. Clarrie was already pouring two pernod and blacks. It wouldn't be my drink of choice, but she won't drink anything else.

We exchanged gossip about some mutual acquaintances while she finished setting up the bar, pushing handfuls of tonic and bitter lemon bottles into the gaps on the shelves and running a duster over the frames of the playbills that lined the basement's walls. The only other customer was an old guy in a cravat nursing a large whisky in the corner: I knew him by sight both from here and from some adverts on the telly when I was a kid. Like a lot of the customers here, he was an actor: like a lot of them that came in to drink at this time of the day, he was doing a lot more 'resting' than he was acting these days. He was reasonably safe in the mornings, but you didn't want to get within groping distance after mid-afternoon.

Finally everything was neat and shining to Clarrie's satisfaction. She tucked her duster away beneath the bar, filled a glass with fresh ice and transferred her untouched drink into it in one fluid movement, and came round the bar to perch on the stool next to mine, lighting up a Virginia Slim. I pulled the Polaroid of Stephen out of my pocket and passed it over. 'Have you ever seen him in here, Clarrie?'

She blew menthol smoke over the picture as she considered. 'No, I don't think I have. I'd never have served him if I did. Ding Ding, it's Lilly Law for Claribel if I started dishing out the veras for chickens like that. Mind you, you weren't much older than that when you first came in here, were you dearie?' She gave me an affectionate pat on the knee.

'I was younger than he was,' I admitted. 'Or at least, younger than he said he was.'

She raised a plucked eyebrow. 'Was?'

'He's dead,' I confirmed. 'Someone killed him last week.'

Clarrie sighed a dramatic stream of smoke over Stephen's photograph before handing it back to me. 'Tragic. Happening far too much these days.' You could always tell she was serious when she dropped the polari. 'What's this got to do with you, Tommy?'

'I'm trying to find out who did it.'

She sniffed. 'Job for the sharpies, that.'

'They're not interested. We went to the police station. As far as they're concerned, it was accidental death and that's that.' I wasn't going to get into the business about Special Branch with Claribel: one word of it to her and it would be all round gay London by closing time.

'I still don't see why you need to be poking your esong into it. Lot of nasty people out there, Tommy. You need to be careful what you go charpering into.'

'I've made a promise,' I said limply. I still wasn't sure exactly who to: Malcolm Crichton, poor sobbing Peter, dead Stephen, or maybe just myself.

Clarrie gave me a considering look, then patted my leg again. 'All right. But you're to take care, Tommy. Your Aunty Claribel worries about you.'

'I will.' I extracted the book from my jacket and leafed through it to the right page. 'What about this bloke, have you ever seen him?' I hadn't even had a chance to indicate which of the four people on the spread I was talking about – she could have opted for Thomases Peter or Ronald, or Tierney, Sydney instead – when Clarrie brought a painted fingernail down

101

decisively on Thorpe, Jeremy. 'Oh, I know *him*. Everyone knows him. He used to be a regular in here, trolling up and down the place in his zhooshy suits.'

'Did you know he was a politician?'

She rolled her eyes towards the nicotine-stained ceiling. 'How could I not? He was always screeching off about it.' She put on an affected voice an octave or two lower than her own: '"You must come and visit me at the House, dear boy"; "As I was saying to the Prime Minister just the other day…" Talk your Aunt Nells off about it if you gave him half a chance.'

That surprised me. 'He was quite open about it?'

She crushed her cigarette into the ashtray on the bar and pursed scarlet lips in disapproval. 'I heard him saying to a blag once – and this is a right bit of rough trade I'm talking about – "Do you know who I am?" Bold as brass. And the blag answered, big butter-wouldn't-melt smile right across his eek, "You're a very nice generous gentleman". And off they scarpered together.'

I pondered this for a few moments as Clarrie went back round the bar to pour out another whisky for the aged actor. Thorpe hardly sounded like the ideal candidate for blackmail if he was as flamboyantly open as Clarrie suggested. In which case, why bother killing Stephen?

'Didn't anyone ever blow the gaff on him?' I asked when she was finished. 'Try and sell a story to the papers or something?'

'Ha!' Clarrie snorted with laughter, but made me wait for an answer as she went through her theatrical routine of lighting her cigarette. '*Someone* did,' she said finally, blowing twin minty streams from her nostrils.

'But they weren't interested?' I prompted. From the way she was lingering behind the bar and the slowing of the conversation, I could tell she was angling for me to buy her another drink. I'd hardly touched my own yet.

A smirk. 'They might have been interested in the story. But they took one look at who was telling it and said "no ta very much me old cove."'

'Who was that?'

I was, quite literally, on the edge of my seat, but Clarrie was having none of it. 'Oh, I see so many of them come and go through here, duckie, you can't expect me to remember all their names,' she trilled, studying her chipped nails nonchalantly.

I gave up. 'Perhaps we'd better have another drink then.'

She was dipping a fresh glass in the ice bucket before I'd even finished speaking. 'Thank you dear, most generous. Keep yours in the bottle, shall I?'

'That's fine,' I said, counting out change onto the bar top. I still had a few more notes, but they were in my sock, and I wasn't about to get them out in front of Clarrie or anyone else that might be looking.

'Now, where were we?' she said, rejoining me in front of the bar. Her glass was considerably fuller this time. She'd helped herself to a double measure.

'Someone was trying to tell the papers about Thorpe.'

'That's right dear. Poor old Norman.'

'Norman who?'

She flapped a hand dismissively. 'Depends what day of the week it was, duckie. It was something French the first time I met him, that was years ago now; then he went all double-barrelled and was telling anyone that would listen he was the orphaned son of an earl or some such. The last I heard of him he was going by Norman Scott: someone brought in an advert he'd modelled for in one of the glossies, starkers as you like with his buns out in front of a window. And very nice buns they were too.' She gave a wistful smile.

'And he tried to sell a story about Thorpe?' I prompted before she got too lost in reminiscence.

'Sell a story, tell a story.' She waved away the smoke between us. 'You couldn't talk to him for more than five minutes without him bringing up Jeremy Thorpe and every wrong he'd done him since the year dot. On and on he'd go.'

'But no one was interested?'

'Oh, they were interested all right. That was, until he got talking.' She put a finger up to her temple and rotated it. 'Dizzy doesn't even begin to cover it. Always going on about how Thorpe had shushed his cards to stop him getting any national handbag and how he hadn't even been a fruit until Thorpe had his wicked way with him. Whereas you've never seen such a born omi-polone in your life. Fruity as a nutcake.'

Crazy or not, it sounded like Scott would be a useful person to talk to. 'Do you know how I might get hold of him?'

Clarrie swirled her glass, making the ice cubes clink. 'I've not laid ogles on him in years now, dear. Last I heard he was supposed to have got *married*.' She made it sound like a fate worse than death.

'I don't suppose you've got a phone number or anything?'

She shook her head. 'He's not the sort to stay in one place for very long, if you get my drift.' She gave me a look that implied everything from debt-collectors downwards.

'Does he have any friends I could ask?'

'Not ones as have stayed friends.'

There was a rap at the door and Clarrie slid from the barstool and went over to let in two more customers. One, a handsome bloke with a handlebar moustache, was definitely giving me the glad eye as he arrived at the bar, but I was too caught up in our conversation to care. 'You can't think of anything that might help me find him?' I demanded.

'Sleeping dogs, dear, sleeping dogs.' Clarrie gave me a disapproving look and concentrated on flirting with the newcomers. I picked up my drink – it was lukewarm by now – and took a sip, wincing at the aniseed taste. It was happening again. Every time I seemed to be getting anywhere, I came up against a dead end.

The new arrivals had apparently not been in since before the weekend, so they needed to be filled in on all the gossip, or the 'cackle' as Clarrie called it. It was a good five minutes before she returned to me, sitting glumly over the cloudy purple depths of my glass.

'Horses,' she announced, à propos of nothing.

'What?' for a moment I thought she was talking about the White Horse whisky jug sitting on the bar top between us, which I had been staring at blankly as I sipped my drink.

'If Norman Scott wasn't talking about how Jeremy Thorpe had ruined his life, he was always talking about horses. How he could have been a top racehorse trainer if it wasn't for Thorpe, or how happy he'd been working in the stables until you-know-who turned up and led him astray in the hay. If you insist on going charpering after him, that's your best bet.'

I gave her a grateful smile. 'Thanks Clarrie. I really do appreciate it.'

She bared lipsticky teeth at me. 'One for the road it is, then.'

I sighed and reached into my sock.

THIRTEEN

IF I LEFT THE Up Your Bum that afternoon feeling like I might actually have some talent for this detective business, I had definitely had the optimism knocked out of me by the end of the evening. I staggered back to Mark's flat some time after ten, light-headed and nauseous from mixing my drinks in the course of my progress across gay London and feeling so down-hearted that the sight of the duffel bag containing the pathetic total of my worldly possessions as I put it down in the crowded cosiness of Mark's lounge was almost enough to bring me to the brink of tears. I had been greeted with plenty of knowing looks as I asked about Norman Scott – he had clearly made quite an impression, even if he hadn't been on the scene for years – but no one had a clue as to his current whereabouts. Finally, in my last stop of the night, the back bar of the Salisbury on St Martin's Lane, a bloke said he thought he had gone to Wales, but he couldn't remember who had told him so. Mark didn't exactly help matters when I asked if he'd ever come across Scott by smirking and saying 'we don't all know each other, you know.'

Still, I woke up the next morning with a renewed determination, a hangover that was milder than expected thanks to the aspirin Mark had insisted I take and the pint of water he had left by the bed for me, and the beginnings of a plan that would keep me busy for rest of the day. Step one: find Norman Scott. One thing I've learned in my years working the street is to trust my gut feeling, and for some reason I felt sure he would be able to help me find out exactly what had happened to Stephen.

I didn't have a lot to go on. A name. A country. And a specialist subject. But, to coin a phrase, I'd started and I was determined I was going to finish. And if that meant calling on the professionals, so be it.

It was just after noon when I climbed the stairs to Harvey's office. It obviously counted as early morning for musicians: the rehearsal rooms were silent save for the sound of loud snores coming from behind the door on the first floor. Apparently I wasn't the only person who used the building as a doss-house.

The relative quiet meant I was able to hear the murmur of male voices from above. I considered turning around and coming back later, but it was raining out and I was already soaked, so I announced my presence with a sharp rat-a-tat-tat on the glass pane and went on in.

There were only three people inside, but the small room felt crowded. Harvey's a fat bloke, as I may have mentioned before, and his secretary Alison could do with losing a few pounds too, but it was the third figure who, despite being a relative streak of piss compared to the other two, really dominated the space. From cap-flattened greasy hair all the way to the crossed black boots that were perched arrogantly on the edge of Harvey's desk, Sergeant Gordon Mullaney of the Soho Vice Squad exuded arrogance and malevolence. Or maybe it was just that I'd been on the wrong end of his truncheon too many times.

The conversation had halted as soon as I had knocked. Alison was staring determinedly at her typewriter, doing her ineffective best to melt into the background completely. I bet if you asked her what the men had been talking about, she would have sworn blind she hadn't heard a thing.

'Tommy,' said Harvey bluntly. 'I didn't call you in.'

'No.' I've seldom felt more unwelcome in a room, but I stood my ground. 'I was hoping you could help me out with something.'

Harvey's eyes darted nervously to the policeman lolling on his sofa and back again. 'What sort of thing?'

'I need to track someone down.' The more nights I'd spent away from his office, the more I'd come round to the idea of using Harvey's services: since Malcolm Crichton thought he was paying for a Lewenstein Agency investigation anyway, the idea of funnelling some of his cash in that direction without either man being aware of it kind of tickled me. Now I was here, however, with Sergeant Mullaney's grey eyes drilling into me, it didn't seem quite as funny. 'I've got a name, and I know he used to live in London, but I think he's in Wales now.'

'What's he done, nicked your handbag?' drawled Mullaney from the sofa.

Harvey at least had the grace to look embarrassed. 'This isn't a great time, Tommy,' he spluttered, rising from behind his desk in an attempt to look like he was the one in charge in the room. 'I was just heading out, as it happens. Could you come back later? Gordon, why don't we go down to the Angel and I'll stand you a pint and a pie, eh?'

Mullaney completely ignored him, leaning back in his seat, and aiming his snakelike gaze in my direction instead. 'Don't see so much of you on the streets these days, Tommy. Your arse too old and tired to flog to the punters now, is that it?'

I scowled at him. 'I'm off the game, sergeant.'

'Is that right? Will wonders never cease?' Sergeant Mullaney has a habit of chucking out rhetorical questions like these. At least I think that's the right term for a question you shouldn't answer if you know what's good for you.

Harvey was hovering over his chair, not sure whether to sit back down or not. Mullaney continued to ignore him. 'And yet,' he drawled slowly, 'you've got enough money to come here seeking out Mr Lewenstein's professional services.'

I shrugged, trying to act more casual than I felt. 'I'm doing all right.'

'Are you indeed.' Mullaney finally turned his attention to Harvey. 'Sounds like I might need to add young Tommy to my little list of successful local businessmen, doesn't it, Mr Lewenstein? Speaking of which…?' He tapped the breast pocket of his unbuttoned tunic significantly.

Harvey clocked his meaning straight away, nodding vigorously as he fumbled the cash box out of his desk drawer and extracted a crumpled tenner from it. 'Much obliged,' drawled Mullaney, opening up his pocket book and sliding the note in among what looked like half a dozen others. 'Now, did someone mention the Angel? A man could die of thirst around here.'

Harvey was into his coat and ushering the policeman out of the office in seconds. He didn't look at me as I stood aside to let them pass, but Mullaney made sure to let his cold dead eyes slide all over me as he put on his cap and stalked past. He smelt of Old Spice and alcohol. I focused my own eyes on his dandruff-flecked shoulders and tried not to react. I noticed the ID number had been neatly snipped from his uniform.

'Urgh, that man gives me the heebie-jeebies,' shuddered Alison as soon as they were safely down the stairs.

I nodded smiling agreement. It was probably the most human warmth the pair of us had ever exchanged. 'He's a proper creep, isn't he?'

'Big time.' She got up and bustled over to the window, pushing it up to let the frigid February air gust in and flush away the policeman's presence.

'When d'you think Harvey'll be back?'

'Not until Sergeant Mullaney has touched him for as many drinks as he can,' she said as she settled back down at her desk. 'But he's only got a fiver in his wallet. He empties it out on Wednesdays specially.'

I grinned. 'Crafty.'

'He's learned his lesson. What did you want him for?'

I sat down on the sofa, at the opposite end to where Mullaney had been. 'I'm trying to find this bloke – it's a favour for a friend. He used to live in London but the last anyone heard of him he'd moved somewhere in Wales.'

'D'you know his name?'

'Yeah. I was hoping Harvey might be able to…well, do whatever it is he does when he's looking for people.'

She rolled her eyes. 'He gets me to do it, that's what! You want to start with the phone book.'

I frowned. 'But he won't be in it. Like I said, he doesn't live in London any more.'

She shook her head. 'But he might be in one of them. They've got phone books for the whole country over at the reference library in Leicester Square. That's where we always start.'

I knew the library she was talking about well. I'd spent plenty of time in there over the past few winters when it was too cold to hang around on the streets. It was always nice and warm inside, although I would have preferred it if they stocked a bit of fiction for the sake of variety.

'Thanks Alison. That's really helpful,' I said, unable to keep all the surprise out of my voice.

She shrugged. 'Only saving myself a job, aren't I?'

'Well, I appreciate it, anyway.' I did. So much so that I even briefly considered giving her her keys back, but you never knew when they might come in useful again. Still, she was doing me a big favour. 'I'll buy you a drink sometime, yeah?' She gave me a scornful look. 'No offence, Tommy, but you're not the sort of man I like buying me drinks.'

And we were back to normal. 'Suit yourself,' I shrugged, and headed for the door.

The phone books were there, just as I remembered them, taking up three full bookcases in the ornate wooden gallery that ran around the first floor of the building. Yellow pages too, for every part of the country. My heart sank slightly when I looked at the scale of them. The only comfort was that the ones for Wales looked to be thinner than some of the others: Manchester came in two volumes, each of them nearly as wide as my hand, and London had no fewer than five.

It took me most of the rest of the day to compile a list of likely candidates, jotting down the very few Scott, Normans I turned up, but also every Nick, Nicola, Neil, Nigel, Nerys or Noreen who had been unhelpful enough to get themselves listed with just their initials. A couple of times I considered breaking the monotony by heading out to a phone box to make a start on the actual calls, but as the list got longer and longer I figured I really ought to wait for the cheap rate to kick in at 6 o'clock or I was going to run out of change pretty quickly.

It was getting on for that time anyway before I slotted Ceredigion back onto the shelf, took Conway over to the table I was sharing with an old man who had been gently snoring over a spread copy of the *Daily Mirror* the whole time I had been there, and opened it to find exactly what I was looking for. Not just a Scott, Norman, but one whose address was the Tal-y-Bont Pony Trekking Centre. It had to be him. Get me: I was practically Sherlock Holmes.

I rushed out of the library in search of a phone box, and had to go all the way down to the bottom of Trafalgar Square, scattering the pigeons before me, before I could find one which didn't have a queue outside. I dialled the number and stood with my 5p poised ready over the slot as I waited to be connected, running over what I was going to say. *Hello, is that Norman Scott? You don't know me but I want to ask you about Jeremy Thorpe.* Going by what Clarrie had told me, he would be only too eager to talk. Maybe I could even arrange to meet him. I still had the cash I'd earmarked for Harvey's services, which would more than pay for a train ticket. Wales wasn't all that far away. In which case, why was this phone box taking so long to put me through?

Finally the clicking on the receiver stopped. But instead of being replaced by a ringtone, I got a solid brrrrrrrrrrrrrrrrrr instead. Number unobtainable.

Fuck. I checked the number I had jotted down and dialled it again. Same thing. Had I copied it out wrong? Maybe I'd gone number-blind after so many hours scanning the grey columns. I put the receiver back in the cradle and turned to open the door and go back to the library and check, then paused and picked it up again.

Brr Brr. Brr Brr. 'Operator?'

'Oh, hello, I'm having trouble getting through to the Tal-y-

Bont pony trekking centre.'

'Checking that number for you.' She sounded brisk and efficient. I only hoped I was pronouncing the name right.

'I'm afraid that number is listed as defunct, sir.'

'What?'

'De-funct, sir,' she said more clearly, obviously assuming I was either deaf or stupid.

'Oh. Right.' All my triumph leeched out onto the damp concrete floor of the phone box. I wasn't Sherlock Holmes. I was barely even one of the Baker Street Irregulars.

'Can I help you with anything else, sir?'

'No. Yes.' She was still there. 'Could you put me through to the local exchange please?'

'They'll only tell you the same thing, sir.'

'I'd still like to speak to them.'

'Putting you through now sir.' The amount of prim disapproval she managed to pack into five polite words was incredible.

'Tal-y-Bont Post Office?' The new voice sounded much warmer. It was the accent I think.

'Oh, hello, I was trying to get hold of a Norman Scott, but the number –' I stopped. There had been an audible gasp at the other end of the phone.

'That man is no longer in the village.' She sounded a lot less friendly now.

'Oh. Right. Do you know where he went?'

A disapproving sniff. 'I believe he's living down in the West Country now.'

'Right.'

A decidedly frosty silence followed, which I tried to fill from my end. 'I'm trying to get hold of him to ask him about something quite important. Is there any way you could help me? Might anyone there have an address or phone number for

113

him?'

'Is this to do with Jeremy Thorpe?'

The question nearly pole-axed me. 'Well...yes it is, as a matter of fact.'

'Then my advice to you would be to leave well alone and not get involved.'

'I...I think I sort of am involved, unfortunately. Sorry.'

The pips went at that moment, and while I had another 5p ready and hovering over the slot, the sudden sound seemed to break some sort of spell at the other end. A great deluge of words came tumbling out, as if the woman at the other end had been keeping them stoppered up for an age. 'That young man has a habit of drawing people into his problems, and it brings them nothing but ill. Gwen was doing very well until he turned up, a fine respectable widow she was, decent and god-fearing with her husband not even six months in his grave. And turning in it, too, I shouldn't wonder, to think of her *living in sin* with someone like that. Took advantage of her, he did. Sought her out when she was vulnerable. Drew her in with all his wild talk and accusations. And took her money, too. Let the poor woman become besotted with him even though there was no way on god's green earth a man like that was ever going to return her affections.' The voice subsided into stifled sobs.

'I'm really sorry,' I said weakly. I wasn't sure who this Gwen was – Clarrie had mentioned something about a marriage – but she clearly meant a lot to the woman on the other end of the line. 'Was she a good friend of yours?'

'Twenty years we'd been working together,' the woman snuffled. 'She started here when she wasn't much more than a girl.'

'And she started...' I searched for the right term '...going out with Norman Scott?'

114

A sharper sniff. 'They *moved in* together.' The way she said it made it sound like they'd been caught shagging in the middle of the High Street.

'And she knew all about him and Jeremy Thorpe?'

'He fed her all his stories, yes. There was nothing unusual about that, he used to carry on about it all the time and most people in the village knew better than to listen, but Gwen – she was a lovely woman, but naïve I suppose you would call her – she got very upset on his behalf and tried to do something about it. She even went all the way to *London* for a meeting about it at the Houses of Parliament.' That tone again: she made it sound like her friend had headed off to Sodom and Gomorrah.

'When was this?'

'Not long before she died.'

FOURTEEN

THE LIGHT butterfly-flutter that had started up in my guts when the woman first mentioned her friend turned into a maelstrom.

'Do you remember who it was she met in London?' I asked, trying to keep my voice steady.

'I know it wasn't Emlyn Hooson, the MP she was expecting to see,' the woman said, a cautious note creeping into her voice. 'When she got to there it was someone higher up in the Liberal party who came to meet her. I don't recall who. Who am I speaking to, please?'

It sounded like she was beginning to regret being so talkative. 'My name is Thomas,' I told her, trying to pronounce it as Welsh-ly as possible in the hope I could win her back round. 'Thomas Wildeblood. I'm a detective.' In for a penny, in for a pound.

'Police?'

'No, a private detective.' It sounded barely convincing from my end. I was just thankful she couldn't see me in my leather jacket, clutching my crumpled notes and the stubby pencil I'd liberated from a bookmaker's on the way to the library. 'I'm looking into the death of another person who was making similar claims to Norman Scott, and it would really help me if I could talk to him. Do you know of any way I could get in touch?'

I could hear her considering at the other end. I'm not sure if it was loyalty to her friend, post office professionalism or a simple desire to be rid of me that won out in the end, but she eventually said, 'I might have a forwarding address I could give you.'

'That would be marvellous, I'd be so grateful,' I practically gabbled. There was the sound of a phone being put down from the other end, footsteps and the rustle of papers. The pips went again before she came back on the line and I fed in more coins.

'It's care of a Jack and Stella Levy. Who they are I don't know, probably some other poor souls he's drawn in with his sob stories.' She read out an address in Devon which I scribbled down. I had to get her to spell out the name of the village for me: South Molton, M-O-L-T-O-N.

'Thank you,' I said, before throwing in a line that showed just how deep I was getting in to this detective act. 'Just one more thing – I'm sorry to ask: how did your friend die?'

Now she sounded decidedly guarded. 'The coroner said she'd drunk herself to death. And there were traces of all sorts of pills in her blood as well. But she hadn't meant to kill herself, he was very clear about that: it was an open verdict. Not that anyone took any note of that: Scott even managed to make her inquest all about himself, blurting out all the sordid details about what he'd been up to in London so that was all anyone was talking about rather than what a fine, lovely woman Gwen had been.

I said as much in my evidence. I said to the coroner, "Gwen Parry-Jones would still be alive if that man had never walked into the village, and that's God's own truth." And there's plenty here would say the same. I can't say there were many folk who were sorry to see the back of Norman Scott when he cleared off out of here.'

I thanked her and put the phone down. The churning in my guts had redoubled. I made no move to retrieve the last of my 5ps that had come rattling through to the unused coins flap or leave the phone box until a loud tapping on the glass brought me to my senses.

'All right, all right, sorry,' I snapped at the woman outside. She just scowled, so I didn't bother to hold the door open for her.

I stamped over to the foot of Nelson's column and heaved myself up onto the cold stone plinth beneath the lions to gather my thoughts. It was now fully dark, and as I watched, the lights on the Whitehall Theatre flickered into life: pneumatic nude women eight-feet-high chased each other round the awning, their nipples and crotches artfully obscured by vast lettering which read *Paul Raymond Presents... Come Into My Bed!* King Porn had already gobbled up Soho: now it seemed he was on his way south, riding towards Parliament on a sea of tits and bums, all good clean fun of the strictly heterosexual variety.

I followed the line of twinkling headlights all the way down the road beyond, to Big Ben's illuminated face at its end. That was where Gwen Parry-Jones had gone, thinking she could right a wrong, thinking she could expose the truth. And, like Stephen, she had ended up dead. Was Thorpe in the building right now, I wondered, plotting away with his Liberal colleagues, thinking his secret was safe forever? How would he react if I took Mark's advice and walked down there to parliament and demanded to see him? Would I be the next one to end up bashed on the head, dumped in the Thames? Or would he just look at me blankly with those dark eyes, and say 'Stephen who?'

And if he did simply deny all knowledge, what could I actually offer in return? Despite the lurid conspiracy theories that had begun to swirl in my mind, all I had to offer by way of evidence was the word of an underage rentboy. Actually, slightly less than that: it wasn't even Peter who had given us Jeremy Thorpe's name, and although there was plenty to suggest that getting involved with the man brought bad luck in its wake, we didn't have any solid evidence that he and Stephen had ever actually met. Admittedly, there were only thirteen Liberal MPs – I'd checked in my *Times Guide to the House of Commons* and been pleased to find Mark had got the number slightly wrong – and the chances that more than one of them was hiding an interest in boys and willing to go to extreme lengths to do so must be slim. But I still needed something concrete to connect the two of them.

Thankfully, I had a plan to get exactly that. And according to Big Ben in the distance, it was getting on for time to put it into action. I swung myself down from my perch and set off for my next appointment.

I'd asked Malcolm Crichton to meet me outside the tube station in Covent Garden, because I didn't fancy hanging around Piccadilly Circus if he turned up late, but he was already waiting on the pavement by the time I got there. He was wearing a long black overcoat with a velvet collar: if you'd given him a walking cane and a green carnation he could have passed for Oscar Wilde, which I'm pretty sure was his intention. I didn't mind: a dirty old man in search of rent boys was exactly the look that was needed for our purposes.

We went over the plan again as we walked past the boarded-up market buildings. I'd outlined the basics to Crichton on the phone that morning – that he needed to extract a friend of Stephen's from Playland, paying the going rate, and bring him to me so I could show him Thorpe's photo in the book to see if he recognised it – but he was twitchy about the whole thing, wanting to know, quite understandably, exactly why I couldn't just go in there and ask him myself. Sticking as close to the truth as I could while keeping my increasingly unconvincing private detective hat on, I'd spun him a story about a previous investigation into the managers of the arcade making me persona non grata. I steered very clear of any mention of violence or threats – there was no point making him any more jittery than he already was – and I did my best to distract him now by going over and over the plan and getting him to repeat details back to me until I was sure he had them down pat. I reckoned it would be fine for Crichton to go into the arcade and ask for Peter by name without raising suspicions. He could claim a friend had recommended him. That sort of thing happened all the time. Certain boys got a reputation for being convincingly enthusiastic, or particularly tight, although neither lasted long.

Meanwhile I would be waiting round the corner in a café on Glasshouse Street for the pair of them to come and meet me. I'd originally proposed that Crichton should hire a room at the Regent Palace where I would be able to speak to Peter in private, but he'd balked at the extra cost – I'd made it clear that all this evening's activities came under the heading of 'plus expenses' – and I wasn't prepared to risk the hotel's bar or any of its other public areas given how easily the boy himself had spotted me there the week before. We should be safe enough across the road as long as I kept my wits about me. I bagged a table at the back of the café which had a good view of the door and the street beyond the steamed-up window, and noted approvingly that the backs of the booth seats were high enough to hide both Peter and his supposed punter from the street if they sat opposite me when they arrived. I was actually congratulating myself on just how brilliantly I had planned the whole thing when the bell above the door tinged, and Malcolm Crichton pushed his way through the rainbow plastic strip curtain followed by a boy I'd never seen before in my life.

FIFTEEN

'Ah!' The old man spotted me and bustled over to the booth. 'Here we are!' He gestured to the boy to slide in opposite me, which he did without much enthusiasm.

'Hello,' I said. The boy nodded a surly greeting.

Crichton was staring rather bewildered at the illuminated menus above the café's counter. This obviously wasn't the sort of place that professors of art history usually hung out. 'Does one order over there, or do they come to us?' he asked.

I slid out from my own side of the table and stood up. 'I'll give you a hand. D'you want a Coke?' The boy looked up at me from under hooded eyes and nodded again.

I ushered Crichton over to the counter, where an assistant was snapping plastic lids onto tubs of sandwich fillings that really didn't look fit to do another day. The old man looked delighted with himself.

'Who's that?' I asked him quietly.

'What?'

'That's not Peter.'

Confused, he looked over at the boy in the booth, who was busy sneaking sugar cubes out of the bowl on the table and into his jacket pockets. 'Yes it is.'

'No it isn't,' I assured him. I turned aside to order our drinks – two bottles of Coke, even though I still had half a cup of coffee left, and, after some prompting, a tea for Crichton. 'Did he tell you that was his name?'

'Yes.' Crichton was chewing his lip, flustered. 'I went in and started putting money into one of the machines as you instructed, and that boy came over. I said I was looking for Peter who'd been recommended by a friend of mine, and he said that was him. I…I did think it was rather a coincidence.'

'Right.' I looked back at the boy. The sugar bowl was empty, and he had gone back to staring blankly ahead, his hands stuffed into the pockets of his jeans. I could have kicked myself. If – when – I'd been in the same situation, I'd have done exactly the same. 'How much did you pay him?'

'Ten pounds.' Crichton looked like he might be about to cry.

'All right, don't worry.' The man banged our cokes, and a pair of grubby glasses, onto the counter, and turned round to rattle a huge teapot under the water boiler. I tried to think. Crichton could hardly go back for another go ten minutes later. And what were we supposed to do with this boy in the meantime? Was one of us going to have to screw him for appearance's sake?

I let out a sigh of frustration, flickering my fringe. The plan might be scuppered, but it wasn't the kid's fault. He'd seen a chance for some cash and taken it. Let him enjoy his Coke and a half hour off duty. I supposed I could chat to him in the meantime, see if there was anything useful he could tell us about

Stephen. I picked up the two bottles, leaving the glasses where they were, and walked back over to the table. 'There you go.'

'Fanks,' the boy muttered, and clamped his lips greedily around the bottle's neck. It was half empty by the time he put it back down on the table, and he let out a burp so ferocious that it obviously startled even him.

'Better out than in,' I said. He grinned.

'What's your real name?' I asked gently. Crichton was still at the counter, counting out change and negotiating what he was meant to do with his teabag.

'Kevin.' The boy stared down, shamefaced, at the shiny tabletop.

'Do you know Peter?' He nodded again. 'Is he all right?'

'Fink so.' He mumbled his words down into his chest so it was hard to hear what he was saying. 'He was already out with a punter, see. And I didn't want your pal to be disappointed.'

'Yeah yeah,' I chided him. 'Don't worry about that, forget it. But I really do need to talk to Peter. The real Peter.'

He glanced up at that, his eyes meeting mine for the first time. 'You came into the arcade. Before.'

'That's right.' I smiled encouragingly. I didn't recognise him, but there had been a whole gaggle of boys in the place when Phil had attacked me: he had probably watched the whole thing.

At that moment Crichton arrived at the table, holding his tea ahead of him at arm's length. Half of it had slopped into the saucer. I motioned for him to sit down, and he chose the seat next to Kevin, who visibly shrank away from him. His eyes flicked downwards again.

'It's all right,' I tried to assure him. 'Malcolm's a friend.'

There was a long silence before the boy spoke again. 'Phil cut your face,' he muttered. The old man looked startled.

I reached up to finger the scar by my eye. 'It's OK, it wasn't too bad. Listen, Kevin, I really do need to see Peter. Do you think you could get a message to him?'

He didn't respond, just sat there, staring down at the table. He hadn't touched the rest of his Coke. I exchanged glances with Crichton, who looked completely out of his depth.

'We have paid you quite a lot of money, Kevin,' I prompted gently.

The boy nodded. I realised his shoulders were shaking. He muttered something too quiet for me to hear. 'What was that?'

We both leaned in to try to hear, and the boy shrank further back into the corner where we had trapped him. 'I said everyone always wants Peter,' he said, his voice barely more than a whisper. 'They always wanted Stephen, and now they always want Peter. No one ever wants me.'

I looked across at Crichton, dismayed. 'No, Kevin, it's not like that. Not at all. Really.'

'You're a very attractive young man,' stuttered Crichton. I wasn't sure this was the best way to help, but he persisted. 'Very attractive indeed.'

Kevin was sniffling now. 'Don't make me give your money back,' he pleaded. 'They'll hit me if I go back without any money.' Crichton, who was poised to slip a comforting arm around the boy's shoulders, withdrew it. He looked absolutely horrified. This was clearly an unwelcome wake-up call about the business he had been patronising all these years.

'We're not going to,' I assured Kevin. 'I promise. It's fine. I just need you to give a message to Peter. I just want to talk to him, like I'm talking to you, that's all. Can you do that for me, Kevin?'

He nodded, wiping a denim sleeve across his damp nose. I pushed the Coke bottle encouragingly in his direction.

'Can you tell him to come and meet me?'

A big sniff and another nod. 'Here?'

I looked around. We were the last customers in the place, and the staff were already mopping the floor and casting resentful looks in our direction. 'No,' I thought for a second, running through my mind for recognisable local landmarks. 'Just round the corner, where the bridge goes over the street, do you know where I mean?' Kevin nodded over an upturned bottle. 'I'll be there at half past seven, and again at half eight if Peter can't make it then. And every hour after that: tell him whenever he can get away, I don't mind waiting. And say there's some money in it for him, too.' It wasn't that I thought Peter needed to be bribed to come, just that I knew he would be as worried as Kevin about what his pimps might do to him if he came back empty-handed.

'All right.' The Coke bottle, drained, clunked back down onto the table. I'd barely touched my own, and I passed it across to him: 'Here. You take this with you.'

A skinny arm snaked out to snatch it. 'Ta.'

'Just don't forget to tell Peter, OK?'

'I won't. Can I go now?'

Malcolm Crichton didn't hang around either. No sooner had we watched Kevin scurry off down Glasshouse Street, his worn-out shoes and the filthy bottoms of his tatty flares scuffing along the pavement, than the old man turned to me and demanded to know exactly what I had got him involved with. 'That boy was frightened, visibly frightened,' he protested.

'How did you think they kept boys like him in line?' I asked.

'Not like *that*,' he gasped. 'He said that they would actually hurt him if he went back without any money. It's disgusting. It's exploitation.'

It was indeed, I was about to point out, and he and punters like him were right up there doing the exploiting – but I bit my tongue. He was still, at least in the make-believe world in which we'd fallen in with one another, my employer.

'That their own innocent desires can be…*abused* in such a mercenary way,' he continued, almost to himself, and I realised Malcolm Crichton's fantasy world extended a lot further than that.

'I'm going to need some more money,' I said bluntly. 'If you want me to find out what happened to Stephen, that is.'

'Oh! Of course.' He fumbled his wallet out of the pocket of his coat and thumbed out another three crisp tenners. 'Will this be, ah, sufficient for your needs?'

'For now.' I folded the notes up and pushed them into the pocket of my jeans. Any reservations I had had about taking money off the old man had now dissolved.

'Goodbye Mr Lewenstein,' he said, fastidiously brushing down the front of his coat as if he could sweep away the events of the last hour. 'I must say I have found this all very disturbing. Very disturbing indeed.' I watched him head off to the Underground entrance, noting that he wasn't so distressed that he didn't sneak a sideways glance at the rough trade leaning on the railings as he descended.

I had a quarter of an hour to kill, so I went for a stroll, keeping clear of Piccadilly Circus itself, where I was still wary of showing my face. On Denman Street I recognised a couple of acquaintances who were servicing punters in the shadows of shop doorways, nodding and waving to one (the other wasn't in a position to see me). All the way up Shaftesbury Avenue the fronts of the theatres blazed with lights: crowds were just arriving for the evening's shows, all dressed up in fancy suits and evening dresses. On Rupert Street the Raymond Revuebar offered an even more colourful alternative: *International Striptease Spectacular: Personal Appearances of the World's Greatest Names in Striptease.* The alleyway beyond it was a rainbow blaze of competing neon, so bright it was actually hard to look at. I thought back to the power shortages a few years ago when the government had ordered all of this switched off: suddenly the whole area became a labyrinth of dark corners, and while the rest of the country worked a three-day week, us Dilly boys had never been busier. 'It's just like the Blitz,' one punter about Malcolm Crichton's age had enthused to me, mid blow-job. 'We used to grope our way across town and the place was full of soldiers, it was *marvellous.*'

It was nearly time for my appointment with Peter, so I circled back down Brewer Street past the porn cinemas and made my way to where the covered bridge crosses Sherwood Street between the wings of the hotel I had until recently called home. I'd picked our meeting place because it's one of the few quiet spots around here: hardly anyone comes up beyond the theatre unless they're up to something they shouldn't be, and I'd brought plenty of punters here for quickies in the past. The only person around now was a kitchen porter sneaking a cigarette outside a door propped open with a cooking oil canister: there was certainly no sign of Peter.

After giving it ten minutes I headed off to a nearby pub, the Crown, where I ordered a half of lager and threw a few darts until it was time to go back again an hour later. If Peter did have difficulty getting away, I could be in for a very long evening. And if Kevin didn't even bother to pass the message on, I supposed I could waste the whole night. There was a payphone in the pub's entrance hallway, and I thought about calling Mark on it, but I'd used up all my change on that long-distance call to Wales a few hours earlier. He said he wasn't bothered when I came and went anyway: here was an opportunity to see if he really meant it.

At half-past eight I strolled back down to the bridge again. The illuminations in Piccadilly Circus were blazing away at the far end of the narrow street, turning it into a dark canyon, the night sky no more than a dull strip between the buildings that towered on either side of me. Peter was nowhere to be seen. The chef had retreated into the warm too, shutting the door behind him. I stomped my feet and zipped my jacket all the way up to my throat against the cold. I would give it five minutes.

We were into March now but my breath was still showing in clouds in front of me. It was starting to feel as if winter was never going to end. We'd better get a decent summer to make up for it. At the top of the street the pub door opened, letting out a brief blare of music and voices, but the man who came out turned left and headed up Brewer Street instead of coming towards me. I turned round and looked down the street in the direction I expected Peter to approach from, but to be honest I had already given up on him, at least for now: I had no way of knowing if he and Kevin's paths had crossed yet.

When I figured enough time had passed I turned around and trudged back up the road towards the pub, already resenting the cash I was going to have to spend there in order to keep warm for another hour, or possibly more. A car had just turned the corner and was coming towards me, but I didn't pay any notice until it drew to a halt beside me and the doors flew open, one of them slamming painfully into me and knocking me back against the wall.

I barely had time to react other than to get my arms up over my face, which only exposed my belly so that the great strapping thug who had clambered out from the driver's side of the car could get in a sharp winding punch, doubling me up. Then he simply reached down to scoop an arm round my legs, wrapped another round my shoulders and bundled me effortlessly into the boot which his companion had gone around and opened.

'Thought you'd come back and have another go, did you?' said the smaller man as he loomed over me. It was Phil from

Playland.

'I didn't, I swear,' I began to whimper, but he reached into his pocket and produced something which he forced into my mouth, pinching my nostrils shut with his gloved fingers until I had no choice but to open up and accept it. As soon as he had pulled the straps tight around the back of my head the other man rolled me over onto my side, yanked my arms behind me and wrapped something round my wrists: the whole thing was done so swiftly and efficiently it might have been choreographed.

'Kevin came straight to us and told us about your little offer,' Phil spat as he tested the fastenings. 'He's ours. Peter's ours: they're all ours. Get one thing straight, there's only one outfit running chickens round here. There ain't no room for competition.' He punched me hard in the face, stepped back and slammed down the lid of the boot. It rebounded painfully off my shoulder the first time, making me howl into my gag, but the second time it caught and fastened, and I was plunged into absolute blackness.

SIXTEEN

THE BOOT STANK of dirt and engine oil and a wave of nausea overtook me as the car began to move. I struggled to take in air through my nose, knowing that if I was to cough or gag I was in danger of choking. I recognised the thing in my mouth: it was a ball gag, the sort you can buy in most of the sex shops in Soho. I'd worn them before – strictly for punters' pleasure, that sort of thing does nothing for me – but this one tasted strongly of someone else, and the straps were set too tight, for someone smaller than me. I didn't even want to think about who had last been made to wear it.

Almost immediately the car went into a seemingly endless turn – I suppose we must have been going around the roundabout in Piccadilly Circus – which crammed me up hard against the wall of the boot, my head crushed forwards and my face buried in the collars of my leather jacket, making it even more difficult to breathe. As we finally straightened out and the pressure on my neck was eased I forced myself to take in long, steady drafts through my nostrils, trying to calm the thumping rhythm of my heart. If I panicked now, I would be done for. A nice hippy girl who had been into meditation had lived at the squat for a while, and although I couldn't be doing with the nonsense she spouted about chi energy and the like, I had let her teach me the basics of tantric breathing, which turned out to be a tonic at the end of a busy day on the Dilly. Now, in a state of considerably more stress, I put her lessons to the test. Feel the cool clean air flow in and fill your belly, your ribcage, your chest, and every part of your body, two, three, four, and out, cleansing yourself of all those toxins and strain, two, three, four. And in, two, three, four, and out, two, three, four. Ironically, I suspected my current sensory deprivation was exactly the sort of meditative state she had been urging me to try and achieve, but I can't say it felt very relaxing right now. The car kept juddering to a halt and then starting forward again, flinging me back and forth in the confined space: each time the engine would roar and the grinding of the gearbox went right through me. Phil's words at our last encounter kept coming back to me: *It won't just be your face I'm cutting, I'll have your cock off as well.*

I tried to manoeuvre my bound hands as best I could beneath me to see if there was any give in whatever was fastened around them. No joy. It was a thick strap of some kind, more bondage gear or maybe just an ordinary belt: I could feel the cold bulk of a buckle against my wrist as I wriggled, but it was way out of reach of fingers which were already beginning to go numb.

No point struggling, then: better to conserve my energy for whatever was coming next. I told myself I had got out of situations as bad as this before – I once had a punter, strung out on heroin and wielding a kitchen knife, lock me in his flat and refuse to let me go for an entire night and day. We had to stop at some point, and then I could try to explain once again that I had no interest, less than no interest in trying to poach any of their boys off them: they had got it all wrong. Assuming, that was, that they actually took this thing out of my mouth so I was able to speak.

For now, I had to keep calm. Concentrate on something else. Go to your good place. With a wrench I realised I didn't have my lucky book on me – I'd taken it out of my jacket pocket that morning so I could fit the *Times Guide* in instead – but it didn't matter, I knew the thing practically off by heart anyway. What had Peter Wildeblood done when he found himself locked up like I was? On his first night in prison he had catalogued the contents of his cell, studied every square inch of it. How did it go? *I shall know the number of fly-specks on the light bulb, and the way the grain of the table-top runs, and the faint smell of this cake of soap, and the disposition of the lumps in the mattress and the shape of the stains on the blankets. I shall experience these things as vividly as though I loved them, which I never shall; but I must guard against hating them, or they will begin to drive me mad.* All right for him to say: I couldn't even see my surroundings, let alone begin to appreciate them. But it was working: I was feeling calmer, not so close to the brink of suffocation.

It helped that the revving and roaring had calmed and our progress got smoother: I sensed we must have moved beyond the city centre and onto more open roads. As the car sped up and the mechanical noises dulled to a low throb I realised I could make out other sounds: the voices of my captors in the front of the car. Yes, that was Phil speaking – I wasn't going to forget the sound of his voice any time soon. And that must be his companion, the bigger man who had lifted me so effortlessly into the boot. But it was too muffled for me to make out what they were actually saying.

I had nothing to lose. Bracing my feet against the back of the boot I tried to wriggle forward a few inches: my forehead rapidly came up hard against the back of the car's seats. But there was light coming through at the furthest edge of the barrier where it met the wall of the car: only the tiniest sliver of dull orange that ebbed and flowed with each streetlight we passed beneath. If I could shuffle just a bit further and twist my head round to press an ear right up against it – yes! I could just make out what they were saying.

'…good lad for coming straight to us. We should make an example of him.' That must be the other man.

'How d'you mean?' Yes, that was Phil all right.

'I dunno, give him a treat. Some new clothes or something. Show the boys loyalty pays.'

Phil snorted. 'Why don't we just make them watch us work Peter over instead, show 'em what you get for being bad?'

My heart sank. Getting Peter into trouble was the last thing I had wanted to do. None of this was his fault.

But it sounded as if there might still be some hope for him. The first part of the larger man's response was muffled, but I made out the words '…don't know if he'd even have gone and met this bloke.'

Phil was having none of it. 'He needs a slap anyway, miserable little shit. He's hardly brought any money in for days now.'

'Yeah well, he's been out of sorts since Stephen died. They were mates, weren't they?'

A grunt. 'Wouldn't surprise me if he was doing business on the side. I know Stephen was.'

'And look what happened to him. I think that might be warning enough for the rest of them.'

'Yeah, well, a slap or two always helps make the message

clear, doesn't it?'

Phil sounded like his usual charming self, but his companion was having none of it. Either he raised his voice, or turned towards Phil, or both, but I heard what he said next with crystal clarity. 'You can cut that shit out right now, Phil. The last thing we need is you flying off the handle. I'm not ending up with another Billy Two-Tone on our hands.'

That name rang a bell. Billy Two-Tone, so called for the blonde streaks that ran through his long brown hair, had been a familiar figure on the Dilly until he disappeared a couple of years ago. But there was nothing unusual in that. People disappear from the Dilly all the time.

I couldn't make out Phil's answer, which came in a sulky mutter. But his colleague – his boss, by the sound of it, carried on in the same fierce tone. 'I mean it, Phil. We've got enough heat on us thanks to Stephen's little scheme. The big man told me if we can't even manage to keep our boys in line and stop them shooting their mouths off without him having to step in, there's no point him wasting his time on us any more. Says if we have any more trouble with the filth, him and his mates won't be doing anything to help this time.'

Another muttered reply seemed to make the bloke really angry. 'What the fuck are you talking about, Phil? You know if it wasn't for him putting in a word last time we'd have all gone down. So no going psycho this time, right? We get this prick somewhere quiet well out of town, then it's a quick in-out, no messing about, and we dump his body in a ditch. Right? If he's rent like you say, he's nothing, no one's going to miss him.'

SEVENTEEN

DUMP HIS BODY. My surroundings seemed to float away, leaving me lost and anchorless in the darkness of the boot. Another wave of panic fizzed through my body, bringing water rushing into both my eyes and my mouth, where it washed uselessly against the back of the ball gag. I started to thrash around, straining desperately at the bonds around my wrists and kicking out against the wall of the boot in the mad hope I might somehow be able to attract attention from any other passing vehicles.

'Shut the fuck up back there!' came a yell from the front of the car – I heard that clearly enough – and there was a sudden burst of pop music, sounding weird and distorted from where I lay. They had switched on the radio to drown out the sounds of me struggling.

It meant there was no chance of making out anything else

they might say, but I had heard enough. This coffin-like space was not just Peter Wildeblood's prison, it was the condemned cell. I was on my final journey.

And the worst of it was, I thought as I exhausted myself and slumped back into a twisted heap, they were right: no one would miss me. Mark might wonder what had happened to me, when I would be back to pick up the few possessions I had left in his flat, but I'd made it perfectly clear to him that he shouldn't rely on my returning. He would most likely just think I had freaked out at the idea of commitment and done a runner. If only I hadn't been so stubborn when he invited me to stay. If only I had made that phone call from the pub. If only. If only.

Would he even get to hear about it if my body was found? At least that way he would at least know my disappearance was nothing to do with him. Or would that just make things worse? I'd seen at the police station how far Mark's righteous fury had carried him over the death of a complete stranger: the worst thing that could possibly happen would be for him to go blundering into Phil's world demanding justice on my behalf. I'd tried hard to shield him from the grim realities of how I'd been living for the past few years: my last hope had to be that he wouldn't get sucked in to it all after I had gone. No, better for me to just slip away, anonymous, an eternal mystery.

As I lay hopelessly in the darkness, I was surprised to find my parents drifting into my thoughts too. Even if my body did get found, and was identified as Tommy Wildeblood, there was no reason for them to ever find out about it. There was nothing to connect that name to them. He was a stranger. How long was it now since I had last seen them – four years, was it, since I had stomped off down the front path, my father puce-faced on the doorstep and yelling his head off about revolting perversions as the net curtains twitched and jumped all the way down our

137

suburban street? And my mum behind him in the hallway, still in her coat and nurse's uniform, having got back from work minutes earlier with nothing more on her mind than what to cook for our tea, only to discover all hell had broken loose in her home.

I wondered if they ever thought about me. Surely they must do. I was their only child, for all my father's loud protestations about 'no son of mine.' Well, here I was about to make good on all his predictions: I was undeniably coming to a Bad End, it was indeed down to hanging around with degenerates, and I really had brought it upon myself.

Calm breathing. Calm breathing. I tried to count out the slow two-three-fours, but it was hard not to match them to the rapid hammering of my heart as it thumped in my ears. If I could only get this damn gag out of my aching mouth. If I could only loosen the strap round my wrists. If only. If only. If only.

I think I must have lost consciousness at some point, because I drifted off into a strange half-dreaming state where those contorted bodies on Malcolm Crichton's walls seemed to float in front of me, their faces tantalisingly familiar but hovering just beyond my recognition. We seemed to have been travelling forever: we must be well clear of the city by now. I'd been a London boy for years, barely able to comprehend life outside of the capital's centre. Now I was leaving the place for the last time: going back to the countryside to die. I wondered who would find my body. Maybe nobody would. Maybe I would just rot away in a ditch somewhere, unnoticed, unmarked, unmourned, unremembered. People disappear off the face of the earth all the time. Look at Lord Lucan. And people were actually bothered about trying to find him.

Oh god: we were slowing down. I slid forwards and up against the back seats, then was crushed up against the side once again as the car turned off the road. The sound from beneath the wheels changed from smooth tarmac to a looser, crackling surface and finally we came to a complete standstill: the engine stopped and for an all-too brief moment there was blissful silence. Then the sound of doors thunking open and slamming shut, footsteps, and the lid of the boot was pulled up. I found myself looking up not at the two men towering over me, but past them to the starry sky beyond. It struck me quite hard that it was the most beautiful thing I had ever seen.

Hands on my shoulders, hands on my legs, pulling me up and out of the car. I couldn't stand up, let alone try to run; my legs were cramped into their bent position and I fell forward painfully onto my knees. I could make out trees on either side of us, black against the deep indigo of the sky. We were in a lay-by, its pitted surface glazed with puddles. Litter everywhere. Piles of cigarette ash and butts where drivers had tapped out their ashtrays; tattered scraps of paper caught in the tatty hedgerow and streaming from the barbed wire tangled through it. Somehow I took all of this in in photographic detail, but it took me a moment to register what Phil was holding in his hand as his companion took a fistful of my collar to haul me upright and face him. A knife. The same knife he had held to my face in the arcade when he warned me – you couldn't say he hadn't warned me – to steer clear. That felt like a lifetime ago. A lifetime that was about to end. Everything seemed to go into slow motion, and I could only watch dumbly as he as he drew the knife back and then plunged it savagely forward, the blade disappearing into my chest.

There was a sudden blinding light all around me, washing over me. I could hear voices, but they seemed to be coming from very far away: there was another noise, too, a great roaring which was getting louder and louder as the light which surrounded my body got brighter and more intense. And then everything was just a confusion of light and noise, and I fell forward onto the cold ground and what felt like oblivion.

Which is when someone grabbed my shoulders, turned me over, and said in a broad Scottish accent, 'Are you all right pal? What's going on? Are you OK?'

EIGHTEEN

MY HEAD FELL BACK onto the wet gravel as I rolled over onto my back, and I found myself staring straight into the blazing whiteness: it emanated from two vast headlights, and between them I could just make out a single word in massive letters: *LEYLAND.*

'The lorry driver started back as he caught his first sight of me face-on. 'Oh. Kinky stuff, is it?'

I shook my head frantically, mumming denials through the ball gag. He nodded. 'All right, hang on, mate.' He pulled my head up, not ungently, and fumbled with the buckle at the back of my head. At last the ball gag came loose, and I sucked in great gulps of the night air, coughing and retching and heaving myself over to spit onto the damp ground beside me. My saviour straightened up rapidly and stepped out of range. He was a big bear of a man with a mass of ginger hair. You could see why Phil

141

and his pal would have thought twice about messing with him.

'Well, your mates have taken off, anyway,' he told me when he figured I had finished.

'They weren't my mates,' I croaked, elbowing myself up in to a sitting position and waggling my bound hands behind me. 'Is there any chance...?'

'Oh, like that, was it?' He squatted down and unbuckled the belt, winding it off my arms. His lorry's engine was still thrumming noisily away just a few feet behind us. 'Lucky I pulled in when I did, then.'

'Very lucky. Thank you. Really, I mean, thank you.' I shook my wrists, trying to force some feeling back into hands that felt like they belonged to someone else. I still couldn't quite work out why I was sitting up and talking. Apart from a general aching throughout my body, I seemed to be fine.

'You want this?' He dangled the ball gag from a finger.

I shuddered. 'No thank you.'

'Fair enough.' He swirled it around by the end of the strap a couple of times and sent it flying, watching appreciatively as it sailed up over the dark hedgerow and into the field beyond. 'See what the farmer makes of that. You get to see all sorts in this job, I tell you. My name's Alan.'

I took the meaty hand he extended in my direction, which he used both to greet me and to haul me to my feet. 'Tommy.'

'All right Tommy. I'm not going to ask any questions. There's a seat in my cab if you want it. You can get yourself dried off and warmed up at least.'

I nodded enthusiastically. There was no sign of Phil and his mate, but that wasn't to say they weren't going to come back when they thought the coast was clear to finish the job. 'Which way are you going?'

'West. I've got a load of pallets that are due in Taunton by six o'clock. I only pulled in here for a piss. Lucky for you I did. Go on, get on up.'

I limped towards his lorry, my legs still feeling the after-effects of the night in the cellar, and swung myself up into the cab while Alan wandered off towards the hedge to attend to his needs. It was nice inside: he'd stretched sheepskin rugs across the seats and hung a lion rampant flag across the back of his sleeping compartment: the whole place had a warm fug of masculinity and tobacco. There were weird crackling noises coming from a box attached to the dashboard and someone calling himself Tomahawk was talking about roadworks on the A38.

Right now I just wanted to get as far away from Playland as possible. Actually, right now all I wanted to do was close my eyes and sleep for about a year. Only then did I feel I might be able to process everything that had happened in the last few hours.

It was warm in the cab, and I unzipped my leather jacket. It flapped open in an unfamiliar way: I ran my fingers down my front and they jagged on a new hole high up on the left side, at about the level of my heart. There was a neat incision in the black leather through which I could feel torn lining and some other strange texture beyond it.

'Fuck,' I whispered to myself. I had had the jacket less than a week and it was ruined. And yet I didn't seem to be: why not? Tentatively, as if the danger was in the discovery rather than the damage itself, I reached inside my open jacket: the skin I pressed down on felt tender, bruised maybe, but my jumper and shirt were intact. What was going on?

And then, as my knuckles came up against a heavy weight and my brain finally took in all the oxygen it needed to function properly again, I realised. I pulled the copy of *The Times Guide to the House of Commons* out of the inside pocket of my jacket.

It was run through from the front cover all the way to a few pages from the back, where the sheer weight of paper had halted the knife's progress. Like some First World War soldier with the bible at his breast, my life had been saved by the book. It was the best thing I had ever shoplifted. If anyone ever tries to tell me crime doesn't pay, I'm going to make them look at every single one of those neatly slit pages.

'You all right? What you got there?' asked Alan as he clambered up into the driver's seat.

'Nothing.' I shoved the book back into its pocket, with difficulty, because in its mangled state it wouldn't shut properly.

As we pulled out onto a deserted dual carriageway, I squinted out at the darkness on either side. 'Where are we, actually?'

'Just south of Reading.'

Jesus. I was only a few miles away from my parents' house. What were the chances?

'Where do you want dropping off?'

I spoke without thinking. 'As far away from here as possible.'

'Fair enough. Well, like I say, I'm going all the way to the West Country, if that's any use to you.'

The West Country. It felt like a sign. Maybe first appearances hadn't been deceptive, and this man really was my guardian angel? I delved into another pocket, and found the scrap of paper I'd scrawled Norman Scott's address on. 'You're not going anywhere near…South Molton, are you?'

He shook his head, red mane swishing from side to side. 'That's a bit further on, over Exmoor way. But I'm sure we can find you someone who's going that way on this baby.' He leaned forward and patted the crackling box on the dashboard. 'You seen one of these before? They're the business.'

He lifted a mouthpiece on a curled telephone cable to his mouth. 'Breaker, breaker, this is Big Dipper, twenty on the

A33 calling out for any good buddies heading West. Got me a hitcher here looking for an onward ride.' For some reason he was putting on a weird American accent, as were several of the men who responded. The ensuing conversation sounded like gibberish to me – there was a lot of *ten-fours* and *Roger Wilcos* involved, and an inquiry as to whether I was a 'seat cover', which I apparently wasn't – but the upshot of it was that he found another driver who was willing to pick me up in a rest area on the outskirts of Taunton in a few hours' time and take me all the way on to South Molton.

'I can't tell you how grateful I am,' I told Alan again when he had made the arrangements and signed off with a cheery 'threes and eights'. 'You really have saved my life tonight.'

'My pleasure.' He slotted the mouthpiece back into its cradle, and I eased back into the fur-lined seat, ready to give in to the drowsiness that was threatening to overwhelm me. Which is when I felt one of those meaty hands come across to rest just above my knee.

I kept my eyes closed to see if it would stay there. It did.

'You know I don't actually mind that kinky stuff, as it happens,' he announced in a slightly croaky voice after a little while.

'Right,' I said resignedly. It looked as if I wasn't going to get to go to sleep after all.

Look, I've had worse experiences hitch-hiking, and you could hardly say I didn't owe him one. It was only a quickie, snatched in another thankfully deserted layby, and he let me stay in his sleeping space afterwards to grab an hour or two's shut-eye. I actually felt a bit sad to say goodbye to him as I clambered down from his cab and watched him drive off into the distance.

There was a dull glow in the direction we had come from which signalled that the sun would be up soon. I had an hour or so to kill before my next lift turned up – Alan had checked in with the driver, who called himself Red Rover, before dropping me off – so I went in to the café at the rest stop to see if a big mug of black coffee and a bacon sarnie smothered in Daddie's Sauce could do what another seven hours' sleep was really needed for and set me up for the day. Turns out they couldn't. When I looked at myself in the mirror in the café toilets after my breakfast my face was grey and puffy, my eyes bloodshot and my hair a greasy mess. My whole body still ached from the abuse it had undergone: there was a livid purple bruise on my shoulder and the skin on my wrists was red and sore. Still, there was nothing to be done about it: I pulled down the cuffs on my jacket, poked back a sliver of lining that was protruding back through the slash in the front so it was less obvious, and went out into the cold morning to continue my journey.

NINETEEN

THANKFULLY, RED ROVER turned out not to want to do anything more to me than bore me to death about the yacht parts he was delivering to Westward Ho!, which, he proudly told me, was the only place in Britain with an exclamation mark in its name ('Came up on *Sale of the Century* last year, that did, and it was for five pound'). I mostly tuned him out and looked out of the window instead, enjoying the landscape, the big winter sky and the bizarre place names that slid past on the road signs: Norton Fitzwarren, Wiveliscombe, Holcombe Rogus. As we drove, the countryside changed and grew increasingly wild: the fields gave way to scrubby moorland, the few bare trees stunted and bent against the wind, an unending vista of brown bracken and gorse like something out of *Wuthering Heights*.

'This is Exmoor,' Red Rover told me, rolling the R proprietorially. 'And they do say there's a Beast of Exmoor, so

you'd best watch out if you're planning on staying in these parts.'
So maybe more like *The Hound of the Baskervilles*.

It wasn't long after that that he pulled up to let me out, directing me down a lane that led off the main road and telling me South Molton was about fifteen minutes' walk that way. The sun was getting pretty high in the sky now, and although there was still a bitter wind coming down off the moor, the bright sunshine and the primroses on the grass verges seemed to carry at least a hint that spring was on its way. I knew we were into March because we'd had the extra day for the leap year the week before, but the sleepless night had left me unsure even of what day of the week it was, let alone the date. I was a man out of time, as well as out of place.

God, it felt good to be out in the open, though. Why didn't I do this more often? Actually, scratch that, why hadn't I done it *ever* in the last four years of stomping along city pavements, eyes down and always on edge, ever-braced for the worst to happen? It felt like out here in the wide open I could stand tall and breathe properly, relax, and maybe get some perspective on everything I had learned in the past week, perhaps even see how it all fitted together. The Playland crew were killers, I had had that proved to me in no uncertain terms, but I still didn't think they had been responsible for Stephen's death. What was it they had been saying in the car? *The big man told me if we can't manage to keep our boys in line and stop them shooting their mouths off without him having to step in… Any more trouble with the filth and him and his mates won't do anything to help this time.* My thoughts went back to the police raid on the arcade last year: it had been the talk of the Dilly for days while the place stayed shuttered and closed, everyone speculating that it was just the beginning, that the Vice Squad had changed the habit of a lifetime and were about to move in mob-handed and arrest the lot of us. Then one morning the place was open again, just like that, with the same old young faces in there drifting between the machines like ghosts.

The big man. Could that be Thorpe? I pulled out the life-saving book and leafed through the perforated pages as I walked until I found his photograph. He was hardly the most physically imposing of men, but then again that might not be the sense in which they meant it: there were all sorts of different ways of wielding power. He was leader of his party, for a start. And even if the party was small, Mark had said it held the key to keeping the country running. You didn't get much bigger than that.

And I was on my way to see someone who could tell me more about him: Norman Scott, who in the space of what must only be 48 hours had gone from being a rumour in a pub, to a name in a phone book, to a flesh-and-blood man in the village I was now approaching. He might not have all the answers, but I was sure he could help me out with some.

The grass verge gave way to a pavement, and before long the few isolated bungalows and farm buildings on either side of the road began to get closer together until I was unmistakeably walking down a street rather than a road. A sign welcomed me to South Molton, encouraged me to please drive carefully and added the information that the place was twinned with Livarot in France. It was chocolate-box pretty. Several of the houses had bay windows which hung out from their top storeys over the street: one or two had big grand porches on the front with pillars, and one on an island in the middle of the road even sported castle-style battlements. I passed both a butcher's and a baker's, and I wouldn't have been in the least surprised to come across a candlestick-maker too: this was the sort of place that seemed more suited to one of Miss Marple's cases than the one I had got myself caught up in.

The feeling seemed to be shared by the locals, too. The early morning shoppers I passed, all of them togged up in country clothes that would have been old-fashioned twenty years earlier, made no effort to hide disapproving stares at my leather jacket and admittedly filthy jeans. One old lady waiting at a bus stop let out an audible gasp and – I swear this is true – switched her handbag on to her other arm to keep it well out of reach as I walked past her. Under the circumstances I decided not to bother asking for directions, but just wander around until I found the address I had written down: the place was obviously tiny, and since the street I found myself on was called East Street and the one I was looking for was South Street I figured that even I might manage to locate it.

The further I walked, the more picturesque the place became: past the battlemented building the road opened into a wide square with the traffic flowing down either side of a paved market full of brightly-striped stalls. There was a grand town hall with a flag and a clock tower too: the place was practically Trumpton. What it did feel, and for this I was very grateful, was safe: the world of pimps and flick knives and violent death felt very far away on this sunny morning. After all, if anything bad did happen, I could surely rely on Pugh, Pugh, Barney McGrew, Cuthbert, Dibble and Grub to be along to rescue me.

South Street turned out to be at the far end of the market, and the little cottage I was after was right at the top of it. It was also, to my surprise, next door to a rather grander brick building with large arched windows and a set of gilt letters above them which spelled out *LIBERAL CLUB*.

It felt like a bad joke. Could it just be coincidence? Something else struck me, and I pulled out the split hardback from my pocket and leafed with difficulty through its damaged pages until I found Thorpe again. His constituency was listed as

North Devon. Unless my geography was completely out – and I had been predicted an A in my O-level, not that I had ever got as far as taking it – I was currently standing pretty much slap-bang in the middle of North Devon.

Had Norman Scott deliberately come and put his head in the lion's mouth? Or was it Thorpe that had installed him here to keep him handy for when he was in the area, conveniently leaving his wife in London? From the way Clarrie had talked about him, it sounded as if the two of them had fallen out for good. But then she had made clear Scott wasn't the most reliable of witnesses. Maybe it was more complicated than that. There were plenty of kept men who resented their lovers just as much as they relied on them. And plenty of queens who were happy to bad-mouth their boyfriends in public and insist everything was all over only to jump back into bed with them at the earliest opportunity.

Well, there was only one way to find out: ask him. I put the book away – I could barely cram it into my pocket now the cut pages were so disturbed – checked the address one last time and then rapped on the door of the little cottage.

Empty houses have their own distinctive sound. I think I knew as soon as I knocked that no one would be coming to open the door. Still, I waited a while, and even tried knocking again. I didn't really know what else to do. After that I tried peering in at the windows, but they had nets and I couldn't make out anything beyond them.

'You after the Levys, my love?' said a bright voice from behind me, and I jumped guiltily away from the pane. A round-faced, friendly woman holding a cardboard box full of cabbages was standing on the pavement next to a van with its back doors open.

'Yeah. Yes,' I stuttered, even though it wasn't the exact truth.

'Friend of theirs from London, are you?' She eyed my outfit appraisingly.

'Um – friend of a friend.'

'Right. Well, they only use the place at weekends, and they're not down much at all in the winter.'

'Oh…right,' I said lamely.

'I can give you their phone number in London if you like,' she offered. 'Tell you what, give us a hand in with this stuff so Bert can get off the double yellows, and I'll look it out for you.'

I went over to the van, hauled out a box of cauliflowers, and followed her into the greengrocers on the far side of the cottage. A bloke in overalls with a nicotine-stained moustache – Bert, I presumed – was just emerging to fetch yet more boxes from the van.

'Right,' said my new acquaintance, dumping her box and indicating where I should do the same. She wiped her hands on the front of her apron and went round behind the shop counter. 'Now, where did I put it?'

'It was actually Norman Scott I was after,' I admitted. 'I think he might have been staying with them?'

'Oh.' She stopped riffling through the mass of papers she had pulled out and gave me a look that I couldn't quite work out.

'Or have I got that wrong?' I said breezily, hoping to restore her former bonhomie. 'He gave their house as his forwarding address.'

'No, no, he lived there,' she said, still strangely serious. 'For a bit. Then he moved on.'

'Oh.' My heart sank. Was I going to end up chasing Norman Scott all round the country? 'Do you know where he went?'

She chewed her bottom lip doubtfully for a moment, then said: 'You're best talking to Mrs Friendship.'

'I'm sorry?'

152

She smiled at my confusion, but with none of the open warmth that had been there before. 'I know, funny name, isn't it? Suits her though. She took Scott in when he...ran into trouble last year. She'd be the best person to tell you about him.'

'And where would I find her?'

'Barnstaple.'

More travelling. She clocked my expression. 'Don't worry, Bert can run you up there, can't you Bert?'

Bert had just staggered back into the shop with two crates of oranges stacked on top of each other. He dumped them on the counter and said sulkily, 'Can I?'

'Oh, don't be daft, you're going that way anyway,' the woman scolded him. Seeing my chance to ingratiate myself, I hurried out to the van ahead of him and made straight for the heaviest-looking boxes.

Bert, as it turned out, wasn't much of a talker at the best of times. Most of the forty-minute journey passed in silence and smoke, half of it from the roll-ups that he sucked on incessantly while driving and half from the van's engine, which belched out black fumes, the latter somehow managing to find its way in through the windows we had rolled down to let out the former. I was frozen to the skin, bronchial and smelled like an ashtray by the time he pulled over to let me out in the centre of Barnstaple, a much larger town than South Molton, and waved me vaguely in the direction of a pub. It was only when I checked the sign above the door of the Market Inn – *Mrs Edna Friendship: Licensed to sell intoxicating liquor for consumption on the premises* – that I was sure I was in the right place.

It was getting on for lunchtime by now, and the place was full of customers, but when I said I was looking for Mrs Friendship the eldest woman behind the bar passed the half-filled pint pot she was holding to one of her younger companions, told them both they would have to manage by themselves for half an hour, and lifted the flap so I could come through to her side and follow her through a door marked *Staff Only*.

'Judy phoned and said you were on your way,' she said, with the same West Country burr as the lady in the greengrocers. 'Go on up.' She indicated a staircase, its treads narrowed almost to impassability by crates of bottles and boxes of crisp packets. 'Better to talk in the flat where we can get a bit of peace and quiet.'

'I'm trying to get hold of Norman Scott,' I explained as I climbed, though Judy had presumably told her that too. 'Is it right that he lives here?'

I came to a small landing. 'Door on the left,' said Mrs Friendship, so I opened it – and something enormous launched itself at me.

I wasn't prepared for it, and with thoughts of my ordeal with the Playland pair still fresh in my mind, I'm afraid I may have screamed. Thankfully the thing resolved itself quite quickly into a dog, but a dog the likes of which I have never seen. It was huge, practically the size of a lion or a Shetland pony. It could have flattened me with just one of its vast paws. Thankfully – because my thoughts had flipped straight back to Henry Baskerville – it seemed more intent on licking me than attacking me, but its affectionate attentions were still enough to drive me backwards until I was teetering at the very edge of the staircase, threatening to fall back on top of Mrs Friendship and send the both of us crashing to the bottom along with everything else that was stacked on the way.

'RINKA!' bellowed Mrs Friendship in a thunderous voice. 'Get down, girl! BAD DOG! Rinka! Get down!'

TWENTY

'SHE WAS STANDING over his body, like she was keeping guard,' said Mrs Friendship sadly as she scratched the dog behind her ears. 'You stayed with your master to the end, didn't you, girl?'

The Great Dane turned and licked her hand as if it understood her, thumping its tail on the carpeted floor heavily enough to make the glasses on the nearby coffee table rattle. We were sitting in the lounge of the flat above the pub. Mrs Friendship had fetched us both a brandy from the bar after she broke the news that I was almost six months too late to meet Norman Scott.

'And he'd been shot?' I asked, rescuing my own glass as it vibrated towards the edge of the table.

She nodded. 'From close range, the police said first of all. Then they changed their story later on. Tried to say it must have been someone out shooting pheasants or deer that hit him from a distance.'

'But they never caught anyone?'

She shook her head scornfully. 'Never tried, so far as I could see. Said it was probably just someone who panicked when he realised what he'd done and took off. Or maybe didn't even realise he'd hit someone. But they've got the names of everyone round here's who's got a shotgun certificate – they must do, it's them as issues them – and there's plenty of farmers drink in here I know for a fact were never asked where they were that day or what they were doing.'

'Did you ask the police about it?'

'Oh, I tried,' she said with vehemence. 'Went down the police station and kicked up a fuss. Said there was no reason for Norman to even be up on the moor. Rinka needs a lot of exercise, bless her, but he never used to walk her up that way: he said the landscape spooked him, it was so lonely. He used to go round the town instead. Besides, the weather that day was filthy. They just told me it was out of their hands. Some lot from London had taken over the investigation.'

'Special Branch?'

She looked at me in surprise. 'That's right. How d'you know that?'

I shook my head. 'Lucky guess.'

She took a deep swig of brandy. 'Well, after that I had a visit from some of them. Wanting to search Norman's room. I'd let him stay in one of the guest rooms here, see, after I found out he'd been sleeping rough – oh, a terrible state he was in.'

'And did you let them?'

She shrugged. 'Didn't give me much choice. I said to the one that was in charge – right shifty bugger he was – that I couldn't see what it could have to do with anything and they'd be better off out looking for whoever shot him, but he insisted. I knew what he was really after: Norman had been writing a book about Jeremy Thorpe and everything he'd done to him, and sure enough, he made a beeline for that and took it away with him, and a lot of his other papers too. And that was the last I ever saw of that.'

'But they're not allowed to just keep stuff,' I protested. I'd been booked in for importuning for immoral purposes enough times to know that. 'They have to give it back.'

She shrugged again. 'When I asked they said it would be "returned to his rightful heirs in due course". I don't know who that would be: he never talked about his family. I know it isn't me.'

'Did they at least give you a receipt?' At West End Central they were scrupulous about signing everything in and signing it all back out again, usually with a few taunting comments about your possessions, or lack of them.

'Ha! Fat chance. The man in charge wouldn't even give me his name.'

'Did he have an ID number on his uniform?' I was clutching at straws.

'He wasn't in uniform. Just a normal suit. Grey. He must have been something high-up, though – it was him giving the orders. And he was old, too. In his seventies, I'd say.'

'His seventies? Are you sure he was police?' I'd never seen a policeman that old. I was pretty sure they got pensioned off at 60, if not before. The joke on the Dilly was that they were getting younger and prettier by the year.

Mrs Friendship shrugged. 'The other ones, the pair that did the searching, they said they were Special Branch. They showed me their badges. But the older one, I didn't see any ID for him. He was a funny-looking bugger. Sticky-out ears.' She cupped both hands beside her head to demonstrate, abandoning

Rinka's own ears, and the dog shuffled round to turn her attentions to me. 'Worse than poor Prince Charles's. I always think it's a such a shame, he'd be such a handsome lad if it weren't for them, although I don't think much of that beard he's got now, do you?'

'I've not seen it,' I said, distracted. Rinka pawed at my leg, and I took over stroking duties. She was actually very friendly once you got over the shock of the size of her, though you had to watch out for the slobber.

'She likes you,' said Mrs Friendship with an assessing look.

'She's got good taste, haven't you girl?' I leaned in for the doggy-talk, and was rewarded with a long wet tongue across the face.

'Norman would have liked you too.' She looked me up and down. 'You're just his type.'

I found myself blushing, I'm not sure why. It wasn't even much of a compliment from what I knew about Norman Scott: he didn't even seem to have a preferred gender, let alone a type. But I muttered thanks anyway, and buried my embarrassment in more fussing over Rinka.

Mrs Friendship gave a sad smile. 'If only you'd come last year. You could have helped bring him out of himself. I said to him, "Norman, you need to stop living in the past, time to move on." But he could never quite manage it, poor soul.'

'You said he was writing a book?'

She nodded, looking down into her brandy glass and seeming surprised to find it empty. 'He really stuck at it too: pages and pages there were.'

'Did he have a publisher?' I was trying to think of other people who might have copies of what he had written.

'No, but he'd been talking to a journalist who was interested: he thought if he could get them to print something, that would get the ball rolling. "They'll be knocking down my door, you wait and see," that's what he kept saying.' She placed the glass carefully back down on one of the coasters with their pictures of country flowers. 'I tried to tell him not to get his hopes up, but he was so full of himself: "At last I've found someone who'll listen to me," he kept saying. It was *Private Eye* magazine, the ones that did all the stuff on Profumo – but you'll be too young to remember that, I expect.'

'No, I do,' I assured her. I sort of did. I'd been at primary school at the time, but you couldn't go anywhere without hearing the name. Or seeing the pictures. There was one, torn out of a newspaper and smudged and grubby from being passed around the playground so many times, of a woman with no clothes on who was somehow involved in it all. Even at the time I remember that while my classmates were thrilled into open-mouthed silence by her nakedness, my first reaction had been to wonder why she was sitting on her chair the wrong way round.

'Christine Keeler.' I spoke her name as I remembered it. It had earned me a clip round the ear from my dad when I'd asked about her at the dinner table.

'That's right, dear.' Mrs Friendship looked like she was lost in nostalgia too. 'Oh, it was a different world then, dear, you wouldn't believe how much everything's changed. Anyway, there's one of our regulars who reads it – *Private Eye*, I mean – and he told Norman his story was exactly the sort of thing they printed. So he wrote to them, and someone wrote back, and he even went up to London for a meeting with them.'

'When was that?'

'Sometime last year. October, perhaps? Not long before he...' She left the sentence unfinished, fishing a tissue out of her sleeve and pressing it to her pursed lips. It came away bright pink.

I busied myself fussing over Rinka to give her time to collect herself. The dog rolled over onto her back, inviting me to scratch her vast expanse of tummy with its twin columns of nipples. She knocked into one of the heavy armchairs as she did so, shunting it several inches across the floor. It felt as if the furniture of my own familiar world was being irrevocably shifted about as well. For one inconvenient boyfriend to die a violent death might be considered a misfortune, to lose two begins to look very much like a conspiracy. Add in a third death in mysterious circumstances and you're well into paranoia territory. And that was before you even factored in the mysterious spiriting away of bodies and jug-eared strangers going over the heads of the local police.

I had to ask. 'Mrs Friendship, do you think Norman was murdered to keep him quiet?'

Now there were tears brimming in her eyes. 'I don't want to. I don't want to think that that sort of thing happens in this country. Oh, Northern Ireland maybe, you read about all sorts happening over there, but here, in Devon? Only I can't think of any other explanation for it, can you?'

'No,' I said quietly.

'He was a lovely man, Norman.' Mrs Friendship plucked a tissue from the sleeve of her blouse and pressed it to her nose. 'You would have liked him. Oh, he had his problems, more than most, but on a good day he could be such fun. And marvellous with animals, too. Only he could never get over this…injustice that had been done to him by that man. I don't mean the sex, my dear, you meet all sorts in this trade and I'm all for live and let live when it comes to what goes on in people's bedrooms. But to be used when he was so young and then just chucked aside – well, it just ate him up from the inside. I always thought it would be the end of him. He told me he'd tried to do away with himself more than once. But I never thought he would go like *this*.'

'No,' I said helplessly. 'I'm so sorry.'

She trumpeted into the tissue and pulled herself together with an effort. 'That's why I got such a shock when Judy rang and said you'd arrived looking for him. And you've come all this way and had a wasted journey.'

'I wouldn't say that,' I assured her. I had at least had my worst suspicions confirmed.

'What will you do now?' Mrs Friendship asked.

I sighed. 'I don't know really.' I couldn't go back to London. But it looked like I had reached a dead end in Devon.

'Why don't you stay for a while? We can't have you just heading straight back again. You could have Norman's old room for a few days.'

'Oh, no, I really couldn't,' I started to protest, but it was half-hearted at best. I was exhausted, and the prospect of a bed – even a dead man's bed – was desperately appealing. I felt like I had been running for days. I needed some time to think things over, take in all the new information I had been exposed to, work out what the hell I was going to do with it.

'Nonsense,' blustered Mrs Friendship, standing up and sweeping up the brandy glasses. Rinka twisted up to attention at the same time, her ears pricked and eyes trained on her mistress, who nodded in her direction. 'You can help me out by walking Rinka, she needs more exercise than I can give her when we're busy. And you can help out downstairs in the evenings too: we're short a potboy. It'll be nice to have a young man around the place again.'

I gave in gracefully. 'Well, maybe for a few days, if you're sure.'

The landlady beamed. 'I'm sure. Now, let's see what we can do about some dinner for you.'

One vast serving of hotpot later, I settled gratefully down between sheets so fresh they crackled with static in the guest room that had until so recently been home to the late Norman Scott. Mrs Friendship's official visitors might have made a good job of searching the place and clearing his papers, but they had left other plenty of other traces of the dead man behind: his paisley-patterned shirts and astrakhan coat still hanging in the wardrobe; a few well-thumbed copies of *Horse and Hound* stacked on the bedside table; a pair of scuffed Chelsea boots placed neatly side-by-side at the foot of the bed. He had left more of a mark of himself than Stephen had on his own spartan quarters in Malcolm Crichton's apartment, but then he had survived longer, had more opportunity to leave his imprint on the world. A wider wake in the water, sending ripples out to crash on distant shores. More mess to be tidied up.

I was surprised to find that the deep sleep I fell into was undisturbed by ghosts.

TWENTY-ONE

Mrs Friendship woke me in plenty of time for my evening shift. 'I've put the immersion on,' she told me as she placed a steaming cup of tea down by the bed, and I took the hint and ran myself a bath, which, along with the afternoon's kip, left me feeling considerably more human than I had when I arrived that morning. Her bathroom was the most feminine space I have ever been in: floral tiles, pink suite, bright pink carpet on both lid and around the base of a toilet topped off with a Cindy doll hiding the spare loo roll in her vast crocheted skirt. The shelf above the sink was crammed with pastel bottles of cold cream and lotions, Yardley soaps in their ruched packets, canisters of talcum powder scented with lavender and lily-of-the-valley. I went downstairs smelling like a tart's boudoir, dressed in a pair of Norman Scott's trousers and the least vivid of his shirts I could find. Mrs Friendship had urged me to help myself to whatever I wanted: 'It would all have gone to the Spastics months ago if I'd only managed to get round to it.'

She showed me to the pub's wash-up and demonstrated how to use the rickety waterboiler above the great square sink, and for most of the evening, punctuated by regular circuits of the noisy pub gathering up glasses, I was left there alone with my thoughts and the sound of Radio One on a tinny transistor hanging from a hook on the wall. I got some funny looks from a few drinkers when I was doing my rounds front of house, but no one questioned my presence. I got the feeling I was only the latest in a long line of waifs and strays that Mrs Friendship – there was no sign of a Mr Friendship – had taken in.

I slipped out to the small hallway beside the lounge bar where there was a payphone at one point when there was a lull and tried to ring Mark, but there was no answer. It was a shame. I was looking forward to telling him I had been right all along.

Bizarrely, now I had got over the initial shock of finding out Scott had been killed too, I felt a strange sense of calm about the whole situation: the idea that there was an organised conspiracy to kill men like me to cover up the transgressions of politicians was somehow easier to handle than the random, pointless violence I had got used to on the Dilly. The fact there was someone out there who could put the frighteners on men like the Playland crew carried its own strange comfort: it definitely wasn't a case of my enemy's enemy is my friend, but I did like knowing my enemy had an enemy who could cast them aside as casually as they had tried to get rid of me. It helped that out here in the country, doing an honest job for the first time in a long time, I felt like I was well out of everyone's reach: maybe I could just stay here in Barnstaple, filling the village queen role in which it seemed Norman Scott had been reasonably well-accepted, steering well clear of bent politicians and corrupt coppers and bullying pimps and all the other horrors of my London life, washing pots and walking dogs and breathing in clean country air for the rest of my life.

Or maybe not, I concluded at some point well after closing time, when my hands were bright red and pruned and my back ached and I was sick of the sound of John Peel's droning voice, and still the barmaids kept on bringing tray after tray of sticky glasses through and dumping them on my draining board with a cheery 'there you go!'.

Mrs Friendship had gone up to bed by the time I was finished, but she had left me a set of keys, a lead and a note asking me to walk Rinka round the block before I turned in, 'just so she can do her business'. It turned out the dog had other ideas, and I was dragged all the way down to a wide river that cut through the centre of the town, along the footpath by its side for what felt like a mile before she led me back by a circuitous route through the silent streets, stopping to sniff at every discarded bit of litter and most of the lamp posts and, given our relative strengths, giving me no option but to stop as well. She did at least deposit a gargantuan turd on the pavement outside W H Smith's, ready for someone to step in come the morning. I had listened to several sets of distant church bells chime one by the time that the Market Inn finally loomed back into sight, much to my relief, given that I was long-since lost by this point and trusting entirely to Rinka's sense of direction.

I didn't get any choice about the dog sleeping in my bedroom that night either – she just barged in and lay down beside the bed, stretching nearly the full length of it. She snored a little and woke me up once whimpering in her sleep but I didn't mind. I suppose she thought her master had come back.

The pair of us joined Mrs Friendship in her upstairs kitchen for a late breakfast the next morning – two eggs, three rashers and a fried slice for me, a whole big tin of Pal and three handfuls of biscuits for Rinka. She said she wouldn't need me in the pub till that evening and encouraged me to get out and 'see the sights.' To be honest, I didn't really fancy her suggestions of the covered market, the park or the museum: instead I told her the site I really wanted to see, if she didn't mind giving me directions, was the place where Scott had been murdered.

'Oh, it was right up on top of Exmoor: too far for you to walk,' she told me.

I was taken aback. 'So how did he get there?'

She shrugged, folding her arms across the front of her housecoat. 'Someone must have driven him. That's what the police reckoned: they said he was found not far from a lay-by on the Porlock road. That's when they *would* still tell me anything.'

My thoughts flickered back to my own recent ordeal, and I frowned down at the greasy plates and the teapot under its knitted cosy to centre myself in the more comfortable present.

'So he must have been forced into a car? Both him and Rinka?'

'I can't see anyone forcing this one anywhere she didn't want to go, can you?' The dog, who had installed herself under the kitchen table in the hope of scraps, sensed that she was being talked about and thumped her tail noisily on the lino. 'Norman could be…quite trusting,' Mrs Friendship said quietly. 'I think if someone had spun him the right story, he might have agreed to go with them.'

I nodded, sipping my stewed tea. Norman Scott and I had both done our fair share of relying on the kindness of strangers.

'Who found him?' I asked after a while.

'Oh, it was Jethro Morgan: he grazes his sheep up there, and he drove up to check on them that afternoon. Said he could see Rinka from miles off: he thought she might be worrying his flock so he went over, and that's when he saw Norman's body.'

'Could I speak to him?'

She smiled. 'You're in luck. It's market day today, and he usually pops in for a pint or two at lunchtime.'

I passed the morning taking Rinka for another walk, or rather letting her take me for a walk, around the town centre. She followed the same route as the night before. There was a skidmark and a set of brown footprints outside Smith's that I took a perverse satisfaction from, though this time she chose to leave her equally enormous deposit outside Fine Fare instead. I dropped off my leather jacket at a saddlery Mrs Friendship thought might be able to repair it: the grizzled old boy behind the counter sucked his teeth a bit and said it was 'outside of our normal line of work', but promised he would do his best with it if I left it there until the next day.

At noon I was back in the snug of the pub, nursing a glass of Tizer and earwigging on the conversations around me, which from what I could make out through the Wurzelish burr, centred mostly on the scandalous price per head Red Rubies were fetching, whatever they might be. It was gone one o'clock before Mrs Friendship waved me over to the bar and introduced me to a stout, elderly man in tweed whose face was ruddy from exposure to either weather or liquor or a combination of both. He had his own pewter tankard behind the bar, like plenty of the other regulars, and when I offered to buy him a drink and he nodded a 'much obliged' Mrs Friendship filled it with Courage Best without even having to check.

I led Morgan back to the table I had chosen, which was well away from the noisy scrum around the bar. 'Have you had a good morning?' I asked him, by way of being friendly, but all I got back was a non-committal grunt.

'Mr Morgan, I wanted to ask you about the body you found

on the moor,' I continued once he had settled himself on a stool and sucked the foam off the top of his tankard.

'Ah,' he said with a nod. I waited, but no more was forthcoming.

'I…I understand you were up there checking on your sheep?'

Another nod, and finally I coaxed some words out of him, although they weren't particularly relevant ones. 'Got a hundred closewool grazing up there, ent'I? Not now mind. Back down in the pens for lambing now, see?'

Slightly disconcerted by the way he answered my questions with questions of his own, I pressed on. 'And you saw his dog first, is that right?'

He shook his head as he sucked up more beer. 'Not me. End of the day it were, and coming on dimpsey, so much you could miss even a gurt big beast like that in the distance. But my dog seen 'ee all right, and she sets off barking. So I goes over to see what she's about, dunn'I?'

'And that's when you saw the body?'

'Thought she had a sheep down, first of all. Had my own gun to my shoulder, I did, ready to finish her off. Then I gets closer and I sees it 'ent no sheep, but a man.'

'Could you tell he was dead straightaway?'

He grimaced. 'Hole right through his head, and blood run out all over the grass. I could tell.' He took a comforting gulp. His pint was mostly gone by now. It had at least made him more talkative.

'How close to the road was he?'

A shrug. 'Hundred yard off or so?'

'So if you hadn't come along, how long do think it would have been before his body was found?'

'Hard to say. He were right down in the bracken so you wun't see him from the road. Plenty of picknickers up on Porlock Hill in zummer' – he actually did pronounce it with a z – 'but not come October. Reckon a hiker might maybe have come across 'ee sooner or later. Or mebbe not. Could be he'd still be up there now if it weren't for me happening by, cuddn'it?'

I couldn't help picturing Norman Scott's body mouldering away on the hillside all through the harsh winter. Would he have become a skeleton by now, or by the spring when the tourists started to arrive? I had no idea how long it took. But the likelihood was that what whatever state it was in, his body would have been found eventually: his killer had made no effort to bury it or even hide it. Even Phil and his mate had talked about dumping me in a ditch, but Norman's killer couldn't be bothered to do even that. Stephen had been left out in the open too. I'd read somewhere that bodies left in water float at first, then sink, then bob up back to the surface again as they start to decay. The Hampstead ponds were so public his corpse was never likely to make it beyond the first stage. Whoever killed them both wasn't fussed whether they were found or not. They were too arrogant to care.

Morgan was staring philosophically down into his empty pint pot. 'D'you want another one in there?' I offered.

Mrs Friendship was in the middle of serving someone else, but she passed his order over mid-round to Sally, one of the barmaids, and came over to speak to me instead. 'How you getting on?' she asked with a wink.

'Better than I thought I was going to at first,' I admitted.

'He gets more talkative the more he puts away,' she told me. 'That one's on the house.'

I accepted Morgan's thanks for the pint when I put it in front of him anyway, and waited for him to swig deep before I continued our conversation. 'So what did you do after you found the body?'

He wiped froth from his lips with the back of his hand. 'Got myself down into Porlock and called for the police, din't I? I'ent on the phone at my farm, see. That were after I got a bit of rope on his dog and got 'er into the back of my van with my own beast.' He smirked. 'Had a hell of a job shiftin'er, din't I? She din't want to come at first.'

I smiled, remembering my own forced march around Barnstaple the night before. 'You weren't worried the police might think you had something to do with it?' He looked at me quizzically. 'You said you had your gun with you?' I prompted.

'Oh.' He shook his head vehemently. 'No, not then I weren't. They could see it weren't no shotgun that did for him as clear as I did.'

'Really?' I made no effort to hide my surprise, but he didn't take the hint. 'How exactly?' I was forced to ask.

'I knows guns,' he muttered darkly, staring down into his beer. 'I were in Malta, and then Normandy. I knows a revolver shot when I sees one.'

'Right.' I looked at him appraisingly. Close up, he probably wasn't as old as I'd assumed on first appearance – maybe in his mid-50s. He'd have been about my age during the war.

'And it weren't no accident neither, I'll tell you that.' Mrs Friendship had been right about the beer loosening Morgan's tongue. With only a few mouthfuls left in his mug, he was practically gabbling. 'Your man from London trying to say he'd just been hit by some stray shot. The state he was in, whoever put a bullet in him must have had the muzzle right up against his head. It weren't no accident, it were an execution.'

The simultaneous translation I'd been running snagged on 'your man from London,' then made sense of it. 'D'you mean the man who came to see Mrs Friendship? The one with the big ears?'

'Came to see me too, dinnee?'

'You didn't get his name, did you?'

Morgan shook his head. 'Din't give me no name. I knows the type though.'

'Oh?'

He curled his lip. 'Officer class. Struttin' around like 'ee owned the place. Ee says to I, "Tragic business, tragic business, but from the sounds of him this fellow won't be much missed around these parts." Morgan's impression of his visitor involved him straightening his neck and raising his voice by half an octave. '"Hardly worth any local losing his licence over, let alone his liberty". All smiling and friendly, but he were letting me know just what I could expect if I went on kicking up a fuss.'

'And did you?'

He shook his head firmly. 'Told him in that case I must have been mistaken. And then it were 'Good man, good man,' and he were asking me all about which battalion of the Devonshire I were with, and where I saw service, and leaving me with no doubt he already knew all the answers.'

The door to the pub banged open as a new crowd from the market arrived, letting a cold breeze in with them which made me shiver.

'Mrs Friendship thinks...' I began, glancing over at the welcoming figure behind the bar, and then amending my words. '*I* think Norman Scott may have been murdered to protect Jeremy Thorpe's political career.' As I said it, I realised it no longer sounded at all outlandish. 'Do you think that's possible?'

Morgan supped up the last of his pint and wiped his mouth before answering. At first I thought he was ignoring my question and carrying on with his military train of thought. 'When I were in Normandy, me and a bunch of my mates had to storm a kraut pillbox. There were twenty of us when we started running up the beach, and the sand were that cledgy we were slipping and sliding all the way like you can imagine, and by the time we got to the dunes there was just me and a couple of the other lads left. I ain't never been so a-veered in my life. The krauts inside were blazing away, and we was running straight into their line of fire. God knows how it was I didn't get hit, but somehow I got close enough to lob a grenade in there, and that's when they stopped firin'."

I nodded encouragingly. I wasn't sure where this was going, but it was at least a good deal more exciting than the army stories my dad used to tell. His national service had come too late for the war, and fallen slap-bang between Korea and Suez, meaning he missed both of them. I don't think he'd ever forgiven the world.

'So in we went, me and these two other lads, only the doorway were narrow and we had to squeeze in one by one and somehow it were me that ended up in front. I won't forget it till the day I die, it looked like a butcher's slab in there, and I knew that were my doing. All the krauts was dead except for one of them, who'd been blown back from his machine gun against the far wall, and as I came in he was scrabbling for his own revolver only his arm were all buggered up and he couldn't get a hold of it in time. And I already had my Enfield out, pointing at him, and he started talking to me in kraut, saying *nein, nein*, and a whole load of other stuff I couldn't understand. And the way the light was coming in through the slit in the pillbox it fell right on his face, and I could see he was a lad no older than me, and just as a-veered as I were. If it weren't for the language coming out of his mouth, he could have been one of ours. Only I knew as it had been him who had just mowed down my mates, lads I had fought alongside, and slept alongside, and eaten and drunk alongside, and he had been sat behind his gun not thirty seconds before blasting them down without a second thought. And it hit me, then, for the very first time in the whole war, that this lad, who must have lined up and Heil Hitlered along with all the rest of them and killed maybe hundreds of Englishmen like me, he was doing it because he thought it was the right thing to do. Because he thought that was what was needed to defend the kraut way of life just like we were fighting to defend the British way of life, and that every single man that he killed was dying for a good reason.'

'But…he was wrong,' I pointed out.

'Didn't matter to them once they were dead, did it,' said Morgan solemnly. 'Didn't matter to *his* mates that I'd killed, neither.'

I couldn't quite bring myself to follow his logic. 'But Norman Scott wasn't a soldier,' I objected. 'We're not at war!'

He shook his head slowly. 'Mebbe there's people out there who still think they're fighting to defend our way of life. There's plenty of people round these parts as think Jeremy Thorpe's doing a fine job. Plenty of people in the country, too. Future Prime Minister, that's what some say.' The old soldier got to his feet and slid the stool he had been sitting on neatly back under the table. 'Thanks for the drinks, boy. Time I were on my way.'

'Sure. Thanks for talking to me.' He gave me a curt nod and headed towards the door.

'Mr Morgan?'

He turned, part way across the busy room.

'What did you do? To the German soldier?'

He gazed at me, impassively, then slowly shook his head and walked out of the pub.

TWENTY-TWO

I TRIED PHONING Mark again before the start of my evening shift. I could really have done with talking all of this through with him, but there was no answer at his flat. Then I remembered tonight was CHE night, got the number of the community centre from directory enquiries and rang there instead.

'Hullo?' I recognised Neil's voice. He sounded wary. We've had a few abusive phone calls at the community centre before: calling us poofs and queers mostly, on one occasion threatening violence convincingly enough for us to adjourn the meeting to the Black Cap instead, where we felt there might at least be safety in numbers.

'Neil, it's Tom,' I told him.

'Tom?'

'Tommy.' My personal re-branding obviously still needed some work.

'Oh, hi Tommy. Are you not joining us tonight?'

'I can't, I'm out of town, sorry.'

'Oh, I'll put your apologies down in the minutes then.' He actually sounded excited about doing so.

'All right. So long as you promise not to have too much fun without me.' The sarcasm sailed right over his head, as I knew it would. 'Listen, is Mark there yet?'

'I've not seen him.' His voice went distant as he turned to address the room: 'Has anyone heard from Mark this evening?' There was a faint chorus of negatives before Neil came back sounding coquettish. 'We wondered if he might be with you, actually.'

So that bit of gossip had spread, as expected. I ignored him. 'Could you give him a message when he turns up?'

'Of course.'

'Just say I'm in Devon – I'll explain why when he calls me. Here's the number.' I read the handwritten numerals off the poster beneath the payphone's plastic hood.

'All right. Will we see you next week?'

'Not sure.' Right now I didn't feel I could plan any further ahead than the next few hours. I was certainly in no hurry to show myself anywhere near London.

There were already several trays of glasses lined up for me when I went through to the wash-up. I kept the door propped open and the radio turned down all evening so I would hear the phone if it rang, but it didn't.

I was kept even busier than the night before. There was a darts tournament in the Market Inn and half the town seemed to have turned out for it, women as well as men: I found myself rinsing out as many sherry schooners and long-stemmed barley wine glasses as I did pint pots. I still had several trays-worth to get through at half-eleven when Sally came through and

175

told me it had been such a busy night that Mrs Friendship was treating all the staff to a drink and I was to leave the rest till the morning and come and join them in the saloon bar. She didn't need to tell me twice.

Mrs Friendship had stoked up the fire, and she and the other barmaid Linda had already made a good dent in a new bottle of brandy (Sally was on the cider because she was driving). The landlady's cheeks were as rosy as the pattern on her blouse, which she had unbuttoned sufficiently to reveal an expanse of crepey cleavage: she had already taken her bra off and hung it over the back of the leather armchair, for which she begged my pardon with a wink and an 'it's been a long day, love.' I fetched a glass and joined them on the brandy, although I was careful to pour my own: Mrs Friendship's personal measures were significantly more generous than those she dispensed from behind the bar, and I've never had much of a head for spirits.

Linda and Sally wanted to know all about London and, specifically, what famous people I had seen there. I think I was a bit of a disappointment, to be honest: they were obviously hoping for George Best and the Bay City Rollers, and the best I could offer was George Melly and the Rollers' manager Tam Paton. But I did manage to impress them with my tale of when Princess Anne drove past me in St James's Park. 'And she was driving herself?' asked an awe-struck Linda. 'Even after what happened? So brave.'

After that we got onto their own claims to fame – Linda had got Dave Hill from Slade's autograph when he had been visiting his grandparents in Holbeton; Sally had been in the audience for *Seaside Special* when it came to Torbay the previous summer, 'and you could actually see me in the crowd.' Mrs Friendship claimed to have shared both a railway waiting room and a charming conversation with Greer Garson, but none of us had ever heard of her. Her explanation led us off into a long conversation about our favourite films (Linda and Sally both plumped predictably for *Love Story*, Mrs Friendship said *Gone With The Wind* and I did my best to convince all three of them to see *Jaws* when it finally made it to the cinema in Barnstaple) which took us all the way through to the point when the clock above the bar chimed one and the barmaids announced they both really should be heading home.

Mrs Friendship was holding up the nearly-empty brandy bottle invitingly when I returned from locking the pub's side door behind them. 'Have one last nightcap with me before you go to bed, dear,' she demanded.

'I'm not sure,' I demurred. I was tired, and quite pissed enough already. 'I still need to take Rinka out.'

'Oh, she's fine,' Mrs Friendship scolded, glugging liquid into my glass so I didn't have a choice in the matter. 'Just remember to let her out into the back yard so she can do her business before we go up.' The dog, who had been let down into the pub after closing time and settled mountainously in front of the fire, did indeed look perfectly content. So I followed her example and settled back into my own position, chinking my snifter against the landlady's conspicuously fuller one and staring into the glowing embers over the sleeping dog's back.

'They're good girls, those two,' Mrs Friendship remarked after a while, her voice soppy with drink.

'They seem very nice.'

She chuckled. 'Clueless of course. I don't think Linda's ever made it any further than Paignton; and I doubt she ever will if she marries that young man of hers. She'll be handing in her notice by the end of the year and pushing out babies by the end of the next, you mark my words.'

I smiled, but didn't say anything. The only role I seemed to be required to play now was appreciative audience.

'Didn't have a clue what to make of Norman, neither of them.' She shook her head, smiling.

'Oh?'

'Sally didn't trust him an inch. "Are you sure you know what you're doing?" she kept asking me. She even wanted me to put a lock on the bottle store. Wouldn't leave the till open when he was nearby, even while she was counting out change. I said to her, "He's no more likely to be dipping his fingers in that till than you are, young lady, and don't think I haven't spotted you charging for singles when you've measured out doubles for the lads from the technical college." That shut her up.'

The firelight was reflected off the glass of the framed prints which lined the walls of the bar, playing over the ploughmen and the steam locomotives and the dogs playing billiards. Mrs Friendship swirled her brandy and smiled at me over the top of it. 'It's good to have a young man around the place, though.'

I wasn't sure if she was referring to Scott or me by this point, and I'm not entirely certain she was, either. Whichever it was, I was definitely making this my last drink of the evening. The bottle was all but empty, and there was a faraway gleam coming into my landlady's eyes. My predecessor might have been AC-DC, but I definitely only flowed in the one direction, and I didn't want to take the risk of either of us being embarrassed.

'Have you got a special friend?' she drawled, as if she was reading my mind.

'I...yes, sort of,' I admitted, and then thought it might be best to clarify. 'He's called Mark.'

She nodded approvingly, which was a relief. 'Known him long?'

'Known him a long time. Only been together...that way, for a little while.' I glanced towards the hallway where the payphone sat silent. 'I've been trying to phone him for the last couple of nights, only I don't seem to be able to get hold of him.'

She waved her glass expansively, spilling some of its contents. 'Oh, use the phone upstairs dear, don't waste your money on that one.'

'Oh, no, I couldn't,' I protested, but she overruled me with a smile.

'I insist, dear. Don't worry, I won't eavesdrop on your love talk, I'll make myself scarce.'

'Oh, it's not really like that.' Realising I was blushing, I turned my gaze back to the fire. I still wasn't quite sure what it *was* really like with Mark. I just knew I would really like to talk over all this stuff with him. I'd try and call him again tomorrow morning. Well, later this morning.

'I think Norman had that too, poor dear. For a while,' said Mrs Friendship after a while. She was definitely slurring her words now.

'Did he? Who with?' I said, mostly for the sake of saying something. Her reply surprised me.

'With Thorpe.'

'Really?' I couldn't keep the shock out of my voice, and Rinka, who had given every impression of being deep in slumber, pricked up her ears and raised her head from the hearthrug.

'Oh yes,' said Mrs Friendship, a mischievous smile spreading across her face. 'They were very affectionate with one another at one point. Very affectionate indeed.'

'How do you know?'

She laughed to herself and drained her glass before replying. 'Oh, I know.'

I couldn't work out quite what she meant by this, but I figured, correctly, that if I left her staring into the flames for long enough, she would tell me.

'They didn't get everything, you see.' There was something like a giggle in her voice.

'What d'you mean?'

She leaned forward and groped for the brandy bottle, nearly sending it tumbling on to the tiled hearth. 'Here, let me,' I urged her, and poured the last dregs into her glass before repeating my question.

'They searched through all through the stuff in his room, and they took away everything he'd written,' she slurred. 'But what they didn't know was that he'd given me some things for safekeeping. And that's what I did with them. Put them in the safe.' She tapped the vast ring of keys which she always kept near, and which were currently sitting on the sticky tabletop beside her.

'And what was it?' I asked, feeling my adrenaline levels perk up to compete with the booze that was washing around my system, and thanking god I'd been taking it a bit easier than she had.

'I'll show you dear.' She swept the keys up and pushed herself up from the armchair, staggering slightly as she tried to pick her way past the spreadeagled enormity of the dog and reaching a steadying hand out to the mantelpiece. 'Whoops!'

'Would you like me to…?' I said, getting up myself.

'Oh yes, perhaps.' She thumped heavily back into her seat and counted through the keys on the ring, holding out one to me. 'It's under the stairs, dear. Look for the biscuit tin.'

I made my way through the darkened bar and out into the cramped hallway behind it. What I had taken, if I had noticed it at all, to be just a cupboard under the stairs – a glory hole, as my parents had hilariously but obliviously called theirs – turned out to contain a built-in cast iron safe: the key slipped easily into the lock and when I pulled on the brass handle next to it the heavy door swung open. The week's takings were inside – Mrs Friendship was a very trusting soul indeed – and on the shelf above, some brown envelopes stuffed with what looked like contracts and legal papers. On top of them was a battered Family Circle tin. I extracted it, closed and locked the safe again, and carried it back through to the pub where an anxious Rinka was waiting for me just on the other side of the bar.

'It's all right, good girl, she gave me permission,' I assured her. Back by the fire, Mrs Friendship had slumped in her seat with her eyes closed. I made as much noise as I could levering the lid off the tin, but she didn't stir.

Inside was a yellowing envelope addressed to Scott at an address in Tiverton, which I knew from reading road signs was somewhere near here. It had a House of Commons postmark on it. Beneath it was a black and white photograph, its edges tatty: glue marks on the back suggested it had been pulled out of an album. I recognised Thorpe straightaway: his face looked younger, but he was dressed in his trademark old-fashioned way: a waistcoat that looked like something from *The Forsyte Saga* and starchy shirtsleeves. Next to him was a handsome young man, about my age, who I assumed must be Scott. It was pretty obvious what Thorpe had seen in him. He was holding a dog, not Rinka but one of those little yappy things that go for your ankles if they get the chance. Thorpe's arm was around Scott, his hand resting suggestively on the younger man's hip. They were both grinning broadly: they looked very happy together, and also very happily together.

I glanced across at Mrs Friendship, but she was dead to the world, a little drool beginning to form at the corner of her smudged lips. Figuring she would not have invited me to fetch this stuff unless she wanted me to look at it, I slid the letter out of its envelope. The same portcullis logo was on the top of the single sheet of notepaper: the letterhead read *From the Office of Jeremy Thorpe MP.*

My Dear Norman, I read. The handwriting was all florid curls and showoffy stuff: I had to lean in close to the firelight to be able to read it.

Since my letters normally go to the House, yours arrived all by itself at my breakfast table at the Reform, and gave me tremendous pleasure.

I cannot tell you just how happy I am to feel that you are really settling down, and feeling that life has something to offer. This is really wonderful and you can always feel that whatever happens I am right behind you.

I turned the sheet over to read the sign-off.

Bunnies can (and will) go to France.

Yours affectionately

Jeremy.

I miss you.

'Bunnies?' I actually said it out loud. Mrs Friendship did not stir, but Rinka pricked up her ears and turned her head inquisitively to one side. 'I know, tell me about it!' I muttered to her.

I read it through again: whatever the bit about bunnies might mean, the rest alone meant there was no mistaking this for anything other than a love letter. I turned it over again to check the date at the top of the letter – February, 1961. Fifteen years ago. And, more to the point, six years before it was legal to be gay. By the look of what Scott was wearing in the photo – it was impossible to tell from Thorpe's outfit – it had been taken around the same time. Between them, they tied Norman Scott to Jeremy Thorpe for certain. This was proof. And that, presumably, meant it would be worth killing for.

I couldn't help myself. Putting the letter back in the envelope, and the lid firmly back on the tin, I went to check that both the front and side doors of the pub were firmly locked. Squinting out through the windows, the street outside seemed to be deserted, though the bottle-end glass in the pub's windows made it hard to be sure. Rinka was certainly not going any further than the high-walled back yard tonight.

I returned to the fireside, where Mrs Friendship was now audibly snoring, and picked up the tin. A clichéd thought – *The evidence is in my hands!* – flickered through my brain. The question now was, what should I do with it?

It was a question for morning and for clearer heads. I scooped up the keyring and headed back to the safe.

TWENTY-THREE

I MANAGED TO GET Mrs Friendship up to bed, or at least as far as the door of her bedroom, from where she assured me to my relief that she would be fine. Come the morning, Rinka and I were up and breakfasted well before she surfaced. It was a relief when she did show her face, because I was starting to worry about opening time.

'I'll be fine, dear, just make me a nice strong coffee while I fetch a couple of aspirin,' she assured me, but when there was a knock at the front door not long afterwards, Mrs Friendship did ask if I would mind going down and letting Sally in and giving her a hand setting up instead of her. There were still the unwashed glasses left from last night waiting for me too, and what with that and the Saturday lunchtime rush it was gone three pm before, having effected a slightly miraculous recovery courtesy of a full face of make-up and two bottles of Guinness,

184

Mrs Friendship locked the door behind the last of her customers and we had a chance to chat.

'About the letter and the photo…' I began as she sawed slices of white bread and ham in the pub's pantry to make us both our belated lunch.

She groaned, closing her eyes. 'I shouldn't have told you about that stuff.'

'Why not?' I asked, with slightly too much enthusiasm. 'Don't you see, it's exactly the proof we needed. It shows that Thorpe and Norman were an item. Put that with what Jethro said about his body, and you've got firm evidence he was murdered, and why!'

'That's Mr Morgan to you,' she scolded me half-heartedly. 'D'you want piccalilli?'

'Please.' I watched her slather the luminous yellow slop over both sandwiches. 'Do you not see what it means, though, Mrs Friendship? We could actually get justice for Norman!'

She slapped two more inch-thick hunks of bread down on top of the fillings, pressed them down viciously and sawed them into diagonals. 'And how exactly would we do that? I've already told you I tried going to the police. They weren't interested. Said it was out of their hands.'

I took the plate she shoved in my direction and followed her through to the bar. 'What about the magazine you were talking about? *Private Eye*? You said Norman had already been talking to them.'

She let out a sigh as she put her own plate down on the counter and stationed herself behind the beer pumps. 'I'm not sure, dear.'

'Why not?' Over the course of the last few hours of deep thought in the wash-up I'd built up the idea of the magazine as our potential saviour. I assumed with a name like that it dealt with murder mysteries as a matter of course.

'I don't think his meeting with their journalist went terribly well, to be honest. Norman came back from London in a dreadful mood. He didn't tell me exactly what had happened, but I got the impression they'd had some sort of falling-out.' She pulled a half pint of mild and held out the glass in my direction.

'Thanks.' I took it and settled on a bar stool to tuck into my lunch. 'Did he show them the letter and the photograph?'

She shook her head as she flipped the lid from another bottle of Guinness for herself. 'He left those in the safe here. He was very keen that they should help him get the book he was writing published, you see, so that was what he took to show them.'

'Right.' Mrs Friendship had told me there were 'pages and pages' of it. There was no typewriter in Scott's room, so they were presumably all handwritten. I wasn't sure that would have been the best way of selling his story to a sceptical journalist: certainly it lacked the immediacy of the contents of the biscuit tin which even I had been able to decipher straight away.

'What about if I were to take the letter and the photograph to London and show them to the journalist he was talking to, and tell him what happened to Norman?' I asked. 'I really think that might get us somewhere.'

'Oh, I don't think I could let you take them away, dear.' She looked doubtful. 'Norman gave them to me for safekeeping.'

'But he wanted his story to come out, didn't he? That was exactly what he was trying to do.'

'Well…yes.' She nibbled doubtfully at the corner of her sandwich. Half her drink was already gone.

'So really, this would be us carrying out his last wishes.' This was laying it on a bit thick, but I really felt the need to persuade her. Something that had only been intriguing when Malcolm Crichton walked into the office ten days ago had now become a full-on obsession.

'I suppose...' She didn't look at all convinced. I was starting to wonder if I should have gone with my first instinct and just taken off with the biscuit tin and its contents, and maybe the rest of the safe's contents too, while she was fast asleep. But I knew I couldn't have done. After all the hospitality she had shown me, Mrs Friendship deserved better than that.

'This is a really great sandwich, thanks,' I overcompensated.

She gave a wan smile. 'Don't mention it, dear.'

We chewed in silence for a couple of minutes, both lost in thought, before I spoke again. 'The 'bunnies' thing. What was that all about?'

'Oh!' She lifted a serviette to her mouth. 'Norman said it was what Thorpe used to call him. Because he said he looked like a little frightened little rabbit the first time he... the first time they had sex.'

'And France?'

'Norman said he was hoping to go there and study dressage at the time. He had a real gift with horses, you know.'

'But he never went?'

'No. Thorpe got him a job at a riding stables near here instead. He wanted to keep him...on hand.'

'So their thing went on for a while, did it?' I still wasn't quite sure how to account for the near decade-and-a-half between the date of the letter and Scott's murder.

'Oh yes.' She washed her mouthful down with the last of the barley wine and pushed the half-eaten sandwich away. 'Thorpe put him up at a flat in London for a while too, somewhere near parliament, so he could have his way with him whenever he wanted. At least that's what Norman told me. Only in the end Thorpe got tired of him, and cut him off, and then when he started making a fuss...well, here we are.' Up came the serviette again, and I realised there were tears brimming in her eyes.

Call me callous, but I decided to press home my advantage. I reckoned the emotion was at least half hangover anyway. 'Mrs Friendship, please let me take the letter and the photograph to London. We owe it to Norman to try to expose what happened. And not just to Norman, either. If people are being murdered because they're a threat to politicians' careers, then everyone needs to know about it. This is 1976, not…the olden days.' I petered out a bit at the end there, I'll admit. The period I had in mind was the Tudor court, and off the top of my head I couldn't date that any more accurately than a few years ago when *The Six Wives of Henry VIII* was on telly. I'd watched it with my mum when I was still at home. We used to like the costumes.

Thankfully my ploy seemed to be working. 'I suppose so, dear. As long as you promise to take care.'

I nodded reassuringly. 'I'll keep them with me at all times: I won't let them out of my sight, I promise.'

She shook her head, the tears now flowing freely and making tracks down her rouged cheeks. 'I don't mean of the letter and the photo, dear; I mean of yourself. I couldn't bear to think of anything happening to you.'

'Oh!' I was taken aback. 'I'll be fine, don't worry. I know how to look after myself.' I mean, it was literally *days* since anyone had tried to kill me.

'It's just it's been so nice having you here,' she flustered as she pressed the serviette to her eyes. 'You will at least come back and visit us, won't you? Rinka will miss you terribly.'

'Of course I will,' I assured her. I was absurdly touched.

'And you won't go until the morning, will you?'

'Not if you don't want me to, no.' I couldn't see it making much difference. Presumably the magazine's offices wouldn't be open until Monday anyway.

'Good, good.' She sniffed, rolled the serviette up into a ball and pushed it into her sleeve, brushing crumbs briskly from the front of her blouse as she rose from the barstool. 'Saturday night's always busy, and I don't know where I'd find cover at this short notice. Are you finished?'

I nodded, looking at her with something close to admiration as she whipped my plate away. Up until ten seconds ago I could have sworn it was me who was doing the emotional manipulation. 'I'll leave these in the wash-up for you to do later then,' she said as she disappeared through the door at the back of the bar.

There were still two and a half hours to go until evening opening, so I took Rinka out for a walk around town to pick up my jacket and search out a copy of *Private Eye* to swot up on ahead of visiting the office. WH Smith seemed to have every magazine under the sun except the one I was looking for, and I had to queue up behind all the kids spending their pocket money on *Whizzer and Chips* and the *Dandy,* only to have the man behind the counter confirm that 'we don't stock that title' while looking at me as if I had asked whereabouts they kept the hardcore pornography. I went out and untied Rinka from the lamp post where I had left her anxiously whimpering, asked directions from one of the crowd of admirers she had acquired in my absence, and eventually found another newsagents where the man behind the counter, the first brown face I had seen since arriving in Barnstaple, was pleased to provide me with a copy. It cost 15p, which seemed a bit steep given that it seemed to be printed on something like Izal toilet paper. There was a picture of the Queen on the front cover, with a speech bubble coming out of her mouth saying something about Princess Margaret and Roddy Llewellyn. I think it was meant to be a joke, but I didn't get it.

I didn't get much of the contents when I leafed through it back in my room at the Market Inn either. It wasn't what I was expecting. It was inky and full of misprints, some of which were clearly deliberate just to be rude, like the Shit of Persia, and some of which, like the Prime Minister being spelt 'Wislon', just looked like mistakes. While some parts were obviously meant to be funny, like the cartoons, there were articles about the leaders of the National Front and a company called Slater Walker which didn't have any jokes in at all. There was a column called Grovel which mentioned Nigel Dempster, who I remembered Mark getting cross about the other evening. *Private Eye* called him 'the Greatest Living Englishman', which didn't sound promising.

Thinking of Mark prompted me to try to phone him again (on the payphone: I felt awkward about taking up Mrs Friendship on her offer), but there was no answer. I knew he worked most Saturdays though, and if all went to plan I should be seeing him tomorrow anyway, when I headed back to London.

According to the timetable that Mrs Friendship kept by the till, the trains on a Sunday were few and far between, and if I wanted to make my connection in Exeter I needed to get one that left Barnstaple just after ten the next morning. At least there was no question of another late night that night – by the time I had finished another busy shift in the wash-up Mrs Friendship was long since tucked up in bed. She was up before me the following morning too, and by the time I stomped into the kitchen she had the most impressive cooked breakfast I had seen yet waiting for me. 'Well, you've a long trek ahead of you,' she said, briskly brushing away my thanks. She had managed to take her make-up off last night, and she hadn't put it back on yet this morning. Without it she looked a good decade older, and sadder.

'I'll come with you to the station: Rinka needs the walk,' was about the sum total of our conversation over breakfast. By 9.30 I was ready in the hallway with my freshly-repaired leather jacket on. The saddler had made a good job of it: although the rip was still pretty obvious in the lining, you could barely make it out from the front. Now all I had to do was not get stabbed again.

Mrs Friendship soon joined me, but it was only once she had finished wrapping a headscarf over her hair, pulled on a waxed jacket from the hallstand and got Rinka's collar and lead on that she unlocked the safe and withdrew the tin to ceremonially hand over its contents. She still didn't look totally convinced she was doing the right thing. 'I promise I'll get them to where they need to go,' I assured her, sliding them into the newly-repaired pocket by my breast (I'd finally disposed of the *Times Guide*, figuring its work was done). She gave a solemn nod, but didn't seem inclined to discuss the matter any further. She unlocked the pub's side door and the three of us made our way out into the cold Devon morning.

It wasn't far to the station, but we had to cross the river to get there, passing over wide mud-flats with a quick-flowing stream of estuary water at their centre. The wind caught us full-on as we crossed the bridge, numbing our faces and driving Rinka's ears back against her head. The train was already waiting at the platform when we arrived. Mrs Friendship explained that this was the end of the line: only quarry trains went beyond Barnstaple these days, 'thanks to bloody Beeching'. I wouldn't let her waste money on a platform ticket: we said goodbye on the pavement outside the station.

'Take care,' she instructed me, pressing a lipstick mark onto both my cheeks. 'Do what you can for Norman, won't you?' Her eyes were watering again, and not just from the biting wind.

'I will, I promise. I'll be in touch.' I leaned down to plant a kiss on Rinka's head, and pulled back before she could slobberingly return the favour. On the platform the engine had begun to thrum in a purposeful way and I could see the guard starting to arrange his flags, so I left my goodbyes at that and hurried through to board.

The train was one of the old-fashioned ones with separate compartments. I walked the length of a few carriages up the narrow corridor to see if I could get one all to myself, but it was surprisingly busy for a Sunday, so I opted for the first one I came to that had a youngish man on his own in it. You never know, you might get lucky.

We left the town behind almost immediately and by the time I had settled in my seat there was nothing outside the windows but muddy fields and bare trees. The river, presumably the same one we had crossed on the way to the station, wound alongside the train, sometimes curving under bridges to emerge on the opposite side of the tracks. My travelling companion showed no inclination to emerge from behind his *News of the World*, let alone while away the journey in an erotic adventure, and I was left surveying what little I could see of him and wishing I'd brought something of my own to read. I'd given up on *Private Eye* and left it behind on top of Norman Scott's pile of *Horse and Hounds*.

Eventually I moved my eyes up from his crotch (clad in blue denim and not particularly promising) to the newspaper itself. The headline read *Ms.ing You Already!* I had to read it twice, and I still couldn't make any sense of it. The accompanying photo, of a hefty-looking woman whose angry expression only served to accentuate her heavy brows, didn't give me much of a clue either.

I leaned forward and put my elbows on my knees, pretending to be looking out of the window in case the newspaper's owner noticed, but really positioning myself so as to be able to make out the text below. There were two smaller headlines printed in white-on-black boxes. *Colquhoun quits with defiant declaration: Yes, I'm Lesbian* read the first. *Loss of Majority Plunges Government Into Crisis* read the second.

Maureen Colquhoun was the Labour MP Mark had mentioned in the pub last week. He'd said the tabloids were trying to drive her out. So, they'd succeeded then. I tried to make out the miniature words of the story below, and got as far as *Women's Lib fanatic Maureen Colquhoun sensationally QUIT the Commons last night complaining of a 'witch-hunt'* before the paper's owner emerged from behind the crinkled page and pointedly said, 'you all right there?'

'Sorry'. I settled back in my seat, blushing.

He glanced at the front page and gave me a conspiratorial leer. 'Not much of a surprise, is it: look at the state of her! It's never the ones you'd want to see doing it to each other that turn out to be lezzos, is it?'

I had definitely picked a bad compartment. I turned pointedly to stare out at the countryside as it went by, suddenly quite keen to get back to London after all.

TWENTY-FOUR

THE CAPITAL DIDN'T SEEM in such a hurry to have me back. The train I was supposed to catch from Exeter was cancelled because the guards were out on strike, the one I did manage to get two hours later was delayed even further by a points failure, and when I finally got to Paddington a bomb scare had put the whole Circle line out of action. It was late afternoon before I stumbled through the front door of Mark's flat, having already worked out from his failure to answer the doorbell – I still wasn't entirely comfortable about just using the key he had given me – that he wasn't in.

The place was freezing. I did a quick circuit to switch on the electric fires, which brought me into the bedroom where it was immediately obvious that Mark wasn't the only thing that was missing. The clothes rail was half-empty too: there were a few shirts and a couple of pairs of trousers left hanging there, but the rest was just a tangle of wire coathangers. And my duffel bag was no longer where I had left it at the foot of the bed either. Had he thrown it out, in a fit of pique at my days-long disappearance? But why would he get rid of most of his own clothes, too? I edged round the bed to check it hadn't just been kicked out of sight, but there was no sign of it at all. What was lying on the carpet, however, was a familiar orange-and-white cover: yes, it was my copy of *Against The Law*. And next to it were a few other things: a cheesecloth shirt, some balled-up socks and underpants, a towel, a deodorant stick, all of which I recognised as mine: here were the keys to Harvey's office too, in fact, the full contents of the bag as I had left it. Just not the bag itself. I supposed I didn't mind Mark borrowing it, but he might have taken a bit more care emptying it out. *Against The Law* was getting fragile enough already without being left splayed open on the floor like that. I picked it up and slipped it into my jacket pocket, tucking the precious letter and photo inside: it felt good to have it back in its rightful place. I scooped the keys up too and put them in the opposite pocket. You never knew when they would come in useful again.

I straightened up and headed out into the hallway. Now I saw that there was a note on the little bamboo table next to the phone. It was addressed to me. *Thomas*. Bit formal.

Thomas,

I've had to go away for a few days. Give me a call on this number and I'll explain.

Mark

The number began with 01, which at least meant he was still in London. I dialled it, and stood tapping my foot on the lino while I wondered what was going on.

Someone picked up after just a couple of rings, or at least, the phone stopped ringing at the other end. But there was no reply to my repeated 'hello?', just a few mechanical clicking noises. Shaking my head – this really wasn't my day – I hung up and dialled again, but the same thing happened. I gave up and went through to the kitchen to put the kettle on. I was parched.

My thoughts ran ahead of me as I stood at the kitchen counter waiting for the water to boil. If Mark was still in London, that ruled out a family crisis at least. Given what he had said about relations with his father I couldn't exactly picture him dropping everything to rush back to Swansea anyway. But if he was staying somewhere in London, why had he taken so much stuff with him? Practically his whole wardrobe was gone, except for...

Except for the cowboys t-shirt, which I had been staring dumbly at for the past few seconds as I drummed a coffee spoon on the countertop. It was still hanging where it had been last week, in pride of place above the television. It was Mark's favourite. He had worn it out on our first date, to the cinema, and he had been wearing it the last time I saw him, too. *I love it,* he'd grinned when I commented on it. *I'd wear it all the time if I thought they'd let me get away with it at work.* All right, there were obvious reasons he would leave it behind if he'd been going to stay with his parents, but I'd already ruled that option out. In all other circumstances, I was certain it would be the very first thing he would pack.

I stopped tapping the spoon. The noise of the boiling kettle was filling the empty flat: I reached over and shifted it off the ring so I could hear myself think. My eyes flicked to the sink, the only one in the flat. There was a mug beside the cold tap that had held two toothbrushes – I'd made a big joke out of putting my green one in there alongside his blue one the week before. Now there was only one left. But it wasn't mine, it was his.

Think. Think. Mark had one of those wipe-clean memo boards that he wrote shopping lists on, didn't he? Yes, here, on the wall by the fridge, with a border of crock-pots and vegetables and roast chickens and bunches of herbs all heavily outlined in black. There were a few words scrawled in the middle: *TEABAGS; Smash; Curry Powder.* I unhooked it and carried it back out into the hall, swiping up the note from the phone table to hold them side-by-side. The two sets of handwriting looked nothing like each other.

And Thomas. Who called me Thomas? Not Mark. He was one of the few people who had bothered to respond to my recent requests to be called Tom, not Tommy, but the only person I could remember identifying myself to as Thomas was the woman in Wales I had phoned when I was first looking for Norman Scott. She might well be the only person ever, actually. I'd had no reason to use it otherwise: it wasn't like it had ever been my real name.

Wait. The policeman. The desk sergeant in Hampstead police station. I had given him the name Thomas Wildeblood. And, although I had needed some prompting, I had given him Mark's full name too. I had watched as he wrote them both down. Oh god. What had I done?

I looked at the number on the sheet in front of me. I had dialled it. Not even just once, but twice. Not only had I dropped Mark right in it, I had walked straight into a trap and obligingly triggered it too. How long was it since I had put down the telephone? Three minutes? Two minutes? Not long enough for the kettle to boil. That was good, at least. But I had to get moving. I had to get out of here right now.

I yanked open the door of the flat and started down the stairs. But I had barely gone more than a few steps when the sound came from below of a key in the lock of the front door. I came to a halt, grabbing the handrail to steady myself. There was a squeaking noise, and a chink of daylight spread across the darkness below.

I hadn't got to the turn in the staircase yet, so I couldn't see the newcomer, and, more to the point, they couldn't see me. But I knew full well what they *could* see right now: that apart from the door they were coming in through, there was no other exit from this hallway.

I bolted backwards, scrabbling the key back out of my pocket to open the door that had only just slammed shut behind me. As soon as I was safely on the other side I rattled the chain into place. That put an extra barrier between me and whoever was coming up the stairs, but it took me further away from where I needed to be too – specifically anywhere but here. My heart was pumping, my armpits prickling. What the hell was I going to do?

The sitting room-cum-kitchen was at the front of the building, its windows above the front door, which rendered them useless. What about the back? I ran into the bedroom, stomped heedlessly over the top of the bed and yanked up the bamboo blind Mark had hung over the back window. There was a flat roof outside, made of corrugated iron, with steam billowing out from beneath it: beyond it I could see a tiny yard cluttered with metal barrels of cooking oil and dustbins. I scrabbled at the window catch – it was an old Victorian fitting with a lever you had to twist, but thankfully it wasn't rusted into place, and within seconds I had the sash open, bringing the cold air and an eye-watering aroma of spice and frying onions gusting into the room. I can honestly say I have never smelled anything quite so sweet.

From behind me came the sound of a key turning in a lock, and the flat door opening only to crunch to a halt at the length of its chain. I swung a leg over the windowsill and tested the firmness of the corrugated iron. It felt like it would hold.

Ducking under the raised pane, I pushed myself out onto the flat roof, pulled my other leg through after me, and said a small prayer of thanks when I didn't instantly plunge through and straight into a boiling curry pot. I turned and tried to close the window behind me, but there was no purchase from this side, so I gave up and began instead to edge my way across the roof. The surface bounced sickeningly as I moved across it, but it held my weight. When I was just a couple of feet from the edge I dropped to all fours, and then turned and dangled my legs over, keeping a wary eye on the open window behind me. Which meant the eruption of angry yelling from beneath took me completely by surprise.

On balance, looking back at it, the poor chef was probably more surprised than I was: he had been quietly getting on with his work when my size nines suddenly swung into view, and given the sharp knives and hot burners he was surrounded by, he was lucky not to do himself a mischief. Furious as he was, he ended up doing me a favour by bursting out of the kitchen to grasp me by the legs and yank me down into the yard: it resulted in a much easier landing than I might have managed by myself. Thankfully, it also put him off balance, and he had to let go of me as he went staggering back into the collection of oil drums, sending them tumbling and clattering together and making such a racket that any thoughts of a silent getaway were gone forever. 'Cheers pal, sorry pal,' I gabbled apologetically as I spotted the wooden gate standing open at the back of the yard and launched myself at it.

I reached the opening at the exact same moment as a burly man coming through the other way. He was moving just as fast as I was and we slammed into one another hard. He was so much bigger that I actually bounced off him and back into the restaurant's yard while he grabbed at the brick gateposts to steady himself. Staggering among the clattering cans I looked desperately to either side for another way out, but there was nothing: the walls weren't high, but they were topped with vicious-looking shards of broken glass set in cement. Realising he had me trapped, the man gripped the gateposts more firmly to block my exit. Even in the circumstances I couldn't help noticing that he was handsome in a rough sort of way: lantern-jawed, close-curled blonde hair tumbling down to the collar of a brown leather blouson. As he watched me squirm a nasty smile slowly spread across his face – then, suddenly and inexplicably it changed to a look of shock as he focused somewhere behind my right ear and I turned instinctively and twisted out of the way of a blade which passed so close that I could feel the rush of air on my face.

'You get out! You get out of here!'

The chef was standing directly behind me, brandishing a large knife in each hand. He had obviously ducked back into the kitchen to grab them: I could see a spilled chopping board and shredded vegetables tumbled all over the floor behind him. A whole onion was still rolling across the tiles towards the open doorway, making a bid for freedom.

I had to do the same. I twisted back: the blond man had stepped forward from the gateway, his hands held up, placatory, his eyes on the chef as he said 'All right pal, take it easy, take it easy'. There might just be enough space for me to slip past him while he was distracted, but he would catch me up easily unless I could find some way to delay him. Any hopes that the chef might oblige were rapidly fading: after his first angry burst of slice-and-dice action he seemed less inclined to take a second swipe; although he was still holding both blades high he was now retreating towards the kitchen door, his foot about to come down on the onion which was now out in the yard and still rolling, rolling…

Idea and action came upon each other so fast I couldn't even tell you how it happened: without even processing the thought I had hooked my foot beneath one of the overturned oilcans and sent it spinning towards the intruder: by chance I picked one of the full ones and it slammed into his legs and sent him toppling forwards, face-first towards concrete, if the outstretched blades didn't get in the way first. I didn't stop to see: no sooner had he begun to fall than I leapt high in the air, right over his splaying legs and the still rolling barrel, landing hard in the gateway and using the impact to launch myself forward and out into the alleyway beyond. There was a confusion of shouts behind me, both from the yard and from somewhere above – Mark's window, I suppose: the chain can't have held up for long – a confusion of English and Asian in which all I could make out were the words 'Stop!' and 'Leave it you Paki cunt', but I was off and running, running, knocking over bins and skidding on their contents, ricocheting off the walls on either side of the narrow alley until I reached the open street at its end. It was filled with people: ordinary people, just going about their business, oblivious to what was going on beneath their noses. A woman in a long coat with a dog on a lead recoiled with a shriek as I erupted out of the alleyway. I spat out a 'sorry' as I launched myself forwards into a gap in the traffic: there was a sound of screeching brakes, but I made it through and on to the other side of the street, turning right and heading for the main road with half a thought of making it to the underground station: I'd become expert at slipping past the ticket collectors over the years, and if my pursuers were less successful and there was a train at the right time as I got to the platform – if, if, if – maybe I might be able to give them the slip that way.

I never got to test out my plan against the Sunday tube

timetable: no sooner had I reached the corner than I saw the front door to Mark's flat swing open and a man erupt out of it. I only had a vague impression of a dark suit and army-short hair before I saw he had spotted me, and I spun on my heels and took off in the opposite direction. I had no idea where I was heading. I know all the escape routes around the Dilly, I've had cause to use them often enough, but I wasn't familiar with this part of town at all. All I could do was hammer down the high street, with nothing but darkened shopfronts to left or right. I wove between groups of pedestrians plodding along the pavement in their Sunday best: somewhere nearby pealing bells provided an incongruous soundtrack, their uncertain rhythm out-of-kilter with the steady slapping of my plimsolls on pavement and their echo from far too close behind. And then I saw it: a bus stopped at a zebra crossing, its back open and welcoming. I caught up with it just as the last pedestrian reached the opposite pavement and it was belching smoke from its exhaust and quivering, poised to move. I got both hands round the pole and hauled myself up onto the platform just as it jerked away, stumbling and nearly going headlong into its interior before managing to steady myself on the handrail of the staircase.

'Careful, man,' called out the conductor from inside. 'Not worth risking your life for, is it?'

I had to gasp down a couple of rasping breaths before I was able to mutter a reply. 'Yeah, it is.' Behind us – further behind us than I had thought, and getting further away by the second – the man in the suit had come to a halt in the middle of the road, hands on his knees, breathing heavily, staring after me with a baleful stare. Any other day and he might have caught up with me easily enough – the traffic was usually bumper-to-bumper outside Mark's windows – but luckily it was a Sunday so the bus had a clear run ahead of it. I watched him recede into the distance, cars honking their horns and manoeuvring around him, and aimed a V-sign in his direction before he was lost to sight.

Still, this was no time to relax. They – whoever They actually were – had got Mark and they were after me next. Where the hell was I going to go? I leaned dangerously out of the back of the bus to crane up and check the number: a 134. That was good. It would take me all the way down to the end of Oxford Street: from there it was a quick scuttle into the rat runs and rabbit warren of back streets around Soho. At least I would be on home territory. Meanwhile, best to sit tight and get my breath back. I hauled myself up the stairs and on to the top deck, which was full of West Indians in formal wear, smart overcoats all round and big hats on the women, all chattering away to each other. They were obviously either on the way to, or back from, church. Perfect. Safety in numbers.

The bus wound its way down through Camden, coming close to the community centre where CHE met. Had Mark ever made it there the other night, or had they already got him by then? And what had they done with him? He didn't know anything, that much would have become obvious pretty quickly. The last time we had spoken – it felt like a lifetime ago now – Norman Scott was nothing but a name to us, and Jeremy Thorpe was barely on the radar. But would that be enough to save him? Was he even still alive? Or had Mark, the man I had wanted to protect above all else, gone the same way as Norman, as Stephen, as god knows how many others?

I couldn't think about that right now. I couldn't. I had to keep my wits about me. With every stop I stiffened and twisted around to face the top of the stairs, scanning each new face that rose into view, but none of them belonged to my pursuers. The churchgoers rose en masse and got out at Camden Road and I took the chance to shift to the back seat so I could squint through the filthy window at the street behind. No sign of blondie or the guy in the suit on either pavement. The traffic was backed up behind us all the way to the bridge with its *G DAVIS IS INNOCENT* graffiti. I was so lucky I had managed to jump on the bus when I did.

I felt in my pocket for the letter and photo I had brought from Barnstaple. They were still there, tucked in tight inside *Against The Law*. So long as I still had them safe, I was ok. And no harm could come to me while I was sitting here. Now my arms and legs had stopped shaking, I could almost convince myself I was taking a perfectly normal journey on the bus. The top deck had filled up again, with sluttily-dressed girls and mod boys heading out for the evening, and shiny-suited Irishmen returning from daytime drinking sessions that had started at some point in the previous decade. Right at this moment I felt a great surge of affection for each and every one of them.

Suddenly I realised the bus had been idling still for longer than it had been at any point during our journey so far. I looked and saw we were pulled up at the stop by the burgundy arches of Mornington Crescent tube: at the same moment came the cheery call of the conductor from below: 'Jus' be a few minutes 'ere, got to make up the time.' I twisted round in my seat again, and to my horror saw that a black car was nosing out of the stream of traffic to pull in to the kerb behind us: I caught a glimpse of brown leather behind the wheel and then my worst fears were confirmed as the passenger door swung open and the crop-haired man in the suit climbed out. A car. Of course they had a car. They must have been following the bus the whole way.

Heart pounding, I jumped up out of my seat but it was too late: he was already on board and rising towards me like a devil through a theatre trapdoor: he had a great smile on his face as he saw me looking down at him.

Then came a commanding voice from beneath: 'Let the passengers off first, please, sir.' His smile faltered, and he stepped back and to the side. After a moment, as I stood there frozen at the top of the stairs, another face leaned round to replace it and peered up at me from beneath a peaked cap. 'Are you comin' down, sir?'

'What? No,' I stuttered, still rooted to the spot. 'Sorry. Thought this was my stop. My mistake.' I turned, and scuttled, stooping, right down the length of the bus to the very front, where by some miracle all four seats were free: if he was coming for me, I could at least make him work for it. I scanned the surfaces around me desperately to see if there was anywhere I could stash the letter and photograph, but no joy: close-moulded plastic stretched from floor to curved ceiling, tight and impermeable. There were no slits in the seat I could slip them into, nothing to greet my groping fingers beneath but sheer plastic and globs of dried chewing gum. And it was too late anyway: I could hear his footsteps thumping slowly, deliberately down the aisle towards me. I sensed, rather than saw, him sit down beside me, ignoring the two spare seats across the aisle. I kept my eyes trained straight ahead at the front window. IN EMERGENCY BREAK GLASS, read the writing across the bottom. It was starting to look like my only option.

'Thomas Wildeblood?' came the murmur in my ear.

I shook my head violently.

'Don't fuck me about,' he hissed. 'Are you going to come along quietly with me, or are you going to make this difficult?'

Finally I turned to face him. He was younger than I had thought from a distance, skin stretched tight over high cheekbones, his shaven head accentuating his skull-like appearance. 'If it's all the same to you,' I hissed back at him, 'I'll make it difficult.'

At that exact moment, as if it was obeying my instructions, the bus shuddered and pulled away from the kerb. My companion started, muttering a surprised 'fuck,' and then grabbed my arm. 'Come on, get up.'

'No.' I pulled back, curling myself into the corner of the seat. The people in the seats behind us shifted curiously, wondering what was going on. I don't think that would have bothered him – he didn't seem the type to be fussed about a bit of social embarrassment – but from further back came another welcome sound: 'Tickets, please, all tickets please.' The conductor had arrived on the top deck.

'Shit.' My would-be-abductor had no choice but to settle back in his seat as the uniformed figure made his way slowly down the bus, and we pressed haltingly on towards town. *Please let him have no money*, I thought to myself, over and over as the ticket machine rattled and clicked its way towards us. *Please let him get thrown off.*

Finally the conductor arrived beside us and plumped down into the vacant seat opposite, shifting his ticket machine into his lap. 'Ah, it's the man who doesn't know if he's coming or going,' he said in that special London way that sounds like a joke and a threat at the same time.

'Tottenham Court Road station, please,' I said loudly and clearly, holding out a handful of change I had managed, with some difficulty, to work from my jeans pocket and aiming a pleading look in the conductor's direction.

'Right you are.' He took my money without meeting my gaze and laboriously wound out a ticket. I slumped back into the seat. We were just passing the end of Drummond Street, and Laurence Corner. I realised it was nearly a week since I had picked up Mark from work there for what I was now definitely thinking of as our second date. Before this bastard and his mates had taken him away from me.

'Just the next stop please,' my companion grunted.

'That'll be sixpence,' said the conductor. The thug delved in the pocket of his suit and came out with a pound note, which the conductor just stared at. 'I can't change that.' For a second my spirits soared.

'All right, hang on.' The goon went back in for another go, and, to my disappointment, came out with a five pence piece and one penny. Click click, rattle rattle, went the machine, and the ticket was dispensed, ripped off and handed over. The conductor got up, called out 'Euston Road; next stop Torrington Place', and made his way back up the bus, both of us craning around to watch him until he had disappeared down the stairs. Then my companion turned back to me, and said in a low voice: 'You and me are both getting off this bus at the next stop, if you know what's good for you. And then you're going to get into the car that's following behind without trying anything stupid. Got it?'

I nodded, mutely, biting my lip. Outside the window the buildings of University College were sliding past. I figured we would soon be drawing level with Russell Square. It was one of the biggest cruising grounds in London: a guaranteed pick-up spot once darkness had fallen. And where there are gays on the pull, there are always police around, too.

The bell tinged, and the bus began to slow down. My abductor reached for my arm again and took a firm hold.

I closed my eyes, took a deep breath and then as I stood up, yelled at the very top of my voice: *'Get your hand out my trousers, you filthy pervert!'*

TWENTY-FIVE

I WILL SAY THIS for them: the police can be very quick on the scene when they put their minds to it. Both passengers and conductor had reacted in just the way I'd hoped: the whole top deck erupted and the old lady in the seat behind us even took her umbrella to my assailant as he tried to push his way through the suddenly rowdy crowd of passengers and down the stairs. He didn't make it that far before the conductor erupted up, grabbed him by the arm and told him in no uncertain terms that he wasn't going anywhere until the cops had been called.

Undoing my jeans was a nice touch. I'd had plenty of practice whipping people's flies open in my time, and it was a cinch to open the buttons on my own under the guise of fumbling for change to pay for my ticket. I'd maybe overdone things by adding an affronted yell of 'and I'm only 16!' when the guy was trying to make his escape – certainly the first policeman on the scene looked sceptical about that particular detail when the time came to write it in his notebook. But there was no way I was risking my would-be abductor getting off with a stern warning and sent on his (which is to say my) way. I needed him, and preferably his pal in the car behind, taken in to the station at the very least.

At least no one seemed to doubt the main thrust (as it were) of my story. 'He followed the poor boy right down the bus and sat next to him even though there were seats free on the other side,' the old lady happily testified as the concerned-looking constable scribbled it all down in his pocket-book. 'And then he was fumbling around with him and whispering in his ear all the way. Poor lad looked terrified.'

I nodded, doing my best to look tearful, which wasn't actually that hard under the circumstances. The crowd around me murmured in sympathy, and someone even patted me consolingly on the back. Everyone had been made to get off the bus, which was parked up with its engine off, and most of them seemed in no hurry to continue their journey on any of the alternative ones that had gone by, preferring to stay and watch the show instead. A few other passers-by – mostly long-haired students from the nearby university – had swelled their ranks, wanting to see what was going on.

The one person who wasn't there was the blond in the black car. He'd pulled in behind the bus all right, and hung around for a good five minutes with his engine idling, ignoring the honking protests of other bus drivers trying to pull in to the stop – but when he saw the uniformed policeman turn up and his companion marched off the bus to meet him, his arms firmly held by the conductor on one side and the driver on the other, he had pulled out again and shot off down Gower Street like a scalded cat.

'All right,' said the constable, slapping his notebook shut once he had got the basic story from me, a blanket denial from the man in the suit, and the sense that the crowd was turning ugly. 'We'll take this down the station, then. I'm arresting you on suspicion of indecent assault on a boy under the age of seventeen and attempting to procure the commission of an act of gross indecency.' He managed to get all of that out in one breath, which I thought was quite impressive, and then rattled through the do-not-have-to-say-anything-unless-you-wish-to-do-so bit with barely a pause.

Finally, as a voice from the back of the crowd threatened to 'save you a job and knock the dirty bugger's block off right here', the policeman radioed for transport, and two panda cars came dingalinging down the street just a couple of minutes later. One for him, one for me. 'Don't worry, you won't have to see him again,' they promised, and I fervently hoped they were right. For the very first time I got to ride in the front, with no handcuffs or abuse like I was used to. The driver even asked if I minded having the window open.

This unfamiliar behaviour continued at West End Central, where instead of going round the back and down the ramp to the holding cells, we drew up at the front entrance and I was allowed to make my own way up the steps and inside with no more than an ushering arm to guide me. From there I was taken straight through to an interview room that had comfy chairs and carpet and everything, though the mirrored window in the door left me in no doubt that the usual rules still applied and I should keep the act up for as long as anyone could be looking in at me. They did, however, bring me the cup of tea I'd been craving for hours now, and a biscuit to boot, and I was left to my own devices for half an hour until a nice lady copper came in to take my formal statement.

I was very aware that this might be a case of out of the frying-pan, into the fire – if I was right, it was details of my last visit to a police station that had led my pursuers to Mark's flat in the first place – so I started off by saying I really didn't want to press charges, in the hope that, tea and biscuits notwithstanding, I could get out of the place as soon as possible. But she insisted she had to take a statement anyway, on the grounds that 'for all we know, this man might make a habit of doing this sort of thing to other boys.' I knew how unlikely that was – he looked as straight as a five-bob note to me, and I can usually tell – but I agreed to tell her my story, which I kicked off by saying my name was Richard Barnicoat, who was a kid who used to bully me at school. I toyed with using 'Scott Norman', but assuming these details might get passed on to my pursuers too, I thought it best not to tip them off as to exactly how much I knew.

I'm my own worst enemy, because as we got going I couldn't resist embellishing things even more with the detail that I'd been taking the bus back from a bible study class at my church youth group. Of course she then asked me what church, and I had to make one up – I plumped for St Matthew's on the grounds that he'd been the best-looking apostle in the *Illustrated Children's Bible* – and then stumped me completely by asking me if I wanted to phone 'mum and dad and let them know where you are?'

'Come again?' I spluttered.

She looked at her watch. It was gone seven o'clock now. 'They'll be worrying about you, won't they?'

'Oh. Yeah. Probably.' I nodded a bit too vigorously, overcompensating.

Thankfully she misinterpreted my obvious discomfort, and leaned forward, her face a mask of comforting sympathy. 'Or would you prefer *me* to tell them what's happened, if it's difficult for you?'

Well, of course, I couldn't have that, so I had to put on my best brave-little-soldier face and let her lead me out to an office where I spent five minutes assuring the speaking clock that there was no need to worry and it really didn't need to come and pick me up.

Still, I was congratulating myself on a job well done and making a start on another cup of tea and a second digestive when the door to the interview room opened again, and a very unwelcome figure walked in.

'Hello, Tommy,' Sergeant Mullaney said, neutrally enough, but with that air of menace he manages to get into the shortest of utterances.

'Hello, Sergeant.' I returned the cup to its saucer, unsipped.

He was in uniform, but his cap and his tie were missing, and with his jacket undone and his hands in his pockets as he loped over to the table he looked like an actor slumming it between performances.

'Or should I be calling you Richard these days?' he asked, still in the same unnaturally friendly tone.

'Oh. Ah,' I blustered, unsure what to say to this.

'D'you know what we call giving false details to the police?' he asked, breezily conversational as he wandered past me and around behind my chair.

'Um…no,' I had to admit.

Suddenly Mullaney turned and grabbed my head, slamming it down onto the tabletop in front of me and holding me there. 'It's called perverting the course of justice, Tommy,' he hissed into my upturned ear. 'Just right for a little pervert like you.'

I tried to reply, but couldn't find much more to say than 'ow!'

'Because, you see, all the perverts that get brought in here come to me in the end,' he continued, his alcoholic breath washing over my face. 'I'm Vice, see? That means I find out about every grope, every gobble, every cock that gets stuck somewhere it shouldn't on my patch. And when I get told that a man's been brought in accused of fiddling with a little boy on a bus, imagine my surprise when I find out the innocent young virgin in question is *you*.'

'I'm sorry! I'm sorry!' I spluttered. Mullaney's only response was to twist his hand in my hair, grinding my face harder into the scratched surface.

'Lucky for you, that's not the only surprise I've had this evening,' he said, and finally let me go. I sat back in relief, rubbing my nose, which was streaming and felt like it might be broken, as Mullaney circled the table and sat down opposite, continuing his story as if we had just been having an amiable chat. 'Because no sooner have we brought you in and before Constable Wickes has even had a chance to start typing up the witness statements he *very thoroughly* took from everyone who was present for your little performance, someone else arrives at our front desk saying he saw the whole thing. He claims what actually happened is that you half-inched his pal's wallet, and all he was trying to do was get it back off of you.'

I shook my head vehemently. 'That's a lie. That's rubbish. You can search me if you want. I haven't got anything of theirs.'

Too late I remembered the letter and photo in my pocket, and came to a gulping halt. But Mullaney made no move to search me. 'Do me a favour, Tommy,' he drawled wearily. 'If I wanted to find someone's wallet on you, I'll find it all right, along with anything else I fancy charging you with possession of. I know he's lying. And he knows I know as well, and the worst of it is, he doesn't give a fuck. Do you know what he tried to tell me his name was? Mr Smith, and his pal in the cells goes by the name of Jones. Which quite frankly is just taking the piss. And as I

213

think we've established, *Richard*, I don't take kindly to that.'

I'd rarely seen Mullaney look genuinely angry – he preferred to stay detached even as he doled out the worst of his violence and menaces – but he looked furious now.

'What does he look like? Mr Smith?' I risked asking, wondering if it could be the same mystery visitor who had dropped in on Mrs Friendship and Jethro Morgan.

'Typical pretty boy,' Mullaney sneered. 'All blonde curls and fancy jacket.'

No, then, it was just my other pursuer, returning to the fray after presumably consulting with his superiors. It sounded like falling flat on his face hadn't spoiled his good looks, more's the pity.

'Who are they?' Mullaney demanded.

I shrugged helplessly. 'I don't know.'

BANG! Mullaney slammed his fist down on the table hard, making both the tea cup and me jump. His face remained impassive. 'Don't fuck me around Tommy. They've got me working Sunday, when I should be at home enjoying my wife's crackling and *Sing Something Simple*. I am not in the mood to be fucked about. Why were they after you?'

'I don't know,' I spluttered. 'Really, I don't. They turned up at my friend's house, and they started chasing me.'

'And you've never seen them before?'

I shook my head. 'Never.'

His nostrils flared. 'So how exactly, Tommy, do you explain surprise number three, which is the phone call I just took from Scotland Yard telling me it's not in my interests to seek a prosecution in this matter, it's all a misunderstanding, and we should let Mr Jones out of the cells quick sharp?' He sat back and looked at me expectantly.

Even if I had my suspicions, Mullaney was the very last

person I was going to share them with. 'I can't,' I said, flinching involuntarily.

Instead of the explosion I was expecting, Mullaney spoke softly, though no less menacingly. 'No. Neither can I. And more to the point, neither could the fella on the end of the phone. "So he's one of yours, is he?" I said to him, and he was very quick to assure me he was nothing of the sort. Bit too quick, as it happens.' He leant back in his chair. '"Well in that case," I told 'im, "I still need to know who he *is*, because he's sat in my cells with his mouth clamped tighter shut than a choirboy's ringpiece at the general synod while everyone else in my station is trying to spin me cock and bull stories." D'you know what he tried to tell me then, Tommy?'

Being taken into Mullaney's confidence felt no less dangerous. 'What?' I asked, hoping this was one of his usual rhetorical questions and my not knowing wasn't going to make him angry again.

A vulpine grin. 'He said it was none of my business. I said that made it even clearer that it must be some of his, and I'd be sure to make that clear in the report which I was planning to circulate to as many of the top brass at the Yard as I could remember the names of. "No, no no," he went, sounding like someone was twisting the rod that's stuck up his arse, "I can assure you this wasn't a Special Branch op, it's got nothing to do with us at all". In that case, I say, in my cells he sits and in my cells he stays until I get a decent answer as to who he is and what he was doing on my patch with his hands down someone else's trousers. And laughing boy tells me if that's going to be my attitude he's got no more to say to me and rings off in a huff.'

Mullaney stretched even further back in his chair, sliding his hands into his trouser pockets, suggesting the interview, such as it was, was moving on to an even less formal footing.

He gave me a long, evaluating look. 'I don't like you, Tommy. I think you're a nasty little queer, and a whore to boot. Probably spreading all sorts of diseases around London with what you get up to.'

I wasn't stupid enough to react to this, so I stayed silent. But it was pretty rich coming from Mullaney, who took payment by way of a freebie in practically every upstairs room in Soho when he did his weekly rounds before heading back home to his poor wife and her pork crackling.

'Only there are some things I don't like even more than you. And that includes being ordered about in my own nick. And I don't much like penpushers sat in cushy offices at Scotland Yard, neither, specially when they start trying to throw their weight around where real coppers are trying to get an honest day's work done.'

'Right,' I said slowly. I was pretty sure Mullaney had never done an honest day's work in his life, but I liked the direction this seemed to be going in.

He sniffed hard, audibly and unpleasantly rolling the results around in his throat. 'Got my old pal George Fenwick up on a charge, for fuck's sake. There's a man who's done more proper police work in a week than any of those office boys'll do in their lifetimes.'

'OK,' I said, since a response seemed required.

Mullaney suddenly lunged forwards, and I shied back, but he was only reaching to tap the tabletop for emphasis. 'Thing is, though, I know how these things work. No office boy at Scotland Yard is going to shove his oar in on a Sunday night ordering me to drop an investigation – an investigation into a very serious crime, that of going about diddling little kiddies on buses – just because one of their bumchums from school or the local lodge is involved. That sort of thing gets sorted out with a funny handshake later on and way above my level. So I ask myself what the hell could a dirty little scrote like Tommy Wildeblood have got himself involved in that's important enough to have the *force's finest* standing to attention when they should be tucked up at home watching *Songs of Praise*? And I start wondering who needs hitting hardest – Richard so-called Barnicoat or No Comment Norma down in the cells – before I start getting some answers?'

He cracked his knuckles unpleasantly, and I felt every part of my body involuntarily clenching.

'So I'll ask you once more Tommy, who are these two jokers really, and why were they after you?'

This question definitely wasn't rhetorical. I had to give him something, if only to save myself from getting intimately acquainted with the tabletop again.

'It's to do with a bent politician,' I said slowly, choosing my words very carefully.

'Bent?' I knew in which sense I had meant the word, though I'd had a feeling Mullaney would take it the other way.

I nodded. 'He had sex with…some friends of mine.' I was prepared to go on, if I had to – surely even Mullaney would manage to come down on the right side when it came to murder – but he appeared to have already taken the bait.

'I got you, I got you.' He glanced round at the door of the interview room, which was still closed, and then shifted his chair closer to the table. 'You got photos?'

How did he know? 'Um…yeah.'

'Right you are.' Mullaney leaned back in his chair and crossed his arms. 'Well, well. Now we're talking. Of course, you wouldn't be stupid enough to try something like that without cutting *all* your pals in.'

He said this as a statement of fact, and I suddenly grasped

217

what he meant. 'Oh…no, of course not.'

'That's good. Because I'm a good copper, Tommy, got my ear to the ground, and if anyone comes into a sudden windfall on my patch, I *do* get to hear about it.'

I nodded vigorously. 'Of course.' I might have known Mullaney's mind would go straight to blackmail – and, what's more, that his first reaction would be to blackmail *me* into promising him a share of the proceeds.

He flashed that disconcerting grin again. 'I mean it, Tommy. I find out everything that's going on on my patch – *everything*, Tommy – whereas that lot barely know what's happening beyond the end of their in-trays.' He stretched out, putting his arms behind his head and gazing up towards the ceiling, talking as much to himself as to me. 'Special Branch: special needs, more like. Didn't manage to spot the paddies coming over from their godforsaken island all tooled up to start planting bombs in places where actual civilised people live, did they? And I didn't see many of their lot in Balcombe Street neither. Too busy sitting in their nice central-heated offices pushing paper and sticking their noses into our business, instead. Trying to tell us what makes for *subversive literature.*' He practically spat the words out. 'I know a dirty book when I see one. And I know a dirty hippy when I see one, too.'

His eyes drifted back down to rest on me.

'So…?' I ventured after an uncomfortable silence.

'So?' he drawled, in high-pitched imitation of my question. 'So, Richard Barnicoat should run off home to mummy and daddy.'

He looked at me expectantly, and I slowly rose from my seat. 'Now?'

'Before I change my mind,' he confirmed.

I headed towards the door, but turned back. 'What about

them? Smith and Jones?'

He exhaled heavily, then twisted in his seat to face me. 'Well, Mr Smith is still sitting in reception, which is why I'd suggest you might want to use the back exit – I know that's the way you like it anyway.'

He gave me a nasty smirk, and I forced myself to smile in return. I knew exactly what he was implying, but the truth was I was more than familiar with the layout of the cells-end of the station. 'What about Mr Jones?'

Mullaney made a great show of looking at his watch. 'Well, would you look at that? Time for my tea break. That means I'm strictly forbidden to do anything for the next half an hour – Police Federation are very strict on these things, and quite right too, it's a health and safety issue, not just a welfare one, as I'm sure I don't need to point out. I expect I'll probably take a stroll down the canteen and get myself a sausage roll, maybe a scotch egg – nothing too heavy, like I say, I'm saving myself for my wife's crackling when I get home, smashing that is, in a bit of bread with a dollop of HP – and a nice cup of tea. Scalding hot, they serve it, so I'll need to wait for it to cool down before I can drink it – that's another health and safety issue right there – so I can't guarantee I'll make it back on duty before, ooh, say, a quarter past eight at the earliest. Then, of course, my instructions from our superior officers at the Yard will be the very first thing on my to-do-list.' He smiled at me – for once, I thought, genuinely, companionably even – and I grinned back before making for the door.

'Oh, and Tommy?' he said when I was half way out of the room.

'Yeah?'

'Fuck off.'

I fucked off.

TWENTY-SIX

I STARTED RUNNING the minute I got out of the police station, without any clear idea of where I was running to. It felt as if London, the city that had seemed so huge and full of opportunities when I arrived here, was slowly shutting itself off to me, piece by piece: the Dilly patrolled by the Playland crew; Mark's flat under surveillance; and now anywhere these mysterious pursuers and their Scotland Yard protectors might lurk. And my possessions were being whittled away too: I had nothing now but the clothes I stood up in, the precious letter and photograph and my lucky book. Thank god I had thought to put that back in my jacket in the few minutes I had been at Mark's.

But hang on – that wasn't all I had picked up, was it? I checked the opposite pocket as I hurtled across Regent Street, heedless of traffic, heading instinctively into the backstreet badlands of

Soho. They were still there. The keys to Harvey's office. I had somewhere to go after all. Back to where it all began.

I made it to Denmark Street by a roundabout route, stopping every few blocks and ducking into doorways to check the pavement behind me and make sure I wasn't being followed. The building was dark, but the same cacophony was blaring out from the first floor. Or maybe not quite the same: I thought as I ascended the staircase that the group might maybe have mastered a minimal number of chords since I had last heard them. I could even make out some of the words that the singer was bellowing along to the racket: *Anarchy in the UK! Anarchy in the UK!* You don't know the half of it, mate, I thought as I unlocked the top-floor door. You don't know the half of it.

Once inside I collapsed onto the sofa, breathing heavily. My mind was whirring at the same rate as my hammering heart: a jumble of fearful thoughts tumbling one on top of the other, none of them forming connections, none of them making sense. Who the hell was after me? Mullaney seemed convinced that the two men who had been chasing me were Special Branch officers. But in that case, why hadn't they just arrested me rather than going through all that rigmarole on the bus, or pulled rank once the uniformed copper arrived? And why would Scotland Yard be so keen to deny any official link to them? Were they just up to a little freelance work on the weekend? And how did Mrs Friendship's mysterious visitor fit into all this? His companions had been happy enough to flash Special Branch ID on that occasion, even if he had declined to give his name. Was he police too? Or did he represent some other organisation lurking deeper in the shadows?

Through all of this, one thought kept coming back to me, slamming through my head, threatening to overwhelm me. *They got Mark. They took Mark. Mark's dead.*

No. I had to stop thinking that. Until I knew for sure otherwise, I had to assume my boyfriend – yes, turns out I was happy to call him my boyfriend now, now that he wasn't around to hear it – was alive somewhere, maybe being held prisoner, but still OK. These people hadn't exactly gone to great lengths to conceal Stephen or Norman Scott's bodies: both had been arrogantly left out for anyone to find, in the knowledge that when that happened they would be able to pull the strings required to tidy things up and ensure there were no awkward questions asked. Until I saw a body – saw with my own eyes that it was Mark – I had to believe he was still alive. Otherwise I feared I was going to lose the plot completely.

And that was what I had to hang on to: the plot Mrs Friendship and I had come up with the previous afternoon. What had happened since was irrelevant, save that it increased the urgency: I still had the letter and the photo, and I still had somewhere to take them. Even better, it was somewhere nearby: *Private Eye*'s office address was printed in the front of the magazine, and it wasn't down on Fleet Street with the other papers like I'd expected: it was just a couple of blocks away in the middle of Soho. I had a name, too, of the journalist Scott had talked to before: Paul Foot. I could get there first thing in the morning and hand both pieces of evidence over to him, leave it to him to know what to do. All I had to do was lie low until then.

And so, after checking several times that I had definitely locked the office door, and keeping my trousers firmly on this time, I settled down on Harvey's sofa once more and tried to get some sleep. It was pretty hopeless, and not just because of the thrashing guitars and off-beat drumming from below. Particles of the day's events kept flashing through my mind, only in this subconscious version everything was against me: the window wouldn't open; the roof wouldn't hold; the gate was locked; the bus pulled away at the last minute; Mullaney wouldn't listen and just kept grinding my face into the table until it popped like a blister.

Paranoia from the day before mingled with paranoia about the day to come and every time I did manage to slip into unconsciousness I seemed to start awake almost immediately, picturing Alison arriving to open up the office for the day and finding me still sprawled on the sofa. I ended up watching the shadows shorten on the polystyrene ceiling tiles as the dawn turned them from grey to nicotine-stained yellow, before giving up on sleep completely at around seven, sitting up and instead trying to find comfort in the well-thumbed pages of *Against The Law*. The hippies back at the squat had relied on the *I-Ching* to guide them in their life choices; more than once this book had done the same job for me. I flicked straight to the cheerier section at the end to find Wildeblood senior musing on how with a gay relationship of any standing, 'there will always be 'corroborative evidence' of some sort; letters, photographs, the sharing of a home' and, within the space of a page, returning to work and pointing out that 'The men and women who work in Fleet Street may be cynical in some respects, but they are generous and delightfully frank. There was not a moment of embarrassment; there was no moral judgement and, I am glad to say, no pity.'

That had to be a sign that I was on the right course. At eight thirty on the dot, armpits scrubbed and hair finger-combed as best I could in the tiny lavatory on the landing, I turned up the collar on my leather jacket, opened the front door a crack to check there was no one waiting for me outside, and set off on the short journey to Greek Street to hand over my corroborative evidence.

Well, it turns out that journalists might be generous, frank and all the rest of it, but they don't keep anything like normal office hours. I quickly located *Private Eye* – it was a side-door marked by a brass plaque reading 'Gnome House', whatever that meant, to the left of Doc Johnson's Love Parlour – but nine o'clock came and went and the door remained just as firmly closed as the sex shop next to it. I hung around for a while by the theatre across the road, which was plastered with posters for *Jesus Christ Superstar*, but I started to feel horribly conspicuous as well as starving, and, deciding that a moving target was safer than a sitting duck, and one with enough energy to run safer than one who was about to fall over from fatigue, headed round the corner and hid myself away at the back of Bar Italia for eggs on toast and two of those tiny coffees that pack as much punch as a pot of the normal stuff. I was feeling a hell of a lot better when I scuttled back to Greek Street just after ten and found the door opened to my push, revealing a dingy staircase from the top of which I could hear the rattle of typewriter keys.

'Hello,' I said to the distracted-looking woman hammering the machine when I reached the top.

'Just a minute,' she said without looking up. Slightly awed – she had one of the poshest accents I have heard in my life – I stood back and tried to make myself inconspicuous, but it wasn't an easy task. Hers was one of several desks crammed into the tiny room, all of them overflowing with piles of paper and yellowing newspapers, some of them stacked in wire in-trays which were all full to the brim. Yet more bits of paper were drawing-pinned on the walls: torn-out newspaper headlines, photographs with speech-bubbles scrawled on them, typed letters on headed paper – a lot of them seemed to be from the *Sunday Times* – and yellowing cartoons. The only areas left un-papered were the windows to the street and a half-glazed partition opposite:

through it I could see another, slightly larger room, its walls painted bright red. It was empty except for a very thin man in a waistcoat who was hunched over one of those sloping stand-up desks. He appeared to be concentrating very hard on cutting up sets of letters with a scalpel.

Tap, tap, ping; and finally she was ready for me. 'Yes?'

'I'd like to speak to Paul Foot, please.' I was holding the photo and letter in front of me as if their significance would be obvious to anyone else.

She looked at me dubiously over half-moon glasses which she wore on a chain round her neck. 'He's not in today, I'm afraid.'

My heart sank. 'Oh… When will he be back?'

'I'm not sure, he comes and goes.'

'Oh.' I looked down at the precious bits of paper in my hand. I had pinned all my hopes on handing them over this morning: my luck had barely held out yesterday, and the thought of having to keep them safe for even longer was almost unbearable. 'Are there any other journalists here I could speak to?'

'Not at the moment, no.'

I wasn't sure I believed her. She had paused before answering, and looked me up and down appraisingly.

'What about him?' I gestured to the thin man behind the glass. 'Is he not a journalist?'

She swivelled in her seat. 'Him? God, no.'

Spirits sinking, my gaze drifted to the partition beneath the glass, which was lined with wooden pigeonholes with names scrawled underneath them: *Sheila, Cash, Richard, Grovel.* 'Could I leave something for Mr Foot, then?'

She sighed audibly. 'I suppose so. He does get sent an awful lot of stuff though, you know.'

I aimed her what I hoped was an ingratiating smile, although from the reaction it got, it wasn't. 'I think he'll be interested in this. It's about someone who came in to see him a while ago to talk about Jeremy Thorpe. His name was Norman Scott.'

The woman's manner got visibly colder, her back straightening and her lips pursing. 'Oh. I remember him. What does he want now?'

'Nothing.' She was starting to irritate me, so I went for broke. 'He's been murdered.'

That got a reaction. Her jaw actually dropped. 'Oh!'

'So can I leave these for Mr Foot?'

'Yes. Yes, of course.' Flustered, she reached out a hand for the envelope and photo. I was about to hand them over, but at the last second I held back. 'Actually, these might not make much sense on their own. Can I write him a note?'

'Of course.' Dropping her glasses to the end of their chain, she spun in her chair to search for a pen and paper. 'Sit over there if you like.' She indicated one of the other desks in the room – the least untidy one, though that wasn't saying much – and I slipped in behind it, pushing the papers aside to give me enough space to write. Now she was all flapping over-friendliness. 'Can I get you anything? Tea? Coffee?'

I gave her the ingratiating smile again. 'Tea would be lovely. Two sugars, please.'

As she bustled off to busy herself with an electric kettle, I studied the blank sheet of paper in front of me, wondering how to begin. With Stephen, or with Norman Scott? Or maybe a personal story would be better, starting with my own recent experiences?

Scanning the desk in front of me for inspiration, my eyes came to rest on a cardboard box file. A single word-title was scrawled across its front: LOONS. Checking that the woman wasn't looking, I used the biro she had given me to poke its lid open. It was stuffed with letters, some on unfolded sheets of writing paper, some not even removed from their envelopes. I scanned the top-most one, which was written in looping handwriting, a vast white space left at the beginning of each paragraph. *Dear Mr Ingrams, I write to inform you of a conspiracy to persecute myself involving top-level figures in the security services, the Conservative Party and the local council. I have documentation going back many years which proves among other things I have been targeted through secret broadcasts via my TV set...*

If I wanted this to get read at all, I should probably just stick to the basics.

Dear Mr Foot,

In October last year you had a meeting with Norman Scott, who you may remember was trying to publicise his past sexual relationship with Jeremy Thorpe MP.

Last October, Norman Scott was shot dead on Exmoor, near Barnstaple where he had been living. You will be able to check this with the local police force, and with Mrs Edna Friendship of the Market Inn in Barnstaple, who he had been living with. Also with Jethro Morgan, the farmer who found his body. I apologise that I do not have an address for him but Mrs Friendship should be able to put you in touch.

Mr Morgan, who is an ex-army man, saw the body close up and is firmly convinced that he was killed at close range with a revolver. However the investigation was taken out of the hands of the local police and handed over to Special Branch, of whom I'm sure you are aware of. Since then the story that has been spread locally is that he (Scott) was shot by accident with a shotgun by a hunter of deer or pheasants.

Many people, including Mrs Friendship and myself, are convinced that Norman was murdered to silence him from talking about Jeremy Thorpe.

Last month a second person, Stephen – surname unknown – was also murdered.

Hang on, I thought, let's be strictly accurate with this.

Last month a second person, Stephen – surname unknown – met with a violent death and his naked body was found in Hampstead ponds on Hampstead Heath. I have evidence

Strictly accurate.

I have been told that he had also had a sexual relationship with Thorpe

Strictly.

I have been told that he had also had a sexual relationship with ~~Thorpe~~ a Liberal politician, whom I assume also to have been Thorpe, and that he was threatening to expose this (the relationship). Again Special Branch took over from the local police force. I have this information first-hand from a sergeant at Hampstead police station. And Stephen's body was also removed from the hospital morgue without an inquest happening. This is first-hand information also.

I paused, and sipped the mug of tea that the woman – all sweetness and light now – had popped down next to me. Set out like this, it all sounded quite matter of fact and plausible. Should I add any of my own experiences from the last twenty-four hours? *I am now being chased by mysterious men who may or may not work for Scotland Yard, and have nearly been arrested for perverting the cause of justice but a policeman let me go because he thought I was a blackmailer.* Yeah, maybe not. If I did that, I might as well just put my letter straight into the file in front of me, and skip the middleman altogether.

> *I cannot give you any contact details for myself due to unforeseen circumstances but I will try to return to your offices later this week*

Although thinking about it, the less I allowed myself to be seen around central London, the less chance there was of Messrs Smith and Jones, or whoever they really were, of catching up with me.

> *or at least to telephone. As I say, if you speak to Mrs Friendship she will vouch for my story and also Mr Morgan, and possibly also the police in Barnstaple.*

Here's hoping. Morgan had been happy enough to talk when he had someone pouring drink down him in his local– I just had to hope he wouldn't clam up if he got a call from a London journalist.

> *I also enclose a photograph of Norman Scott and Jeremy Thorpe together and a letter which I think speaks for itself. Please take great care of these as they were among Scott's most precious belongings and they are the only proof that he was telling the truth about their relationship.*

That sounded a bit like I was telling the journalist how to do his job, so I added another line.

> *At least the only proof I have been able to find although I*

am sure as a professional you will be able to find out more. Police from Special Branch removed other papers from the Market Inn: Mrs Friendship will tell you all about that.

I felt I was beginning to ramble, so I signed off, and was just about to fold the sheet of paper around the envelope and photo when something struck me: this would have been so much easier if I had been able to do it face to face.

PS – This is not because of me objecting to them being homosexuals at all. I am a homosexual myself.

'Finished?' asked the woman brightly as I stood up. She took the paper from me and gave it a quick scan. I might have been mistaken, but she seemed to focus particularly on the postscript before she said, 'I'll put it in an envelope, I think, keep everything together.' I watched it until it had been safely enclosed and stowed in one of the pigeonholes – marked *Footy*, which was rather sweet – and then said my goodbyes, checking one last time if she knew when I might be able to catch the man himself.

'I really can't say: he only pops in occasionally to see Richard, the editor,' she apologised.

I thanked her and set off for the stairs. But I'm still not sure if she was being entirely truthful with me: as I was leaving the man in the room next door started coughing, and a tremendous thumping noise came from the ceiling above, so there was definitely someone upstairs. I almost turned back to ask if she was sure there was no-one else I could talk to, but I'd already stepped aside to let an elderly man in a belted mackintosh come up the stairs and she was greeting him with such enthusiasm – 'Tom! How lovely to see you! Have you brought us the crossword? I'm afraid Steve's not here yet' – that I left it and descended to the street and out into the considerably more dangerous open.

The bright spring sunshine hit me like a spotlight after the murk of the office, and I crouched back against the wall of the building, shielding my eyes as I glanced anxiously up and down the street. I set off up towards Soho Square, to keep moving as much as anything else: after they, whoever they were, had found me so quickly at Mark's the day before, it felt as if staying still for too long was an invitation for them to pounce again. My plans had only gone as far as handing over my evidence to *Private Eye*: now that was done I didn't have the first clue what to do with myself next.

I crossed Old Compton Street and scuttled along the vast side wall of the Casino Theatre, decked out with posters for Danny La Rue. There was a man who could hide himself away if he wanted to: out of his slap and in street clothes, you could walk past him on the street and never be any the wiser. Sadly the opposite option wasn't open to me: Claribel had let me try on some of her wigs once, but told me sadly that I'd never have the figure to pass as a woman. Nor was there much else I could offer in the way of disguise: I was incapable of growing a decent beard or moustache even if you gave me a week to work on it, let alone on the timescale that circumstances demanded. I had to accept that as long as I stayed in London I might as well have a target painted on my back.

Was there anywhere safe for me to go? The world I had moved in for the past few years, the 'gay community' as Neil at CHE liked to call it, was suddenly too small for comfort: everyone I knew knew everyone I knew, and anyone asking after Tommy Wildeblood would find their way to all my usual haunts before too long. In fact for all I knew the thugs I had run into yesterday had already done so: it might only have been my unscheduled visit to Devon that had kept me out of their clutches so far. And it wasn't even as if they were the only ones who would be looking for me: the Playland gang would surely want to finish the job they had started, and now, to boot, Sergeant Mullaney was going to be after me for his cut from a blackmail plot that only existed in his own imagination. Doors were closing to me all over the city, and they were slamming hard.

I needed a place that would take me in and keep me hidden. Somewhere far away from the city, somewhere Tommy Wildeblood was a complete unknown. Mrs Friendship's fitted the bill, but there was no way I could go back there without the photo and letter I had promised her I wouldn't let out of my sight. Which meant there was only one place on earth left that fitted the bill.

'You've got to be joking.' I actually said the words out loud to myself as I arrived at the top of Greek Street where it opened out into the leafy canopy of Soho Square.

No. It was out of the question. Wasn't it? Surely it was. Except that, if you put all emotion aside and looked at the problem with logic instead, it was the only solution that made sense.

No. Sod logic. That wasn't the way I was prepared to play it. I crossed the road into the little park, sat down on one of the benches, reached into my jacket pocket and pulled out my personal *I-Ching* instead. It had told me what I needed to hear this morning, and I was confident it would do the same now, and then I could rule this nonsense out completely and maybe come up with something else.

The book fell open on the same two pages as before. I must have cracked the spine or something. But my eyes went straight to a different paragraph this time.

When I went to the country to stay with my mother and father, I thought that meeting their friends was going to be the worst ordeal of all. There is probably no group of people more conservative, or less likely to understand a predicament like mine, than the middle-aged inhabitants of a small country town... I was surprised and moved to discover that I was quite wrong. They welcomed me back as though nothing had happened.

'Oh, shit,' I said out loud again.

TWENTY-SEVEN

ALL THE WAY ON THE train I was giving myself get-out clauses. Maybe they wouldn't let me past the front door. Maybe they would be away on holiday. Maybe they'd moved house. After arriving at Reading Station – it was less than an hour away from London, which seemed incredible given the gulf that seemed to gape between the two places – and catching the familiar bus through unchanged streets, I started to focus and fret over smaller practicalities: if my mum was on days they would both be out at work; should I maybe go to the hospital first and try to find her there instead; oh god, what if my father had lost his job or was off sick and it was him who answered the door instead? As I walked up the actual road with its neatly-trimmed verges and high privet hedges the whole monologue in my mind was reduced to one simple thought, repeating over and over: What am I doing back here? What am I doing back here? What the hell am I doing back here?

Even as I walked up the crazy-paved path towards the front door – painted red now, it had been blue when I left – I was telling myself it wasn't too late to turn back. It was only the fear of what lay behind me feeling more acute than the deep-seated dread of the past which pushed me on to the porch and forced my unwilling finger onto the doorbell button. Its synthetic imitation of Big Ben's chimes brought me abruptly shuddering back to full awareness of what I was doing: I was actually poised to turn and launch myself back off the step and start sprinting away when the door creaked open.

My mum didn't meet my gaze at first: she was scrabbling in her handbag for her purse, an Avon catalogue clutched in one hand. I had time to take in the fact that she looked somehow both older and younger than when I had last seen her, her face more lined but her hair a deeper chestnut shade than the grey-streaked brown I remembered, before she looked up and her eyes met mine and widened and wettened in quick succession.

'Alex!' she gasped, and then reached forward to grab me and hug me and pull me inside all in the same movement. For a fleeting moment it struck me how keen she was to get the door shut so I was out of view of the rest of the street, but then all I was conscious of was the force with which she was crushing my body against her own.

For the first minute or so all she could do was keep repeating my name over and over again, her voice catching. I found I was crying myself, sniffling into her new hair, which smelled of fresh shampoo with an undertone of something much more familiar and primal.

Finally we managed to disentangle ourselves, but she wasn't ready to let go of me yet, holding me at arm's length by the shoulders and looking me up and down with amazement.

'You're so *big*!' she kept saying, even though I didn't think I'd got any taller since I had left home, and 'I can't believe it!'. Eventually she ushered me through into the lounge, which had a new three-piece suite but was still laid out exactly the same, and pushed me down onto the sofa where she finally let go of me. Even then she didn't sit down herself, but stood over me shifting her weight from foot to foot and wringing her hands together until I had to ask her to sit down as well because she was making me nervous.

'Oh! I'm sorry love,' she exclaimed, perching on the edge of one of the armchairs, although not the nearest one. That was my father's. If I didn't know that from the fact it was in the exact same spot as before, the side table next to it with its stack of neatly-folded newspapers, ashtray, pipe and tobacco pouch would have told me.

Nothing else in the room seemed to have changed either. Same ornaments, the china lady with her parasol and the glass birds and fish and Bengo the boxer pup laid out in the exact same spots on the mantelpiece. Same knight in armour guarding the fire irons beneath; same crying Pierrot in his frame above. *Radio Times* and *TV Times* still stacked on the shelf beneath the telly, with the former carefully placed on top because it was more respectable.

'Everything's just the same,' I said, to explain the way my eyes were wandering round the room while she still had hers fixed upon me.

'Well.' She was still holding her handbag, and she fished inside it to find a tissue and mop the mascara that was smeared down her cheeks. 'You know how your dad is about change.'

'Yeah.' It came out with more meaning than I meant it to.

'Oh Alex.' She looked as if she was biting back more tears, and then she suddenly stood up again. She couldn't seem to keep still. 'What can I get you? I'll make some tea. Have you eaten? I was just about to have some lunch. Nothing special, just a sandwich. I could open a tin of soup though? Or do some cheese on toast?'

'I'm fine, Mum, don't worry,' I assured her, trying to get her to settle, but she was already bustling through to the kitchen, saying the kettle had just boiled and it would only take a minute to brew some tea. She pushed the door to behind her, and I realised what she really wanted was a moment to get herself together, so I left her to it.

Her nervous energy was infectious, and I found it quite hard to sit still myself. I got up and walked to the window, looking out at the street where I had spent the first 16 years of my life. The conifer in the middle of the lawn was nearly the height of the house now. I remembered helping my father plant it. There was a photo somewhere – it would be in one of those albums on the shelf – of me standing next to it, the tree and me exactly the same height (at least if I stretched up on tiptoes in my muddy wellington boots). I hadn't thought about that day in years, but I could recall the rich smell of the compost right now as clearly as I could picture the photo itself: it was on the same page of the album as the one of us in our England scarves ready to watch the World Cup final on telly that same summer. I could remember mum dragging us out into the sunshine to take it, my dad grumbling all the way that we would miss the start of the match. I could remember the feel of his arm around my shoulders as we posed on the front step, too. I couldn't recall a single thing about the actual game.

'Here we are,' Mum announced, pushing her way back into the room tray-first. As well as the teapot and mugs she had piled a plate high with biscuits: not just Blue Ribands but Viscounts too. It was a wonder she hadn't got out the best cups and saucers.

'I've not got much in,' she chattered apologetically as she set it down on the side table next to the sofa and started fussing over plates and pouring milk. 'Your dad was going to take me up to the cash and carry at the weekend but the car's playing up. We were going to have chops tonight but there won't be enough to go round. It's all right though: I've got some mince that will stretch. You are stopping, aren't you? Oh Alex, it's so good to see you.' Abruptly she burst into tears again, great heaving sobs that shuddered through her whole body.

'It's all right Mum,' I told her, taking the milk-jug from her hand and putting an arm around her shoulders. 'Come on. It's all right. I'm sorry to give you such a shock.'

'We didn't know where you were!' she wailed, all composure gone. 'We didn't have any way of getting in touch with you! We didn't know if we'd ever see you again!'

'Sshh, shh,' I said, rubbing her back as if my life depended on it, my face hot and embarrassed. 'I'm here now.' There was no reason for her to know that was only because I was finally running away from something even more frightening.

She reached a hand out to clutch my leg, her long nails digging into the denim. 'You are staying, aren't you? You aren't going to disappear again?'

I shook my head. 'No, no. I'll stay for a few days if you'll have me.'

'Of course we'll have you!' Her voice was all thick and snotty. I'd never heard her like this. 'Your dad never meant you to leave! He's never forgiven himself! We could have sorted everything out if only you hadn't run away.'

'Really?' My father had made his feelings pretty clear on the day I walked out. It had never occurred to me that they might have changed in the intervening years. 'He's said that?'

'Oh, you know what he's like.' Getting herself under control, she sat back and blew her nose. 'He doesn't like to admit when he's got things wrong.'

So he hadn't said so, then. That sounded more like him.

I pushed back into the cushions myself, increasing the space between us. 'Nothing's changed, you know. I'm still gay.'

She sniffed into her tissue, but said nothing.

'So if you've sill got a problem with that, I might as well leave now,' I warned.

'Oh, don't be so pompous, Alex' she said sternly, and I felt myself deflating. 'Honestly, you're as bad as he is. Neither of you ever change once you've set your mind to something.'

'It doesn't really work like that,' I protested.

'No? Well how does it work then? Because you never gave me the chance to ask.'

I was reddening again. That was a fair point. I'd stormed out of the house after my father had found *Against the Law* and my small collection of other gay books stashed under my mattress – he'd never usually have looked there, only the cold water tank had sprung a leak over my bed and he'd gone in to clear up the mess. The whole thing had exploded while mum was still at work, and before I knew it I'd walked out, at the time, I thought, forever.

Tucking her tissue away, Mum reached over and started to pour the tea. 'I've done my best ever since. I got some books out of the library. And I watched that *Civil Servant* thing, too.'

This was gobsmacking. 'Did you watch it with Dad?'

She was doling out sugar, and rattled the spoon angrily around the cups. 'No. I had to go over and watch it at the nurses' home with Janine and the girls.' Janine was a friend from the hospital, a bit younger than my mum. She was the first divorced person I had ever met.

'Did you like it?'

She passed me my cup, and held out the biscuits. 'It was OK. I wasn't shocked, if that's what you're thinking. Although I have to say he didn't much put me in mind of you.'

'No.' I took a Blue Riband and began to unwrap it. 'I think he's quite...an extreme case.'

She nodded, curling both hands around her own mug to bring it up to her lips. 'Have you got a boyfriend?'

I nearly choked on my biscuit. 'No.' Then I thought about it. 'Yes.'

'Good.' She nodded firmly, but didn't ask any further, which was a relief. I sipped my tea, my biscuit forgotten as I did my best to adjust to this new reality.

'So where have you been living?' she asked after a while.

'Oh, here and there,' I said vaguely, before realising this was just my stock answer and she deserved something a bit more specific. 'In London.'

She nodded. 'We thought you might be. The police said that was where most runaways go.'

'You went to the police?'

'When you were first missing. Once we realised you weren't coming back.' Her lips were tight, her emotions now held well under control.

'I'm sorry,' I muttered, staring down at the pattern on the sofa cushions.

'We went down a few times to try and look for you. In the early days. But of course London's enormous, and we didn't know where you might be, so it was a waste of time.'

I tried to picture my parents walking up and down the Dilly, searching the crowds for a familiar face, but I couldn't. The two worlds just wouldn't fit together. It was mad that I had never stopped to think of my parents worrying what had happened to me. Just as the layout of the lounge was unchanged, I'd somehow assumed that everything else would have just carried on as normal too. I'd taken my dad literally when he ranted about 'no son of mine', but I suppose actually the absence of a son might have been as difficult to live with as the presence of this particular one.

And a part of me couldn't help thinking, *serve him right*.

But my mum was correct: she had never been allowed a choice in the matter, and that was both of our faults. 'I'm sorry,' I said again.

She reached out and took my hand, squeezing it hard. 'Just, please, don't go again without telling us where you're going. Telling me. I need to know you're safe.' Now I looked at her properly, Avon might be doing their best but it wasn't fooling anyone: the lines around her eyes had thickened and multiplied, and there were deep worry lines across her forehead. That was probably down to me. I felt terrible about it. And I felt even worse for lying to her now.

'Don't worry, I'm fine. Totally safe,' I told her firmly, squeezing her hand back. 'Now, what was that about cheese on toast?'

I wasn't even that hungry, but it seemed better to keep mum busy than let the conversation drift on to more dangerous ground. We managed to witter away about nothing much all afternoon, as I helped her hang out the washing and then make a start on dinner, enthusing over the prospect of cottage pie ('It was always your favourite') and peeling the potatoes and carrots while she braised the mince. That was about the extent of my cooking ability, but it didn't stop her from raving about it. It was just one of the ways she kept over-complimenting me about how much I had grown up, while I kept steering the conversation well away from the precise nature of the adult skills I had acquired while I was away. Both of us were talking too much and saying too little, each aware of the clock steadily ticking towards quarter past five when my father, his routine honed to split-second precision over thirty years in the same job, would arrive home from work.

At least it turned out to be mum's day off before a week of night shifts, which meant there was no danger of the two of us being left alone. But I was dreading seeing him, nonetheless. My anxiety got a big boost mid-afternoon when, sent back through to the lounge to relax while Mum made another pot of tea for us both, I had picked up the newspaper on the top of the pile next to his chair, the previous day's *Sunday Express*, and found it folded open on John Junor's column. I read:

"Ms" Maureen Colquhoun seems very insistent that we should all know the revolting details of her sex life, writing in her resignation letter that she is an 'out and proud Lesbian'. Pass the sickbag, Alice! I know what the good people of Auchtermuchty will make of her claim that it makes no difference to her ability to do the job she was elected to do. They will say that those other good people of Northampton North deserve a normal woman – better yet, a normal man – to represent them, rather than some hairy-legged gender-bending women's libber whose contempt for the family is so brazen that she walked out on her own husband and children to wallow in a cesspit of her own making.'

I put it back on the pile next to his pipe, feeling rather nauseous myself.

When the kitchen clock rolled round to ten past five, mum suggested I 'go and have a stroll round the garden so I can have a chance to speak to your dad first'. I was out of the back door practically before she'd even finished speaking. She'd mentioned that he was on pills for his heart now, and remembering the colour he'd gone the last time I'd seen him, I was genuinely worried he might drop down dead if I was the first thing he saw when he walked in.

There wasn't actually much back garden to walk round – it stretched maybe twenty feet to the fence between us and the identical house on the street behind – but nevertheless I stuck my hands in my pockets to stop them shaking and paced up and down the beds of neatly planted vegetables a few times, pausing to force myself to read the block-printed plastic labels at the end of each regimented row: *RADISHES; ONIONS; POTATOES; LETTUCE (BUTTERHEAD); LETTUCE (LEAF)*. He was still growing the salad stuff, then. Every year as far back as I could remember he'd dutifully planted his seeds and battled the slugs and snails for months on end, only to push the end result aside when it got served up on his plate and complain about 'this rabbit food.'

At a quarter past five on the dot, I heard the car pull up at the front of the house, and the front door open and slam. Mum had obviously intercepted him in the hallway and taken him into the front room, because I couldn't hear any of their conversation, and I was left treading the grass at the end of the garden in the last of the sun, feeling like a trapped animal with nowhere left to run. I couldn't stop myself shaking, and it wasn't even cold.

If I'd been frightened as Tommy yesterday, it was nothing to how I felt as Alex right now. He might have proved he could face down gangs and goons and secret policemen, living on his wits and threading his way through the capital's back alleys unseen, but all his street smartness seemed to have been left behind in London. Now I was a scared teenager again, exactly the same boy as I had been four years previously, everything raw and too close to the surface. Turned out the person I had been running from all these years wasn't the angry man inside the house: it was the little boy shivering in the back garden.

The sun dipped behind the house, plunging the whole garden into shade. The strip light in the kitchen was blazing out through the slats of the blind on the window and the frosted panel in the back door. As I watched, a silhouette appeared upon it and grew taller, bigger, sharper, closer, until finally the handle clicked down and the door swung slowly open.

TWENTY-EIGHT

'Alex.'

He gave me a curt nod, which I returned slightly too promptly. He looked older, too. The Bobby Charlton comb-over was more obvious now even less of his hair remained. His moustache was flecked with white, making him look like he had just downed a glass of milk. He was wearing the thick brown and cream cardigan with the elbow patches that he kept hanging up in the hallway: every evening as soon as he stepped through the door the first thing he did was to swap it for his work jacket. As ever, he had zipped it up right to the top and kept his tie on: there was no reason to start going crazy just because work was over for the day. I, who could barely get beyond the school gates before my tie was off and stashed in my pocket, had never understood this need to stay literally buttoned-up, but the only time I had ever dared ask about it I got a half-hour lecture on army uniform drill and the fact me and my friends didn't know we were born.

Mum was hovering behind him in the doorway, urging him onwards. We both started forward at the same moment, meeting in the middle of the path between the vegetable beds, each unsure of how we were going to greet the other until he stuck out a hand which I took and shook as if I was being introduced to royalty rather than seeing my own father for the first time in four years. His grip was firm but fleeting: he obviously didn't want to maintain contact for longer than was strictly necessary.

'Alex,' he muttered again. He might actually have been introducing himself: it was his name as well as mine. Perhaps he thought I'd forgotten.

'Hello.'

'I'm glad you've come back to see us.' He didn't exactly sound it. 'Your mother's been very worried about you.'

'Yeah.' I'd already apologised to her: I was damned if I was going to apologise to him.

'Worried sick,' he emphasised, jutting his chin forward in the way he always does when he's about to lose his rag, but at that point mum jumped in and said 'Why don't we all have our tea?' and we both trooped back into the house with no blood spilt on the root veg at all.

Naturally, the return of the prodigal son wasn't allowed to interfere with dad's usual routine, and with little more than the preliminaries done – partly thanks to both of us washing our hands unusually thoroughly, grateful for the opportunity to put a locked bathroom door between us – we sat down around the kitchen table on the dot of half past. 'Alex helped me make it, he's quite the cook these days,' Mum said brightly as she ladled out the cottage pie, but this got no more from my father than a grunt and a slightly curled lip. I could have told her he would see kitchen skills as evidence of effeminacy rather than self-sufficiency, but it was nice of her to try anyway.

I might not have deserved much of the credit for it, but god, that was the best meal I had tasted in a very long time. The very first mouthful brought a rush of emotions with it: not just nostalgia for childhood meals gone by, although there is no one who can cook a cottage pie as good as my mum's, but a warm feeling of comfort and safety which flooded my stomach to force out the sick fearfulness that had taken residence there. I polished off my portion within minutes, mum happily helping me to seconds while my father was still picking out the carrots from his first and laying them on the side of his plate (he put on his reading glasses to be sure he got every last one). 'Anyone would think you hadn't eaten all the time you were away,' she commented, and beamed when I told her in return that I hadn't – 'at least nothing as good as this.' There was Cremola for afters, with tinned pears (he had his without), and then, just the same as ever, Mum started making the coffees while he stomped through to the lounge to watch the evening news.

'Go with him,' she said, as I hovered uncertainly in the kitchen, and then, when I still looked unsure, gave me an actual shove, 'Go *on*.'

I got another curt nod when I went in and settled on the sofa. He was already in his own chair, which almost seemed to mould and close in around him like a shell, waiting for the TV to warm up. It was a relief when Angela Rippon swam into view, preventing any possibility of conversation.

'The Prime Minister, Mr Harold Wilson, today ruled out calling a general election, despite the fact that the Labour party has lost its majority in the House of Commons,' she announced brightly. 'Mr Wilson said that he intends to carry on in government, and will be holding discussions with the minority parties in order to ensure that the government has the necessary parliamentary numbers to push through their programme of legislation. The unprecedented circumstances are the result of the resignation of Mrs Maureen Colquhoun as the MP for Northampton North, after she lost the support of her constituency party over allegations about her private life. Tonight we look at the prospects in this new and surprising parliamentary situation.'

And he was off. 'It's a bloody disgrace,' my father spat. 'Socialists just can't accept when they're beaten, that's the problem.' He wasn't addressing his remarks to anyone in particular – presumably he knew Angela Rippon couldn't hear him – but Mum, who was just coming into the lounge with a tray of coffee mugs, took it on herself to reply anyway.

'Would you rather he stepped aside and let that nice Mrs Thatcher be in charge, dear?' She popped the tray down and, to my surprise, aimed a big wink in my direction.

'No I would not!' my father barked. 'Although I suppose even *she* wouldn't be able to do a worse job than this shower.'

At that moment the woman herself came on the screen, announcing that the Prime Minister's 'decision is really against the nation's best interests. He's lost his majority, and when that happens, I think you really lose the authority to govern.' She was wearing a funny green blouse with a pussy-bow at the neck, and looked as if she had had her hair done specially. She put me in mind of a headmistress at a posh girls' school.

'Your dad doesn't approve of a woman being leader,' Mum said as she passed me my mug.

He grunted, shifting in his seat. 'Ridiculous. Keith Joseph should have stuck at it: I couldn't see what all the fuss was about. If you ask me the Tories started going down the drain the moment that pansy Heath sacked Enoch.' He realised too

248

late what he had said, flushed red and shot a stricken look in my direction, but, unwilling or perhaps unable to apologise, blustered on instead. 'There was a man who wasn't afraid to say it like it is.'

My mum's tone was icy. 'You'll be voting for him next time, then, will you dear?'

My father's eyes were nearly popping out of his head. 'I bloody would, if he hadn't buggered off to Ulster!'

Enoch Powell was among the few politicians I had definitely heard of, although all I could tell you was that he was a racialist. I remembered a big fuss over a speech he had given not long after I started at secondary school, and a singular lack of fuss over a nice kid in my class called Ashraf being surrounded by bullies in the playground chanting 'We're with Enoch' and calling him a Nig-Nog and a darkie. I'd wanted to intervene, but been too ineffectual a presence to do anything but run and find a teacher, who at least dispersed the crowd, although he seemed to have suddenly developed deafness as to what they were actually yelling. I did at least try to comfort Ashraf afterwards. These were the people my father was apparently lining up behind. He'd obviously got worse since I'd been away.

'I rather like her,' my mum said pointedly, as she stirred her own coffee. 'She puts me in mind of Barbara Castle.

From the armchair came an apoplectic sound like a lilo makes when you pull the stopper out. Mum didn't seem to notice quite how red her husband had gone. 'I quite like that Shirley Williams, too,' she murmured.

'*Some of us are trying to watch this,*' my father spluttered through gritted teeth, signalling the discussion was definitely over. Mum took a big sip of coffee at this point, hiding her face behind her mug, but I could have sworn she was smiling.

Later, when he was safely stowed in front of *Nationwide*

with the door closed, and me and Mum were doing the dishes together – her washing, me drying – I said to her, wonderingly: 'You were winding him up in there, weren't you?'

'Oh, he needs to be teased, sometimes.' She smiled to herself as she ran a scourer round the pie dish.

'You never used to stand up to him.'

She snorted, 'Didn't I?', and then thought for a moment as she ran the dish under the tap and then passed it across. 'No, you're probably right. I used to walk on eggshells more. Trying to keep the peace between you two, most of the time.'

'I'm sorry.' There had certainly been plenty of mealtime bust-ups in the last few years I had been living at home. I'd spent much of my time up in my room, to avoid my father's company as much as anything else. At least it meant I got plenty of reading done.

'No, you were a teenager, I understood. And you were sensitive, you take after me that way. I was always rather proud of the way you stood up to him when he…well, when he got like that.' She jerked her head towards the lounge.

'Really?' This thought stopped me in my tracks, letting a glut of foamy water run off the plate I was holding into the sleeve of my shirt. I always thought Mum had disapproved of me talking back to my father.

'Mmm.' She nodded. 'I'd have preferred it without all the shouting, don't get me wrong. But you were growing up to be your own man, and I liked seeing that.'

This cast pretty much all of my memories of home in a different light. 'I always thought you took Dad's side on everything.'

She gripped the side of the sink with Marigold-clad hands and turned an incredulous face towards me. 'Really Alex? You really thought I felt the same about the world as he does? I work

250

in a hospital, for goodness's sake! I have to actually look after some of the people he only reads about in the sodding *Express*!'

'No, I...' I tailed off. I'd never really given much thought to how Mum's work must affect her outlook on life. I'd never really been bothered with it beyond what shifts she was on, and whether it meant she'd be around to cook our tea or if I was going to be sent out for fish and chips. 'I just... there were some things you said.'

'Such as?' She returned to the washing-up, slooshing the pudding bowls around in the soapy water. Somehow it was easier to talk when we were focusing on our own tasks rather than sitting facing each other.

'Well...' I started, then stopped. Was it worth going there, when we seemed to be getting on so well? It probably wasn't. 'It doesn't matter.'

'No, go on.' She scrubbed the first bowl and passed it to me.

'Well. OK. I remember when it was on the news that it was being made legal to be gay.'

She let out a soft 'ah,' and I paused, worried I had taken us into territories that were better left out of bounds. But she rubbed a rubbery finger across her nose, sniffed, and said, 'Go on.'

'Well, I remember dad ranting and raving about it and how disgusting it was.' If I dried this bowl any harder I was going to rub the pattern right off. 'And I remember you being quite upset too.'

She nodded, head down over the sink, but didn't say anything.

'In fact,' I said carefully, my ears burning and a strange prickling at my eyes, 'you said it made you feel 'physically sick'.'

She dropped the bowl she was holding so hard that it banged on the bottom of the sink before bobbing back to the surface. 'Oh, Alex, love, do you not remember why?'

I was severely regretting going down this route now. Why couldn't I just have kept my mouth shut? 'No,' I stuttered.

'It was your dad. The way he was talking. Look, for a start, it wasn't them making being gay legal that they were talking about, at least not like that, the reporter kept going on about 'the act of buggery', and your dad was furious, not just about the law changing but them saying that word on the news too, and he started ranting about what they used to call it in the army, and he said…'

She stopped, putting her hand to her mouth. 'What?' I prompted, my voice coming out all high and trembly.

She turned to face me, heedless of the water dripping off her gloves onto the kitchen floor. 'He was calling them "shit-stabbers". He kept saying it, over and over again, and I could see how upset you were, and I had a good idea why, because believe it or not I'm not as stupid as you think and a mother always knows, and I shouted at him to stop it, and yes, I did say he was making me feel physically sick, because he sodding well was!' And, yet again that day, she burst into tears, and I would have felt guilty about it only I was crying as well, and the pair of us were making so much noise that my father actually came to the door of the lounge – no further, mind, and he only opened it part way and stood looking through the gap – and said 'Everything OK in there?', and I was about to say yes, fine, which was all he wanted to hear but before I could, my mum absolutely shrieked at him '*Go and watch your programme!*' and he shut the door again very quickly.

The bowl turned out to be chipped. I felt bad because it was one of the set that Mum and Dad got as a wedding present, but she said she really didn't care.

TWENTY-NINE

THE NEXT COUPLE of days passed in a weird, slightly dream-like way. It felt like I was living in two separate realities at the same time: simultaneously the teenager sleeping in his old room beneath his Marc Bolan posters and the grown-up visitor looking at the place with new eyes. The days were fine – I slept in in the mornings until my father was safely out of the house, which also put me in tune with Mum as she moved onto her nightshift routine, and the two of us enjoyed afternoons together doing the household chores and the shopping and getting used to each other's company again. On Wednesday we took the bus into the town centre, and she insisted on treating me to some new clothes in Littlewoods: a shirt and some new pants and socks as well. This was very welcome, because the money I'd had from Malcolm Crichton was running low now, and while I'd been able to dip back into my teenage wardrobe, most of the stuff in there didn't fit me too well any more. I seemed to have broadened across both the chest and thighs, although I had shed enough inches around the waist that I had to wear a belt if I wanted to stay decent. There was also the issue of it being all the stuff I'd actively opted not to take with me because it was too unfashionable even in 1972.

The evenings were a different matter. Mum headed off to work at five thirty, giving her just enough time to get my father's tea on the table and say hello to him before catching the bus from the end of our road. That left him and me to eat and spend the rest of our evenings in the house together. We got through the first part of the ordeal by wolfing down our food (chops on Tuesday, sausage and mash on Wednesday) at indigestion-causing speed, and the second by staying out of each other's way as much as possible. His solution to the washing-up was to dump it in the sink for Mum to deal with when she got back, exhausted, at eight o'clock the next morning, so I took over doing that, finding I could stretch it out to last a full half hour if I really put my mind to it. That still left four hours or more to fill before bedtime. He managed it by not shifting from in front of the telly – there was pro-celebrity golf on Tuesday night, so he was in his element – while I mooched around upstairs, leafing through books I hadn't thought about in years and blowing the dust off records I was both proud (*Abbey Road*, *Hunky Dory*) and slightly ashamed (Lieutenant Pigeon) to have spent my pocket money on. When Wednesday night rolled around, however, I couldn't resist *Morecambe and Wise*, and the initial awkwardness when I joined my father in the lounge soon melted away when the pair of them came on in kilts and Ernie started prancing around while Eric pretended to play the bagpipes. We were both soon laughing fit to burst. We'd always watched *Morecambe and Wise* together as a family, it was our favourite, but I hadn't seen them in years. I didn't even know they were still on telly.

'Oh, that was grand,' he said, taking off his glasses and wiping his eyes as they finally skipped off to 'Bring Me Sunshine'. 'I like the Ronnies too, but there's no one that can touch that pair.'

'It was really good,' I agreed. It had been. Seeing him relax and actually show some pleasure in anything had been good, too.

Letting out a few last chortles, he slid his glasses back on and shifted forward in his seat to reach for the button. 'Hughie Green's on the other side.'

I interrupted his movement: 'Can I just watch the headlines? Is that OK?'

He gave me a curious look, but shrugged. 'Have it your way.'

'Thanks.' The jabbing theme of the *Nine O'Clock News* was already beginning. I had a vague feeling that I ought to be keeping on top of politics ready for the conversation I was hopefully going to have with Mr Foot: I had phoned the *Private Eye* office that morning and been told he had been in and collected his post, and I should try again later in the week if I wanted to speak to him.

'Crisis talks at Number Ten continue as the Prime Minister attempts to shore up his government ahead of a possible vote of confidence in the government,' announced the frowning newsreader. 'Tonight Mr Wilson met with the Liberal leader, Mr Jeremy Thorpe, as they discussed the terms of a deal which could see him agree to lend his party's support to Labour until the end of the current parliamentary term.' My ears pricked up as the screen was filled with footage of the familiar gaunt figure loping out of the famous doorway, raising his hat to the cameras as he went. 'Although Downing Street refused to comment on the terms of any such "Lib-Lab Pact", options range from a so-called confidence and supply agreement, which would see the Liberals pledge to vote with the government on key areas such as budgetary and security issues, or a fully-fledged coalition which would see Mr Thorpe and some of his Liberal colleagues take positions in the cabinet.'

'Outrageous,' came a snort from the armchair. I was so caught up in what was going on on screen that I actually shushed him, earning me a furious glare. I didn't care.

'There has been speculation this evening that discussions have reached a sticking-point over Mr Thorpe's insistence on taking one of the great offices of state for himself. It is thought he is holding out for the position of either Foreign or Home Secretary.'

At that point they cut away to another headline about a sterling crisis, and I turned to my father in frustration. 'What does the Home Secretary do?' I'd heard the phrase before, but I wasn't quite clear what the job involved.

'Well,' he spluttered, still put out at being told to be quiet. 'It's the department in charge of law and order. The police, and courts and prisons and all that.'

'What?' I couldn't believe my ears. 'You're joking?'

He scowled. 'No.'

'Jesus!' I thumped back against the sofa cushions, flabbergasted. Thorpe in charge of the justice system. Giving orders to the police. It was just unthinkable.

'What's got into you?' My father was staring at me, befuddled.

'He can't be. He can't be put in charge of the police.'

'Why not?'

'I… he…' Unable to sit still, I sprang up and paced over to the window, then back to the hearthrug, while my father stared up at me. What the hell. If I didn't talk to someone about this, I was going to pop. I took a deep breath. 'Because he's a murderer, that's why.'

His mouth fell open. 'What the bloody hell are you on about?'

'He's killed two people. Or at least, people working for him, trying to protect him, have. I've been investigating it for weeks now.'

'*Investigating*? What are you talking about? Sit down.'

I stayed standing. 'I know how it sounds, but it's true. One of them was drowned, the other one was shot. It's all been covered up.'

He shook his head and jabbed a finger at the telly screen. 'Why would a fellow like him get himself involved with anything like that?'

'Because they were a danger to him. To his career.' In for a penny, in for a pound. 'They were men. He'd had sex with them. I know for a fact he'd had a long-standing relationship with one of them: they were boyfriends. And he was threatening to go public about it.'

Instead of the explosion I was expecting, my rather furrowed his brow, looking from me to the television set and back again. 'You...' he began saying, then stopped, rubbing a fretful finger across his moustache, which is something he always does when he's nervous. 'He – ?'

I sighed and sat back down on the sofa, my panic dissipating and being replaced by a dull, helpless feeling. 'It's true, dad. I've spoken to people who knew them. I've seen evidence.'

That was when something really unprecedented happened. My father shunted himself forward in his chair and reached out to turn the volume down. The only time I could ever remember him willingly silencing the telly before was when they announced Winston Churchill had died.

'So you're saying Thorpe is a...' I could see him searching for the right word, and failing. 'A homo?'

257

I let him off with no more than a raised eyebrow. 'Yes, Dad. Like me.'

He gave me an uncomfortable twitch of acknowledgement, without quite meeting my eye. 'And people have been done away with to hush it all up?'

'Yep.' I couldn't help feeling this was the more important revelation, but at least he'd got there in the end. 'He's got people covering up for him. People high up in the police, and maybe other politicians too.' I was thinking of poor Gwen from Wales and her meeting at the Houses of Parliament.

My father was sitting up in his armchair, rubbing his moustache so hard he was risking a bald patch. 'Typical,' he announced.

This was just as unexpected. 'What?'

'Well, they're all at it, aren't they?' He turned and began to scrabble through the pile of newspapers beside his chair. 'Looking out for each other. Doing each other favours behind the scenes.'

'What, gay people?' I said, bristling myself now.

He flapped a hand dismissively, keen for me to carry on listening. 'No, no, all of them. Liberals; socialists; communists; anarchists. "Fellow Travellers", they call them. Here, you should read this.' He extracted a paper from the pile and thrust it towards me: not the expected *Express* but one I hadn't seen before, its neat grey masthead reading *The Free Nation*.

'What is it?' I took it gingerly from his hand. A strap across the top of the page read 'Newsletter of the National Association For Freedom': then came a headline shrieking 'OUR CHARTER' over a numbered list that began '1. We have the Right to be defended against the country's enemies; 2. We have the Right to live under the Queen's peace.'

'It's a new thing, I joined it at Christmas,' my father enthused.

I'd never seen him so excited. 'Look inside,' he continued, flapping a finger and then snatching the paper back to rifle through the pages himself when I didn't move fast enough. 'Here. Look. They want us to report evidence of "*subversive elements* in local government, the education system, Whitehall and the public services." Well this is exactly the sort of thing you're talking about, isn't it?'

I looked at the box-out he was jabbing an insistent finger at. It was headed *NAFF Needs You!* I smothered a smile. 'And what exactly would they be able to do about it?'

He gestured excitedly at the paper again. 'They can expose it, can't they!'

I folded the paper back to scan the front again. Point 11 on the paper's list read 'We have the Right to Freedom from oppressive, unnecessary or confiscatory taxation,' which certainly sounded more like my father: I've never heard anyone moan so much about the taxman.

'And who are they, exactly?' I said doubtfully, flicking through the pages.

He sat up straight in his seat. 'Patriots. Old soldiers like me. Businessmen. And some politicians, too, proper Conservatives from the old days, not like the namby-pamby lot we've had lately. And them too, the McWhirters.' He indicated a photo of two familiar faces on the page I'd just turned over.

'From *Record Breakers*?' I couldn't stop a giggle from escaping.

'Well, it was both of them, until the bloody IRA blew his brother up,' he sniffed, offended. 'And *he* was trying do the job the police should be doing and bring the buggers to justice, too.'

'Right,' I said absently. I wasn't sure how I felt about being bracketed together with the editor of the *Guinness Book of Records* in a noble quest for truth. The opposite page was filled with an article about trade unionists, from which the phrases 'red wreckers' and 'Soviet stooges' stood out. The whole tone of the magazine put me in mind of the file I had peeked into at *Private Eye* the other morning.

'To be honest, I've actually already gone to the press,' I admitted reluctantly.

That shut him up. 'What? Who?'

'I went to *Private Eye*. I'm talking to one of their journalists tomorrow. Paul Foot.'

His mouth dropped open. 'Oh, no, Alex, you don't want to bother with that lot. It's a joke paper, that rag.'

'It's not,' I said defensively, though to be honest I still wasn't entirely clear as to exactly what status the magazine held. It definitely had jokes in it. I overcompensated: 'He's very interested in the story.'

'I bet he is.' My father's forehead crinkled suspiciously. 'What did you say his name was? He's not related to that commie Michael Foot is he?'

That was the Labour politician Mark was such a fan of. The coincidence of the names hadn't struck me till now. I ignored it and pressed on. 'It was them who exposed Profumo, remember?'

'Aye, and that's where the rot set in. Well, on your own head be it.' He snatched his paper back, his face reddening. 'You'll end up locked up for slander, I shouldn't wonder.'

I couldn't help laughing. 'Hang on – a second ago you were all for publishing!'

'Yes, well. It's probably all a load of nonsense in any case. London putting all sorts of ideas in your head.' He looked thoroughly embarrassed by his momentary enthusiasm. I should have remembered that the thing he hated above all was being laughed at.

'So that's it, is it?' I asked, my voice coming out more harshly than I intended. 'It only counts as truth if its coming from your side?

He brandished the paper with one hand while jabbing the other in the direction of the silent TV screen, which was showing footage of black soldiers and a map of Angola. 'Don't talk to me about sides. I tell you what, I'd trust what this lot tell me over the *Bolshevik Broadcasting Corporation* any day.'

I was about to retort, but I bit my tongue. When I spoke, it was as calmly as I could manage. 'What about those of us who are actually out there, Dad? Actually out in the real world, finding things out for ourselves?'

He was red as a beetroot now. 'Oh, give over. "Out in the real world". You want to try working for a living, son.'

It was a familiar phrase. He'd thrown it at me regularly all through my schooldays, when it made even less sense than it did now. But I noticed he couldn't say it to my face any more. Instead he was staring at the TV screen, reaching forward to change the channel and turn the volume up loud enough to drown out anything else I might want to say. He looked as if he was trying to pretend the last ten minutes of conversation had never happened. Hughie Green was back on the screen, he was safe in his armchair with its wall of newspapers around it, and everything was all right with the world.

I took a deep breath and got up from the couch, taking my time leaving the room, enjoying the discomfort it caused him. 'Night night, Dad.'

Maybe my mum had been right. Maybe I had got bigger after all.

THIRTY

'HELLO, *PRIVATE EYE*?'

'Oh hello,' I gabbled as the coin thunked through the slot and into the machine's innards. 'It's Tommy Wildeblood. I came in earlier in the week with some stuff for Paul Foot?'

'Oh yes.' It sounded like the same posh woman I had spoken to before. 'He's just come in: let me see if he's free to talk to you.' Her voice went muffled. I guessed she was cupping a hand over the receiver. '*Paul? It's that chap who came in with the stuff about Jeremy Thorpe.*'

Another faint voice, just as posh but male, came from the background. '*Oh yes! Here, I'll take it here. What was his name? Tommy?*' With a clunk he came through loud and clear. 'Tommy, hello, thanks for calling back.'

'That's fine.' I'd been trying the office number all morning, doing circuits round the block my parents lived on and back to the phone box by the recreation ground. With my father safely at work mum would probably have let me use the home phone, but I knew they tried to avoid making daytime calls, and anyway I felt better making this call in private.

'And thanks so much for dropping off that stuff for me, it was fascinating. I've already spoken to the police down on Exmoor. They were very helpful.'

I perked up. 'They were?' I'd spent the last two days, and the whole of a sleepless last night, worrying over various scenarios: that Foot wouldn't be interested in my story, or that official stonewalling would kill the whole thing as dead as poor Norman Scott and Stephen were.

'Very much so. Officially they wouldn't do anything but confirm finding the body, of course, but I spoke to one of their superintendents off the record, and he was very sore about having the case taken off his hands. He says there was absolutely no doubt that Scott was shot at close range: they were investigating it as a murder before the big boys from London moved in and froze them out. And he knew all about Scott's claims about Thorpe as well: apparently there'd been some business about an unpaid hotel bill earlier in the year and Scott blurted the whole thing out under questioning. He thought the whole thing was very fishy indeed.'

'Wow.' I didn't know what else to say: it sounded like things could not have been going better.

'Plus we've got your letter of course: there's no way Thorpe can wriggle out of that. No, I'd say we've really got the bastard this time!'

I couldn't help giggling: not only is it always funny to hear posh people swearing, it was such a huge relief that he was taking the whole thing so seriously, enthusiastically even. 'So do you think you'll be able to write a story?'

'Absolutely, definitely. I put a call in to Thorpe's office yesterday asking for a comment from him, and we've already had a letter from his solicitor hand-delivered threatening to sue – ha! ha! – so he's definitely got the wind up him.'

Foot was guffawing with surprising delight, but this sounded like a worrying development to me. 'Will that not stop you?'

'Oh no. His lawyer's Lord Goodman, this is typical of him, trying to put the frighteners on us. It never works, and he never learns.'

I felt my shoulders slump in relief. 'That's good. Because I saw on the news last night…'

He cut across me. 'Yes, yes, I know, it really couldn't be better timing. It's perfect. We won't be able to tie Thorpe directly to the murder of course, not yet, but we can at least lay out all the circumstances surrounding it and pose a few awkward questions for him. Tommy, is there any chance you could come into the office for a chat? I'm going to call those other people you mentioned down in Devon this morning, but I'd like to run through all the details with you too before I start writing it up.'

'Sure. Of course. When? Today?'

'Ah, no, I've got something on this afternoon that I can't get out of. Could you manage tomorrow? In the afternoon?'

'That's fine.' Mum was sure to lend me the money for the train fare, and I would just have to keep my head down and take my chances getting across London.

'Great. You know where we are? Of course you do. I'll see you tomorrow, then.' He rang off with another flurry of thanks, and I exited the phone box feeling happier than I had in days. I'd liked him. His enthusiasm had been infectious, as had his confidence: he really sounded like he knew what he was talking about. At last, I seemed to be getting somewhere. After all those doors shutting in my face, finally I had found someone ready and willing to stack up the dynamite that would blow them all open again.

When I got back to the house, mum was up and in the kitchen eating Shredded Wheat in her housecoat. 'There's tea in the pot.'

'Thanks.' I sat down at the table, but she stayed standing, leaning against the cabinet next to the sink. She watched me pour and add milk and sugar before speaking again.

'Did you and your dad have a row last night?'

'Oh.' I stopped with the mug half way to my mouth. 'Not a row exactly. A bit of a discussion about politics. Why, what did he say?' The pair of them crossed over briefly when she got back from her night shift and he was getting up to go to the office.

'He said he'd been awake half the night worrying about you.'

'About me?'

She clocked the surprise on my face and gave a wan smile. 'Yes. About who you'd been hanging around with in London and the silly ideas they'd been putting in your head. His words.' She raised her eyebrows towards the ceiling conspiratorially and turned to spoon her uneaten cereal into the flip-top bin.

I'd been too wired to sleep much either. At some point in the early hours, at that crazed point when you're staring into pitch blackness and everything seems out of proportion, I'd managed to convince myself I held the Fate of the Nation in my hands, pronounced in capitals like that in my head. It all seemed a bit silly in the light of day, especially after the way Foot had seemed to treat the whole thing as a tremendous bit of fun.

'Mum?'

She had her back to me as she rinsed her bowl at the sink.

'Yes love?'

I chose my words carefully. 'If you had evidence of someone committing a crime, what would you do about it?'

She was drying her hands on the tea towel. 'What sort of a

crime?'

'A serious one. Murder… say.' I added the last word when I saw the look of alarm on her face.

'Well, you'd have to go to the police, wouldn't you?' She folded the towel up neatly and hung it back over the oven door handle.

'But if the police weren't willing to investigate. Or they couldn't, for some reason.'

She looked at me curiously. 'Why would that be?'

I traced a finger around the top of my mug. 'Say they were overruled. Or they just thought that the person who had been killed wasn't worth bothering about, that he…deserved it.'

'Ah.' She looked like she had caught my drift. 'Well, I don't know. The law's meant to apply to everyone, isn't it? Equally.'

'Well, yeah, but…' I wrinkled my nose sceptically, trying to think of an acceptable example, my own experiences on the Dilly definitely not fitting the bill. 'Look at all those people that got shot in Northern Ireland on Bloody Sunday.' The row over that incident had been notable both for being one of the last I had had before leaving home, and one of the few where I remembered Mum speaking up on my side, or at least expressing doubt about my father's assertion that they were all terrorists who had it coming or they wouldn't have been out on the streets in the first place. I can't say I followed the ins and outs of the story closely, but I seemed to remember the authorities had come to pretty much the same conclusion.

'Fair point.' She pulled out a chair and sat down opposite me, pouring a second mug of tea for herself. 'Well, if it was me, I would want to see justice done. I think I would kick up a fuss about it if I could.'

This was what I wanted to hear. 'Like maybe going to the press?'

'Maybe. Yes, I think so. If that was the only way.'

'Good.' I sat back in my chair, relieved. 'Um…is there any chance I could borrow some money?'

'What for?'

'I need to buy a train ticket to London tomorrow. I have to meet someone.' She looked doubtful, so I shamelessly turned the screw. 'I suppose I could always hitch-hike…'

'No, I'll buy you a ticket.' She stood up, scraping her chair back across the kitchen floor, but paused. 'There's one condition though.'

'What?'

'It's got to be a return.' She smiled, down at me, but I could see the worry in her eyes. 'Ok? I don't want this to be the last time I see you for another four years.'

I nodded and did my best to smile back, trying not to think about what might await me in the city and horribly aware that coming back wasn't something I could necessarily guarantee. My voice caught in my throat as I said, 'It's a deal. It might not be for a few days, though.' I didn't know exactly what my movements would be after I had been in to see Foot. The safest thing would be to scurry straight back to anonymity here, but I wasn't sure I could handle any more of my dad's company on top of the suspense of waiting for the story to come out. If possible, I would like to be on the scene as soon as the next *Private Eye* was published, even though I wasn't sure exactly what was going to happen as a result.

Mum didn't say anything, just leaned forward across the table to press her lips to my head and ruffle my fringe with her fingers. Which gave me another idea.

'Could you cut my hair for me, too, Mum?'

So it was that I got on the train at Reading station at lunchtime the next day looking markedly – though not nearly as much as I would have liked – different to how I had arrived. Mum had cropped my hair so short she had stopped to ask me twice if I was sure about it. 'You're going to look like a skinhead,' she objected, but I assured her this was how everyone was wearing it in London these days: I obviously couldn't let on that it was a disguise. She was worried enough as it was, fussing over making me sandwiches for the trip and even asking me if I was sure I would be warm enough before apologising when I gave a look and reminded her I was twenty years old. It was an especially silly question given I had put on the old green parka I had used to wear to school. I still had my leather jacket with me, folded up and stashed in the bag I used to use for my PE kit along with a few other bits and pieces, but I thought it was too big a risk to go back into town in the same outfit Messrs Smith and Jones had last seen me wearing. Whereas with the parka's hood zipped right up leaving only a little fur-trimmed porthole to peep out of, there was very little chance of anyone recognising me at all.

Mum came with me to the station, claiming she had to do some shopping in the town centre anyway, but by the time she had accompanied me all the way to the platform neither of us were bothering to keep up the pretence. 'Are you sure you can afford this?' I asked her doubtfully as she counted out the cash for my fare, suddenly guilty about the money she had already spent on me.

'It's fine. I've got my own account now,' she told me as the man slid the ticket through the grille and she passed it on to me.

'Really?' Dad used to count out the housekeeping for mum every Monday morning, and give her hell if she said she needed more before the weekend.

'It's my wages, isn't it?' She pushed her purse back into the depths of her handbag as we made our way out of the ticket office and onto the platform. 'I opened an account with the

Building Society – they'll let you do it without your husband's signature – and arranged with the hospital to have my wages paid straight in.'

'Wow.' I gazed at her, impressed. 'What did Dad have to say about that?'

She shrugged. 'He doesn't like it, but he'll have to lump it.' She shot me a sly sidelong glance. 'You're not the only one allowed to stretch your wings, you know.'

My father and I had managed to avoid each other pretty effectively during my last twenty-four hours at home, helped by the fact that Thursday was Rotary night, so he had been absent for most of the evening. Learning over breakfast that I would be leaving today, he had offered another limp handshake and a surprisingly heartfelt 'Take care of yourself, son.'

'I just – I suppose I always thought of the pair of you as a unit, you know,' I said, staring across the empty rails to the opposite platform. 'That you just agreed with him on everything, and did what you were told.' I risked a cheeky glance in her direction. 'Now it turns out you've secretly been a Women's Libber all along.'

She smiled. 'I've read my Germaine Greer.'

Now I really was surprised. 'You haven't!'

'I have. Janine lent it me. I found it quite hard-going, to be honest, but I did like leaving it on the bedside table, just for the look on your dad's face.'

I let out an involuntary snort of laughter, which she joined in with. At that moment my train appeared around the bend in the track and began to pull in to the platform. 'Take care,' said Mum, hugging me so tight that she practically squeezed all the air out of me. 'I mean it. Don't do anything silly.'

I couldn't promise her that, so I just shook my head mutely and got on the train before we both dissolved into puddles.

The journey seemed even shorter going this way, the fields whizzing past and soon giving way to the factories and tower blocks of the capital's outskirts. The madness of the previous week had seemed to fade away while I had been safe back home, but as we approached the city my anxiety began to grow again, and while I knew there was no earthly reason for my pursuers to be waiting at Paddington I still tied myself in knots over the possibility. At least the light drizzle that was running down the windows of the train gave me the ideal excuse to put my hood up and draw the drawstrings tight before disembarking.

The heaving concourse meant safety in numbers too. I moved with the crowd towards the underground entrance, heading for the Bakerloo line, which would take me all the way to Oxford Circus, from where it was only a short scuttle through familiar streets to the *Private Eye* office. The flow was mostly in the other direction – people with suitcases making an early escape to the country for the weekend – but I managed to tag along in the slipstream of a big group of what looked like students, hoping I would pass as one of them if anyone did happen to be looking, all the while trying to assure myself no one possibly could. I'd got halfway across the concourse before I remembered the vast Victorian arched roof covering the whole station, and realised the only way I could make myself stand out more was if I actually opened an umbrella, so I lowered the hood and opted for just keeping my head down and hoping for the best instead. At this rate I was going to be a nervous wreck long before I got all the way to my destination. The *Evening Standard* placards standing at the entrance to the tube read 'WRITS ISSUED OVER LORD LUCAN', and I thought enviously of him as I headed for the steps: he had managed to disappear without trace, so why shouldn't I?

Then my eye jagged on something else and I stopped dead in

my tracks. A man walking behind me cannoned into my back and swore: gabbling apologies I ducked out of the flow of bodies and doubled back to where the newspaper vendor was standing, a rolled-up copy at the end of his outstretched arm as he bawled '*Stan-ad! Stan-ad!*' over the heads of the oncoming crowd.

'I'll take one, please.'

'Sixpence, guv.'

I searched my pockets for change: pulled together a handful of coppers and passed them over, my fingers scrabbling to unfold the paper before it had even left his grubby hand. I hadn't imagined it: there the words were, in a vast headline covering half of the front page:

GOLDSMITH SWEEPS *PRIVATE EYE* OFF SHELVES OVER 'LUCAN LIES'

Someone bashed heavily into my shoulder, jerking me round: I was standing right in the way of the other customers as they filed past, coins at the ready in a well-oiled routine. 'Come on mate, move along,' the paper seller snapped at me, and realising that I was behaving ridiculously for someone who was trying to blend in with the crowd, I pressed the paper to my chest, stepped back into the flow of people and let it carry me on down the steps and into the underground station.

It was only once I was safely on the right-hand side of the escalator rumbling down towards the platforms that I could read the front page properly.

James Goldsmith, the millionaire financier, announced this morning that he has issued writs against the satirical magazine Private Eye *over an article concerning the disappearance of Lord Lucan, which he says contained false and libellous statements about his own behaviour.*

Mr Goldsmith says that the magazine's article was not only inaccurate, but consisted of 'malicious libels of the most grave manner imaginable.'

He has today launched legal actions not only against Private Eye *itself, but its printers, SW Litho Limited, and thirty-seven distributors, wholesalers and newsagents concerned with the sale of the magazine, who, under English libel law, share liability for the magazine's contents. Mr Goldsmith has required the companies to sign an undertaking that they will cease dealing with* Private Eye *immediately or face further action.*

Mr David Cash, Private Eye's *managing director, this lunchtime confirmed the receipt of the writs. He said: 'We will be resisting this action using all the legal means at our disposal, but as things stand, it seems unlikely that we will be able to get our next edition out and on sale as scheduled early next week.'*

In all Mr Goldsmith had issued no fewer than 63 writs over the article by 1pm today.

What the hell? All this must have happened since I had spoken to Foot at the *Private Eye* office only yesterday, or he would surely have said something about it. It had to be just a coincidence, didn't it? Foot had said the magazine was always tangling with lawyers: maybe this was just run-of-the-mill stuff for them and I had been spectacularly unlucky with my timing. Still, *no fewer than 63 writs*. That sounded like a lot more than was normal, otherwise why would they bother to write it? And going after the printers and newsagents too. That sounded like someone who was really determined to stop people reading it.

I arrived at the platform just as a train was pulling in and, once aboard, shuffled through the paper until I found the inside page the story continued on. It was dominated by a photograph of a tall man in a suit accompanied by an almost impossibly glamorous blonde woman. The caption read *James Goldsmith with his companion Annabel Birley in the South of France*. He had an almost perfectly round bald head, and a wide mouth crammed with more teeth than seemed natural: he reminded me of nothing so much as the shark on the *Jaws* poster.

[continued from front page]

Mr Goldsmith recently replaced Jim Slater as chairman of Slater Walker Securities following the crisis which obliged the Bank of England to step in to guarantee the group's lending book in order to prevent insolvency. He also heads the multinational company Cavenham Foods, owner of brands including Bovril, Marmite and the Liptons supermarket chain.

In a statement released through his solicitors, Mr Goldsmith said: 'Private Eye has lied about me, and it has falsely accused me of criminal behaviour. I will not allow such libels to stand. For too long Private Eye *has served as a pus in the body politic. It is a mouthpiece for a conspiracy of Marxists and trendies who are poisoning the well of public truth. Tolerance of extremists who are trying to destroy our society is not a virtue. I believe that it is cowardice and treason.'*

Blimey. He sounded like he would get on well with my father. I wondered if he was a *Free Nation* subscriber too.

He pointed out that SW Litho Limited, the printing company

273

which he also today served with a libel writ, is owned by the revolutionary newspaper Socialist Worker, *edited by* Private Eye *journalist Paul Foot.*

A shiver went down my spine as I read the name. But surely it was ridiculous to think this could have anything to do with what I had been talking to Foot about? The article even said as much: it was all to do with 'an article concerning the disappearance of Lord Lucan'. That had been a massive story for months now: his murder of his children's nanny and subsequent vanishing had even percolated through to the boys on the Dilly, who had had fun speculating that one of their regular punters, a bloke they called 'Fumbly Barry' who happened to have shaved off his moustache at around the same time, was really Lucan in disguise.

No, it had to be a coincidence. I was just being paranoid. Wasn't I?

THIRTY-ONE

I TURNED BACK to the front page and scanned the article once more.

> 'As things stand, it seems unlikely that we will be able to get our next edition out and on sale as scheduled early next week.'

Coincidence or not, yet another door had slammed shut. The same thing kept happening. It was as if I was stumbling through a maze, and every time I spotted a path that might lead to freedom it was closed off, again and again, boxing me in to an ever-decreasing area, running out of ways to turn. And it wasn't just space I was running out of, but time too. The second story on the *Standard*'s front page was headed *Thorpe Holds Out for Home Office*: as if it had been put there just to mock me it detailed how a deal with the Liberal leader was expected 'early next week.'

The train came to a halt in a station and the doors rumbled open. Lost in my own thoughts, I realised too late that we were already at Oxford Circus, and had to twist and shove my way through the oncoming passengers, managing to stumble out onto the platform just as the doors were closing on my heels. I stood there, numb, as the train hissed onwards and out of sight and the crowd flowed around me towards the exits, not knowing what to do next. Should I press on to *Private Eye* in the hope there was something that could be done to salvage my story? Or just abandon it all, cross to the opposite platform and repeat my whole journey in reverse, making my way back to Reading and obscurity and an acceptance that my father was right, that this sort of thing was not for the likes of me to tackle?

No. Fuck it. So what if I was up against a millionaire as well? Could he really be any more frightening than the politicians and policemen and pimps I already knew were lined up against me? It didn't make what I was fighting for any less right. In the end they were just another bunch of bullies, like the boys tormenting Ashraf in the playground. Bullies acting out of fear. And I had proved to myself this week that I was strong enough to stand up to bullies now.

Shouldering my bag, I strode up the emptying platform. Goldsmith or no Goldsmith, I was going to keep my appointment. Foot and his colleagues sounded as if they were up for a fight: they deserved to know why they were being targeted, and they were better-placed than anyone else I could think of to help me get to the bottom of all this. Besides, I really didn't have anywhere else to go.

My resolve carried me all the way up the escalators to the surface, and only faltered a little once I was out in the open air and felt the need to hide my face inside my hood to prevent being spotted by the increasing multitude of people I was trying to avoid. I was helped by the fact that the drizzle had now deepened to pelting rain, so I hardly looked out of place. Another advantage of the downpour was that the streets were relatively empty. Even the ever-present touts had retreated inside the doorways of their strip shows for shelter, and I guessed as I passed the entrance to the public toilets at the top of Carnaby Street that they would be busy with men seeking shelter just as much as sex.

It was only as I turned the corner from Old Compton into Greek Street to be faced with a forest of umbrellas fanning out from the doorway to *Private Eye* across half of the street that my courage abandoned me, and I did a quick about-turn. I had gone no more than a few steps, however, before I forced myself to stop and duck in under the eaves of the pub across the road, the Coach and Horses, so I could at least scope out the situation. I knew better than to hang around there too long without buying a drink – the landlord's a foul-tempered old sod who's barred me more than once – but there were plenty of other people sheltering there and keeping an eye on proceedings across the way.

'What's going on?' I asked one of them, a chubby bloke who was nursing a half of lager and sucking on a cigarette.

'It's *Private Eye*. Jimmy Goldsmith's suing them,' he said, without taking his eyes off the crowd.

I glanced down and saw a wire-bound notebook sticking out of the pocket of his mackintosh. 'Are you a journalist?' I asked.

He nodded. 'We're waiting for the editor to come out, see if he'll give us a statement.'

'Right.' I looked gingerly at the mob around the office's doorway. Several of them had cameras on straps around their necks. There was even one bloke with what looked like a TV camera trained on the doorway, his companion holding a microphone on a long pole which protruded above the clustered umbrellas. I didn't fancy trying to shove my way through the mob. Ending up with my face splashed all over the evening news didn't exactly seem the best way to stay incognito.

Time for a change of plan, then. I wondered if I could phone Foot and ask him to meet me somewhere else instead? He was almost certain to say he was too busy. With all this going on, he had probably forgotten all about our appointment anyway. But it might be worth a try. Where was the nearest payphone? I squinted through the window of the pub. There was a phone on the far side of the bar, under its plastic hood, but there was someone using it just at the minute. Besides, I could see the landlord glaring balefully out from behind the bar: I would have to go past him to get to the phone and he was almost certain to shout at me that it was for customers only. I had hardly any money left, and certainly not enough to waste on a drink that I didn't even want. Better to see if any of the phone boxes on Shaftesbury Avenue were free instead.

Just as I was about to turn away from the window, a door opened in the wood-panelled wall directly next to the payphone and a man emerged from the gents. Blonde hair, lantern jaw: I recognised him straightaway as the man I had last encountered in the back yard of Mark's flat, and watched speed off down Gower Street. Mr Smith. Even worse, his eyes met mine across the pub, my horrified face perfectly framed by the circle of my hood, and I could see he recognised me, too.

Both of us stood stock-still for a second, frozen in recognition. And then it was as if the spell broke and I spun round and ran. I sprinted across the road, faintly aware of faces at the back of the crowd turning to look in my direction as I passed them, and on into Romilly Street, heedless of where I was headed, just wanting to get as much of a head start as I could before finding somewhere, anywhere to crawl in and hide. The rocket-ship spire of St Anne's Church stabbed up into the sky directly ahead of me, but it would offer me no sanctuary. What about the Golden Lion on the corner just before it? Could I run in there and throw myself on the mercy of the customers, maybe claim the men after me were queer-bashers? No: as I got closer I could see there were no lights on inside, the place was empty: I scudded to a halt and rattled the door as I reached it but it was firmly locked against me. Too late I remembered that they'd had their lunchtime licence taken away after complaints from the neighbours about 'indecent behaviour' going on on the premises, as if there was any other sort of behaviour going on anywhere else in Soho.

There was a shout and I risked a quick glance back up the street behind me: the blond man was further behind than I'd feared, not yet across Frith Street, and limping heavily, I fervently hoped thanks to the oil drum I had punted in his direction on our last encounter. But to my horror I saw that another figure had joined the chase and was coming up fast behind, heedless of the puddles and poised to overtake. It was the man with the shaved head who went by the name of Mr Jones. He must have been waiting in the huddle around the magazine's office: thank god I had not tried to push on through. Although I hadn't done much better by holding back and putting myself slap-bang in the path of his companion's piss-break.

All these thoughts went through my head in a fraction of a second: I gave the pub door one last despairing tug before hurling myself onwards round the corner and down Dean Street, heading for the roaring traffic and crowds of Shaftesbury Avenue. Ahead was Chinatown, but that was no good to me:

always cluttered with vans and great pallets of produce in the way, no one to help or even understand, alien territory in every respect. Instead I gave in to what I realised had been my homing instinct all along: I turned right and headed for the Dilly. The pavement was thronged with people, too crowded to run on: I side-stepped into the road instead, scanning for spaces in the double stream of traffic that I could swerve and skip through to get to the opposite side. My peripheral vision was hindered by the hood of the coat and I misjudged badly, feeling the onrushing blast of a vehicle before I saw it. I leapt wildly, a motorbike's wheel missing my flailing legs by inches, the screech of its brakes and the outraged yell of its rider filling my ears as he swerved, tipped and crashed to the wet tarmac behind me, his bike spinning on into the middle of the road even as I reached the far pavement and carried on running. I caught a brief glimpse of Jones on the opposite pavement before my view was blocked by a bus screaming to a halt to avoid the motorbike: hopefully that would slow him down a little. My own breath was coming in sharp rasps as I thundered on, my heavy bag thumping painfully against my side and sharp jabs of pain stabbing up through the thin soles of my plimsolls every time my feet slammed down on the pavement. I could feel the beginnings of a stitch coming on – my mum had been feeding me rather too well over the past few days – but I didn't dare slow down. I could see Anteros ahead and the illuminations tracking their endless course across the vast façade, and in my head I was scanning through all the familiar escape routes: every underground entrance; every shop where I had successfully shaken off store detectives; each alleyway, back way and closed-off corner where I had discreetly hidden away to service a punter in the past. I reckoned my best bet was to make for the closest set of steps down to the tube station, just around the corner on the Circus itself: once I was safely down in the rabbit warren I could re-surface in any one of half a dozen different places.

That was so long as I could keep up this pace. My side felt ready to split open now and my legs were like jelly. More than once as I dodged round pedestrians my swinging bag threatened to pull me right off-balance: I unlooped its strap from over my head without breaking pace and, unwilling to throw it away, clutched it close to my chest with one arm. If nothing else, it was heavy enough to swing as a weapon if – or as was starting to feel increasingly inevitable, when – they did catch up with me. Gasping for breath I rounded the corner beneath the huge Wrigleys hoarding and saw the station steps ahead of me. And there was another welcome sight there, too. A friendly face.

'Ray!' I gasped in panic. 'Help!' My voice failed me and as I came skidding to a halt all I could gasp was 'Chase…chasing me!'

A host of emotions crossed Ray's handsome black face in a matter of moments: wide-eyed shock at my sudden appearance, crinkle-browed concern at what I was saying, and then the clench-jawed decisiveness that signalled action. He reached out and grasped me by both shoulders, using the last of my forward momentum to practically lift me off the ground and swing me in behind the newspaper kiosk he was standing beside, pushing me up against its wooden wall so hard that the very last of the breath was knocked out of me. Stupefied, I watched as he knocked my bag from my hands and began to bundle me out of my coat, yanking the zip down and sliding the smooth material off my shoulders and down my arms: the crazy thought went through my head that I'd always quite fancied Ray, but this was hardly the moment. Without even looking round he barked an order – '*Simon!*' – and held the coat out at arms length to the teenager who materialised at his side.

'Put it on and *run*, boy,' he spat, and Simon, a skinny lad I'd seen around with Ray's lot before but never spoken to, instantly obeyed, slipping the coat on and whipping its hood up over his close-curled black hair in one fluid movement as he set off from a standing start to sprint across the road. The traffic lights, amazingly, were in his favour, and the pair of us watched as he pelted past Anteros with a turn of speed that was way beyond my own capabilities.

'Him a runner,' Ray nodded approvingly, one meaty hand still keeping me pressed back against the slats of the news kiosk as we watched the boy go. At that moment there was a clatter of running feet and Mr Jones shot past us, just feet away, and made straight for the crossing himself. The lights had turned amber and the traffic was beginning to pull forward again, but he hurled himself on, heedless of blaring horns, his eyes fixed on the parka-clad figure who had already cleared the traffic island and was dodging the cars on the other side, headed for Piccadilly itself.

Ray's head swung round again and he shot me a look of urgent enquiry. 'There more?'

I nodded frantically. 'One.'

'OK.' With a last shove to indicate I should stay flat against the wall, he stepped casually to the corner of the kiosk, assuming a wide-legged stance with his hands onto his hips to peacockishly block me from view. He was wearing a suit, as usual, three piece in brown nylon today, the trousers flared as wide as the lapels on the jacket. He didn't look like he had even broken a sweat.

All of us – me, Ray, his boys spread out along the railings – watched and waited, and after probably the best part of a minute, long enough for Simon to be sprinting past the front of Simpsons and Mr Jones havering at the edge of the traffic on the far side of the statue, seeking a split-second chance to follow him, Mr Smith came running past and headed after them. He was limping quite badly, his face screwed up in pain. I found this more pleasing than I can say.

As soon as he was safely across the road, Ray turned, grabbed my arm, scooped up my bag in his other hand and pulled me around the railings and down the underground steps. Still breathless, I tried to gabble my thanks, but he just gazed grimly ahead, and muttered 'you not safe yet, boy.' Although he let go his grip on me as we descended, it was only to slide his arm through mine, and for all the appearance of friendly companionship he kept it there as strong as a padlock as he marched me across the crowded concourse, his eyes flicking from side to side, scanning the mass of people who milled around us. As we approached the barriers I was about to protest that I didn't have a ticket, but Ray produced a whole bunch of them from his pocket. He keeps hold of everything for his boys while they're working the Dilly. He insists it's for safekeeping, but they pretty soon realise it's also his insurance policy.

He let go of me when we got to the escalators, but only so he could steer me briskly down the left-hand side ahead of him. His arm went back through mine as soon as we got down to platform level, and we ran the gauntlet of curious looks from tourists as he steered me all the way up to the far end where there was hardly anyone waiting.

It was only once we were finally safely on a train – sitting opposite one another as the only passengers in the very last carriage – that he finally seemed to relax, and said to me: 'Tommy, man, what the hell you been playin' at? There been people all over axing questions about you.'

THIRTY-TWO

It seemed that Mr Smith and Mr Jones had been doing the rounds of the Dilly for days now, asking both boys and punters if they knew a Thomas Wildeblood and where he might be found. Ray assured me that none of his 'family' had told them anything – 'We look after our own, Tommy', he told me, offering me a hand-clasp so heartfelt it brought a lump to my throat – but he couldn't speak for any of the other lads on the meat rack, most of whom would sell their own grandmothers for a wrap of speed or a spoonful of smack. That was why he had been so keen to ensure no one spotted the two of us together, because – and this was the point where I really got emotional – we were currently heading for his house in Brixton, where he said I was welcome to lie low for as long as I needed.

'It's too much to ask, Ray, these are dangerous people, I don't want to put your family at risk,' I protested, but he waved it away.

'We can sort sometin' out,' was all he would say on the topic.

'Did they say why they were looking for me?' I asked, once it had become clear that the subject was closed.

'Them sayin' it was you killed that boy Stephen,' he told me bluntly.

'What?' I sat back in my seat, flabbergasted, my nausea redoubling. 'That I killed him? Why?'

Ray shrugged. 'Jealousy; money; maybe just because you's a psycho-killer. Whatever the person them talking to want to hear. Them want to make sure if you seen, they get to know about it.'

I shook my head slowly. I couldn't believe it. As all the evidence had come tumbling out about Norman Scott, I had somehow allowed myself to forget about Stephen, who this had all started with. I had barely given him a thought since I had headed down to Devon. But everything I'd done, all that had happened to me, had been a result of my going against my better instincts and trying to get justice for him, to find out who was responsible for his death. And now these bastards were going around telling people – people I knew, people I had lived and worked with side by side for years – that it was me.

Ray was gazing at me with a mixture of sympathy and pity. 'What did I tell you when you came axing about him? You getting yourself into other people's trouble.'

It was true. That was exactly what he had said, right back when I had been making my very first enquiries on the Dilly. And boy, had he been right. What had I earned for trying to do the right thing? I'd lost Mark. I'd lost my independence, sent scurrying back to hide away in my childhood home. I'd lost all belief in law and order – though I'd never had much faith in that to start with – but in any kind of natural justice, too. And now they'd even taken the Dilly from me. I was never going to be able to show my face there again. I would be spending the rest of my life on the run.

At that moment it all got too much for me. Maybe it was coming down off the adrenaline of the chase, maybe it was the belated realisation that the salvation I had been hoping for through *Private Eye* had been snuffed out in turn. I leaned forward and buried my face in my hands. A series of sobs shook my body like spasms, guttural noises came from my throat that I could barely recognise, let alone control. My whole body was shuddering as I gulped involuntary mouthfuls of the dry underground air, my body taking over the most basic work of keeping me alive because my mind no longer cared. I gave myself over completely to despair.

I don't know how long I stayed like that – it might have been minutes, it could have been hours – but eventually I was recalled back into the present by Ray's touch as he cupped a hand tenderly but firmly around the back of my bowed head. 'You need to get yourself together, man,' he murmured, close to my ear. 'We nearly in Brixton, and I can't have you drawing attention.'

I sat back, rubbing my wet cheeks with the heels of my hands and sniffing, trying to will my breathing back into regularity. A tight tension headache had settled across my brow and the tops of my eyes: emotional anguish translating itself into genuine bodily pain just as effectively as my aching legs betrayed my recent physical exertions. I was like a limp rag as Ray led me off the train, trailing along behind him up the escalator and out into daylight, through the clamour and din of the market and the haze of spice and cooking smells and on up Coldharbour Lane to the house where he and his ever-evolving family lived. On the few occasions I had visited previously the three-storey terrace had been heaving with life, reeking of dope and vibrating with bone-shuddering bass beats, but now, on this rainy March afternoon, it was as silent as the grave. Nothing but the profusion of roaches piled in the ashtrays in every room to show that there had ever been anyone there.

'Lie down and get some sleep,' Ray ordered me, leading me upstairs to a bedroom and pointing at one of the three beds crammed inside. Obeying him in all things seemed much the easiest option right now, so I did as I was told and crawled in beneath the musty blankets, not even bothering to take off my clothes, and lay staring up at the cracked plasterwork on the ceiling. Ray stood for a moment looking down at me, then sucked hard on his teeth and left the room, coming back in with a couple of pills which I swallowed without question.

I don't know what they were, but they did the job. No sooner had he left the room again, telling me he had to get back to town and would see me later, than I fell into the sort of deep sleep, untroubled by dreams or external noises or worries, that I couldn't remember having in weeks. Not at Mark's, and certainly not at my parents. Probably, in fact, not since I had been kicked out of the squat and found myself forced onto Harvey's sofa. I stirred at one point, surfacing into darkness and an awareness that someone was getting into the bed with me, but his intentions were not sexual – I'm not sure I would have cared, or been in a position to do anything about it, even if they were – and I soon slumped back into oblivion. I didn't wake properly until some time the next day, and the bed was empty again. So were the other two in the room, although I had the feeling they too had been occupied at some point in the meantime. My parka was folded neatly and draped over the foot of the bed.

There was no one in the rest of the house either. When I made it as far as the kitchen the clock said it was early afternoon. I must have been unconscious for the best part of twenty-four hours.

I pottered about for a bit, exploring the other rooms, most of which featured the same cramped sleeping arrangements as the one Ray had put me in. Only the main bedroom at the front of the house had just the one bed in it, a double, which I knew from my previous visits was where Ray slept with whichever of the house's other inhabitants was currently floating his boat. When I was last here, at Christmas, it had been a slim Trinidadian called Kenneth who had dreams of being a professional disco dancer. He had displaced a guy called Lee, who was still living in the house as one of the family. I heard Lee had tried to slit his wrists not long afterwards, and although they got him an ambulance in time to save his life, he never returned from the hospital.

In the kitchen I found some bread and some cheese – French brie, with the stamp of the Fortnum and Mason food hall on it, although I'd be surprised if it had been anywhere near the shop's tills on its journey here – and a tobacco tin nearly full of some good-quality grass, which got me through the rest of the afternoon, knocking me almost immediately into the welcome state of not being able to think about anything even if I wanted to. The most activity I could manage was to leaf through the collection of LPs in the front room, looking for something that might be suitable to soundtrack my hazy state, but they were mostly Trojan records by people I'd never heard of, and the couple I managed to de-sleeve and successfully navigate on to the turntable were way too heavy for me to cope with.

Somehow they sounded more appropriate after Ray and the rest of the family returned at some point after it got dark. The rest of the evening passed in a raucous and relaxed atmosphere that I was content to observe as an outsider rather than an active participant just so long as the joints kept on rolling. I know I wound up sitting next to Simon for some of the time, and I thanked him profusely for his help the day before and heaped praise on his athletic prowess. I started to worry about what might have happened when Smith and Jones caught up with him, but he assured me they hadn't and he'd been able to double back through Green Park unscathed. I'm pretty sure I started telling him how worried I was about them catching up with him later on in the evening, too, at which point he gave me a funny look and moved to sit somewhere else. Someone cooked some food at some point, and though I wouldn't be able to tell you who or what, I definitely ate more than my fill. The ganja had made me ravenous.

After a while I realised that people were drifting off to bed, and I decided to do the same. When I managed to get upstairs there was a lad called Theo already asleep in the bed I had slept in the night before, so I went off to tell Ray this, and he said something about having to 'top and tail', which seemed fair enough since I was a guest. He gave me a couple of the pills again to help me sleep, so it really wasn't a problem.

The next morning wasn't so great. This time I woke up at the same time as everyone else, and had to sit at the kitchen table with a stinking headache and a swirling stomach watching them all get ready for a day on the Dilly in the knowledge that I was going to be stuck here alone all day, too frightened even to stick my head out of the door in case my pursuers were lurking out there. To earn my keep I tried at least to do a bit of housework, washing up the pots from the night before and clearing out all the ashtrays, but it was difficult because there was no washing-up liquid or tea towels. I switched on the radio for a while to keep me company, but the music was too jangly and relentlessly upbeat for my nerves, and when the news came on it was all about whether Harold Wilson would be able to get approval from his party for his Lib-Lab Pact and I couldn't get across the room to the off-button fast enough.

That left me in a terrible mood, so I went searching for something to settle the jitters that were threatening to overwhelm me. The grass was all gone, but I found some resin in a wooden box in the sitting room which turned out to be so strong that a couple off puffs on the resulting joint was plenty enough to blast me straight back to oblivion. I was still flat out on the sitting room floor when the rest of the family got back that evening, and when I tried to get up the room started spinning and I had to be helped, much to everyone's amusement, to the bathroom where I threw up for so long that I was bringing up nothing but bile, scalding the back of my heaving throat. When I was sure it was finally over, I stumbled straight to my bed, but I couldn't get to sleep, thanks partly to the noise from downstairs, but mostly by a vivid and never-ending replay of my pursuit down Shaftesbury Avenue which kept looping through my fevered brain every time I shut my eyes. Not long after my sleeping companion came to bed I got up and went and knocked on Ray's door, but he wouldn't give me any more of his pills, no matter how much I pleaded with him. So I stomped back to my bed and resigned myself to a night of tormented sleeplessness, only to eventually fall into a dream about Mark so intense that I actually woke up thinking that he was lying next to me, only to turn around and be faced with the swiss-cheese stink of Theo's feet on my pillow instead.

The next morning I just skulked in bed until everyone was gone, unable to face their breakfast bonhomie. I pretended to be asleep while my roommates were putting the final touches to their outfits, and kept my eyes screwed shut while I listened to the thunder of feet on the stairs and the high-spirited conversations in the hallway as everyone prepared to leave. It was only once the front door had banged safely shut that I emerged from under the blankets, swung my feet down onto the slightly sticky carpet, and prepared to face another day of doing nothing. The first of a long lifetime.

Or so I thought. It was only mid-morning when I heard a key in the lock and Ray came strolling back into the house, having safely delivered all of his charges and set out their tasks for the working day. I was sitting at the kitchen table with a mug of tea that had long since gone cold. It had turned out once I had already starting making it that there was no milk in the house, and it was undrinkable without.

'You feeling any better, boy?' Ray asked, ruffling my hair as he sat down beside me.

I pulled a face. 'Not great.'

He nodded, his face serious. 'I come back because we need to talk about how you gonna earn your keep, Tommy.'

I sat up, flustered and embarrassed. 'I'm sorry, Ray: I tried to do some housework yesterday, but if you tell me what needs doing I'll be really happy to help out. I could cook for everyone, if you like, although obviously I can't go out to the shops, so...'

He held up a hand to stop my chattering. 'No, man, I don't mean housework. We all get by here fine. I'm talking about *work* work.'

It took me a moment to realise what he meant. I'd been off the game for a good few months now, but I could hardly say it was a matter of principle. I suppose I'd always been aware it was there to fall back on, and I couldn't exactly argue that there were any other options open to me now. Thorpe and his cronies had taken everything away from me. It seemed I had no choice but to go crawling back to square one.

But there were certain practicalities involved. 'But how can

I, Ray?' My heart was beating fast, my nausea had redoubled and when I spoke my voice had a strange wheedling tone that I hardly recognised. 'You said yourself, I can't go anywhere near the Dilly while they're still after me?'

He shook his head. 'No, you can't. I'm talking about house calls.'

'Oh.' I knew a few rent boys who saw regular clients in their own homes, and usually got paid pretty well for it. Myself, I'd always taken my chances with whoever turned up on the 'Dilly, and it had always – mostly – worked out all right for me. But even if I was going to start up such an operation, I'd surely have to advertise my services somehow, which was the last thing I could do in my current situation. 'How would I…?'

Ray grinned. 'I got just the man. You gonna like him. I send him round a boy every Monday, regular as clockwork, and all he want to do is suck him.'

I was surprised. 'Suck *him*?'

His delighted grin widened. 'Yep! He convinced the sperm of a strong young boy just what he need to keep him young. He thinks it's like the *elixir of life*.' He leaned forward and slapped me on the knee. 'He got a particular thing about African sperm, but I think he make an exception for you. More you can pump out the better. And all you got to do is lie back and think of England!'

'That's all?' Surely there had to be a twist. It was usually the punters who claimed they were only after a bit of a cuddle who turned out to be into the roughest stuff of all.

'Him the perfect client!' Ray slapped my leg again. 'Ease you back in gently, eh?'

'Right.' I smiled weakly. 'Where does he live?'

'In that new place in the City. The Barbican.' The name sounded particularly spectacular in Ray's Jamaican accent. 'He living up in the *sky*.'

I hadn't been to the Barbican before, but I knew vaguely where it was, and it was a long way from Brixton. 'What if someone sees me on the way there?' I asked doubtfully.

'That's the best bit. He pay for a *car*. You travel in the lap of luxury, you get blown, you brought back. All arranged. And when you get back, nothing to do but relax. Maybe I even let you have some of them pills so you can get a good night's sleep. Eh? Don't Ray look after you?'

I nodded. 'You do. Thanks, Ray.' I could hardly say anything else.

He gave me a curt nod. 'Don't mention it. Now go get cleaned up. You look like shit, and you leaving in half an hour.'

THIRTY-THREE

THE BARBICAN was like nowhere else I had ever seen. The place was just an emptiness of underpasses at ground level, but when I entered a lift opening directly on to the pavement and travelled up one floor I emerged into a whole new world. Nothing was where you expected it: the buildings seemed to extend up, down and in every other direction at once. One of the hippies back at the squat had decked the place out with a bunch of posters by a guy called Escher, and this place looked like them impossibly rendered into real life. There were concrete staircases and walkways everywhere, slicing in hard geometric lines across the fronts of buildings to which they weren't necessarily connected. Sometimes they opened out into wide, paved courtyards filled with trees and plants, apparently unconcerned to find themselves growing several storeys above ground level rather than out of it. There was even what looked like a school playground high on the roof of one block – thankfully it had a fence around it – and at one point I turned a grey concrete corner to find myself standing in front of a traditional old-fashioned church which looked like it had time-travelled into the middle of some alien planet. Three great towers loomed high over it all, their silhouettes jagged with zig-zag balconies. Other lower blocks were topped off with equally unexpected shapes: arches, hoops and semi-circles, as if the whole thing had been piled up by a giant kid desperate to use up every shape in his set of building blocks. It looked like he had run out, too: the place was only half-finished. You would turn a corner – there were so many corners – and find your way blocked by construction hoardings, paved walkways giving out to a mess of raw concrete spiked with metal rods, excavators and cement lorries roaring beneath the skeletal arms of cranes swinging to and fro.

The strangeness of it all was increased by the fact that other than the builders, there seemed to be no one there. My footsteps echoed back at me from far-off walls as I schlepped along endless walkways searching for any clue that might lead me towards the address Ray had written down for me. After a while I managed to locate the block I was looking for, Mountjoy House, but just as I thought I was finally approaching it the walkway I was on took a sharp right turn and carried me off in another direction entirely.

Finally I found a ramp which promised to deliver me to both Mountjoy and Thomas More House, and eventually I made it to the sixth floor of the former, where I rang the bell on one of a dozen identical doors, hoping desperately that my very average cock would not prove a disappointment after all the time I had kept my client waiting. But I needn't have worried: the old man who opened the door looked delighted to see me, spreading his arms wide and declaiming fruitily: 'Welcome to Sodomite's Walk!'

'Come again?'

'It was the Tudor name for the area we are standing on, or rather many yards above,' he explained. 'Come in, come in, do.'

'Are you Mr Richmond?' I checked before committing to crossing the threshold.

'Mm? Quite so, quite so.' He looked to be in his 70s, although if his self-prescribed diet was doing the job I supposed he might have been decades older. He was wearing a silk dressing gown with a Japanese design on it, underneath which he appeared to be fully and quite smartly dressed. There was something familiar about him, although I couldn't put my finger on it. I'd probably just seen him on the prowl round the Dilly. Hell, I might have had sex with him for all I knew: there had been so many punters I couldn't remember most of them. Although I think his particular proclivity might have stuck in my mind.

'I'm Tommy,' I told him as I stepped into a hallway that was crowded with as many framed artworks as Malcolm Crichton's. I wondered if the two of them knew each other. It wouldn't do to ask, obviously. On second glance their tastes seemed quite different: Mr Richmond went more for brightly-coloured abstracts or what looked like political cartoons, although I didn't recognise any of the people in them.

'Delighted to meet you, Tommy,' he told me as he ushered me into the sitting room. 'Did, ah, Ray explain what I require?'

I was about to say yes, but the view in front of me prevented me saying anything but 'wow!' Most of the long wall of the sitting room was glass, and from up here you could see what looked like the whole of London laid out beneath you: the great dome of St Paul's in the foreground just a few streets away, and beyond it a great profusion of buildings both ancient and modern all jumbled in together, all the way to where I could faintly make out at least two of the chimneys of Battersea Power Station in the distance. I could see Centre Point, too, stabbing up into the sky to the west like a reflection of the Barbican's own towers, the closest of which filled the entire right hand side of the window. Even when I walked right over and pressed my face up against the glass I couldn't see all the way to the top.

'It *is* rather impressive, isn't it,' said Mr Richmond modestly, as if he was actually responsible. 'Perhaps you'd like to enjoy the view whilst I…?'

He gestured towards the antique sofa that ran along the opposite side of the room, and I recalled my reason for being there. 'Yes, of course. Sorry.' I walked over, undoing my belt.

'All the way down, if you wouldn't mind,' he murmured, and I shucked my jeans and underpants – one of the new pairs my mum had bought me, which thank goodness had still been clean in my bag – down to my ankles before making myself comfortable among the cushions. Mr Richmond lowered himself with some difficulty down to his knees on the carpet in front of me, and with an appreciative grunt went to work.

Well, he knew what he was doing, I'll say that much. It felt as if he'd had plenty of practice. Although I couldn't have fancied him less – he was at least four decades above my preferred age range – I quickly responded to his touch and was soon peppering the sound effects I always put on for clients with some genuine involuntary gasps of pleasure. He was making plenty of noise himself, too, going at it like a starving man at an all-you-can-eat buffet, and it was only the slightly revolting sight of his bald head with its border of waved grey bobbing up and down in my lap that prevented me from giving myself over entirely to the experience. I tried to look past it and lose myself in the epic view beyond, but my eyes kept going back to the egg-like dome. Where had I seen him before? It was bugging me now. The answer seemed to be dancing just on the edge of my blunted consciousness, taunting me with a sense that it was somehow significant. Then a hand worked its way up to gently squeeze and play with my balls, just – how did he know? – the way I like it, and all thoughts of everything else dissolved from my head as I threw my head back over the back of the sofa and gave myself over completely to an approaching orgasm.

'I'm going to – I'm going to –', I felt I had to warn him, but rather than pull away he pushed himself chokingly forward and the room swam around me and vanished completely and right at that moment I somehow remembered.

'P – P – *Private Eye*!' I gasped noisily, spasming forward and clutching blindly at the cushions, my fingers digging deep into their embroidered covers.

'Did you say something?' asked Mr Richmond some moments later as he disengaged, drawing a handkerchief from the pocket of his dressing gown and pressing it to his full lips.

'Sorry.' I was suddenly acutely conscious of the ridiculousness of my position. I had never shouted *that* during sex before. 'It's just – I don't want to be rude, but didn't I see you at the *Private Eye* office the other day?' I had suddenly recalled exactly where I had seen that bald dome before: bobbing up the staircase towards me as I was about to leave. The posh woman had greeted him with all the enthusiasm she hadn't bothered to display for me, talking about – what was it? – crosswords.

He gave a modest little cough, and offered the handkerchief to me to clean myself up. I noticed that it had a monogram stitched into one corner: an elaborate *T* and *D*, neither of which, it struck me, stands for Richmond.

'That's…possible.' He pushed himself back on his haunches and reached for the coffee table behind him to help himself up.

'Here, let me.' I stood, my trousers still round my ankles, and hooked my hands under his shoulder to help him rise.

'Very kind, thank you.' Once up, he brushed down the knees of his trousers before sinking back into a leather club chair with an audible gasp of relief. 'Do…you frequent their offices?'

'Oh, no.' I bent over and pulled my own trousers up. The buttons were as fiddly as ever. 'I just went in with a story for them. Do you work there?'

He smiled, as if at some private joke. 'I'm an occasional contributor.'

At this point I really should have been heading out of the door – Ray told me Mr Richmond had paid upfront, and the first rule of rent is you don't hang around once the business is finished – but I found myself sitting back down on the sofa instead. Ray would probably be angry if I was late back, but we could cross that bridge when we came to it.

'Do you know Paul Foot?'

His bushy eyebrows shot up, and he looked at me with new, or at least a different interest. 'Yes, the whole Foot family are great friends of mine. Is Paul a friend of yours?'

I shook my head. 'No. I just talked to him about…well, this story I was trying to get out.' The black mood that had been lowering over me for days began to close in again. 'Only it doesn't look like he'll be able to do anything now. You know, with the court case.'

He nodded solemnly. 'Of course. Dreadful business. If Jimmy Goldsmith wants to dictate what is written about him, he should at least have the decency to do it the traditional British way and buy a newspaper of his own. There is no more humbug spoken on any subject in this country than there is about freedom of the press.'

I opened my mouth to agree, but found my voice catching in

my throat. Maybe it was the feeling that I had nothing more to lose, maybe it was just the atmosphere of post-coital intimacy, but I suddenly felt the urge to unburden myself to this relative stranger.

'I…I think it's all my fault.' I stared down at my shoes, trying to hold myself together. I'd done nothing but brood over it for the last couple of weed-wired days, and by now I was fully convinced that everything must be connected.

'How so?'

'This Goldsmith man, and a lot of other powerful people, are trying to cover up something that happened. Something awful.'

'And what's that?'

I risked a look up at the old man. He had perked up, sitting forward eagerly in his chair, his eyes gleaming. Maybe he was right about the invigorating qualities of young semen. Or perhaps the only thing he liked ingesting more was some good gossip.

I told him the whole thing. More than I had put in my letter at *Private Eye*, more even than I had admitted to Mark when I still – god I missed him – had him around to help me make sense of it all. I started with Stephen, making up for my neglect of that side of the story, telling him all about Malcolm Crichton coming to me for help and my subsequent discoveries from Shirley and at the police station. I told him about Peter's revelation, being careful to get the details right of what exactly he had told about Stephen's blackmail plot rather than fill in the gaps myself – an important politician, always on TV, who would want to 'pay up unless he wanted to find out just how liberal his voters really are.' I went through what I had learned from Clarrie about Jeremy Thorpe – he didn't look surprised at that, just pursed his lips and nodded wisely – and the whole story of my search for Norman Scott. I detailed what I had learned in my phone call to Wales, about the woman who had travelled to Westminster to raise the issue with 'someone high up in the Liberal party', and been found dead not long after. And I told him about the letter and the photo which Mrs Friendship had given to me, and which I had passed on to Foot, and what he had found out from the police superintendent down in Devon, too. And I repeated what Jethro Morgan had told me about finding Scott's body. *Whoever put a bullet in him must have had the gun right up against his head. It weren't no accident, it were an execution.*

He looked at me with grave, dark eyes. 'And you think that Goldsmith is suing *Private Eye* to prevent the story coming out?'

'He has to be.' I explained about Smith and Jones turning up at Mark's flat, and then at the *Private Eye* office on the very day the writs were served. 'That can't be coincidence.'

'It would seem not.' The old man steepled his fingers and pressed them to his lips. I had been talking for the best part of an hour now, all thoughts of Ray and everything else forgotten. It felt so good to unburden myself, to tell all this to someone who took it seriously, didn't tell me, as I'd been telling myself for so long, that I must be mad, that this wasn't the sort of thing that could really happen, not in this country, not these days. I hadn't had that since Mark...since Mark.

'You do believe me, don't you?' I asked after the silence between us had stretched to an uncomfortable length.

'I have no reason not to.' Mr Richmond tapped his fingers against his lips. 'I've had occasion to warn Jeremy of the need for discretion in the past, but I never thought he would resort to such... extreme measures.'

I was shocked. 'You know him?'

'In passing. Not intimately.' The old man dropped his hands to the arms of the chair and levered himself up and out of it with some effort. 'You'll permit me to telephone Paul to, ah, hear his side of things?'

'Of course.' I stood up, but he waved me back into my seat. 'No please, make yourself comfortable. The telephone is in the other room. It's rather cramped.'

I was pretty sure he just didn't want me to overhear the call, but that was fair enough. The man didn't know me from Adam; to him I was just another rent boy with a sob story, albeit one that was definitely not along the usual lines. I was lucky he was the type to listen. Most punters would have kicked me out long before.

He shuffled out into the hallway, and I heard the sound of a nearby door opening and closing. A few seconds later came the sound of his voice, too indistinct to make out what he was saying, but obviously speaking on the phone. A sudden fear overtook me – could I have stumbled into yet another trap? Mr Richmond had admitted he knew Thorpe: was he even at this moment phoning the man himself to grass me up?

Panicking, I tiptoed to the sitting room door, which he had left ajar. Although the door of the next door room was firmly closed, I could hear his voice more clearly from here. *And he tells me you spoke to the police in Devon yourself?* It sounded like it was Foot he was talking to after all.

I realised I'd been holding my breath, and I let it out in a sigh of relief as I drew back into the sitting room. I could feel my heart beating ten to the dozen in my chest. It was hardly surprising I was getting paranoid, given everything that had happened to me in recent weeks – not to mention the massive amounts of cannabis I had been consuming over the past few days. That would have to be knocked on the head, I told myself sternly. I needed my wits about me if I was going to rescue myself from this whole wretched situation. And for the first time since in what felt like a long time – certainly since I learned fingers were being pointed at me for Stephen's murder – I felt maybe somehow I could. Laying the whole thing out loud for the first time, and having someone listen and treat it seriously, had helped reaffirm the righteousness of my cause. And surely fate wouldn't have dropped me into Mr Richmond's lap – or to be strictly anatomically accurate, him into mine – unless he was meant to help me in some way?

The phone conversation was still going on next door. To try to calm myself down as I waited I strolled over to the floor-to-ceiling bookshelves that lined the back wall behind the sofa, and scanned the leatherbound spines displayed there. One whole shelf was filled with identical volumes in red leather, *TRIBUNE* picked out in gold leaf on each of their spines along with a date: the latest was just last year, 1975, but they stretched all the way back to 1937 at the far end. There were a lot of books about church history, and loads about politics, too, by people whose names sounded faintly familiar – George Lansbury, Emmanuel Shinwell, Aneurin Bevan. I pulled the last one – *In Place of Fear* – out to look at it. On the flyleaf in spidery handwriting was written 'To Tom, in solidarity, Nye'. Did Mr Richmond and I share a first name? I peered inside a few more books to check. Yes, here was one, *The Book of the Law* inscribed 'To True Thomas of the Eildon Hills with all best wishes from Boleskine and Abertarff,' whoever they might be. It was a handsome volume, the cover decorated with Egyptian hieroglyphs. I bet you could get a fortune for it on Charing Cross Road.

Ashamed of my unworthy thought, I slid the book back into its place and stepped quickly away from the bookshelf. As I did so I bumped into the edge of a small fold-out writing desk beside it, and disturbed a pile of envelopes on its leather-topped flap. I didn't really mean to read the names on the front, but I couldn't help seeing them as I reached out to prevent them cascading on to the floor. The top one was addressed to *Lord Bradwell*, the second to *Tom Driberg*, both at the Barbican address. Like me, it seemed Mr Richmond was a man who went by more than one name.

I heard a door click open and twisted away from the desk, pretending to be admiring the view from the window as my new confidant came shuffling back into the room. 'Well,' he said, easing himself back down into his armchair. 'Paul confirmed everything you told me, though he's as bemused as I am as to what the connection between Thorpe and James Goldsmith might be. We both thought of him as a Tory, if he was anything, although Paul tells me he has heard rumours that he has been making social calls on some of the, shall we say, more amenable figures at the top of my own party of late. But Paul does agree that the timing of the action seems most suspicious.'

'So what can we do?' I asked helplessly.

'Well, there is only one thing to do,' the old man said. 'We must tell the Prime Minister.'

THIRTY-FOUR

'YOU'RE JOKING!' I sank back down onto the sofa.

He regarded me gravely. 'On the contrary. If Harold is about to tie the government of this country to Jeremy Thorpe's party, he deserves at least to be apprised of the truth about the man.'

I couldn't argue with that: I'd been saying as much, although in not quite such impressive words, for days now.

'But how can we get a message to him?'

The old man gave a modest cough. 'I still retain some influence in the Labour party, I hope.'

I looked at him, then at the bookshelf, and back again. 'You're a politician?'

'For my sins. I was a Labour MP until two years ago; now I sit on their benches in the Lords. I even served as chairman of the party for a while, although,' – he looked down bashfully – 'that would be long before you were born.'

'Oh.' I shook his hand, dumbly, unsure what to say. 'Gosh.' I really did seem to have landed on my feet: Ray might have thought he was making a simple business transaction this morning but he couldn't have played matchmaker more effectively if he'd tried.

'You'll forgive my subterfuge, I hope,' Driberg continued. 'There have been some recent incidents with my young visitors, ah, purloining items once they realise that I have some small reputation in the outside world.'

'Of course.' I thought guiltily of my own covetousness at the bookshelf.

'Harold and I are not on the best of terms, but there are certain…intermediaries who I believe could persuade him to take a call from me in the circumstances,' Driberg continued, dropping my hand and shifting to the front of his chair in preparation to rise. He winced as he got to his feet, and I jumped up to help him. 'Most kind. Perhaps you would…?' He gestured to the doorway, and I let him lean on my arm as we went out through the hallway together and into the room where the telephone was. It turned out to be his bedroom. A vast unmade bed filled most of the room: once I had manoeuvred him into the only chair, next to the small table with the phone on, I had to perch on the edge of it in preference to looming over him as he consulted a small black address book and dialled the number he located in it.

'George? It's Tom Driberg. Are you well?'

It didn't sound as if the man at the other end was very pleased to hear from him. I couldn't hear his half of the conversation, but Driberg sounded rather testy as he said 'No, no, not Northern Ireland, I don't want to discuss that now. In any case the motion has already been listed, it's far too late to withdraw it… Well, perhaps he deserves to be embarrassed. George, if you would shut up and permit me to speak for a moment, I'm calling to save him from a much greater embarrassment.'

I sat there amongst the rumpled bedclothes as he sketched out the basics of what I had told him, impressed by the economy with which he boiled down the details of my long and complicated tale into something more vivid and urgent. The man at the other end interrupted a couple of times early on – he wanted to know my full name, which I supplied and Driberg passed on, and whether I was still with him – but as the story went on he fell silent and let the story flow. By the end of it he even seemed to need nudging to speak. 'So you see, Harold must at all costs not sign this ridiculous, shabby little deal,' Driberg prompted. 'It could bring no end of disaster down on the government.'

He listened for a moment, then consulted his watch. 'Well, I did have a dinner engagement, but under the circumstances… Yes, I would imagine so. Yes. Well, I'll wait to hear from you.'

'Well?' I prompted as he replaced the receiver in its cradle.

'That was George Wigg.' He pulled a face. 'Lord Wigg, if you'd prefer. Not my favourite fellow, but he is one of the most effective drains that flow into Downing Street, as well as carrying the effluent out again. He saw the seriousness of the situation at once, and promised to get a message to the Prime Minister.'

'That's great!' I was beaming from ear to ear. The relief and happiness were almost unbearable. Talk about taking it right to the top. 'So what happens next?'

Driberg nodded at the phone. 'We wait to hear back.' He turned in his chair to face me. 'Since we have some time to while away, I wonder if I might be permitted…?' His gleaming eyes slid down from my face all the way to my crotch.

'Oh! Yes, of course.' The old goat was insatiable. I stood up and undid my trousers. In the circumstances, it seemed like the least I could do.

Wigg phoned back about fifteen minutes later. Any earlier and things might have got very awkward indeed: as it was, Driberg took the call on his knees while wiping his mouth with another monogrammed handkerchief (it turned out he kept a supply of them in a drawer in the bedside table). I'd been worried about sustaining a repeat performance so soon, but Driberg was such an expert operator that he managed to coax a second helping out of me, even if it was more of a light snack than the hearty pudding he might have preferred.

'They're sending a car for us,' he told me as I replaced the receiver for him and helped him up to his feet.

'Us? Me too?'

'The Prime Minister is apparently very keen to hear your experiences first-hand.'

'Blimey.' I couldn't believe it. This day just kept on getting weirder: I had started out on a bummer in Brixton and it looked like I would be ending it with a personal audience in Downing Street. I looked down at my outfit – jeans, red t-shirt, leather jacket retrieved from my old PE bag – and sent another brief mental note of thanks in the direction of my mum for ensuring I was wearing clean underwear.

Driberg smartened up too, swapping the dressing gown for a double-breasted blue blazer with gold buttons, but I was surprised to notice he didn't bother to brush his teeth. He locked up the flat and together we took a lift down to street level, emerging somewhere completely different to where I had gone in. We made our way over to a low wall where Driberg could sit while we waited, and watched a neat line of businessmen in suits by the bus stop on the opposite side of the road. It had dwindled away and replenished itself three times before a sleek black car with *Princess* picked out in silver letters across its front grille pulled up at the kerb on our side. My companion hauled himself upright with a grunt as the suited driver jumped out and came round to open the back door for us.

'I could get used to this,' I joked as we watched Driberg clamber awkwardly in.

'It's actually just that the handles can be a bit awkward,' the driver said with a wink. 'And best leave the windows alone, if you wouldn't mind, the whole pane fell out the other day and the Minister for Trade nearly froze to death.' It was hard to tell if he was joking or not.

Driberg at least looked as if he was travelling in the manner to which he was accustomed, settling back into the black leather interior and gazing impassively out at the city streets as they slid past. For my part, I felt as nervous as I could ever remember. My armpits were prickling and I could feel sweat running down inside my leather jacket. I slipped a hand into its pocket to wrap my fingers around *Against The Law*: its comforting presence helped calm me. Come to think of it, it had been Harold Wilson's government who had changed the law back in '67 to make people like me legal (well, not exactly like me: I still had a few months to go before the state would be ready to acknowledge my right to exist). Rather than reassuring me, the thought just ramped up my terror. I had still been a kid then. Wilson was a figure who had been around for literally as long as I could remember, the most important man in the country, someone who belonged in news bulletins and history books, not in my real life. How the hell was I supposed to conduct myself in his presence?

It was only my absolute determination to get the truth out that stopped me from opening the car door and making a run for it as we slowed at every junction. Well, that and those dodgy handles. I had come this far, and been thwarted every time I had tried to get my story out. If I had the chance to take it all the way to the top – to the one man who couldn't be overruled, or denied his say – then I had an absolute duty to do so. For Stephen. For Gwen. For Norman. And for Mark.

If only he could see me now, I thought. Me, who had been so innocent and clueless about politics only a couple of weeks ago that he had needed the basics of parliament explained using beermats. Me, on my way to see the Prime Minister in person and tell him to his face what was really going on beneath the surface of his country. What powerful people thought they could get away with. God, I would have given anything to have Mark by my side right now.

Beside me, Driberg was stirring uncomfortably, looking round at the dual carriageway we had pulled out onto. 'Where are you taking us?' he enquired sharply.

'I've been told to drop you off at her ladyship's place,' the driver said over his shoulder.

'Eeurgh.' Driberg didn't sound pleased at the prospect.

'Are we not going to Downing Street?' I asked as I recognised the front of King's Cross going by on our right.

'Apparently not. I suspect Harold wants to keep us well out of public view.' He pursed his lips and stared determinedly out towards the turrets of St Pancras.

'Right.' He didn't seem in the mood to chat, so I didn't ask who 'her ladyship' might refer to. We sat in silence as the car took us down through the Euston underpass and on past Madame Tussauds and the Planetarium before turning left into the maze of streets around Marylebone. Finally, when my sense of direction was totally shot, we pulled up next to a panda car which was parked across the entrance to a sidestreet. The policeman in the driving seat raised a hand in recognition of our own driver and drew forward so that we could turn in, and we trundled slowly down what I was surprised to see was a cobbled alley lined mostly with garages. They were evidently attached to the tall houses on the streets on either side, and I guessed they had originally been stable-blocks: we were in a very posh area. As we got to the end of the mews, however, there were a couple of buildings that had been converted into houses, and it was one of these that we drew up in front of. Its front door was flanked by carriage lamps and its large windows criss-crossed with metal security shutters.

'There you go. And that's me done for the weekend – you'll be making your own way back, I'm afraid gents,' said the driver brightly as he came round to open the doors for us. Driberg ignored him, marching up to the building's front door to rap on it, but I thanked the driver profusely enough for both of us and got a nice smile in return before he drove off. I only hoped you weren't supposed to tip.

The door was opened by a woman with a sharp, pinched face and a coiffed helmet of bright blonde hair. 'Oh, it's you,' she said without enthusiasm. Driberg didn't look any more pleased to see her than she was to see him, pushing past her into the hallway without waiting to be invited.

'Hello, I'm Tommy,' I said as I stepped over the threshold, offering my hand and my most winning smile.

'Yes,' she said, without responding to either. 'Wipe your feet please.' She was wearing a tight, cream cardigan, buttoned all the way up to her throat. A gold pendant hung from a chain round her neck, which she clutched at as I passed, turning it anxiously over and over in her fingers.

Driberg was standing impatiently at the foot of the staircase, glowering in every direction but hers. 'He wants to see you first,' she told him, and held out a hand towards one of two doors at the back of the hall before turning back to look doubtfully at me. 'And you'd better – well, perhaps you wouldn't mind just waiting here? Oh!' The last was directed at Driberg's back as he disappeared through the door and shut it firmly behind him. A look of cold fury passed across her face.

'That's fine. Don't worry about me,' I said brightly. The hallway was pleasant enough: a fanlight above the front door let in plenty of the late afternoon sunlight, there were fresh daffodils in a vase on a side-table, and the stairs were fitted with the same thick cream carpet as the floor, which would mean they were perfectly comfy to sit on. But the woman wasn't interested in my comfort. She barely glanced in my direction as she marched determinedly after Driberg, throwing the door wide open in a pointed attempt to make an entrance. I caught a brief glimpse of two other suited men in there as well as Driberg – I didn't recognise either of them as the Prime Minister, but I guess he doesn't go anywhere without advisers and staff with him – before the door was firmly closed again. If the atmosphere inside the room was half as awkward as it had been out here, I was quite glad to be left on this side of it.

I sank down on to the stairs, all my nerves flooding back now I was alone. The gravity of what I was about to do all but overwhelmed me: any minute know I was going to stand in front of the Prime Minister of the country and accuse the leader of one of the other political parties of having people killed to protect his own reputation. I was going to say that a major-league businessman was in on the whole thing, and that parts of the police force were, if not actively helping to cover it all up, perfectly happy to turn a blind eye to corruption and murder. This was so far out of my comfort zone it was barely even on the same planet. But it was too late to back out now. Driberg was already in there, laying out the basics of my story: all I had to

312

do was follow him and answer any questions Mr Wilson might have for me. I just had to tell the truth. And somehow find the courage to do so.

I closed my eyes, forcing myself to take some of those deep tantric breaths I had been taught back at the squat. I could do this. Breathe in. Breathe out. Breathe in. Breathe out. I could do this. I can do this. I was ready.

Behind me the door clicked open and a voice said 'Would you like to come in now?'

THIRTY-FIVE

I STOOD UP. Driberg was coming out of the doorway, along with another old man, one of the ones I'd caught a glimpse of. His face was heavily lined, but his back was ramrod-straight: he held himself like a man much younger. 'Come on, Tom,' he was saying as he ushered him on up the hallway. 'Let's see if we can find you a taxi. Can't have you missing that dinner reservation.' I stepped back onto the foot of the stairs to let them past, Driberg giving a nod and an encouraging smile as he passed. The stranger – George Wigg I presumed – had his hand pressed into the small of his back. As they approached the front door the low sun coming through the fanlight caught both of them, highlighting the taller man's most striking feature: a pair of ears so large and prominent that the sun shone right through them, making them glow pink.

I nearly said something – I don't know what, a word of

warning maybe, or an urgent request for a quick word with Driberg in private before I went in, or perhaps both those ideas only occurred to me long after the moment had passed – but somehow I was too intimidated by the circumstances to open my mouth at all. I just watched them walk down the hallway, open the front door and leave. And then, as the woman came to the door to repeat my summons more impatiently – '*He's ready for you*' – I turned and went into the room at the back of the house.

Harold Wilson was smaller than I expected. That's what everyone always says about famous people, isn't it? He was, though. He was sitting in a big leather wing-back chair, and he seemed somehow to have slumped in on himself, chin into chest, chest onto stomach, shoulders drooping as if he no longer had the strength to hold their burden up. He looked like a toad squatting there looking up at me with hooded eyes. But somehow he was also exactly like he was on the telly: same wide face, great oblong forehead stretching between the dark eyebrows and swept-back grey hair. The only difference was that the great plumes of smoke that hung throughout the room like fog were coming from a fat cigar rather than the pipe I expected. He had to clamp it in his mouth to reach out and shake hands, because he was holding a brandy balloon in his other hand: a decanter, half-empty, sat on the table in front of him.

'It's a great honour, sir,' I stuttered as I clasped his hand, which felt limp and surprisingly cold. I didn't know what else to say.

'How d'ye do.' That flat Yorkshire accent too, so familiar from the news. He pulled the cigar from his mouth and waved it towards the back of the room, which was laid out as an office, in the direction of a man in glasses who was carefully wiping another brandy balloon out with a handkerchief. 'This is Joe

Stone, my doctor.'

I nodded at the man, who looked about the same age as Driberg and Wigg: this was a geriatric's convention. Still, if the Prime Minister wanted a pensioner as his physician, I guessed he was allowed. Now that he mentioned it he didn't look well: he had a sickly pallor, like a man who had been cooped up indoors for weeks without seeing sunlight.

'And Lady Falkender, my political secretary, you've met.' The cigar swerved towards the woman who had let me in: I tried another encouraging smile, but still got nothing in return.

'Will you have a drink with us?'

Stone stepped forward and plucked up the decanter, but in the circumstances booze was the last thing I needed. 'No, I'm fine, thanks.'

'Are you sure?' The two men exchanged glances. 'Some tea then. Perhaps, Marcia, you'll oblige?'

Lady Falkender looked very put out by the request, and from the look on her face I thought for a moment she was going to refuse, but instead she gave a huffy sigh and stalked out of the room. Stone, who was watching her anxiously, realised he was still holding the decanter, and looked for a moment as if he didn't know quite what to do with it until the Prime Minister held out his glass for a top-up.

'So.' He tilted his head at the chair opposite, indicating that I should sit. Stone, his medicinal duties over for the moment, withdrew and leant against a desk in the far corner which was dominated by the shrouded bulk of a typewriter. 'It seems you've stumbled into something very grave indeed.'

'Yes.' I could feel the hairs on the back of my neck prickling: it was as much as I could do to keep my voice steady. 'I couldn't quite believe it at first.'

'No. You did very well to bring it to us.' His eyes, a liquid blue, seemed to be boring in to me as I sat there. I don't think I've ever felt quite so uncomfortable in my life. 'Tell me, how did you come to be involved?'

'Oh.' I let out an inappropriate snort of laughter and hid my embarrassment by looking down at my shoes. 'It was silly really: I was spending the night in an office that belongs to an associate of mine, he's a private detective, just off the Charing Cross Road. And someone came in, thinking that I was him, and told me about Stephen, a…prostitute that had been murdered, and wanting me to investigate. So that's how it all got started.'

'Ah.' Wilson puffed thoughtfully on his cigar, the smoke swirling in rings around his head, his expression inscrutable. 'And that led you to Jeremy Thorpe, did it?'

'Yes. Well, indirectly.' The smoke was catching in the back of my throat, and I had to fight not to cough.

'Indirectly?'

I nodded, not wanting to risk opening my mouth. I wished Dr Stone would open a window – surely this thick atmosphere couldn't be good for anyone's health? – but I felt too nervous to ask.

'So tell me.' Wilson leaned forward, closing the space between us. 'Do you believe he is the only politician involved? Or do you think there are others?'

I was taken aback by this. 'I… I don't think so. I haven't really thought about it.'

'Good.' The Prime Minister sat back again, sucking hard on his cigar. 'Good,' he repeated. He turned his head slightly to address Dr Stone through the fog. 'You see what we have here, do you, Joe? A blind man on the Charing Cross Road.'

I looked at the doctor, but he remained silent, inscrutable behind his glasses. Wilson continued to stare at me as he puffed more smoke into the space between us.

317

'I'm sorry,' I said when it became painfully apparent that neither of them was going to explain. 'I don't understand.'

'No,' said Wilson. 'Sadly I don't think you do.' And for a moment, a look of what seemed like genuine sadness seemed to pass across his face, but then it was gone, and the mask returned.

'Where has George got to?' Dr Stone muttered from the corner.

'He'll be back,' murmured Wilson without looking in his direction. 'He'll just be seeing old Tom off safely.'

'I was very lucky meeting Mr Driberg,' I said, for want of anything else to say.

'You've been very lucky all along,' drawled Wilson. He lifted his brandy glass and began to swirl the liquid around inside. I couldn't help admiring the expert way that he kept the wave just lapping at the rim of the glass, not a drop spilling out.

'Tell me, do you know a great deal about politics, young man?'

'I don't, really,' I admitted, watching the liquid go round and round.

'This country is in a perilous situation. Democracy as we know it is in grave danger. The government I lead is walking a difficult path, beset by dangers on both sides. If I were to stumble, it could send every one of us crashing to disaster.'

'Right.' This had strayed so from what I had expected that I didn't feel capable of contributing anything more. Wilson didn't seem interested in asking me any more questions about what I had found out, or discussing what he was going to do about it. Round and round went the brandy. Round and round.

'The left on one side. I'm speaking not just of the left wing of my own party, though lord knows they are as restive as they have ever been. I'm speaking of those who would throw over our whole way of life, tear apart our nation, destroy everything

318

we have built over centuries.'

I nodded, dumbly.

'And on the other side, something just as inimical to the spirit of Britain,' Wilson continued. 'Private armies and dirty tricks brigades, all heavily-financed and masterminded by men who would like to make another Greece or Portugal of us. I am being absolutely serious, make no mistake about that, when I say that democracy itself, as we know it in the West, is in great danger.'

Were the blue eyes beginning to glaze over, turn misty, or was that just the smoke that was swirling between us?

'I have the privilege – though sometimes it feels more of a curse than a privilege – of knowing more than is ever reported in the newspapers, or on the television bulletins. If you could see some of the information George gathers for me – you would scarcely believe some of what is going on in the shadows. Malign forces on every side. Traitors within our own security services, devilling in the dark. I have it on personal authority from the very top in Washington that some of our recent visitors to Downing Street are not who they seem. I have sat as close as you are now to a man who does not exist! And I hear it all, what they are saying. A communist cell at the heart of government. Moscow gold, and Pretoria photographs. Both sides bugging and burgling their way across London. Oh yes, I could tell a tale or two.'

He extended a finger upwards from his cigar to tap the side of his nose, eyeing me beadily all the time. I glanced towards Dr Stone, hoping he might help me out and say something, but he just looked away.

'Make no mistake, there are dark actors at work,' Wilson continued, seeming to be talking to himself as much as he was to me. 'I hear reports of them every day. Our country's enemies, bending our own countrymen to their will in the name of our country's good.' I could see little flecks of spittle flying from his downturned lips, catching on the surface of the revolving glass and hanging there like jewels.

'And so I go on,' he continued, the passion of his speech suddenly drawing back into the usual flat vowels. 'Not on an easy path, and not always in the company I might choose. But it is the path that must be taken. As they deploy their skulduggery and slush funds, so too must we deploy ours. For the greater good.' Abruptly, he swept the brandy glass to his lips and drained it in one great gulp.

'I'm not sure I understand,' I said slowly, although I had a horrible feeling that I did.

'No.' He shook his head, his chin slumping down towards his shirtfront. 'No. You didn't understand at all. You see what I have become, Joe? The great fat spider in the corner of the room. Drawing all the strands of my web towards me.' His voice dwindled away.

Dr Stone stepped forward and laid a hand on the old man's shoulder. 'Try to stay calm, Harold.' He looked far from well himself: his own face was a sickly grey colour. But that might just have been his professional reaction on realising what you didn't need a medical qualification to tell: the Prime Minister of Great Britain had gone totally and utterly barmy.

I stood up, my heart beating fast. 'I'm going to leave now.'

'No. Please!' Dr Stone turned round and held out both arms as if he was actually going to push me back down into the chair. 'George will be back soon. And look, here's some tea!'

The door had creaked open, and the woman, Lady Falkender, was awkwardly manoeuvring through it holding a large tray. Stone, thankfully, switched his attention from me to her, rushing over to pluck the tray from her hands. 'Here, let me be mother!' he exclaimed.

'I'm perfectly capable of serving the tea in my own home, Joe,' she complained, but she stopped when she caught sight of Wilson, who had slumped even further down into his chair and was looking like death. 'Oh for goodness' sake…have you been getting him worked up again?'

'He'll be fine, he'll be fine,' stammered Stone brightly. He had taken the tray over to the sideboard and was shovelling sugar into cups with a slightly manic air. 'What we all need is a nice hot cup of tea!'

'I really think I'm going to go,' I said, addressing myself to the room in general since no one was looking at me any more. Falkender was leaning over Wilson, shaking him by the shoulder and loosening his tie.

'NO!' Stone practically yelled from the corner. 'Please just sit down. I insist.'

His shout made the woman stand bolt upright. 'Joe, *really!*' she said in a shrill voice. And then, as I watched, her eyes widened in shock and her mouth fell open. I followed her gaze, but Stone had curled away from us both, trying to hide whatever it was she had spotted him doing. 'No!' she shrieked. '*No!* How *dare you*, Joe! In my own house!'

There was a staccato rattling as a shower of pills spilled out of Stone's clenched hand and bounced all over the china cups and metal tray. He turned, his face anguished, gabbling 'Marcia, I can explain, he doesn't have a choice, it's a matter of national security…' But she wasn't looking at him at all. She had turned back to the Prime Minister, who was shrinking back yet further into the depths of his chair. No, that wasn't quite right. He was *cowering*.

'You little *cunt!*' she screamed in an ear-piercing voice, and she drew back her hand and slapped Wilson with amazing force right across his face. 'What do you think you are doing! In my own house!' she wailed, as he pulled his arms up in front of his face to defend himself and both Dr Stone and I stood there, transfixed. '*In my own house!*'

I had seen enough. I strode over to the open door, stomped out through the hallway and yanked the front door open. The daylight was blinding after the gloom of the study. There was a big black car parked outside the house. And a man was lounging against its bonnet, soaking up the last of the sun. He snapped to attention as I erupted out onto the doorstep and stopped in horror. It was Mr Jones.

'Uh-uh,' he barked, spreading his arms to block my path. 'You're not going anywhere.'

THIRTY-SIX

I STOOD WAVERING on the doorstep, scanning vainly for an escape route. The panda car that had been parked across the entrance to the narrow mews had been replaced by another vast black one, and as I looked, Mr Smith opened the door and stepped out, folding his arms and standing squarely in front of his vehicle as a second line of defence. In the opposite direction was a dead end, a sheer brick wall at the end of the mews. There were nothing but shuttered and padlocked garage doors to be seen to either side. I was well and truly cornered.

I took an involuntary step backwards into the hallway as Jones closed the gap between us, a nasty grin spreading across his face. But at that very moment there was a screech from behind me that stopped both of us in our tracks. 'Get out! Go on, out!'

Assuming it was aimed at me, I turned to face Lady Falkender, but I swiftly had to flatten myself against the open door as she bundled Joe Stone bodily past me and out of the building. She stood a good head smaller than the doctor, but she made up for it with the ferocity of her anger: he stumbled over the threshold and might have gone head first onto the cobbles had Jones not been there to catch him. It was hard to say which of the two of us looked more surprised.

'And stay out! You're not welcome. We don't want you around any more,' she hissed after him.

'But Marcia, I can explain,' Stone gabbled as Jones helped him regain his balance and turn to face us. 'He knows too much. He's dangerous.' He gestured emphatically in my direction. 'It's in the national interest he be put down.'

'*Put down!*' She gaped at him, apoplectic, and then seemed to acknowledge my presence beside her for the very first time. I felt her hand lock, vice-like, on my arm, 'This is a *human being*, not some sick dog, Joe!' With that she yanked me backwards into the hallway and slammed the door in the faces of the two men outside.

'Thank you,' I said, weakly.

She didn't say anything for a few moments, just leaned back against the wall and closed her eyes. She was practically panting with rage, worrying away at the locket that hung from her neck, turning it over and over again. I took the chance to glance to the back of the hallway. The door of the room we had been in was hanging open, but from where we were standing I couldn't see the Prime Minister.

When her breathing was finally under control, Lady Falkender opened her eyes again. They were completely dry. 'Could you wait in here please?' she said briskly, opening the door at the front of the hallway as if nothing out of the ordinary had happened.

I stood my ground. 'Not until I get some answers. Who was that man outside the door?'

An irritated look. 'It was one of the Prime Minister's security team. In here please.'

I still didn't move. 'A policeman?'

She nodded, impatiently. 'From Special Branch. Just go in here please.'

I took a step back, my own fury rising. 'I'm not going anywhere!' I protested. 'Not till I find out what the hell's going on here!'

'*That is what I am trying to establish,*' she barked, her voice rising by at least an octave before returning to the same clipped, reasonable tone. 'Now would you *please* wait in here while I talk to the Prime Minister.'

I looked at the door she was indicating, then back to the locked front door behind me. Every part of me wanted to be about a million miles away from this house and its crazy occupants, but right now I didn't seem to have a choice. I stepped forward and into a chintzy sitting room, all floral-patterened wallpaper and antimacassars. I was just taking in the incongruity of it all when the door closed behind me and I heard the sound of a key turning in the lock.

I turned and rattled the doorhandle. 'Hey. Hey!' There was no reply. Faintly, from the back of the hall, I could make out the sound of another door closing.

Sighing, I turned back into the sitting room. My first impression had been right: there were even painted plates hanging on the walls and ornaments sitting on doilies. It was like being back at Mrs Friendship's, or my late grandmother's. With the very important difference that I was a prisoner here, and no one at either of their houses had ever tried to kill me.

I strode over to the window and pulled back the net curtains. The criss-crossed security shutters I'd noticed on my arrival were firmly locked and wouldn't budge. Beyond them I could

325

see Jones the policeman remonstrating with Dr Stone, who looked like he could do with some medical attention himself: he was sweating heavily and kept running his fingers through his damp hair, making it stand on end. Although by their gestures it seemed both men were talking quite animatedly,

I couldn't make out a word of what they were saying, no matter how close I got my ear to the pane. I supposed the place must have reinforced glass. Not surprising if it belonged to one of the Prime Minister's top advisers: the building was probably fortified against the worst the IRA could throw at it. As well as anyone inside trying to get out.

As I watched, both men broke off their conversation and turned in my direction. Impulsively, I let the net curtain drop and jerked back from the glass, but they were looking past the building towards the entrance to the mews, and a second or two later it became obvious why, as the great bulk of Wigg came striding briskly into view. He was clearly demanding to know what the hell was going on: the policeman was shrugging and pointing at Stone, who redoubled his frantic explanation, gesturing to the front door of the house.

'Shit. *Shit.*' I swore out loud as I backed away from the window. Wilson was mad; Falkender's motives I was not yet clear on, though I wasn't about to give her the benefit of any doubt. But Wigg I knew for certain was dangerous. *Officer class,* that's how Jethro Morgan had described him. *Let me know just what I could expect if I went on kicking up a fuss.* That was just after he'd been talking about executions.

I looked frantically around the room for anything I could use to defend myself. There were some photos in silver frames on a side table – Wilson and Falkender posing alongside various famous faces like David Frost and, how appropriate, Richard Nixon – but when I plucked them up the frames turned out to be some sort of flimsy plasticy stuff with no weight behind it whatsoever. The porcelain figurines of shepherdesses and their suitors on the mantelpiece didn't look up to the job either. But hang on: beneath them in the fireplace was a familiar figure, the same knight in armour who stood guard on my parents' own hearth. I bounded over, tipped him forward and rifled, clattering, through the irons that hung from his back until I located the poker. It wasn't quite as long or robust as I would have liked, and hefting it in my hand I suspected it wasn't quite as deadly a weapon as Agatha Christie had led me to believe, but it would have to do.

It wasn't a moment too soon. Barely had I turned around than there was a great hammering on the building's front door, a furious thumping that didn't let up even when Falkender erupted into the hallway yelling at her visitor to be quiet. There didn't seem to be any problem with the acoustics inside the house: I could hear her clearly as she passed the door of the room I was locked in, reached the front door and unbolted it.

Wigg started barking at her immediately. 'What the hell's going on, Marcia? Joe says you threw him out. What are you playing at? You'd better not have let that little toerag get away, my men have been after him for days. Let me in, I need to talk to Harold.'

I took an involuntary step back, my heels coming up against the fireplace. But to my surprise, rather than coming into the building, the voices stayed where they were.

'You're not welcome, George,' said Marcia. Her voice still had that edge of shrillness in it, but it stayed firm. 'He won't see you. He won't see you ever again. I *said* it was a mistake letting you worm your way back in. I told him so again and again, that you and your dirty tricks brigade were nothing but trouble. If I'd had any idea – if I'd had the first clue what you were up to...'

'Oh, do me a favour!' Wigg spat. 'Half of this came from you in the first place.' He put on a snide, wheedling voice. '*We must protect Jeremy, Harold. If they come for him, they'll come for you next.*'

'How *dare* you!' she gasped, her voice cracking and veering alarmingly close to his impression. 'I was never a party to any of this. Not one word.'

'Of course you weren't,' Wigg sneered. 'Haven't you worked it out yet? You still think he tells you everything, don't you? He's not that stupid. Why do you think he keeps you out of the way here, Marcia? It's because he's finally realised what the rest of us have been telling him for years: you're a bloody liability. A jumped-up typist with delusions of grandeur. Now get out of my way and let me talk to him.'

There was the unmistakeable sound of a scuffle, and I gripped the poker more firmly. But the noises didn't get any closer than the front doorstep before I could hear someone else – it sounded like Mr Jones – intervening, saying 'all right, that's enough now,' and a second later the front door slammed shut and all I could hear was the sound of heavy breathing in the hallway. It sounded like Falkender was just on the other side of the door. I could have spoken to her without even raising my voice: demanded to be let out. But right now, shut in here seemed by far the safest place to be.

Instead I approached the window, moving as stealthily as I could, trying to make out as much I could through the net curtains rather than risk pulling them aside. Wigg had stepped down from the doorstep and looked to be deep in discussion with the other two men. The one who had twice tried to abduct me, the one who had tried to poison me, and the man who had evidently been giving the orders all along.

My legs suddenly felt weak and wobbly, and I sat down

heavily in one of Lady Falkender's patterned armchairs, grasping the poker firmly in both hands. No one would believe the situation I had got myself into. But then that didn't matter anyway, because nobody knew I was here. Not my mum, not Ray – the only person who knew my destination after leaving the Barbican was Driberg. A momentary flutter of hope stirred in my chest before I remembered that brandy glass that Stone had been wiping out so carefully when I went into the room straight after Tom had vacated it. Somehow I didn't think he would be making his dinner reservation tonight.

I lowered my head in despair for a moment, then suddenly jerked it upright again as I made out a strange noise. It was coming from somewhere within the house. It was weirdly familiar, but somehow I couldn't place it: a sharp rhythmic tapping. Slowly I rose to my feet and crept across the room to the locked door, pressing my ear to the wood: yes, it was definitely coming from the back of the house, either from what I presumed was a kitchen or the room Wilson had received me in and where, since I had heard nothing more from him, I supposed he must still be sitting. Surely she couldn't be slapping him again? No, the sounds were too frequent and too fast. And then I remembered the shrouded shape on the table against which Stone had been leaning, and realised what the sound was. Someone was *typing*.

What the hell? Was this Falkender's response to the insult Wigg had thrown at her? It was inexplicable, so inappropriate that my brain had refused to recognise it for what it was. It made no sense. I strained to make out anything else, but only the sharp clacking of the keys penetrated this far: someone might have been talking in a low voice too, or that could just have been the blood rushing in my ears.

Shaking my head, I moved back to the window, risking a

brief twitch of the nets this time to get an idea of the lie of the land. I could see Wigg over on the far side of the car talking to Jones, who was practically standing at attention, making it obvious just who was in charge of whom. I couldn't make out Stone at all until I glimpsed a movement in the car's interior: the doctor was sitting in the back, shoulders slumped, his head in his hands. At least it didn't look like a full-frontal assault on the house was imminent.

It was getting dark now, but no lights were visible anywhere else in the street: there were no neighbours to come to my aid even if I could make them hear me through the toughened glass. Besides, what could I shout? *Help, the Prime Minister tried to kill me!* That would get one of us instantly dismissed as a lunatic, and it wouldn't be the one who showed every sign of actually being one.

Back to the door, and the rhythmic clacking of the typewriter keys continued at just the same pace. Surrounded by hostile men, the woman – the Lady – seemed like my best hope of survival. She was the only one who had raised any objection to my murder. Admittedly they were mostly against the principle of it taking place on her own property. But that had to mean that right here, right now, was the safest place I could be.

I hauled the armchair closest to the centre of the room around so it would give me a view of both door and window and slumped down into it with the poker across my lap, its handle gripped loosely in my hand. And waited.

THIRTY-SEVEN

HOURS PASSED, measured out by the rhythmic click-clack of the keys from next door. Darkness fell outside, and inside too, the bright clashing colours of the floral wallpaper and the three-piece suite fading to a grey monotone. I didn't dare switch a light on, for fear of revealing my location to the men outside. It seemed they had nothing to do but wait either: furtive forays to the window revealed that Wigg had joined Stone in the back of the vast car, leaving only Jones kicking his heels in front of the house, his jacket collar turned up against the cold of the March evening.

Eventually the sound of the typewriter stopped, and the house fell into an eerie silence. I got up, to stretch my legs as much as anything, and crossed the room to press an ear to the door, but all I could make out were the faint noises of someone moving about in a distant part of the house. Did anyone else live here, I wondered? Did Falkender have a husband, kids? Or was this some kind of show home, maintained for unparliamentary business at a safe distance from Downing Street?

The sound of approaching footsteps startled me, and I jumped back, colliding with some heavy piece of furniture in the darkness as key turned in the lock and the door swung open.

'Oh!' said a silhouetted figure in surprise. 'What are you doing in the dark?'

Falkender flicked the switch by the door and my garish surroundings sprang back into life as she turned and stooped to pick up a tray she had put down on the carpet to unlock the door, tutting as a large handbag she had hanging on her bony arm slid downwards and threatened to capsize its contents. For a moment she was off-balance, off-guard and utterly vulnerable, her frail figure all that stood in the way of me finally getting out of the room.

And I did nothing. I hid the poker I had been holding ready all this time behind my back, and as she passed me to put the tray down on a spindly side table I took the opportunity to slide it out of sight between the cushion and arm of the sofa. It would still be safely to hand should things turn nasty again, but as long as Wigg and his murderous companions remained safely on the other side of a heavy front door, the last thing I wanted to do was to appear threatening to the house's occupants.

'I thought you might be hungry,' she said in that same determinedly everyday tone, indicating the tray. There was a round of roughly-cut sandwiches on a plate, and an open bottle of beer.

I looked at her in disbelief. 'You have got to be kidding.'

She sniffed and gave me a tight-lipped look, as if I was the one being offensive. 'What d'you mean?'

I stretched out a furious arm towards the next-door room. 'Have you forgotten your friend trying to poison me in there?'

Her eyes flashed. 'Joe Stone is no friend of mine.' The

momentary fury seemed to pass, and she sank down into one of the armchairs, brushing down the front of her skirt with a deep sigh. She looked exhausted. 'Oh, suit yourself.'

I sat down myself, at the furthest end of the sofa from the tray, which also had the advantage of concealing a tell-tale sooty smear the poker had left on the cushions. I hadn't eaten since my meagre breakfast in Brixton what felt like a hundred years ago, and my mouth was desert-dry too. But nothing would compel me to touch anything prepared in this house.

'What are you going to do with me?' The collective 'you' took in everyone both inside and outside the building, but it was fairly evident who was the one wielding the power here. Not to mention wearing the trousers.

'You'll come to no harm while you're under my roof,' she said bleakly.

'And what about after that?' I demanded. 'Or are you just going to hand me over to…them?' I waved towards the window.

Falkender glanced round and seemed to notice the car outside for the first time. Wigg had got out, and I could make out the shapes of both him and Jones peering in at us. She got up and brusquely pulled the curtains closed on them.

'The Prime Minister is going to order them to end this… operation that's been going on,' she said, her voice quavering slightly. 'He is going to make it very clear to George Wigg that we no longer require his services.' She slumped back down into the chair, and I glanced round at the open door to the hallway. There was no sign of movement from the next-door room.

'And I'm supposed to just trust you that that's the end of it, am I?'

She glared at me. 'I have a personal assurance.' She fumbled at the lock of her handbag and extracted a wad of paper. It was a pale purple colour, the front sheet covered with closely-typed text.

I started forward, expecting to take it from her and read it, but she shook her head and slid it back into the bag, tapping the leather significantly. 'It's all in here. A full, signed confession. One call and he'll be finished.' Her eyes flashed again, but this time with a weird look of triumph rather than anger.

'You'd really do that?' I asked in disbelief.

'Oh, I'd do it.' She seemed to be talking to herself more than me, a manic smile creeping across her face. 'I made him. And I could destroy him, too.'

Oh god. The pair of them were as mad as each other.

'And what about me?' I asked after several seconds had passed.

Abruptly, she recalled herself from whatever twisted fantasy was playing out in her mind. 'You. Yes. Well, that's what we need to resolve. We certainly can't have you going around making wild accusations against the Prime Minister.'

'Even though they're true.' It was a statement more than a question.

She gave me a sour look. 'As if you'd find anyone who would believe you. Not even *Private Eye* would dare print that.'

That brought me up short. 'How do you –?'

The hint of a smile was playing at the corners of her pursed lips, but she ignored the question. 'Nevertheless, we would prefer to have your discretion assured.' There was that royal we again. These people might be perfectly prepared to turn on one another and fight like dogs for their own advantage, but when it came to outsiders, their first instinct was to close ranks. These were their secrets to tell, not mine.

'So what will it take?'

I genuinely didn't know what she was getting at. 'What d'you mean?'

She sniffed impatiently. 'We have friends who are prepared to be very generous in such matters.'

It took me a second to catch up. 'What – oh!' I remembered what Driberg had told me back at his flat. 'One of these friends wouldn't happen to be called Jimmy Goldsmith, by any chance?'

'That's none of your business,' she snapped, looking at me like I was something smeared on the bottom of her high heels. 'Just name your price. We haven't got all day.'

I considered the magnitude of the secret she expected me to keep, and the capacity of Jimmy Goldsmith's pockets. A millionaire, the *Standard* had called him.

Then I thought about Stephen, and Malcolm Crichton's helpless grief when he had begged me to get involved in this whole awful thing in the first place. But I remembered, too, that I had only said yes to him because of the cash in his wallet, and the prospect it offered of helping me get off the game forever.

Which is when I gave an answer that surprised us both. 'I want Mark Adamson back,' I said.

'Who?' asked Falkender, bewildered.

'He's my boyfriend,' I said, with increasing confidence. 'My lover. They' – I stabbed a finger viciously towards the window – 'took him away. I want him back. If they've killed him, I want his body. He deserves a decent burial, not to be dumped in some field or given a pauper's funeral somewhere no one even knows his name. He believed in you lot. Your party. All the stuff you've forgotten you were supposed to stand for. He might not have been a Lord or a Lady but he was worth a hundred of you. And if I don't get him back, or if it's already too late because of what those bastards have done – then I will make sure I do everything I can, *everything,* to make sure the world knows exactly what you all are.'

I sat back and folded my arms defiantly. Lady Falkender

was regarding me with a look of infinite distaste. 'Think very carefully. I won't offer again. As I say, we can afford to be *extremely* generous...'

'No,' I said bluntly, looking around at all the ornaments and photographs she'd surrounded herself with. 'Maybe that's how things work in your world, but not mine. I've got one condition, and that's it. Take it or leave it. Oh, and I want to hear him' – I jerked my head back towards the back of the house – 'give the order to Wigg himself, too. The organ grinder, not the monkey.'

Falkender shot me a look of cold fury, but she rose from her seat anyway and went out of the room. 'Leave it unlocked,' I barked as she stopped in the doorway. There was a pause, pregnant with unspoken anger, but the door stayed open.

No sooner had she left the room than I stood up myself, strode over to the window and threw the curtains open. Wigg was leaning against the side of the car, only a few feet away from me on the other side of the glass. I was suddenly full of a reckless courage – maybe because I knew I had nothing left to lose – and I gave him a sarcastic smile and a wave. He bared his teeth in a sneer and ran his index finger across his throat. I extended my own middle finger in return.

Only a couple of minutes went by before Wilson came shuffling out into the hallway. I watched him pass the open door of the sitting room, but he didn't so much as glance in my direction. Marcia was hovering behind him, worrying once again at the locket that hung from her neck. I heard the sound of the front door being opened.

'George.' That same flat familiar tone. Wigg started forward and out of my range of vision, and I made a panicked move towards where I had hidden the poker, but Wilson spoke again, more commandingly. 'No, stay where you are. It's over. I've given my word that the boy won't be harmed. Stand your men down.'

'But Harold!' came the protesting reply.

'No. This has all gone far enough. We've reached the end. You're to do exactly as Marcia says.'

There was a long pause before he spoke again, sounding suddenly withered and pathetic. 'I'd like to go home now.'

I turned back to the window in time to see Wilson making his way towards the parked car. He was stooped, dragging his feet across the cobbles like a man twenty years older. Stone came rushing forward to take his arm, a look of panicked concern on his face, as Jones hurried round to open the car door. The last glimpse I caught of the Prime Minister was as the pair of them guided him unsteadily into the vehicle's dark interior.

From the hallway I could hear Marcia addressing Wigg. There was that strange note of triumph in her voice again. 'He wants to know what you did with his boyfriend. And I warn you, George, if you've harmed him, neither Harold or I will be answering for the consequences.'

Wigg replied in a low grunt, too quiet for the man in the car to hear him. 'Don't you get all high and mighty with me, you bitch. If I go down, I'll make damn sure I take you with me.'

'I don't think so.' The tap of finger on leather echoed through the hallway. 'Harold's told me everything. He made it very clear who came up with this disgusting little scheme, and who was giving the orders. All it would take is one call... No, don't be a fool, there are plenty of copies safely filed away where they'll be found if anything should happen to me. After all, that's all I'm any good at, isn't it George? Being a *typist*?'

She spoke in a tone of white-hot fury, but his reply, when it came, was one of grudging admiration. 'Well played, Marcia.

Well played. Now all you have to hope for is that he keeps his word. Because he's never called your bluff before, has he?'

'The boyfriend,' she spat back, suddenly sounding a lot less sure of herself. 'Now.'

And the front door slammed shut with a tremendous bang.

I waited for a few seconds for Falkender to reappear, but there was no sign of her. Eventually I went out into the hallway myself, and found her leaning against the wall behind the front door, shoulders slumped, eyes closed, breathing heavily. She looked as if the confrontation with Wigg had taken everything out of her.

'Are you OK?'

Her eyes opened and she gave me an exhausted grimace. 'What do you care? Who on earth *are* you, anyway? You're nothing. Nothing.'

Thrown by the abrupt change in her mood, I made no answer. She shook her head disgustedly and stalked straight past me and up the stairs. 'I've passed on your message. He listened. What he'll do about it I don't know. And I don't want to know any of the sordid details, either. The whole thing is making me ill. I'm going to lie down.' She turned the corner on the staircase and disappeared from view.

Not knowing what else to do, I went back into the sitting room. The last thing I had seen from the window was Mr Jones starting to reverse the car out of the narrow mews, but I was surprised to see it still in place. Wigg was standing by the driver's window, a radio mouthpiece pressed to his face, its curly cord stretched out to its full extent from the dashboard. He spotted me looking out at him and narrowed his eyes.

Somehow the advantage I had briefly seemed to hold had skittered out of my grasp. So, too, had my trump card: as I watched, Wigg passed the radio back, rapped on the top of the car and stood back as it began to reverse out of sight, taking the Prime Minister away. Wigg, however, stayed exactly where he was, glaring at me as I stood in the middle of the empty sitting room. It was just him and me now.

I don't know how long we stayed like that, just staring each other out through the bullet-proof glass. It could have been minutes, it might have been half an hour. But eventually the old man turned away and stomped out of view in the direction of the front door, prompting me to panic and rush out into the hallway to check it was safely locked. When I went back into the window I could just make out his feet stretched out on the cobbles: he was sitting on the doorstep, his back to the door, on sentry duty.

After a while clouds of smoke began to drift across the silent mews. I wondered if he had brought enough cigarettes with him. I wondered how long he was expecting to wait.

I could have done with a fag myself. Not as much as I could have done with a drink: my mouth was parched and my head was starting to ache. I looked enviously at the beer bottle sitting on the side table next to the sandwich, its edges beginning to curl, but I still wasn't prepared to risk it. I supposed the taps in the house's kitchen could at least be trusted, but rather than go exploring, something kept me hovering by the sitting room window where I could be sure of Wigg's whereabouts. The pair of us might have played all our cards, but somehow it still felt safer to stay at the table.

So I was still standing there staring out when a wave of blinding light swept across to illuminate the mews, and a dark car drew up outside the building, Wigg scrambling to his feet to greet it. For one confused moment I thought it was the same car as before, bringing Wilson back for some reason, before I caught a glimpse of who was sitting in the back.

339

Even then I didn't recognise him at first, so pale and thin and anguished did he look. But then a great wave of relief came washing over me, drenching me utterly. It was Mark. My Mark. And he was alive.

THIRTY-EIGHT

THE EVENTS OF THE next few hours were so fraught and so frantic that I find it hard to put them in order in my mind. I remember throwing open the front door and rushing out into the street, forgetting the weapon I had stashed away, forgetting Wigg's presence, forgetting everything except the necessity of getting to Mark and throwing my arms around him. I remember the dazed, bewildered look he gave me, as if he could not believe his eyes either. I remember that it took a moment before he returned my embrace, and the weakness of his arms as they finally locked around me, and how thin his body felt beneath the shapeless grey overalls he was dressed in. And the feeling of his stubble – no, it was more like a full beard – against my own skin as I pressed myself into his neck, gasping into his ear how relieved I was to see him, how I had never expected to see him again.

And I remember his strangely absent response – 'Is that – ?', and how I turned to look where he was looking and saw Marcia

Falkender standing pale and drawn in the entrance to her house like a ghost before she shut the door on us.

'I'll explain it all later,' I whispered.

Wigg was standing just a few feet away, regarding us with utter disgust. When he was sure he had my eye, he stalked over to us and spoke in a low, threatening voice.

'You'd better just hope you never run into me again, sonny. It's not in my nature to leave a job unfinished.'

I searched for the appropriate riposte, but in the end I think I just told him to piss off. The last I saw he was folding himself into the back of the car as the driver turned in his seat to reverse back out in the direction he came.

What I don't remember properly is how we got from there across London to Mark's flat, or how I somehow managed to summon up food, hot tea and brandy to revive us both before leading him, meek and unprotesting, into his bedroom, where the window was still gaping open, and gently helping him out of his clothes and trying not to look at the livid bruises all over his emaciated body, tucking him gently beneath the covers and curling up by his side.

I do remember waking in the night, and knowing by the sound of his breathing that he was awake beside me, and the way that when I slipped a comforting arm around him he flinched at the touch. But I remember as well the moment when he finally began to talk, pouring it all out into the darkness as we lay there entangled around one another.

They had come for him on the Thursday, the first day I had spent down in Devon on the trail of a dead man. Two men, claiming to be police officers – they had flashed ID, but not slowly enough that he could see what it said – saying they were following up on our visit to the station in Hampstead. He'd been so pleased that someone was taking the case seriously he'd invited them straight in. Only it had rapidly become apparent that the only thing they were interested in investigating was my whereabouts, and how much the pair of us knew.

'I didn't tell them anything,' he kept saying, over and over. 'I didn't know anything. I didn't know where you were. I didn't even know the name of the guy who'd told you about the kid being killed in the first place, you never said.' But they hadn't believed him. And after threatening him with all sorts of consequences at the flat – charging him with obstruction and withholding information, telling everyone at his work, his family and all his neighbours he was a queer – they had realised it wasn't getting them anywhere, and bundled him into the back of a car to try out some new techniques.

He didn't know where they'd taken him. It wasn't a police station or prison, he was sure of that. 'I think it was just an ordinary house, somewhere out in the country,' he told me. 'They made sure as we went in that I could see it was in the middle of nowhere, so I knew there was no point calling out for help or trying to get away. And they took me down into the cellar and put me into a room with no windows and nothing but a bed and a bucket, and they left me locked in there in the dark for days at a time before dragging me upstairs to knock me around and ask me all the same questions again and again. But I still couldn't tell them anything, because I didn't *know*.'

'It's all right,' I kept telling him. 'It's over now. It's over.'

From my description he thought Smith and Jones might have been among those interrogating him – there were more than two men involved, he was sure of that – but he was certain he hadn't clapped eyes on Wigg before that very evening. *Officer class*, I thought grimly to myself.

I held back on the questions, wary of putting him through it all again. And Mark was too beaten down and exhausted

343

to show much curiosity about what I had been up to in the meantime, although he did admit that he, too, had spent much of the previous few days convinced I must be dead. Eventually he fell asleep, leaving me to stare into the darkness, my mind whirring crazily over everything I had learned over the past twenty-four hours.

I finally dropped off myself around dawn, and was only vaguely aware of him leaving my side a few hours later. I was dozily conscious of the radio coming on somewhere in the flat, but nothing beyond that, so it came as a rude surprise when Mark burst back into the bedroom at some indeterminate point later demanding, 'Did you hear that?'

'What?' I burbled, pushing myself upright, still not fully aware of where I was.

'The news, just now!' Mark exclaimed impatiently, his face radiating excitement and shock. 'Harold Wilson's resigned! He's resigned!'

FOUR MONTHS LATER...

THIRTY-NINE

THE HEAT WAS unbelievable. I'd thought it was hot at home, but as I stepped down from the train at Paddington the air beneath the great glass roof was like a furnace. Thank goodness I wasn't trussed up in a parka this time, trying to hide myself in its hood: now I could walk proud down the platform in the tight t-shirt and denim shorts I had selected specially for the occasion.

The tube was even worse, the intense heat barely relieved by the fetid air that blew in through every yanked-down window. There were posters up everywhere telling passengers to carry cold drinks and avoid travelling at busy times, or at all, if they were elderly or pregnant. The sun had beat down relentlessly for the whole summer. The news was full of stories about people having to fill buckets from standpipes and wildfires raging through the countryside. I couldn't remember the last time it had rained. I could barely even remember what rain felt like.

Still, at least the weather was welcome today, I reflected as I surfaced into blazing brightness at Westminster. The sun had brought out way more people than I had been expecting, at least half of them probably drawn in by the prospect of bared flesh on the other half. What looked like several hundred people were milling around in Victoria Gardens, pointedly greeting one another with hugs, kisses and ostentatious displays of enthusiasm over one another's outfits. Banners were busily being threaded onto poles and unfurled: here a *How Dare You Assume I'm Heterosexual*, there a *3,000,000 Gay People Demand Justice*. It was our banner that I spotted first: *CHE CAMDEN*, standing proud at the far end of the park, and as I wound my way through the crowd towards it I could make out Neil ticking things off on a clipboard and looking happier than I could ever remember seeing him. Shirley was there, too, her arm around a woman I didn't recognise, but she detached herself when she saw me approaching and came forward to greet me with a hug of my own.

'Hi, Tommy, it's so good to see you!' she beamed.

'You too.' I patted her back in a slightly brusque show of affection. Her friend, a very attractive black girl in dungarees, was eyeing us suspiciously.

'Here, look what we made.' Shirley let go of me and stooped to delve into a rucksack. 'This is Anita, by the way. This is Tommy, who I was telling you about.'

The girl looked relieved, and offered me a hand to shake. 'Actually, I mostly go by Alex now,' I told her.

'Sorry, sorry, force of habit,' Shirley muttered, and straightened up, sliding a rectangle of stiff cardboard out of the bag.

'It doesn't matter,' I started to tell her, but I tailed off as she turned the placard around to reveal what was unmistakeably Stephen's face. I'd sent her the Polaroid when she'd written to propose her plan a few weeks before, but this was the first chance I had had to see what she had done with it. It was incredible. All right, the poster paint may have rendered his hair a slightly too garish shade of yellow, but she had got his expression perfectly, improved it, even: that slight anomaly in the eyes was absent and he looked, at last, to be smiling like he really meant it. By contrast, I found I had a lump in my throat.

There was writing beneath it, in big block capitals:

'STEPHEN'
KILLED FEBRUARY 1976
A VICTIM OF PREJUDICE

'It's…it's amazing,' I spluttered, pulling Shirley forward into a more heartfelt hug this time.

'We thought you might like to carry it,' she said. 'Here, Anita, can you fix it to the pole for me? We didn't want to put the staples through until you'd seen it.' She spotted my eyes scanning the crowd behind her, and lowered her voice. 'He's here. He's volunteered to carry one end of the banner at the front of the group, so you don't have to march alongside him. Unless you want to.'

I'd just clocked Mark myself, emerging from behind the material as he hoisted his pole higher under Neil's bossy direction. He looked well.

'Thank you,' I said, squeezing her arm. At that moment Mark spotted me, gave a sheepish half-grin and passed his end of the banner to a slightly put-out Neil. I braced myself as he made his way over.

'Hello.'

'Hi Tom.'

We stood awkwardly for a second before going in to hug one

another. Our bodies joined in an A-shape, slightly too distant, but even through the limited contact I could tell he had regained a healthy shape. Slightly too healthy, if anything. The inevitable cowboys t-shirt was stretched over the beginnings of a belly.

'How are you getting on in Reading?' he asked once we'd let go.

'Really well.' I ran my hands through my hair, which I'd let grow long over the summer. 'I'm really enjoying the job.'

'I knew you would,' said Shirley with a delighted smile. She'd acted as my referee for an interview my mum had managed to wangle me at the hospital, and I was now a full-time ward porter. The job came with accommodation too, in a hostel at the furthest end of the hospital grounds from the nurse's home to prevent any mischief going on, as if that was going to be an issue with me. That meant I could keep a safe distance from my father while still seeing my mum almost every day. It felt like a whole new life had been handed to me on a plate.

'I'm going to college in September, too,' I told them, grateful to be able to haul Shirley into the conversation too. 'Evening classes. Going to finally finish my 'O' levels. Then maybe think about 'A' levels and even going on to Poly, if my results are good enough.'

'That's brilliant, well done!' said Mark, slightly too enthusiastically, but I wasn't going to let anyone's patronising bother me. I'd been worrying about how well I'd fit in and whether I'd be able to keep up with my fellow students right up until a few days ago, when I'd been sent the reading list for the English class and realised I'd already read every single one of the set texts on it, some of them twice.

'And how are you?'

'I'm all right. Much better. Settling in to the new place.'

'Good. Good.' He hadn't wanted to stay in the flat in

Kentish Town after everything that had happened, which was understandable. Once he was back on his feet he'd found himself a new place somewhere up towards Wood Green. It was a bedsit, with less room than before, which had given him the perfect excuse for suggesting it would be an idea for me to look for somewhere of my own, too. I'd agreed, maybe a bit too readily. Although if I was honest, I hadn't totally ruled out the idea of sleeping there tonight.

'How's the family?'

'All right, yeah. Mum's talking about taking some evening classes too actually, maybe even an Open University course.' She'd only sprung this news on me a few days ago. I was pleased for her, obviously, but I couldn't help wondering what my father thought about the plan. She'd told me it would 'do him good to get some practice at coping by himself.' So make of that what you will.

'That's brilliant,' Mark over-enthused again. He'd never actually met my mum. We hadn't got anywhere near that far.

The weight of what we weren't saying hung between us in the heat before Shirley rescued us again. 'Here, take these, it's one between two and I'm meant to be *very strict about it,*' she said, reaching back into her bag and pushing plastic bottles of squash into both our hands. 'Neil says it's very important for us all to *keep hydrated* on the way. I think he's probably worked out the perfect sip-per-mile ratio if you want to ask him.'

We both grinned at her impression, and I felt the ice cracking a little. 'I should get back before he throws a wobbly,' said Mark, looking back to where our dear leader was jiggling his clipboard impatiently. 'Listen, Tommy, it really is good to see you. I'm sorry about the way things worked out…'

'Forget it,' I assured him. 'It was a weird situation. The weirdest.'

We'd *done* our best to make a go of things, but it hadn't taken long for it to become apparent that even the points we were starting from were poles apart. Once Mark had emerged from the near-numb state Wigg's goons had reduced him to, all his righteous sound and fury had returned with a vengeance. Problem was, there was nowhere for it to go. No one left to fight, except for me. Neither of us wanted to let the other one out of our sight, but all we could do when we were together was snipe at each other. He kept wanting to go over the whole thing again and again, insisting there must be more we could do to bring what had been going on to light. I kept telling him it was over, we had got as far as we ever would, that no one would believe us and he should just let it go. Round and round the argument went. Christ, relationships are difficult. Things are a lot easier when they work on a basic transactional level: you give me money, I give you sex: I give you money, you give me a hotel room.

There had been a brief respite when he threw his energies into the battle for the Labour leadership, but when his chosen champion, Michael Foot, had lost, it just made everything worse. That's the big difference between the two of us: Mark's an idealist who will probably spend the whole of the rest of his life trying to change the world, and good for him. Me, I was able to accept that I actually have.

Still, it was good to see him again. I leaned forward impulsively to peck him on the lips. 'Forget about it, honestly. It wasn't to be. Let's just enjoy the day.'

'All right.' He grinned, and I watched him stroll back through the crowd to his rightful place. I couldn't help noticing his arse was filling his jeans even better these days as well.

'Well, *that* wasn't awkward,' said Shirley sarcastically, pushing a pole into my hands. I looked up at Stephen's face above me.

He, at least, I hoped would appreciate that I had done the right thing by him. He understood the code of the Dilly. You couldn't expect anything from the law, but sometimes, if you got lucky, you could manage a kind of natural justice.

'This really is brilliant,' I told Shirley. 'Did you do it all yourself?'

'I had a bit of help.' She smiled in Anita's direction.

'Is she…?'

Shirley smirked. 'Work in progress. I'll let you know by the end of today. Christ, if you can't pull on a Gay Pride march, you really might as well give up and go back in the closet.'

I laughed along with her. I certainly hadn't failed to notice the sheer amount of beefcake surrounding us. Many of the men around us had already stripped to the waist, and most of them were wearing shorts that were barely there to start with. Feeling like part of the crowd for the first time in my life, I slipped my own t-shirt off and tucked it in to hang from the back pocket of my shorts. Three months pushing trolleys and wheelchairs around the hospital had given me muscles in places I'd barely had places before, and I wasn't going to get many better opportunities to show them off than this.

The atmosphere in the little park was beginning to change: there was an air of expectation going through the crowd. Most of the banners were fully erect now. I could see *End Police Harassment of Gays*, *Sissies Unite*, *Gay Rights for Northern Ireland Now* and *Homosexuals are Revolting!*, which I thought was quite clever. As I looked around, a whistle shrilled, and a moustached man who had clambered up onto the base of a statue hollered through a megaphone at everyone to get themselves in line and start moving up Millbank towards parliament. There was a long line of policemen in shirtsleeve-order stretched along the pavement, and for a moment I assumed they were trying to block our way, but as the crowd began to shuffle out onto the road the cops started to move with them, and I realised they were there to form a protective barrier between us and the other people in the street. Whether they were shielding us from them or them from us, I'm not totally sure.

I held Stephen's placard high as we passed the Houses of Parliament, brandishing it defiantly in the direction of Big Ben, though I doubted there was anyone important inside the building to see it. The place had seen some changes over the past few months. Wilson's sudden resignation had taken the whole country by surprise. There was such wall-to-wall coverage that the passing of poor old Tom Driberg – found dead in the back of a taxi; no foul play suspected – had been relegated to a small spot somewhere near the back of the papers where I might have been the only person to notice it. Meanwhile the guessing games about why Wilson had really gone filled pages for weeks. None of them even got close.

To be honest, I still wasn't totally certain myself. Had his departure been part of the deal that Falkender had brokered over her typewriter while I was still locked next door? Or had it been his last triumphant move in the vicious game the whole mad mob of them had evidently been playing for years, quitting just as she thought she had gained the upper hand? Maybe his conscience had just got the better of him. Probably no one would never know.

One thing I was certain of: the country was better off without him. Not that it seemed like it at the moment. His successor Jim Callaghan seemed to be making a terrible job of things, with half the country threatening to go out on strike and everyone predicting we were about to go bankrupt unless we got a loan from the International Monetary Fund. People were saying an election was inevitable any day now and we would soon have our first female Prime Minister, at which point I think my father would probably explode. I'd started reading the papers and following all this stuff now. It turns out politics is actually really interesting once you know a bit about what goes on behind the scenes.

Wilson himself seemed to have gone to ground. Not long after he stepped down he put out a resignation honours list with a knighthood for Goldsmith and rewards for all sorts of other dodgy-sounding businessmen who had been doing god-knows-what in the way of favours for him. Falkender had taken much of the blame for it. Rightly or not, I didn't really care.

Private Eye, meanwhile, had managed to defeat at least some of Goldsmith's legal actions: the magazine had gone back on the shelves at the beginning of April with the full story of Norman Scott's murder inside, photo, bunnies and all. Thorpe had resigned as Liberal leader a month later, still loudly denying any involvement. A few weeks later he'd been kicked out of the party entirely by his successor, Cyril Smith, for failing to give his colleagues a full explanation of his relationship with Scott – or as Smith put it in one of his characteristically blunt TV appearances, 'for telling me bloody lies.'

Things seemed to be moving on that front too. I'd spoken to Mrs Friendship on the phone a few days earlier, and she was full of praise for the local police, who'd been in to take a full statement from her and told her London were now being very cooperative and they expected to make arrests 'in due course' for Norman Scott's murder. She'd asked if that included Jeremy Thorpe, and the policeman had told her he 'wasn't at liberty to say it does, but I certainly wouldn't say it doesn't,' which she took as a very firm yes.

Whether the police would be able to follow things any further up the chain remained to be seen. I suspected ranks would automatically close around the ex-Prime Minister, but god knows what other cock-and-bull story the powers-that-be would come up with to explain things away. Still, Watergate wasn't uncovered in a day either, and I felt I had earned myself the right to relax. And that's exactly what I did that afternoon as the march wound its way up Whitehall. People on the pavements might have been jeering at us all the way, but only the occasional 'dirty queers' or 'filthy beasts' made it through the racket of the steel band leading the procession from the back of a flatbed lorry. I recognised a couple of Ray's boys among the musicians, though the man himself was nowhere to be seen, which was a bit of a relief. I know poor old Tom had paid upfront for the last blow job he would ever give, but I had a nasty feeling Ray might somehow feel I still owed him.

One friendly face I did spot was Clarrie, who was dressed to the nines in a sequinned blue dress, hair plumped up on top of her head and held in place with a sparkling tiara. She was strolling along on the outside of the line of people – she didn't seem to be with any particular group – spinning a union-jack parasol over her left shoulder and using her right arm, clad in a white glove that went all the way up to her elbow, to alternate a regal wave with a jabbed V-sign at any onlookers who fired abuse in her direction. 'I'm practising for my jubilee, darling' she told me when she spotted me and came mincing over to press a lipsticked mouth to my cheek. To which the only suitable answer seemed to be, 'God save the Queen!'

It had never felt better to be out and proud than it did that afternoon. There were gay men and gay women of all shapes and sizes, every age and every colour marching together under the blazing sun. It was my first Pride march, but I'd heard one of the organisers saying it was the biggest one yet, and as we turned into Trafalgar Square and flowed past the startled tourists with their instamatics snapping away, it truly felt like we were growing in both numbers and strength to the point that we could take on the world and demand to be seen 365-days a year, not just this one. I'd made peace with my mum, to the point that she'd given me her blessing to be here today (in the most British way possible, by saying nothing more than 'be careful' but packing me some sandwiches for the train). I could even get through a Sunday lunch with my dad now without an eruption.

And the route seemed to be lined with little sights to keep my mood boosted along the way: we filed along Coventry Street towards Piccadilly Circus, past the front of Playland, all boarded-up, the bulbs dead in its illuminated frontage. The police had raided the place in June, and five people had been arrested and charged with 'procuring acts of gross indecency' and various other offences. The press coverage had focused mostly on one of them on the grounds that he was an old Etonian and Lloyds 'name', whatever that meant, but I'd been pleased to note that one of those in the dock was called Philip, not to mention the fact that all of them had been remanded without bail ahead of their trial. I'd heard on the grapevine that Mr Smith and Mr Jones had quit the area just as suddenly as they'd arrived, and I was reasonably confident I was no longer a subject of gossip around those parts any more. I strode through the Dilly with my head held high. Mostly, anyway – I ducked along with the rest of the marchers when a group of blokes erupted up from Ward's Irish House and started chucking bottles in our direction and yelling that we should be ashamed of ourselves. The policemen marching to either side of us swiftly peeled off to calm things down, although I noticed they didn't actually appear to be arresting anyone.

By the time we had made it all the way up Regent Street I was pretty much immune to the reaction of the crowds. Someone had got up a chant of 'Hooray! Hooray! It's a nice day to be gay!', which went down well with the Saturday shoppers in Oxford Circus, although the subsequent chorus of '2, 4, 6, 8, One in ten of you's not straight' was met with considerably less enthusiasm. But I was past caring. Drunk on the sun – not to mention the vodka that a giggling Shirley finally admitted she'd spiked Neil's bottles of lemon barley with – I was having the time of my life, waving Stephen's portrait from side to side in time with the music and singing along at the top of my voice. I could see Marble Arch up ahead, the mass of banners peeling off to the left just before they reached it, the crowd heading into Hyde Park, where a picnic and an afternoon's entertainment were promised. I was ready to party with the best of them.

And that's when I saw him. A face in the crowd, over on the far side of the pavement, fixed in a derisive sneer as he stood watching us pass by. But I'd know those ears anywhere. It was the man I'd last seen in a Marylebone mews not so very far from here. It was George Wigg.

FORTY

'JESUS!' I GASPED out loud. Shirley had skipped a few feet ahead and was out of earshot amongst all the racket that was going on, but Anita heard me and turned back in concern.

'What's wrong?'

'Someone I wasn't expecting to see. Who I don't want to see me.' I was hunching my head into my shoulders, ridiculously thinking that might make me less conspicuous when I was marching down the middle of Oxford street holding a placard on the end of a six-foot stick.

Anita glanced round at the crowd on the pavement, not knowing what she was looking for. 'Oh dear. Ex, is it?'

'No. No, definitely nothing like that.' I glanced forward to where Mark was marching at the head of our little group. As luck would have it, he was holding the left hand end of our banner, on the far side of the street to where Wigg was standing:

even better, obviously tiring as we neared the end of the march, he had allowed the pole to droop and the material was sagging round the back of his head, obscuring him from view.

It was a split-second decision with very little thought behind it. I sidestepped out of the marching throng and began to wave my own placard from side to side above my head. 'Coo-ee!' I yelled, ridiculously. 'Coo-ee!'

'That's enough, son, back in the line or out of the march,' snapped one of the attendant policemen who had been trailing alongside us for the past few hot hours.

'I'm out,' I told him, and took another few steps towards the crowd on the pavement, brandishing Stephen's image at the one person there who I knew it should mean something to. Wigg's beady eyes were locked on mine. I had got his attention.

'No you don't,' barked the red-faced copper, grabbing my arm. He looked like he was melting beneath his helmet. 'You take one more step with that' – he pointed a finger at the wooden pole – 'and I'm nicking you for carrying an offensive weapon'.

I looked at him, then back at Wigg, and then at the marchers. My own group were long past us now. I could see the back of our banner bobbing away twenty yards or so up the road.

'Fair enough,' I told the policeman, and turned back, thrusting the pole in the direction of a bloke from Lewisham Gay Lib who was passing by. 'D'you mind taking this for me?'

'Yeah, sure. Where are you going?' A young guy with shoulder-length hair, he looked bemused but friendly – hopeful even. Under different circumstances I might have hung around. But I didn't even bother to answer, just stepped past the fuming policeman and, keeping eye contact with Wigg all the way, walked purposefully across to the pavement. Seeing where I was headed, he moved to intercept me, but I took a sharp left at the kerb and pushed on towards Marble Arch, with far less thought as to where I was going than on keeping him on my tail. A swift glance back confirmed he was following just a few yards behind as I wove in and out of the Saturday shoppers thronging the pavement, most of them heedless of our progress as they stood gawping at the mob in the middle of the street. It felt like I was going at a hell of a lick, but judging by the sideways glances at his reflection which I kept stealing in the plate-glass windows sliding past on our right, the old man had no problem keeping up the pace. I'd been reading up on Wigg since our last run-in: a military man through and through, he had seen service in the deserts of Palestine and Egypt, so the oppressive heat would pose no problem for him. As long as I kept walking, he would follow, his eyes on me, oblivious to the rest of the marchers who were already peeling away to our left, the sound of their chanting fading as they headed down Park Lane and spread out onto the parched grass beyond. Plan A – drawing him away from Mark – had succeeded. Now all I had to do was work out what the hell plan B was.

For the moment at least, I was safe. The police presence was even heavier here at the parade's end, and these were proper police, coppers in uniform, not the deep undercover type who took orders from him. But I was hardly about to throw myself on their mercy: in my experience that didn't tend to work out well. I was on my own, like always.

Somehow I had to shake Wigg off my tail. The entrance to the tube station was coming up, but it was shuttered, a grille drawn across the steps and a guard turning people away and talking about overcrowding: no escape there. Ahead I could see the Odeon, and beyond that the bottom of Edgware Road, a vast four-lane junction with two sets of traffic lights to negotiate. Once I got there I would have no choice but to stop walking, and then Wigg would be on me. Could I make a dash across the marginally-less busy road to our left instead, make it into the park that stretched on the other side for as far as the eye could see? Fit as he might be, I still reckoned I could easily outpace the old man across open country. Besides, the place was rapidly filling up with Pride revellers: if he did catch up with me it would give them the perfect chance to put the day's mantra of standing shoulder-to-shoulder against oppression into practice. No, though, that was a mad idea: every moment he spent searching the crowd would increase the chance of him running into Mark, who was still blissfully oblivious to the danger. *It's not in my nature to leave a job unfinished*, Wigg had told me, and both of us counted as unfinished business.

So, I realised as the panic grew within me, did he. In all those endless arguments, Mark had been right. Thorpe was disgraced, Wilson was gone: Wigg was the loose end that was left, the one that had got away – and that meant that unless I did something about it he would always be out there, waiting for me. For god's sake, this was the first time I'd set foot in the capital for months, and here he was, like an avenging angel.

No, I suddenly realised, stopping dead in the middle of the pavement. It was time to stop running. Time to end this, once and for all. I turned around, and as Wigg came thumping towards me, raised a hand in a wave, and once again, horribly conscious of what a rubbish choice I was making if these turned out to be my last words, called 'Coo-ee! Fancy seeing you here!'

And with that, I disappeared down into the subway entrance beside me. From the pavement behind me came a muffled shout – '*Oi you, stop, I want a word with you*' – but I ignored it and, head down, started to run through the dank underpass.

It was like entering another world, the chaos and noise above forgotten as the cold air goosepimpled my flesh and the slip-slap of my plimsolls echoed around me. I hadn't got far in before another set of footsteps joined them, but I didn't turn around. There was no turning back now. I had taken a gamble, and it would either pay off, or be the end of everything.

I concentrated on remembering my way through the piss-stinking labyrinth: straight on, then left at the next set of stairs, heading deep beneath Marble Arch itself. The tunnel bent to the left again, and now in the light of the flickering fluorescents I saw the sign I was looking for: a stick figure, legs splayed in an instantly-recognisable symbol which really didn't need the large cock and balls someone had helpfully added in permanent marker. The gents' toilet. Its door stood invitingly open, and I dived in.

It was empty, so quiet inside that you could hear the drip of the cisterns. One of the most notorious cottages in London, but deserted today, thanks to everything that was going on above. I came to a halt on the tiled floor and turned to face the entrance, listening as the footsteps behind me got louder and louder and my pursuer finally appeared in the doorway.

'You've kept fit for your age, I'll give you that,' I told him.

Wigg was sweating bullets, his shirt sodden, but he barely seemed to be out of breath. 'Got to stay in shape in this line of work.'

I snorted. 'What work? You're out of a job. I watched you get sacked.'

He nodded menacingly. 'That you did.' He took a step forward, and I backed away towards the row of cubicles.

'So this is how you fill your time now, is it?' I sneered, more defiantly than I felt. 'Wandering around town, seeing the sights? Having a good look at the boys?'

A flash of anger and his arm shot up, a meaty finger extended in my direction, sending me another stumbling step backwards. 'You wash your mouth out, you little queer.'

'What's the matter?' I demanded. I was backed up right into one of the toilet cubicles now, cold porcelain nudging the back of my legs. 'Didn't you see anything you liked? How about now?' And with that, I unbuttoned the front of my shorts and let them fall, weighed down by the t-shirt that was still dangling from the back pocket, all the way to my ankles. A look of mingled disgust and fury swept across the old man's face as he glanced down, then rapidly up, and drew back a vast fist.

Nine elephants. Ten elephants.

'All right gents, that's enough,' came a voice from the doorway. I gasped and fell backwards, sitting down heavily on the lavatory seat. Wigg swung at thin air, and off-balance, had to grab at the side of the cubicle to stop himself from falling on top of me as he twisted around to see who was behind him.

'You're both under arrest for gross indecency.' The policeman yanked Wigg back out of the cubicle and snapped handcuffs around his wrists. He shot a disgusted look in my direction. 'Christ, you dirty old bugger, he's young enough to be your grandson.'

The old man, his mouth a round 'O' of shock, was hauled out of the way and a second constable stepped forward to take his place. 'All right, make yourself decent. Come on.'

I stood up, my legs still shaky, pulling my shorts up and slipping my t-shirt back on before holding out my arms so the policeman could snap my own set of cuffs around them. The old tricks are always the best.

I could hear Wigg's furious voice from outside the toilets. 'Get these off me right now, sonny Jim, or you won't believe the trouble you're going to be in! I'm not a bloody queer! You'll regret this, I've got some very powerful friends at Scotland Yard!'

'That's what they all say, sir,' came the reply from the

policeman, and I could tell even from the other side of the wall he was grinning as he said it.

'Come on son.' My own copper took me roughly by the arm and hauled me back out and into the underpass. A protesting Wigg was being marched off up the tunnel. But there was another figure coming in the opposite direction: the man I had spotted back up above lounging on the bonnet of a panda car, marshalling his troops and keeping an eye out for trouble on his patch.

'Hello, Sergeant Mullaney,' I said cheerily.

'Tommy, you dirty little fucker,' he drawled by way of greeting. 'You can't keep it in your trousers for five fucking minutes, can you?'

He transferred his gaze to the constable who was clutching my arm. 'All right, Davies, you can leave this one to me. Go on and give Paterson a hand, and see if between you you can get the old bastard into a wagon without the fairies up there starting a riot about their civil rights. Go on!'

The policeman went scuttling off after his colleague and Wigg, who was yelling at the top of his voice now. I heard the phrase 'do you know who I am?' echoing back down the underpass before they disappeared from sight.

'Right.' Sergeant Mullaney flattened a hand against my chest and pushed me up against the tiled wall. 'Where the fuck have you disappeared off to lately? You owe me, Tommy, and I'm not one to let a debt go.'

So he hadn't forgotten the whole blackmail thing. 'Sorry sergeant.' I did my best to look contrite. 'Things didn't work out quite as expected. The, er, target didn't pay up.'

A warm gust of halitosis washed over my face as Mullaney hissed: 'Not my problem.'

I closed my eyes against the onslaught, and then snapped

them open again as an idea struck me. 'Thing is…' I nodded in the direction Wigg had disappeared in. 'That's him.'

Mullaney glanced up the underpass. 'Him?'

I nodded vigorously. 'He's a politician. Look him up when you get him back to the station. Used to be in the cabinet. And now he's in the House of Lords.'

Mullaney's piggy eyes gleamed. 'Is he indeed?'

'Yep. And that's not all. *He's* the one that got Special Branch on your back that time.' That bit even had the benefit of being true.

A mirthless grin. 'Oh is he?'

'Yes. Watch, I'll bet you he tries to pull some strings to get out of this, too. Friends in high places.'

Mullaney removed his hand from my chest, absent-mindedly dusting down the front of my t-shirt where he had rucked it up. 'Well, that won't work. As you know, Tommy, I perform my duties without fear nor favour. Got a bob or two, has he?'

I nodded enthusiastically. 'I'm sure you could persuade him to make a donation to police funds to make this whole thing go away. Or at least to change the charges to something a bit less embarrassing.'

'Well, there's not *much* we could do in that direction,' Mullaney muttered, half to himself. 'Justice has to be seen to be done.'

'No, I mean, obviously, it's not like you could just let someone go. Under the circumstances.' I said pointedly, lifting both arms up to scratch my chin.

'Of course not.' Mullaney drew a key from the chain on his belt and unlocked my handcuffs, both of us carefully not acknowledging what he was doing. I rubbed my wrists.

'You'll be wanting to run along to your little party now, I expect,' said Mullaney conversationally.

'If you don't mind,' I agreed.

'Oh, I *mind*, Tommy. If I had my way you lot would all be in prison, not prancing around the streets upsetting the public with offensive banners. But my job's just to enforce the law, not make it.'

I nodded thoughtfully. 'That's a very good attitude.'

Mullaney gave me a look as if he was weighing up whether or not to hit me, but in the end he just turned on his heel and stalked off back up the underpass. I waited until he turned the corner and was out of sight before setting off in the opposite direction.

FORTY-ONE

THE ATMOSPHERE in the park was amazing. It was like some topsy-turvy world where gay people were in the majority and could behave like everyone else is allowed to all the time. Couples lolled on the yellow grass, their arms around one other, walked hand-in-hand, or kissed openly right out there in the sunshine. There were picnics spread out on blankets, and bottles of beer and cider being passed around, and every so often you would walk through a cloud of dope-smoke so strong it made your eyes water and your senses tingle. I couldn't spot Mark or my other friends from CHE – with the banners furled and discarded it was much harder to locate people, and besides, the individual groups from the march had split up as everyone began to mingle and make new friends. But I was content just to wander around, soak up the vibes along with any bottles or joints that were passed my way, and enjoy the flirtatious looks and comments that floated in my direction. I felt like I was floating on a cloud of happiness: safe in myself, satisfied with a job well done, every loose end neatly tied up at last.

There was a small stage set up beneath the trees in one corner of the park, and while I mostly stayed out of earshot of the earnest-looking speakers who took turns on it during the first hour – they seemed to be mainly talking about politics and police brutality, both topics I felt I already knew more than enough about – they were followed by a bloke with a guitar who looked like he might be worth a listen.

He was wearing baggy white trousers and thick, round glasses, and he had the nerdy look of someone who read too many books to fit in at school. A bit like me, in other words. I worked my way through towards the front of the crowd in time to catch him announcing a song 'I wrote specially for today, and this is the first time I've performed it.' It had some really clever lyrics about queerbashers and the way the newspapers write about gay people, none of which I can actually remember now, but the chorus was catchy enough, and before long he had most of the crowd singing along with it. I found myself singing along too.

Sing if you're glad to be gay
Sing if you're happy that way
Sing if you're glad to be gay
Sing if you're happy that way!

He got a massive round of applause when he'd finished. People were actually standing up and cheering, and I stuck my fingers in my mouth and gave him a few wolf-whistles, which has always been my party trick. Although the crowd were calling out for an encore, one of the organisers came on stage to say that the terms of their licence from the police meant we weren't allowed any more 'amplified entertainment' today – cue boos from the crowd – and we would have to make our own fun from here on in, at which point the boos turned into cheeky whooping.

I joined a general movement away from the stage, but I'd taken no more than a few steps before I spotted yet another familiar face. Peter, Stephen's friend from Playland, was sitting on the grass a few yards away, looking considerably happier and healthier than the last time I'd seen him.

I threaded my way through the crush to say hello, thinking of Mark's sarcastic comment when I had first brought up Norman Scott: 'we don't *all* know each other, you know.' Well, today it seemed we did: it felt like every gay and lesbian in London was here.

'Hi Peter,' I said cheerily, but the poor kid still jumped like a startled rabbit.

'It's all right, it's me, from the hotel, remember?' I tried to smile reassuringly, but he still looked wary as he scrambled to his feet to face me.

'Oh. Hello.' His eyes were darting from side to side, as if he was looking for a way to escape. He'd filled out a bit – god knows he'd needed to, he'd been so sickly-looking – but his eyes still had that sunken, haunted look.

'You having a good day?' I persisted.

'Yeah. I suppose,' he said grudgingly.

'Here we are!' said another familiar voice, and I turned to see Malcolm Crichton approaching, wearing a sort of long kaftan affair and carrying two Mr Whippy ice creams. For a stupid moment I thought he had got one for me, but then he clocked my presence and his own face dropped too. 'Oh. It's you.'

'Hello!' I was determinedly keeping up a pretence of brightness. 'They look good!'

'Hmm.' Crichton passed one of the cones to Peter, raising

the other to his mouth to lick up a sticky trail that was already sliding down the side. He had a badge pinned to his kaftan: a simple three-letter logo, P.I.E.

'Oh – are you two here together?' I asked, and then the penny finally dropped.

'Peter is living with me now,' said Crichton. His tone was as cold as his ice cream.

I did a quick calculation in my head. March, April, June, July – it hadn't taken him that long to replace the supposed love of his life.

'Right.' I turned back to Peter, who had already wolfed down most of his own cone. 'So, no more Playland, then?'

'Closed it down, didn't they?' he muttered, his mouth full.

'Yeah I… I know.' I turned back to Crichton. 'Listen, I'm sorry I haven't been in touch.'

'I went back to your office,' the old man said brusquely. 'I spoke to another Mr Lewenstein, who told me he doesn't have a son, or indeed any junior partner.'

'Ah.' I felt myself squirming. 'Yeah, I should explain about that.'

'He also seemed to know nothing about the case on which I engaged you.' Crichton had given up on his ice cream, and passed it wordlessly across to Peter, who accepted it eagerly. The old man pulled a handkerchief from his pocket and began to fastidiously wipe his fingers.

'Look.' I could feel sweat soaking through the armpits of my t-shirt. 'I may not have been totally honest when I took your case on, but I promise you, I did a proper job of investigating it. I followed it right up to the top – the very top, as it happens, to some very senior politicians – and I can assure you that the men responsible for his death, every single one of them has faced some serious consequences. They've lost their jobs over it.'

Crichton was giving me a look of disdain, but that was

nothing as to Peter's reaction. 'No they haven't,' he suddenly exploded, his voice a reedy treble that made me spin around, startled. 'You're such a *liar!*'

People around us in the crowd were staring in our direction. 'I don't know what you mean,' I muttered, my face flushing, not just from the heat of the day. 'It was you who set me off in the right direction, Peter. You remember, you told me about the politician, the one that Stephen was trying to get money from?'

The boy stood his ground, furious. 'And he's the *leader* now, isn't he? You didn't catch him. He's been *promoted!*'

'Wh – what are you talking about?' I turned back to appeal to Crichton, but he pushed past me to throw a comforting arm around Peter, who was shaking with anger. 'I don't understand – it was Jeremy Thorpe, wasn't it? Norman Scott was killed because he was talking about his relationship with him, and the same thing happened with Stephen? Didn't it?'

But at that moment something that Wilson had said on that crazy afternoon came back to me.

Do you believe he is the only politician involved? Or do you think there are others?

'Peter,' I said in a faltering voice. 'Who was the politician that Stephen was talking about?'

'I told you,' the boy spat. 'I said he was on telly all the time.'

Oh god. He was right. If you'd asked me back before all this began, when I barely knew one party from another, which politicians I could name, it would have been a very short list, but there would definitely have been one man on it: one man who never seemed to be off the TV, appearing on every chat show, comedy or kids' programme going, never missing a chance to dress up and make fun of himself, a man who was instantly recognisable thanks to his broad Northern accent and the sheer, unbelievable size of him. The man who, thanks to my own actions, was now leading the Liberal Party.

'But... how?' I whispered.

'He was in charge of the home. The one Stephen grew up in.' Peter was sobbing now. 'And when they left he used to send them down to London, saying he could find jobs for them. Only when they got there...' His voice faded away as Crichton pulled him into his chest and began to stroke his back, making soothing noises.

I didn't say anything. There was nothing to say. How could I have been so stupid? As if Wilson would have undertaken such an operation just to save the career of one man. There were probably dozens of them, MPs from his own party too: men too useful, too important to lose over such petty issues as spurned boyfriends, battered wives or abused children. Not when the whole machinery of the secret state could swing in to save them; not when friendly millionaires stood ready and willing to meet whatever expenses were necessary. He had said it himself, not long after he had berated me for my blindness. *I am the great fat spider in the corner of the room, drawing all the strands of my web towards me.*

'Come on, darling, I'll take you home,' Crichton cooed to the sobbing teenager. He shot me a look of pure venom as they turned and walked away.

'I'm sorry!' I yelled after them. 'I thought I was doing the right thing!'

They didn't turn around. 'I did my best!' I added, but it was too quiet for them to hear even if they had wanted to listen.

I stood there for a long time as the crowd melted away around me.

AFTERWORD: TRUE STORIES

I'VE TOUCHED ON the endlessly fascinating facts of the Jeremy Thorpe scandal and the dying days of Harold Wilson's administration in three out of the four non-fiction books I've had published so far (*Private Eye: The First 50 Years*, *The Prime Minister's Ironing Board and Other State Secrets* and *The Lies of the Land*) and since few of those involved could actually agree on what those facts were, in 2017 I decided to sit down and create my own version. A first draft was very nearly finished when, in May 2018, the BBC broadcast Russell T Davies' *A Very English Scandal* and re-acquainted a new generation with the whole unlikely tale. Our versions don't cross over that much, but the fact that the one major character (other than Rinka) who appears in both was Mrs Friendship, and he had her played by Michele Dotrice, better known as Betty in *Some Mothers Do 'Ave 'Em*, felt like a sign that the mid-70s was the right place for me to carry on spending my time.

Harold Wilson's sudden resignation, the precise role of Marcia Falkender and whatever may or may not have been going on behind the scenes were the subject of lurid conspiracy theories at the time, and they have multiplied ever since. Some surfaced in the writings of Auberon Waugh and his fellow travellers in the 1970s, others (eventually) went public courtesy of Peter Wright in *Spycatcher* in the 1980s, and some of the less fantastical (though no less unbelievable) facts have been revealed by Downing Street colleagues in the decades since.

Lady Falkender continued to object fiercely to any accounts of her own career which differed from her own, using the law firm Carter Ruck in 2006 to extract £75,000, an apology and a promise from the BBC to never again broadcast my friend Francis Wheen's excellent fictionalisation of her final days in Number 10.

She was the last of the high-profile politicians who feature as characters in my story to pass on: her death was announced in February 2019 (the real Norman Scott, I am glad to say, still survives, unlike my one). Depending on your familiarity with the English laws of defamation, it may or may not surprise you to learn that the drafts of this book I sent to my publisher in January and May that year were significantly different.

Far from fading with time, the conspiracy theories about what was really going on beneath the surface of the 1970s and '80s have metastasised in recent years. The terrible revelations about the activities of people like Jimmy Savile and Clement Freud have somehow still not been enough for the public, who have needed to perceive something even more awful, even more secret lurking in the darkness. Every paedophile must come complete with a ring; each sordid brutality in a children's home must come complete with a celebrity perpetrator, political for preference. This public need for amplification – and fictionalisation – came to a head with the revelations of 'Nick', real name Carl Beech, whose knotting together of Ted Heath, Harvey Proctor, the heads of both MI5 and MI6 and numerous other establishment figures in an orgiastic, murderous fantasy was thorough enough to convince senior Met detectives that his tale was 'credible and true', only for it to turn out after many months of investigation to be neither.

Meanwhile, a very credible and true story had been hiding in plain sight for over thirty years: it was not until Cyril Smith died in 2010 that anyone bothered to follow up the impeccably-sourced stories the *Rochdale Alternative Press* and *Private Eye* had printed in 1979 about his habitual physical and sexual abuse of children. A local police sergeant in Rochdale had been overruled and ordered to stop his investigation into Smith a decade before that; three separate files detailing the politician's abuse would eventually be submitted to prosecutors, and every one of them ignored.

Worse than turning a blind eye, the authorities actively covered up his crimes. Officers claiming to be from Special Branch intervened when police from another force were on their way to interview one of his victims, and made it clear it was 'not in the national interest' for them to believe anything the young man said. Smith's behaviour was even flagged up by the Political Honours Scrutiny Committee when he was nominated for a knighthood in 1988, but ignored. The youngest of his victims that police have been able to identify was eight years old.

* * *

More than once as I was writing *Beneath the Streets* I heard that nagging voice at the back of my mind asking 'is this a bit too far-fetched?', only to recall that the plot point in question was something that actually happened. I've tried to stick to real events and chronology as much as possible, except on the occasions when I chose to throw them completely out of the window.

It's unlikely anyone other than me will ever care that Tommy and his father sit down in chapter twenty-nine to watch the actual programmes that were broadcast on the night in question, or how punctilious Neil's agenda for the CHE meeting in chapter seven actually is, but the following is a run-down of a few of the more significant bits of non-fiction I wove in along the way:

Tom Driberg's death – in the back of a taxi, from apparently natural causes – actually occurred a few months later on 12th August 1976. He spent the last few years of his life offering hospitality to young rent boys in exactly the manner described.

Tom Robinson's first performance of *Glad to be Gay* did indeed take place at the Hyde Park party following the Pride march in 1976: you can watch footage of the day in the film *David Is Homosexual*, made by CHE Lewisham that year, for free on the BFI website.

Aspects of Harold Wilson's ramblings in chapter thirty-five echo briefings he gave to the journalists Barrie Penrose and Roger Courtiour shortly after his resignation. The line 'You little cunt! What do you think you are doing!' is one that Wilson's press secretary Joe Haines claims Marcia Williams, Lady Falkender, genuinely shrieked at the Prime Minister on a different occasion: she denied it. Haines also wrote that in 1975 Joe Stone, Wilson's personal physician, had offered to 'dispose of' Falkender and 'make it look like natural causes and sign the death certificate.' Another Wilson aide recalled Stone suggesting 'it was in the national interest she be put down'.

George Wigg served as Wilson's 'Spymaster-General' with access to secret service records on politicians during his first term in office: the PM later wrote that he 'did more for our security services and their place in the system of government than has ever been guessed at. For obvious reasons it can neither be described nor fully evaluated.' He had fallen out of favour with Wilson (and, possibly more importantly, Falkender) by the mid-1970s. Wigg's arrest at Marble Arch actually occurred in September 1976. He was subsequently tried for kerb-crawling, and acquitted.

James Goldsmith's first blizzard of writs against *Private Eye* actually came two months earlier, in January, and his multiple actions against the magazine were not concluded until the following year. But he did get his knighthood in the middle of it all – Wilson's resignation honours, compiled from Lady Falkender's notorious 'Lavender List', were announced in May 1976.

Norman Scott did visit the *Private Eye* offices in an attempt to interest them in his story: Paul Foot interviewed him, but took offence at a sexist remark Scott made about one of his female colleagues and told him to leave. Foot went on to break the news that police wished to charge Thorpe with conspiracy to murder Scott in *Private Eye* in July 1978. At a subsequent trial, Thorpe and his rum collection of co-defendants were subsequently found not guilty.

Famously, it was actually Rinka who was killed in October 1975 while her owner survived: it was the evidence of Edna Friendship that led police to the gunman, Andrew Newton, who served a brief prison sentence without (yet) revealing who had paid him for the assassination attempt. The definitive versions of the story appear in Michael Bloch's biography *Jeremy Thorpe* and John Preston's *A Very English Scandal*.

Of the Labour MPs Mark mentions in chapter eleven, John Stonehouse's attempt to fake his own death was unsuccessful and he was arrested in Australia shortly afterwards by police who thought they had bagged Lord Lucan; and Maureen Colquhoun resisted attempts by her constituency party to de-select her for several years before losing her seat to the Conservatives at the 1979 general election.

The real Lib-Lab pact was negotiated a year after my fictional one, in March 1977, but when Thorpe was holding talks with Ted Heath about a possible coalition after the February 1974 election the outgoing PM said he had 'expressed a strong preference for the post of Home Secretary'.

The National Association for Freedom really did exist, and it really did call itself NAFF.

Sergeant Mullaney's much-admired colleague George Fenwick, head of the Obscene Publications Squad, was jailed in 1977 along with a number of other senior policemen after a massive clean-up operation instigated by Met chief Sir Robert Mark revealed officers from top to bottom were regularly taking bribes from Soho pornographers.

Five men who frequented the Playland Arcade in Piccadilly were found guilty of various charges including conspiracy to procure acts of gross indecency by persons under the age of 21 following a nine-week trial at the Old Bailey in 1975: the youngest victim cited in evidence was 12. In another trial the same year three other men were given life sentences for the torture and murder of 20-year-old Billy 'Two-Tone' Mcphee, a resident in one of a string of supposedly charitable 'hostels' for runaways which were run by a paedophile. McPhee's body had been dumped in a ditch on the road between London and Brighton. Both cases featured in a famous Yorkshire TV documentary in 1975, *Johnny Go Home,* which is also in the BFI's collection.

The Sex Pistols spent several months in early 1976 rehearsing, and often sleeping, at number 6 Denmark Street, before exploding into national notoriety courtesy of their television interview with Bill Grundy that December.

Ray and his 'family' were inspired by accounts in Jeremy Reed's *The Dilly: A Secret History of Piccadilly Rent Boys*, which also supplied several other details.

* * *

Tommy Wildeblood will return in *The Enemy Within*.

ACKNOWLEDGEMENTS

IT'S HIGHLY UNLIKELY this book would ever have been written if it weren't for my friend and colleague Francis Wheen. As well as his books *Strange Days Indeed* and *Tom Driberg: The Soul of Indiscretion* and the aforementioned banned TV play, I drew on countless conversations with him over the years. It is a privilege and a pleasure to share an office at *Private Eye* with him. I was also lucky enough to spend seven years working alongside Paul Foot there: lightly fictionalising my own workplace, albeit from many years before I joined the staff (I would have been slightly under one year old at the time), was one of the weirder writing experiences.

Thanks also to Sheila Molnar, Alwyn Turner, Dominic Sandbrook, Ed Howker, Daisy Asquith and the members of CHE Lewisham for inspiring various aspects of the story, and to staff at the Bishopsgate Institute and the BFI National Archive for their help with research. And to Adam Curtis, Maisie Glazebrook, Andrew Hunter Murray, Tina Jackson, Michael Tierney and my agent David Smith for their encouragement along the way. Simon Edge was my wise and thoughtful editor for Lightning Books: it's a much better book now than it was before he got involved. Clio Mitchell did an excellent copyediting job, and spotted an anachronistic howler that probably would have gone unnoticed by most readers, but bugged me for the rest of my life. Any that remain are entirely my fault!